I0760860

FALLON

KINGDOM OF FAIRYTALES
SEASON SIX

You all know the story of your favorite fairytale, but did you ever wonder what happened after the fairytale ending? Well we know. Not all afters end up happily, sometimes the real adventure starts much later...

Following famous fairytale characters, eighteen years after their happily ever after, the Kingdom of Fairytales offers an edge of the seat thrill ride in an all new and sensational way to read.

Lighting-fast reads you won't be able to put down

Fantasy has never been so epic!

URBIS PRISON
SHIPLEY
BADALAH
THE VALE
AZREN
DESERT
DRACONIS
KISBU
ZHORE
MOSA
ELDER
ABORIA
AZURE
ENCHANTIA
AIRE
URBIS
EMERALD CITY
SKYLA
OZ
FLORIS
TULIS
THE FORGE
W
E
ARCADIA
RENAIS
S
MELFALL
ATLANTICE
ANTLA
KINGDOM
OF
FAIRYTALES

ISBN: 978-1-989997-28-4
Enchanted Quill Press

Contaact the author at www.enchantedquillpress.com
Cover by Enchanted Quilll Press
Interior Formatting by Enchanted Quill Press
Editing by Rose Lipscomb

KING OF BEASTS

20TH MAY

"All hail The Party Prince of Aboria." Kalmin hoisted his glass of ale above his head, foam sloshing over the side and covering his hand. He passed it to his left and sucked the foam off his fingers, raising the glass again. "To Prince Fallon."

"To Prince Fallon," the crowd echoed, as they clinked glasses together and let out boisterous cheers. Kalmin took the barstool beside me and slapped his palm on my back. My own ale burned as it gushed down my windpipe. "Thanks, Falls."

I coughed and cleared my throat. "You don't always need to make a spectacle out of me, you know?"

"Why not? The crowd loves it. They feel privileged to be drinking with the prince. Just imagine how they'll react when you become king."

King. I shuddered. The icy chill of the word slithered

down my spine. It's good to be king, or so everyone told me over and over again. But the label of Prince was enough for me. My father could deal with bickering shepherds and tax complaints, I'd rather enjoy the bounty that Aboria had to offer. After all, someone needed to inspire the people, show them the privilege that came with being royal, and I was the perfect person for that job.

"Did you save a seat for me?" A sweet sugary voice whispered in my ear, slow and deliberate to make sure her full lips brushed against my skin.

I twirled around on the barstool as Sophia's dress tangled against my legs and pulled her in closer. Her knees suddenly gave way and dropped her into my lap as an arm wrapped around my neck—a little too dramatic to the accidental, but I gave her credit for trying.

"Afraid there are no stools left, but it looks like you found a seat all on your own." I winked and slipped my arm around her back to steady her.

She laughed and cast her eyes toward the floor. Her long lashes batted playfully as the tips of her fingers found the small curls at the nape of my neck, sending delicious sparks to other parts of my body.

"And I see you haven't come alone tonight, who is this?"

A raven-haired beauty in a rich burgundy gown curtsied politely in front of me. Soft ringlets tumbled over her naked bronze shoulders, as her dark ebony eyes drew me in.

"This is Alessandra, she's visiting from Badalah," Sophia grabbed my chin and tilted my head to look at her, my interest in her new friend more obvious than I'd hoped. She fought a frown, trying to win back my affections with a flirtatious smile. "But she won't be staying long."

"Welcome to the Kingdom of Aboria, Alessandra. I would love to show you what our beautiful kingdom has to offer while you are here. That is if you aren't intimidated by being seen on the arm of a prince?"

Alessandra's eyes looked uneasy at Sophia, the corners of her mouth sinking until she turned and locked stares with me again. "I'd love to, Your Highness."

"Well then, we mustn't deny the people a chance to look upon your beauty. Might I suggest we start tomorrow?"

Sophia launched herself from my leg and huffed into the corner. I twitched, my body wanting to chase after her. But what courtesy would that show to a visitor? This was duty after all.

"I see your hands are empty, miss." I turned back towards the bar and the graying barkeep, Mr. Takka. "Another round for the fine company." I raised a finger in the air and circled my arm.

Mr. Takka shook his head. "You're running quite the tab tonight, Your Highness."

"Just giving the people what they want."

He quickly flipped the glasses on top of the wood-grained bar and pumped the taps of their sweet, amber ale. He handed two overfilled glasses to me. I took a large gulp, letting the heady foam fly down my throat and handed the second glass to Alessandra. She took my gesture with a slight bend of her knee and nod of her head. I liked this one. Maybe a trip through town with me might convince her to extend her time here.

Smash!

"For the last time, I said I don't want anything."

I glanced over at the corner where a petite mousy

girl sat at a solo table, a pile of books spread out in front of her and a pool of beer on the floor. Shards of glass littered the foam. I launched from my stool and slid through the bodies toward the serving girl and the patron.

"I told you I didn't want it." The girl repeated as she bent to help the serving girl pick up the broken pieces.

"Is there a problem?" I asked.

"No sir." The serving girl glared over at her unwanted assistant and rolled her eyes. "Just a mountain girl refusing the prince's good ale."

"Prince's ale. Right." The patron scoffed as the serving girl nudged her out of the way.

"Have I offended you in some way, miss?" I folded my hands behind my back and rolled my shoulders high. Even the dull tavern lights glinted off my gold buttons and differentiated me from the common crowd. The regal stance. The power position.

The patron stood, her feet planted shoulder-width, her arms taut at her sides. "You have not offended me, Your Majesty, but your actions and those of your sheep in fine clothing are offensive to all."

I expected a timid voice from the slight girl in a shapeless tunic, but she roared with the veracity of a lion, garnering the attention of the other patrons.

"Is that so?" I bit the inside of my cheek to stifle a laugh. "Please indulge me. I offered you a drink, was that not a kind gesture?"

"Your kindness is not in question sir, but the gesture was not one for you to give. You do not drink the prince's ale, you drink the ale made from sweat and tears of the people of Aboria. This is the taxpayers' ale." Her hands flew to her hips as a snarky smile curled across her mouth.

"Are we not all taxpayers?" Kalmin joined the fight, his full glass held high as he staggered slightly from the bar, his dress shirt sleeves rolled up to his elbows. "And you should know better than to speak so candidly to our future King." He hoisted the drink higher. "To Prince Fallon, the next great King of Aboria."

The girl shook her head, a few strands falling from the nest of hair she held at the top of her crown with what appeared to be a crisscrossed set of twigs. "The next great King? How can someone who is not even a great prince expect to be a great king?"

A hushed "ooh" cycled through the crowd. The entire population of the tavern now hung on her every venom dripping word. I squeezed my hands together into fists and nudged my chin higher as red flushed my cheeks, and this time not from the drinks.

"And how do you propose to know what kind of King I will be? I've never seen you before. How do you claim to know me at all?"

"You may not have seen me, but I have seen you. I'm in this tavern nearly every night, as are you and your entourage. I've seen you waste the money of the hard-earned people of this Kingdom. I've seen you and your harem of ladies traipse around town like a pack of pretentious fools. But not once have I seen or heard you do anything of value for this kingdom. You are not your father's son, you are weak and vain and have no idea what you are getting into as ruler."

"I know plenty. I know the people, and I've been a son of Aboria my entire life. I don't hide up on the mountaintops like you and your people, I'm here with them every single day."

Cheers elicited behind me and I smirked. This girl was tough. Not the typical drunk rabble-rouser who wandered in here and decided to lay their hard days story on my royal shoulders. But this room was mine. She'd never break that bond and, in the end, she'd be the one to walk out of here as the buffoon. A small tinge of guilt bubbled up in my chest, but I quickly willed it down.

Her thin lips dropped into a frown, but she didn't waver. "Then tell me, prince, what are you going to do about the coming darkness? Are you going to let your people suffer?"

"What darkness?" I scanned the faces of everyone in the bar. Jaws dropped open and stares went vacant but not one seemed to understand her words. "Are you trying to cause a rebellion? One can be held accountable for treason for that kind of remark."

"Oh no prince, the threat is very real. Storms have reached epic levels in Atlantice, wolves are murdering again in Elder, and the dark black clouds over Urbis gather thicker every single day. Those clouds inch closer and closer to our border, while you sit in this tavern handing out ale like water. What happens when Aboria is next? What happens when disaster strikes here?"

I swallowed hard. If what she'd said were true then Aboria needed to be on alert and ready. My father hadn't said anything, neither had my mother, but they often kept me out of the more important matters. Which until now, suited me fine.

"Well, I appreciate your concern and welcome the voice of my citizens, however, this issue would be best left for the monarchy. Be assured we are taking whatever steps necessary to ensure the safety and well-being of our people."

The promise seemed to revive the crowd, pleasant

murmurs and subtle cheers rumbled through the room. I puffed my chest out slightly and smiled the perfect royal smile I'd been trained to use since birth. What did one little girl know about me? I could go toe to toe with the best of them.

"So you've got nothing, do you?"

Her gaze narrowed burning through me like hot iron pokers, searing the truth upon my skin.

"I... We..."

"Fallon, she's boring." Sophia marched her golden head between us, her arms crossed and lips pouting. "Can we please just go somewhere else?"

The room erupted in laughter as the mountain girl shook her head and retreated to her chair and into her books. Her hand scratched feverishly along her parchment, either giving up or maybe knowing she had won but choosing not to claim the title.

I wrapped my arm around Sophia's shoulders her head sliding against mine. "Of course, my love, let's find a more suitable venue."

The door burst open, and a familiar face appeared, the dim light casting shadows from the lines of worry etched across his face as the dark night spread out behind him like a cloak.

"Griswold?" I rushed to grab the hand of the castle's oldest butler. A man who'd cared for me my entire life. "What is it?"

"It's your father, sir. You must come home immediately. Your mother is waiting."

"What's wrong? What's happened?"

Griswold leaned in closer, the smell of the castle rolling off him.

"I'm not at liberty to say, but trust me, it's bad."

~

I thrust open the castle door and rushed through the foyer nearly tripping on the lush red carpet leading to the grand staircase.

"She's in the library," Griswold called from behind me.

I raced up the stairs two at a time and sped into the east wing of the castle. The door to the library creaked as I turned the knob and slid in. The familiar mahogany and gilded bookshelves stared down at me.

Mom startled at the noise then turned toward the door. She forced a smile of greeting behind her wall of tears as her hand clutched at the locket around her neck. She slid it back and forth on the simple gold chain, faster and faster, to the point where it might snap in two.

"Griswold said—" I watched my mother's tears fall harder, each one searing a hole in my own composure, "—are you okay?"

I rushed across the room and wrapped my arms around her shoulders and buried my face in her neck like I did when I was a boy, even though the foot of height between us made it more difficult now.

She squeezed back, her rose-scented curls brushing against my cheek.

"It's your father. I don't even know how to tell you this. We've been keeping a secret from you, from a lot of people. I never thought I'd need to tell you."

"Tell me what?"

"It's your father," she said, between tearful hiccups. "He's...the curse has returned."

I pulled back and sandwiched her cold dainty hands inside my long fingers. "What are you talking about?

What curse?"

She tugged her hands from my grip and started to pace the small room, gripping her forehead.

"It was a long time ago. So long I sometimes forget." Mom craned her neck towards the skylight and exhaled. The air drained from her body like a deflating balloon as her memories washed over her. "When your father was younger, before you and even before me, he made some bad choices. Choices that angered a dark fairy and she put a curse on him that changed him into a ferocious beast. He was more animal than human. He was the prince of Arboria, but after that he moved to the deepest part of the forest to live out his years."

"What?" I ran my fingers through my hair, trying to take in what she had just told me. "You're trying to tell me that Dad, my dad, was once a monster. Are you okay, Mom? Do you need to lie down or something?"

"This isn't a joke, Fallon" She slammed her hand on desktop and the smack echoed through the room.

"I don't quite understand what you mean by beast."

"A beast!" she said waving her hands in the air. "You know. Hairy body, big teeth, angry expression. He's an animal, a monster. He's not human anymore."

I jumped back. This wasn't Mom. She never yelled. Even when I'd been a petulant child or a rebellious teenager, she always still held her decorum.

"But it doesn't make any sense," I said trying to find reason where there was none. "Dad is a pretty upstanding guy. He's noble and always does the right thing. The entire kingdom loves him."

Mom resumed her pacing. Faster. Shorter steps. "Now he is, but back then he was a different person. It wasn't until he fell in love with someone who could see past his beastly form that he changed and the curse was broken."

"You?"

She nodded as a few stray tears leaked from her eyes.

"You have to be kidding." I gripped my hands in my hair and tugged then started racing my own loops around the library. Like mother, like son. "I don't believe this. This sounds like some kind of horror story. Why didn't you tell me?"

Her tears came harder, spilling down her face as her cheeks burned red. "Because we didn't want to upset you. It was all supposed to be in the past. A chapter closed and forgotten. But tonight, when we were walking through the garden, your father just started screaming and fell to his knees. I tried to help him up but he started to change. His hands became claws. Swaths of fur covered his body. And now..." She gazed off toward her favorite bookcase, the one I always saw her standing by when I came in here. As if it unlocked another world that I couldn't see. "The curse has returned. The king has turned back into a beast."

A beast? A real live monster living in our home. Our castle. The papers would be all over this news. The humiliation of it. My father's reputation would be ruined. My reputation would be ruined.

"But he can still rule, right?"

She shook her head, an almost maniacal look in her eyes. "No. Not like this. This time is different. Last time he was angry at the curse, but he was still functioning as a human. But this time, something has changed. He's more animal. The curse is changing him and I'm not sure how to control it. I don't know what to do Fallon. He was fine this morning. Everything was normal. This came out of thin air. I'm not prepared."

I closed my eyes and tried to picture the image from my mother's words, but I couldn't. None of this made any sense. If my mother wasn't so devastated I would've thought this was some sort of cruel joke. I could already feel my world falling out from under my feet. My reputation centered on me being a prince. If my father was a beast, did that mean he was no longer king? "So what does that mean?"

"It means we're going to have to figure this out. I don't know why this is happening again. Your father has led a good and true life since the last curse was broken. He's a good man. He's changed." She walked over and opened her locket. The one she'd worn as long as I could remember. Inside two photos, a young man with dark eyes and a stubborn jaw that I knew too well and the other a hideous furry beast, with a stare that burned at my soul. "I wear this to remember, but I never thought it would happen again. I never thought..."

She raked her fingers through her hair and fussed with her sapphire gown as if she had no idea what to do with her hands or how to keep herself still. I placed my hands on her shoulders. "What do you need from me? I'm not sure what to do?"

She sighed. "I don't really know right now. I just needed to tell someone. To let it out."

I held my arms open and she fell into my chest, her tears soaked my shirt as she trembled. She let the sadness take her for a minute as I held her up while the strength in her body waned. My ribs closed tight around my lungs and my eyes welled, but I didn't cry. Mom kept this family in line. I'd never seen her break. Not once.

After a few moments, she jerked her head up and wiped her face with the back of her hand. Her posture slid back into place, the time for letting go passing as she fell back into her role as queen.

"Thank you," she whispered then let out a short huff as the red drained from her cheeks. "But we need to keep this quiet so the citizens of Aboria don't find out. When the curse was lifted the collective memory of the beast vanished except for those in the castle. It would cause mass panic and we can't have that without the king in place. I can only do so much without royal blood. In the end, I'll always be the commoner who ascended so we need total discretion until we can figure this out."

"Of course." Besides, it wasn't like I wanted anyone finding out about this either.

Smash. Crash. Thump.

A deep menacing roar echoed through the castle.. I shivered. Mom placed her a dainty hand over mine on her left shoulder and forced a reassuring smile.

"I better go. Sounds like he might need me." She patted my grip and turned to go but I gripped tighter on the satin of her gown.

The reality of our situation hit me. My father was not only a beast, but he was here in the castle...with us. The way my mother described him made him sound dangerous. The photo of the way he used to be was enough to convince me that this was no small problem.

"You can't. What if... What if he hurt you? Maybe we should send a guard?"

"My sweet boy. This isn't their problem to bear, and until we have better answers, it isn't yours either. Please promise me that you won't try to see him. Not like this. It wouldn't be good for you or him. I've been through this before and I can handle it. Please, promise me."

She was asking me to let her go into the beast's lair... literally. She gave me a pointed stare and I knew that nothing I could say would convince her not to go.

"I promise."

She pulled me into another hug and I squeezed her tight until she gasped for breath.

"Mom, be careful."

She slipped out of my arms and hurried to the door. "I will. Let's hope we figure this out quickly. I'll be fine."

She slammed the door behind her leaving me alone in the cavernous tomb of books. I glanced at their spines, each one meticulously cared for and in their place. Each title in a beautiful embossed script, like sideways smiles leering at me.

"What are you looking at?" I huffed at them.

I stormed out of the library and down the hall toward my room. A beast. An actual beast. This was seriously going to mess up my street cred.

Griswold appeared ahead of me as if he'd been instructed to wait in that exact spot.

"Is there anything I can get for you, master."

I slumped against the wall my head banging against the stone, the pain oddly providing comfort.

"No. Unless you happen to have a magic wand."

"No wands, sir." He responded stone-faced. "But I'm sure it will all work itself out. I don't particularly look forward to returning to stone if I can help it."

"Stone?"

Why was everyone in the castle in on this secret but me? My father was a beast, his servant was apparently petrified. What else were they keeping from me?

The old man placed a wavering hand over his lips. "Clearly I've said too much."

"What is going on Griswold? You obviously know about my father. why has no one told me any of this? I'm the King and Queen's only child. Don't I deserve the courtesy of the truth?"

"The king and queen have loved you since the moment they laid eyes upon you. I don't think it's a matter of trust, but a matter of protection. You'd be well-served to remember how much they care for you as the coming days may be difficult for everyone."

I scrubbed my hands over my face wishing to erase the last two hours of my life. With any luck this will all be an effect of the alcohol I'd consumed in the tavern in the town and I'd wake up with a throbbing hangover and this would all be a dream...a bad one.

"You are dismissed, Griswold."

He bowed his head, "Yes, sir." Then he scampered off down the hallway before I could question him further.

I reached for the doorknob. Another ear-splitting growl echoed through the corridor. I cringed as I ran through my mother's story again. The one of nightmares. The one she tossed on me, then asked me to stand by and do nothing.

Forget this. I couldn't sit and listen to this all night, not knowing what to do. I let go of the doorknob and raced out of the castle into the night.

Empty seats filled the tavern. Most of the regulars already gone home, and those that remained sat lost in silence entertaining their ghosts. Without the royal tab, the party must've shut down, or maybe just moved elsewhere with closing time looming soon.

I stood in the doorway half considering roaming the streets until I found Kalmin and Harding, but the heaviness growing in my limbs won out.

I pulled up to the bar on my regular stool and

motioned to Mr. Takka.

"Graced by his highness twice in one day, to what do I owe this honor?"

"To a rough night and a cloudy head."

He nodded, the lines around his eyes crinkling in a knowing way. "Well let's see what we can do about that then."

I ran my fingernail through the wood grain of the bar top as Mr. Takka poured a drink and set it down in front of me. "On the house, Your Majesty."

"Thank you. You're a good man."

He retreated to the far side of the bar stacking glasses and wiping down counters, either avoiding the potential of me telling him my problems or maybe knowing better and simply leaving me to my thoughts.

I wrapped my hand around the glass, the cool condensation doing nothing to ease the burn in my flesh.

My father, a beast? Why had no one bothered to tell me? And what did it all mean? My father ruled with a strong fist but with a kindness the people adored. I sometimes wished I'd turned out more like him, but being king always seemed like a lot of hard work.

"Excuse me, Your Highness." A voice, familiar but lacking a certain disdainful vigor, interrupted my wallowing.

I glanced over my shoulder, my body disinterested in fully turning around. The mountain girl in her sloppy, grey tunic.

I sighed, my shoulders collapsing into my chest, with zero energy to deal with her drama right now. "If you have any more concerns might I suggest sending a letter to the castle, or attending a session of court. I'm not sure how much more I can help you without a formal complaint."

Her face scrunched up like one does when they've bitten a sour grape but haven't thought to spit it out yet.

"Actually, Your Highness," she gave the slightest nod of her head and bend of her knee. "I wanted to apologize."

I swirled the ale around in my glass stamping a wet circle across the bar top. "Everyone is entitled to their opinion."

"True. But I didn't have the right to air it out like that. You are the Crown Prince of Aboria after all. My mouth tends to run away on me sometimes and if I forget to catch it, it gets me into trouble."

No surprise there. I let go of the glass and rubbed my damp palm across my thigh, then spun on the stool to face her. If she had the decency to apologize, I could at least meet her eyes. Not many would have the courage to admit they'd wronged royalty, but yet, not many people had the fire to stand up to a royal in such a public way either. A slight shadow of a girl like her would normally fade into the background, but something about the way she stood, her hip jut sharp to the left and the weight of a thousand lifetimes balanced on her proud shoulders sparked an odd challenge in my gut, both terrifying and strangely invigorating.

"Well, again, I'm very sorry." She fidgeted with her hands before narrowing her stare and pointing to the table in the corner. "I better get back. Please forgive me for my lack of decorum."

"I appreciate the apology miss..."

"Veda, Your Highness. Veda Macario."

I extended my hand, but she shook her head.

"I've interrupted enough of your evening. I'll leave

you alone."

My right leg twitched as a restless electric buzz pulsed through my limbs. Alone. The word fell from her lips and detonated like a bomb at my feet--each syllable hollow, empty, and terrifying.

"No rush. Why don't you take a seat and tell me a little more about yourself Miss Macario?"

A bewildered frown etched across her face and she cast her eyes to the floor as a tinge of pink blossomed along her cheeks. She had so much to say, but when she wasn't the one leading the charge her instincts seemed to fail her. The glimpse of vulnerability actually seemed somewhat charming.

She slipped onto the barstool at my left, her elbows on the wooden top and her fingers gently pulling at her frizzy strands of hair tucked behind her ear.

"What would you like to know? I'm sure my quiet life is dreadfully boring compared to living in the castle."

"Maybe. But the castle is all I've ever known." Even if everything I've ever known might be hiding a massive secret. A mystery I didn't have the brainpower, or maybe just the courage to face right now. "Indulge me."

"I'm amazed. For someone who hasn't been outside of Aboria, you sure know a lot about the world."

I scratched the back of my head and gazed over at Veda bathed in the light of her enigmatic glory. She'd done as I asked, spilling her stories with flare and taking me away from this tiny tavern and my own head. But she'd also made one thing very clear--she was smart. Really smart. Her perception and insight rivaled at least half of the top advisors on my father's council, but even her know-it-all attitude didn't feel like an assault. Her straightforwardness came from an altruistic place, instead of one of pride or arrogance, like most who deemed themselves worthy to argue with the crown. Annoying as hell, but also strangely refreshing.

"And for someone who's seen it all, you seem to know very little."

She laughed and leaned forward smacking her hand on my thigh. I glanced at her dainty fingers and her cheeks blanched as she ripped it away, sliding her palm down her thigh as if to erase the action.

I shrugged and gave a reassuring chuckle until a crooked smile crested her lips. "Someone needed to keep my father entertained."

And apparently, keep his secret.

"Closing time. Sir. Ma'am." Mr. Takka appeared in front of us and nodded toward the clock on the wall. His kind stare flitted between the two of us. "But if you need me to stay open I can?"

I glanced at my nearly empty glass, the gravity of going home and dealing with my abomination of a father sitting heavy between my shoulders just in the fleshy spot beneath my neck and pushing me down to the stool.

"I've probably had enough for tonight." I turned to Veda, a slight kernel of anticipation growing in my stomach. "Unless you'd like to stay?"

She leaned back and stretched her arms, a soft squeal coming from her throat. "I should probably get home too."

She slipped her hand into her pocket and slid a wrinkled twenty baht across the bar.

I slammed my hand on top of the bill. "You don't have to pay. It's on me."

"I'd rather not." She wriggled the paper from beneath my fingers and leaned over the bar to deposit it on the lower counter, out of reach. "I prefer to pay my own way."

She gave me one last lazy smile, loose and carefree, a sudden pang surging through my chest.

She rested her hand on my arm, her fingertips cold through the thin cotton of my sleeve. "And about what I said before, about being king. I never said you didn't have the potential to be a great king, I just don't think you're there yet."

She cast another smile my way, then retreated to the corner, piling her books into a perfect stack.

I gulped the last mouthful from my glass and closed my eyes concentrating on the frothy ale as it slid down my throat. Veda's word cascaded through my head, every one of her stories replaying in a calming loop. How she lived by herself up on the mountain. The dreams she had about one day leaving Aboria. Her hopes for a better future. As I recounted each of her words, a peculiar feeling washed over me. I didn't want her to leave.

"Hey, Veda." I spun around on my stool, the ale and the lateness of the evening kept my head on the carousel even after my feet stopped moving. The single table in the corner sat empty, only the click of the front door in its frame answered for her.

21ST MAY

You have the potential to be a great king...just not yet.

Veda's words echoed on a loop in my mind, twisting and writhing through my brain like the matted high thread count sheets wrapped around my body as I tossed and turned. Who did she think she was anyway? No one in the kingdom would have the tenacity or sheer gall to speak to me that way. Is that why I couldn't stop thinking about the strange slip of a girl who lurked in the corner of my favorite tavern? Or maybe it was the lack of malice? When she'd ripped into me earlier, I could see the rage seething beneath her skin, but when she whispered those words in the dim light of early morning they lacked venom. Her wide emerald eyes twinkled with hope. Honesty. She actually believed in me. Why? Who the heck knows?

I unraveled myself from my bed and hung my feet over the side, digging my toes into the softness of the brocade rug covering the cold stone floor. But what if she was wrong and I'd never be great? Groaning, I rubbed my hands over my face trying to scrub out the memory of last night. Of Veda. Of everything.

Grrrrr!

A loud growl accompanied the smash of breaking glass off towards the west wing. I jumped to my feet and grabbed a robe from the armchair by my bed and rushed into the hall. Staff scurried through the corridors, heads down, or grim expressions held tight in fear from the ones who dared to make eye contact.

"That's it. Thank you all, but we will not be needing your services today. Please head back to the servant's quarters." Griswold clapped his hands as his voice boomed over the pending chaos. "Thank you. Move along."

I tugged at his jacket. "What's happening? Is it...?"

Griswold nodded, his lips in a tight grave line.

"But I thought my mother said she was taking care of things. That it would all be okay?"

All the light left in his expression drained. His advanced age showed even older than usual. "Things are worse than she expected. She's gone to fetch a doctor."

"She left him alone? Why couldn't they send someone else?"

"This situation requires the utmost discretion, Your

Highness. Besides, she has been by his side all night, she needs the break. Now I recommend going back to your chambers, at least for the time being."

I stomped down, the smack of my bare foot on the stone surging through my leg. "I want to see him. My father. Take me to him, Griswold."

"I can't." He placed a shaking hand on my shoulders and gently pushed me back down the hall.

I whirled around and planted my feet, the robe billowing around me like a cape. "I am the Crown Prince of Aboria and I demand to see my father."

"And I am on strict orders from Her Majesty the *Queen* of Aboria that no one is to see the king--not even you." Griswold crossed his arms and widened his stance to cover more of the hallway as if I couldn't outmaneuver an old man if I wanted to. "You can take it up with her when she returns, otherwise, please return to your chambers at once."

Shifting my weight from foot to foot, I pondered the value of challenging Griswold. He'd served this castle far longer than anyone else and I doubted a temper tantrum would persuade him to let me get my way. His loyalty to my family seemed superhuman, but it didn't mean that it didn't disrupt my plans on occasion. Unfortunately, today was one of these occasions.

"Fine." I tossed my hands in the air and retreated, Griswold's ever-watchful eye weighed down on the back of my head as I stormed down the hall to my room. I slammed the door and leaned against the wooden panels, banging my head so that it echoed like the knock of an unwanted guest.

Griswold might have my mother's wishes at heart, but it didn't mean I actually had to listen.

I dressed quickly in casual grey pants and a loose

white shirt, hoping to pass as one of the servants from a distance and peeked back out into the hallway. An eerie stillness radiated through the stone corridor, not a footstep or even a whisper, just a strange nothingness. Instead of risking another confrontation, I slipped down the hall heading east and into my mother's library. The rich heavy scent of parchment and ink wafted out as I opened the door and carefully shut it again without a sound. Like always, I scanned the grand bookcases from the floor to the ceiling as if the books could see me. As if they stood guard and recorded all the things that had come and gone in this room and whispered about it to each other when no one was looking. Hopefully, they wouldn't tell on me this time.

Closing my eyes, I searched my memory for the combination. The sing-song of one of the greatest weapons royalty had--an escape plan.

Three Aborian maidens fair,
with silvery voices and golden hair.
Wandered into the wood one day,
left the path and lost their way.
They met a group of goblins five,
then only two maidens came out alive.

Perfect. Three shelves up, one book to the left, five books to the right, knock two times, then pull. I followed the directions and as the second knock died in the silence of the library, the bookshelf creaked open to the secret passageway hidden behind. I grabbed the lantern on the edge of my mother's mahogany desk and slipped through the opening, closing the door behind me. Ducking my head as the passageway narrowed,

I followed the pathways down under the belly of the castle. So many times I'd snuck down here to avoid the lessons taught by my army of tutors—not one bold enough to tell my parents the truth about my lack of academic interest. Instead, I would head east, out to the edge of the forest and to my freedom. Except now I headed west, back into what disaster I didn't know. Besides, after a while, no one stopped me as I came and went from the castle anymore so secret passages lost their usefulness.

I followed the turns as they led deeper into the darkness, the damp stone pathways worn and foreboding as I neared the west wing, the heavy weight bearing down on my ribs growing more heft with each step. Inhaling the musty air, I took one last deep breath before charging up the narrow stone steps to the top floor, the walls tighter than I remembered as a boy. A sliver of light cut through the break in the wall at the top of the stairs, marking a jagged lightening-shaped line across the floor. Almost there. One last chance to turn back and listen to Griswold and my mother for once. But since when did I ever do what I was told?

Thick spider webs filled the single handhold to pull back the passageway door, but I slipped my hand into my sleeve first then yanked hard, the door groaning as it awoke from its slumber. I peeked out to find the hallway empty and emerged into the fourth-floor hall tucked behind a menacing stone lion statue, concealing the passage from anyone who might happen on it by accident. I set the lantern on the floor and started to slip the door back into place.

Crash.

I jumped and slammed the door shut. A loud boom echoed off the arched castle ceilings. I grabbed the lantern, concealing it with my body as I pressed behind the statue. Footsteps fell in the distance but disappeared until I wasn't certain I'd even heard them at all. I slipped out and the lion's side-eye glared down at me, the majestic stone creature likely disgusted by harboring such a coward.

At the end of the hall, I creaked open the door to my father's chambers, the outside vestibule looked ready for war with all the furniture piled along the far wall. Delicate wooden tables from Elder and intricate metalwork from The Forge cast aside as if they were cheap toys instead of one of a kind antiques. Through the second door, my boots crunched on shards of glass and splinters of wood sprinkled across the floor. Paintings sat torn and tattered along the walls mixed with a pile of bedclothes and tapestries. All around broken tables and chairs littered this battlefield and I ran my hands along the thick black marks on the walls from where they must have been launched into like cannonballs, the grit from chipped stone catching in my fingernails.

A deep sigh emanated from the far corner of the room, the sadness so thick I felt it cloud around me before the actual sound hit my ears. In the far corner, a large furry body cowered near the fireplace, motionless save its back slowly rising and falling with each haggard breath. It couldn't be. Could this be the beast my mother spoke of? Even though I heard her words, part of me didn't actually believe them to be true.

"Dad?" I whispered, not sure what answer I hoped to hear back.

The beast glanced over its broad shoulder, a flash of gnarled horns peeked out from underneath its sorrowful stare, but then it simply turned back pulling tighter into itself as if trying to hide or move into a cocoon-like a caterpillar in the spring.

"Is that you?" I took a slow step in the direction of the beast, the sound of the shattered glass crumbling beneath my feet breaking the awkward silence between us. As I reached the side of my parent's grand bed, the fear of what I might be walking towards started to sink into my bones. What if this wasn't really my father?

"Go away, Fallon, I don't want to see anyone right now," the gruff voice said, but with a waver that fought against the postured aggressive tone.

"Mom told me about the curse, that you needed help. I wanted to see for myself. See what I could do."

Another sigh, the same grim sadness, but ten shades darker.

"I can't control it, Fallon. Not this time. It isn't safe for you to be here."

"You don't look very dangerous to me. C'mon Dad, why don't you get up. I'll have the kitchen staff make you a bowl of your favorite Aborian stew and you can tell me about it. Or maybe just get some rest. You must be exhausted from being up all night."

My father's shoulders fell then he stood, finally exposing his new form and I jolted backward. Fur covered his entire body, and the horns I'd only glimpsed protruded from above his bushy forehead curled and twisted in horrific shapes like the shadows that spread across the room from his immense size. At least three feet taller than my human father, and nearly twice as wide. He'd be a beast from size alone, even without the deformities.

I bit the inside of my cheek trying not to be afraid. To be the brave soldier that royalty needed to be in times of crisis. The quality I'd never managed to test and hoped I never would.

“See. That’s better. Why don’t you come sit on the bed, it’s more comfortable than the floor? Plus...well... you’ve run out of chairs.”

“You need to go,” he repeated, the words coming out more brusque this time around.

“Maybe tell me what’s going on first. I deserve that.”

He stood stoic but didn’t argue, although his silence shook me with the same level of terror.

“You’d probably feel better if we cleaned up some of this mess.”

With slow movements, I inched over to the other side of the fireplace to the haphazard pile of books shredded on the floor. My mother’s heart would break to see such disregard for her things, especially since they may have come from her private collection. I didn’t share her love for literature, but at least I could respect it, even if the thought of reading more than necessary for survival built tension in my neck and shoulders.

“I told you to go,” my father bellowed again, accompanied with a growl straight from his gut, menacing and deadly.

I froze, a book split clean through the spine dangled from my hand.

“I just wanted to help.”

He shuddered, his feet lost control as he fell back a few steps, and he staggered in tight circles between the wall and the fireplace, his massive arms swinging out for anything to steady him or worse something to throw. He shook his head, his stare unfocused and his eyes flipped through shades of fear and anger like a kaleidoscope of his soul.

I dropped the book and eased toward him, my hands held out in front of me. “Easy. It’s going to be okay. What can I do?”

His head snapped toward my voice. "Who are you?"

"It's me, Dad, Fallon. Your son."

"I don't..." His voice broke until his words came out in a series of growls and snarls, a stone mask slipping over his expression until the small part of him that I still recognized disappeared in the dusky light.

"What do need me to do?"

He growled again and buckled over, his face scrunched tight.

"Run, Fallon. I need you to run."

"I'm not just going to leave..."

He reared his head back with a howl, brandishing lines of sharp pointed teeth. Fangs. Like ones you'd imagine dripping with blood on the monsters of horror stories. Crimson daggers ready to rip the flesh from your bones. A thing of nightmares.

Blood pounded in my ears as my throat parched. "You don't want to do this."

He stalked toward me, and I matched each step with one in reverse. His snarl morphed into a half-smile, but not the kind I'd ever hoped to see. No joy or happiness, just delicious evil curling across his lips like his body could no longer contain the feeling.

"Just calm down, Dad. It's me. I'll go get Mom. It'll be okay."

My pleas fell from my lips to the ground, completely missing their mark. The human inside was gone.

I twisted toward the door and raced at my freedom, my stare still locked on the monster. Step after step landed on the uneasy ground, and my ankles tweaked left and right as the beast's hungry breath crept across my shoulders. Kidnapping, war, assassination, these were the worthy deaths for royalty, not at the hands of their own father--or whatever my father had become.

Six feet to the door, maybe five. I pushed harder, forcing all the strength I had in to my legs to save me. Three feet. My knee slammed against the side of an armchair and I faltered. My stomach hollowed as weightlessness took over and I plummeted to the ground. Glass carved my palms as I held up my body. Shards dug through the fabric of my pants and ripped my knees. A claw ripped into my shoulder and flipped me over to face the devil that owned my father. A red rage pulsed through him, my legs pinned beneath his lion-like foot.

Flailing my arm above my head, my fingers grazed a larger piece of glass and I grabbed on as a stream of wet blood from my hand threatened to make it slip. The beast reached back, his razor claws steadying for the death blow and I closed my eyes, poised to strike even if I didn't survive.

"Please," I begged as tears flooded my face. "Don't do this."

The beast growled. My muscles tensed, the makeshift glass dagger cutting deeper into my flesh.

"Ezra. Stop that right now!"

The voice of an angel pierced through the terror. Light appeared in the doorway along with the swish of satin.

"He's your son. You love him. Ezra. Just stay with me."

The weight on my legs lifted and I gulped a fresh breath laced with the salt of my own fear. My mother rushed past my body on the floor. The beast staggered backward as if a sniper's arrow had pierced the window and sent him reeling. He raced back to the corner I had first found him, the savage beast transforming into a quivering pup before my eyes. She followed after him, the gold thread of her gown twinkling against his matted fur, her fingers gently stroking the back of his head as her lips whispered a calming hush.

"It's going to be alright, my king. I'm here."

~

I paced between my dresser and my bed, my head dizzy from the short laps or maybe still hazy from trying to process my near-death. The heat of his breath on me. The sharp claws swiping just past my face. I'd been warned to stay away, but I hadn't thought how bad it really could be. How dangerous. Was this really how it was the first time? What did that mean for me?

I kept pacing, but a short flash of my reflection in the mirror stopped my feet, and I grabbed my head to keep from falling over from the abrupt halt. A face, worn and older stared back at me. I blinked. The face disappeared and my heart slowed again. I inched closer and pulled at the skin around my eyes. Just the same as always. Odd. I must've hit my head when I fell. Or now I was just seeing things.

A low knock wrapped on the door and my mother crept in the room, her usual sunny smile trying to force its way through for me, even though her broken heart painted its hurt across her face. She gathered her hands in front of her and concentrated on his fingertips as they rolled against each other.

"How's your hand?"

I held out my gauzed palm, small splatters of red had already started to show through the layers of stark cotton. She cradled it in her fingers, gentle and easy as she turned my wrist from side to side to inspect the injury.

"If it keeps bleeding make sure to replace the gauze

and keep it clean. It'll heal faster."

I nodded. She stared at the gauze, unable or simply choosing not to make eye contact.

"How are you?" I asked, tugging my hand away and denying her the distraction.

She turned her head toward the wall and glided over to the bed then flopped down so her skirt puffed out beside her across the plum duvet. She held her hand to the middle of her forehead and bowed for a moment as she took a slow deliberate breath. For the first time, a trident of wrinkles spread out from around her eyes, the enormity of this situation, or maybe years of dealing with my father that they'd kept from me, etching its anguish into her skin like an unwanted trophy for a sport no one wanted to play.

"I'll be okay. Once we figure out what's caused this, we'll fix it and everything will be normal again. "

"Was it like this the last time? When he, you know, turned?"

"No. He had a temper, but he was still more man than anything. A sad, lonely man, but still human." She stood and grabbed the bedpost swinging herself around. "This...this thing he's becoming is something different. Something new. Besides, your father is a good man now. A strong and kind leader that the people of Aboria look up to for guidance. He's not the same person he was before the curse. And they wouldn't understand. When the curse broke the kingdom magically forgot about the king's curse and it was better that way. I'd hate to see what happens if they start to remember. It would be anarchy."

She stopped trying to keep a positive tone for my sake, and instead fussed with the row of swords and daggers I had in cases near the door. My collection from around the world. Keepsakes from the many trips I'd taken with my father. Trips I didn't know if I would ever get to take again.

"He would've killed me if you hadn't shown up, wouldn't he?"

She stopped, her thumb resting on the blade of a particularly expensive stingray skinned short sword, her eyes closed tight.

"I don't know for sure. But yes, it's possible. Promise me you won't go back up there until I tell you it's safe, okay?"

I walked over and took her hands, the cuts in my palm burning from the pressure of her skin against mine. "I promise. But you need to be honest with me when things like this happen. I need to know the truth."

She glanced up to the ceiling and paused, a cloud cast a shadow over her face as bad memories attacked her. "Of course."

"But I think we have another problem."

I pulled back the velvet drapes and sunlight beamed through the window. Down below a line of villagers stood outside the castle gates. Cameras flashed. People peeked through the bars and tried to maneuver around the guards, parchment in hand. Our own private hell might not remain private for long.

22ND MAY

The photo spread across two full pages of the Aboria Weekly. A distant image, but unmistakable, my father in front of the open castle window his beast form visible to the entire world. The headline, "What Monsters These Royals Be" emblazoned in a bold font right under the familiar masthead. My family's secret shame now front-page news.

I tossed the paper, picture down, on the table and slid my half-eaten eggs away from me. My appetite faded fast as my stomach churned and acid built in my throat. "Any word on my father this morning, Griswold?"

"No, sir. The west wing has been strangely quiet since yesterday and the queen has not been seen since dusk. Would you like me to fetch her for you?"

"Thank you, Griswold, but that won't be necessary." I swallowed my last gulp of tea, made of the best aromatics from Floris, but even they couldn't comfort me this morning. "If my mother asks for me, I'll be out for the afternoon."

I doubted she would ask as she probably wouldn't resurface from my father's side until a cure had been found. But me, I needed to get as far away from both of them as I could. Clear my head, or better yet, hide until all of this nightmare ended. This whole thing would probably kill my reputation.

Outside the front gate, nosy newspaper journalists swarmed like locusts before the end of the world. One even bore the royal crest from far off Arcadia on his sleeve. Great. We weren't just local news anymore; this scandal had gone national. I held my breath and kept my head down as the guards pulled the gates back to let me through. The horde pushed forward, but the guards quickly drew their swords and they retreated.

"Excuse me, Prince Fallon, could you answer a few questions?" a voice called from within the crowd.

I dipped my head lower and charged forward, no one brave enough to touch me with guards standing within a safe distance.

"What's going on in the castle, Prince?"

"No one has seen the King in days. Is something wrong?"

"Is it true that Aboria is being invaded by mountain monsters?"

The voices intensified as people edged closer, but I marched on, my balled fists plunged deep in my pockets. No response would be just as awful as a bad one once it hit the morning papers. As much as a picture of my right hook landing in the face of one of these vulture reporters might look amazing, the negative publicity wouldn't do my father or the kingdom any good. Especially not in his current condition.

The greedy flock of reporter sheep followed on my heels until I reached the golden bridge connecting the castle grounds to the city of Mosa. One by one, they finally dispersed as they realized that I wasn't turning back and they'd gain no more information from me. Besides, they couldn't risk being scooped by someone else sitting at attention back at the castle gate.

I pulled the hood of my cloak over my head and down over my eyes, then crossed the bridge and meandered through the quiet morning streets toward the market. Few people bothered to look at me, likely caught in their own thoughts about the potential threat they saw in this morning's news, or gazing up at the gathering of dark clouds swirling above our heads.

The fragrance of cinnamon and chai wafted from the center of town. My mouth salivated knowing those smells would soon be overtaken by the sweet earthy scent of roasting pecans. I closed my eyes. The thought of their warmth already eased some of the tension building in my shoulders. My feet darted left toward the market stalls, instinct, desire, or maybe hunger from skimping on breakfast plotting my course, but I forced myself to stay to the right. I didn't feel like taking the risk to be recognized today, even though it might just be worth it.

Instead, I headed for the black and white checkered paint spread across the center of the square. The oversized chessboard had been a gift to the city from my father, but everyone knew it was really for his queen. The citizens used to crowd around, filling the rows of seats surrounding the board to watch them play for hours, challenging each other. I'd sit on the ground next to the board watching my mother's gown swish from square to square as she maneuvered the sizable silver and gold filigree chess pieces into position. My father's curious crooked smile would follow her every move, his brow furrowed as his brain twisted to find a way to outsmart her. Occasionally, he'd managed to win a match, but even as a kid I knew she probably let him win.

My parents hadn't played here in years and the delicate craftsmanship on the pieces had tarnished to a greenish hue that gave the lion-shaped knights more menacing glares. I stood back, hands deep in my pockets and watched my friends as they navigated their way around the board. Late nights out always followed with late morning chess games in the square. For the elite, ritual kept the days from dragging until we had to assume our parent's responsibilities. Some dreading that day more than others.

Harding watched the game, his body stretched out from a front-row seat and holding his head. Without even looking, I pictured his bloodshot eyes after another long night his body couldn't handle. His shoulders sagged low to support my theory.

In contrast, Kalmin stood stick straight, his hand on his chin as he studied the game with the shrewdness of a judge. Except, unless he could perform a miracle, Sophia would take his king in about three moves. Maybe he'd finally found a worthy opponent, or maybe something had him distracted this morning.

"I'd suggest moving that bishop Kal before you're outdone by this lovely lady."

I joined the group and slid my arm around Sophia's waist. Her muscles stiffened under my hand. She glanced at me with wide eyes as her body shivered in my grasp.

“What a pleasant surprise, Your Highness.” The words glided off her tongue like a rehearsed melody as she slipped from my embrace and off to the far side of the chessboard, her lingering lavender perfume following close behind her.

“Am I no longer welcome?”

She twisted her fingers in front of her and glanced at Kalmin, then Harding, then back down again, refusing to meet my questioning gaze.

“Of course, you’re welcome. It’s your kingdom after all.” Kalmin smiled, but the edges of his mouth twitched as he forced it. “It’s just...”

The hum of the bustling market amplified as Kalmin searched for words on the tops of his shoes.

“Everyone’s afraid of you.” Harding scoffed and shifted in his seat.

“Afraid of me?” I laughed, but no one laughed with me. “You can’t be serious?”

All three of them stared off in different directions, none anywhere near me.

“Is this because of the story in the paper this morning? About a beast in the castle?”

The collective groaned in agreement.

I crossed my arms and pulled my cloak tighter around me, trying to hide my family’s shame like it was tattooed across my chest. “Do I look like a beast to you? That newspaper story is a bunch of lies. You should’ve just come to me and asked for the truth.”

“I wanted to.” Kalmin’s lips tightened along with his shoulders. “But there were all those reporters outside the castle after the story came out. I didn’t want to be in the way.”

"You know the guards would've let you in. They always do."

"Right," Kalmin nodded. "Next time. For sure."

Sophia's hands twisted faster, as she dared to glance over at me. "But what if that thing came after one of us? That would be awful."

So it was. The real truth. "Except none of you cared if it came after me?"

No one responded as their silence punched into my gut and stole my breath.

I flung my arms in the air. "That's real nice. What if I was hurt or maybe even dead? I would've helped you if you needed it."

"Would you though?" Kalmin finally stepped forward, his hands curled into fists and anger settled into his clenched jaw. "You're Prince Fallon. You always help yourself first."

Every cutting word flew straight from his mouth and pierced my skin like tiny razor-sharp arrows.

"Wow. Okay." I shook my head as my body seethed in pain from the attack. "I didn't realize I'd been such a burden."

I turned sharp and started to walk away.

"You're not a burden. You just never seem like you really need any of us. It's always about you." Kalmin called over my shoulder, the edge smoothing off his tone. "Falls, wait."

In the distance, thunder rolled. I quickened my pace, but no footsteps followed behind. I slowed again, hoping to feel Kalmin's hand clasp down on my shoulder, but it never did. They all just let me go.

Head down, I hurried through the city streets. Gossip and chatter about the ferocious castle beast blew past my ears on the gusting wind. *I always helped myself first.* What did that even mean? Had I not given them everything they had ever asked for? A thin sheet of light rain started to fall, misting the miserable world around me. Maybe I should let my father loose on the city and see what happens. I'd bet they'd be begging for my help then.

I approached the bridge as the drizzle began to seep into my bones, and I ached to close myself up in the castle and forget about everyone in the world outside. Ahead, the throng of reporters still lurked outside the castle gate. Scavengers. I glanced back toward town and my ribs contracted tight around my lungs, my breath hard and labored. Stuck between two places I clearly didn't quite belong. I leaned against the bridge's railing and dropped my hood letting the mist wash over my face.

"It's the prince," someone shouted. "Prince Fallon, what is that thing in the castle?"

Not again. I flipped the hood back up, ignored the voices, and ran the opposite way toward the towering cluster of trees up the hill on the far end of town. People shouted as I ran against the foot traffic and nearly knocked over a half dozen citizens. Shame fueled my run, and wouldn't let me stop. I didn't want to see another person for the rest of the day if I could help it. If they didn't find a solution for the curse soon, I might never leave the castle again. No one wanted a monster on the throne. I didn't want a monster for a father. But I guess none of us would be getting our way, so why couldn't they all just leave me alone.

Just outside the edge of the forest, I buckled over and grabbed my knees. My gasping breaths echoed in the air. Looking back over my shoulder, my body relaxed as no one had bothered to follow me. The crazy prince from the haunted castle running through the streets like a mad man. I'm sure that would make for fantastic gossip to humor the Aborians. I crept down the hill to the right of the main pathway and stood outside the familiar small abandoned cave. Moss grew over the rocks and provided camouflage to the one unknown access point to the castle. The end of the passageway. A safe way home. Except, the thought of going back didn't provide the calm I'd hoped for. The tightness in my chest squeezed harder. Not yet. I wasn't ready. I stared up into the sky, waiting for something, an answer, a calmness, anything to make this hopelessness go away. A weak beam of sun cut through the black clouds and led deeper into the forest. I sighed. Not what I'd expected, but maybe getting lost for a little while might help me find my way.

~

Spring had blossomed in the forest and the fresh foliage protected it from the rain. I wandered underneath the meandering rows of towering teak trees down the lesser worn paths deeper into the heart of wild Aboria. Sunlight peeked through the dark clouds and created misshapen shadows across the dirt pathway as it filtered through the canopy. Thick emerald leaves of the lower flora hung just over my head and the sweet scent from the delicate white buds clustered at the end of their branches swirled around me in the afternoon breeze. The whole aesthetic hummed of an otherworldly calm, but its brilliance dimmed under the black thoughts churning through my brain.

No one cared if I lived or died. Even people I thought were my friends. My best friends. But did it mean nothing? Did they simply hang around to be amused by me? Bathe in the royal glow and reap its glories? But I guess, why not? That's what I'd done. Years of living in the luxury of who I was without knowing the price that it might come with. How it might have been earned.

An image of Veda flickered in my mind. Her charming awkward smile when she told me I had potential. The only person who didn't treat me like a prize to be won or a cow to be milked and she probably hated me. She didn't care about all the things I stood for. If anything, it repulsed her. I repulsed her. If only I had a chance to talk to her again. Ask her about what she saw in me that everyone else didn't. I grabbed the back of my head and groaned looking up toward the sky. She's the last person I needed in my thoughts right now. I had my father to deal with. I had to keep my mother together. I didn't need some know-it-all mountain girl telling me about things she probably knew nothing about. But why did I suddenly want it?

I let the mist of the forest paint across my face, the coolness soothing the burn in my cheeks. How did everything get so complicated? I started to take my next step down the same old route, but a strange unsettled fury bubbled up inside me and I tramped off through the bushes into the unknown.

The remaining sunlight vanished under the denser bush, better matching my mood. The sharp branches and thorns ripped at my legs as I trudged deeper, the pain providing an odd satisfaction. Anything to pierce the veil of the numb dreamlike state I'd been stumbling around in.

I stopped near the gnarled roots of an old banyan tree to catch my breath. Odd-shaped mushrooms gathered in clusters creating an almost perfect circle around the clearing. I dropped to the ground and pulled my knees to my chest. The darkness of the forest surrounded and provoked me like an itchy blanket. I closed my eyes and breathed in the damp musty smell of moss and wet leaves. If I lost myself in here, would anyone even bother to come looking?

"Princes shouldn't venture far from their castles."

The words whispered through the treetops. I snapped my eyes open, but no one appeared. I shook my head. Probably just the rustle of leaves and my distracted imagination.

"The woods aren't safe. Nothing is safe anymore," the whispers returned, louder this time. "Pretty princes should walk in the light."

"Who's there?" I clambered to my feet and bunched my hands into fists, ready to strike.

A chorus of giggling bounced around me from every angle. "Silly Prince, trying to fight the fairies. Don't you have bigger battles?"

Fairies. Great. Tricksters lurking in the woods, sending people in the wrong direction just to laugh at them wandering around lost. Stealing fruit from hiker's packs then throwing it at them for amusement. Just what I didn't need right now.

I started back the way I came, the day getting bleaker as it stretched on. Wings fluttered past my face, like a hummingbird, but more annoying. I swatted my hand in front of me and kept moving forward through the brush.

My head yanked back as my hood flew off my head, but I refused to stop. The bushes and treetops erupted as flocks of fairies burst out of hiding and zig-zagged to create a living wall of limbs and wings to block my path. Tiny lights of every color flickered back and forth.

"You don't believe us?" the chorus chimed.

"Why would I?"

"Because we speak for the trees. The trees know things."

I surveyed my other options. I could plunge deeper into the forest, but they might just chase after me. Waiting them out seemed unlikely. The only way out was through. I continued forward, arms extended to push the fairies to the side. Hopefully, they would be smart enough to move. I'd never heard of anyone dying by fairy bite, but knowing my luck it could happen.

"The trees speak of the coming darkness. They've seen it before. They can feel it coming."

The words coursed through my blood. My pulse pumped faster at my temples. I let my hands fall to my sides, my feet rooted still like the banyan tree.

A shrill cry split through the air and the fairy shield dispersed, a cool current from the fleeing wings blew over my skin as they all disappeared into the forest. A single fairy remained. She flew back and forth between me and the way out.

"The heartless prince might have feelings after all," she said, gliding through the treetops as a silver trail streamed behind her. "Wealth cannot buy kindness, you know. But I think maybe something struck a match. But how many tick...tick...ticks, until our prince goes boom?"

A flash of glitter exploded. I jumped back, and tripped, falling to the ground. The fairy laughed and zipped over my head as I struggled back up to standing, her tiny voice echoing through the trees.

"Enough. What do you know about the darkness? Does this have anything to do with my father?"

"I guess that depends. Who is your father again?"

She tittered and zipped straight up in the air then dropped like a stone back to the forest floor before she changed direction and cut across the tops of the long wild grass, lobbing off the heads of a few flowers in her wake.

"Always so funny. My father. The king."

"Ah. The king. Maybe it does. Maybe it doesn't."

"That's a huge help. Thanks." I crossed my arms and pushed up to my feet, then started to stomp off again. Even my escape plan hated me. I shouldn't have bothered getting out of bed today. Besides, no one ever believed the fairies, why should I?

"No. Don't go." She flew in front of my face and pressed on my nose with her small hands. I stopped, finally seeing her tiny body close up. Her wavy rose gold hair blew in the draft from her beating wings, her silvery skin glowing in the dim light and illuminating the faint lines of fairy symbols painted or tattooed on her shoulders and down her arms. I held out my palm and she took the gesture, resting on top of the gauze still twined around my hand.

"You're hurt? That just won't do." She dug her bare foot under the first layer of gauze and attempted to pull it up and peek underneath.

"It's fine. Don't worry about it. Just tell me what's coming. What does it have to do with me and my family?"

"Patience, prince. You'd learn much from looking beyond yourself. Nature is a web of connections. We rely on each other." The fairy bent over and planted her hands on the gauze. A blue glow came from grip as her petite face squished together. Pain jolted down my arm as a deep burning raged in my palm. Invisible flames ripped through my skin, devouring it, consuming.

"Ow!" I snatched my hand away. "What did you do

to me?"

The fairy tumbled through the air and crashed into a pile of dead leaves.

She huffed and regained her stance, flying back up into my eye line. "I think the words are 'thank you'. We don't just heal anyone, you know."

I unwrapped the gauze but the huge gash from the glass was gone, except for a few crumbles of dried blood still left from yesterday. I flexed my hand. No pain. Nothing.

"You're welcome," the fairy said, peeling a leaf from her hair and tossing it behind her. "Now can we move on. You have much work to do."

"Me? I don't think you get it. It's my father that's the problem. Not me. He's the one who needs to get better."

"But you need to defeat the coming darkness. The darkness is what's affecting your father. It poisons the blood, brings out the evil."

"So you're saying he's been poisoned?"

She shook her head, a glittery cloud puffing into the air around her. "The darkness is many things. Many bad things. But things are changing. Moving. We can feel it. The forest feels it. And you need to save us. Why do you think you came here?"

"Ha." I stomped my foot and pointed at the ground. "I came here to get away from everyone else's judgments, not to find more. And I'm not exactly the hero type. Why do you think I would be the one to save you?"

"Because that's what the forest is telling us. They know the stories. The ancient ones. The ones others don't dare to tell. There is a plan for you, even if you don't know it, even if you don't want it. You have potential, Prince of Many Faces."

Potential. A dirty word. I definitely didn't see it.

“Besides,” her wings slowed and she hovered ethereally in the air, her tiny eyes welling until she blinked and pushed the tears down. The weight of a thousand stares bore down on my shoulders as the rest of the fairies edged in toward us.

The silver fairy narrowed her stare toward the onlookers than flitted near my ear as her squeaky voice dropped low. “You might be our last hope.”

23RD MAY

I looked in the mirror and tilted the crooked crown straight again. The thick gold frame and ring of sapphires weighed nearly as much as a brick. It strained my neck and constantly slid off to the side. How did my father ever wear these things? So uncomfortable. Even the golden rings in my eyes seemed tarnished next to the large hunk of gold on my head.

I slid a few jeweled rings on my fingers. The large rubies looked massive next to my simple signet ring, but Griswold insisted that I needed to be in full dress. Not just a prince, but not quite a king. Something in between that I didn't know how to be.

"You look great, darling."

Mom slid into my room, her beautiful raw silk gown in deep shades of midnight blue and gold swept across the floor, the skirts swishing around making her look the regal queen even without the sash across her shoulder emboldened with our family's royal crest. The lion in the center stood for bravery, but I didn't feel I lived up to the legacy, especially not now. My aching stomach seemed to agree.

"As do you. The kind and gracious queen." I leaned down and kissed her cheek, her skin dry and tired as the brightness in her eyes snuffed to an exhausted glaze. My throat closed and I struggled to swallow the words of pity she didn't want to hear. The toll of caring for a monster slowly painting its horror across her face.

"How's Dad doing?"

The sash sagged as her shoulders fell, the heavy sigh collapsing her posture. "It's getting worse. Sometimes he doesn't even know who I am anymore. The doctors have taken to sedating him most of the time, but if we don't find a solution soon..." Her eyes welled, but she turned away before wiping the tears and flicking them to the floor. "Let's just stay positive okay. Are you ready for your big debut?"

I wrung my hands, my thumb tracing over the thin white scar running down my palm where a huge gash should be. The fairy thought I needed to be some sort of hero, so why did I feel like a scared little boy? "I think so. But why can't you make the announcement? I will always be there for you, but you're the queen. I'm just a prince."

She sighed and shifted the hefty crown back into place on the top of my head as it had already slipped again. Casting her stare to the floor, her already ashen cheeks paled further, almost as if she'd been replaced by a ghost. "Because, I don't know what's going to happen, Fallon, and you may need to take on the role as king much sooner than any of us expected. If your father...if he doesn't get better, you will need you to step in and take his place."

"But what if I'm not ready?"

She placed her hands on the sides of my face and forced me to look at her. "Of course you are. You've been training your entire life for this. All your lessons. All your time here in the castle has been grooming you for this moment. It's your destiny."

My destiny. I swallowed against the thickness growing in my throat. Every part of my body seemed to weigh more today. Heavier. Harder to carry. "And if I can't?"

"Rumors are already spreading throughout the kingdom. We need to address this now or there will be chaos." She let go of my face and hesitated with her hand on the doorknob, her shoulders heaved before she turned back to face me. "The announcement is at three o'clock, I'll meet you in the foyer at quarter to three. Please don't be late."

I watched her slide back out the door, her posture stick straight and demeanor flawless, even though her insides were being torn apart. I'd never be that polished. I knew my duty to the family, but I never actually thought I'd have to do it. I'd falsely believed that my father would just live forever and take care of things, even if I became king I wouldn't actually have to do the work. I should've paid more attention to my studies. I should've behaved. I should've spent more time with my father when I had the chance. I should've done a lot of things that regret wouldn't be able to fix.

The mirror on the wall showed a kid playing dress up in the king's clothes. I fixed my collar and adjusted the crown again, the honor still not sitting right on my head.

~

Sun beat down on the courtyard as transparent waves of heat shimmied in the golden afternoon. The layers of pomp and circumstance cocooning my body did nothing to relieve the tension in my neck and shoulders as I paraded to the makeshift stage, a crowd of people several yards thick already waited at attention. A wooden podium stood in the center, but I couldn't help picturing stocks, as if I were marching to my execution instead of just a simple speech. I'd made this short journey a thousand times before, but the people didn't come to see me, they came to listen to my father. To be inspired. To be led.

The swish of satin amplified as my mother sped up beside me and whispered in my ear. "Remember to breathe and don't lock your knees or you might faint."

I forced a smile, as I tried to grab onto the small speck of levity in her tone and calm myself down. She smiled back, both of us pretending, each one trying to be what the other needed and not quite knowing how.

We reached the edge of the stage and her gentle hand nudged my lower back, urging me forward, but polite enough not to push. The guards took their positions next to us as their careful stares scanned the awaiting horde.

I shook my hands behind the podium, sweat beading on my palms and against the back of my neck. Almost everyone in the city had come, but as I scanned the crowd I didn't recognize the faces I wanted to see. My friends hadn't bothered to support me. Part of me even hoped I might see Veda standing in the crowd, but as I searched row on row of faces, her dark soulful eyes did not appear.

"Er...ah...Welcome citizens of Aboria."

A derisive laugh swam through the audience. I closed my eyes and took a deep breath as an unsettling quiet fell over the crowd.

"I'm sure you are all surprised to see me addressing you all today instead of His Majesty King Ezra, and I wish my first public address were under better circumstances."

A low murmur rose as people began to shift and shrug. I swallowed, the neck on my coat seeming to shrink around my vocal cords.

"The king has fallen ill. We have enlisted the best doctors in the land to attend to him and we hope that he will be back at this podium again soon. He sends his regards, but asks that you provide him the time and space he needs to recover."

The rumbling of voices grew. Waves of sound crashing against the shore.

"In his absence, Queen Abigail and I, along with the help of the advisory council will be consulted on all matters."

No turning back now. The wave of mumbling voices peaked again and rushed toward me. I moved my weight from one foot to the other as sweat dripped down my spine. Questions garbled and meshed as the news of the king settled on the crowd.

"What about the monster in the window? The one from the newspaper?" a man's voice called from the middle of the pack. A chorus echoed his questions, repeating the words over and over but with their own accusatory tone.

I glanced over my shoulder. Mom stood tall and

nodded me to continue, although her encouraging smile didn't reflect in her eyes.

"The pictures aren't real. There is no monster in the castle."

The murmurs erupted into a full-blown assault, my head ricocheted back and forth at the questions coming from every angle: *What about the loud noises and smashing in the castle?; Who's looking after the servants?; What if the monster gets loose? Why don't you tell us what's really going on?*

My tongue stuck to the roof of my mouth as the citizens became more enraged, spreading out and getting closer to the stage. I cleared my throat.

"Thank you all for coming here today. We'll provide more details as they become available."

Boo!

The sound rose through the crowd, picking up momentum as it echoed through the courtyard adding voices as it moved. The guards flanking the stage snapped to attention.

"You're a coward, not a king," a voice yelled.

A pomegranate whirled through the air and smashed on the stage in front of me. Seeds and juice splattered my dress shoes. Another pomegranate flew toward me. It slammed against the podium and shot berry guts on my cheek. I wiped it with the back of my hand, my white gloves staining bright blood red. A troop of guards raced from the castle and assembled in a thick line between the stage and the townspeople, swords drawn for anyone foolish enough to keep going. The boos and jeers intensified as the crowd disbanded and started to make their way out of the square and back towards the city. A flood of comments, none positive, added to the noise and seeped into my brain.

You don't deserve this. You'll ruin us. You'll never be our king.

And as I watched them all retreat, my heart knew they weren't wrong.

~

I pulled my hood tighter around my face as I strode through the shadows on the cobblestone streets. The anonymity of night did little to soothe the embarrassment seething beneath my skin since the guards marched the residents of Mosa out of the castle grounds, but at least if I kept my head down and avoided the lantern light I might avoid any unnecessary confrontations. Hiding seemed the only option after how badly I'd handled my first public appearance as acting king. Cowardly, but effective.

The cool breeze nipped at my cheeks as the wind picked up. A spring storm loomed in the dark clouds overhead, providing another reason I should've stayed back in my room, but locking myself away only made the memory of the mocking voices louder.

The fairy said I needed to save them. Veda said I had potential. How could they both be so wrong, or was this simply some cruel joke intended to destroy me? Either way, I needed answers or I'd go insane pacing the halls of the castle trying to make sense of it all.

I reached for the handle of Takka's Tavern, but my hand hesitated and shook at the door handle. I'd spent so many hours here, almost like a second home, but I doubted I'd still be welcome. If I didn't need to see Veda one more time, I'd likely turn around and head straight back the way I came.

I placed my hand across my chest and breathed

deeply feeling my lungs rise and fall against my ribs, trying to force them into calm. *Keep your head down and make it quick.* I yanked open the door and stepped out of the dark into the den of familiar voices. I clung to the back wall and glanced at the corner table where Veda usually haunted, but tonight her chair sat empty, the tabletop bare without her stack of books. My heart sank into my stomach. The sudden urge to see her hit me hard, overwhelming, like a strange addiction, desperately needing another fix. Probably just the insecurity after my complete disaster as king. It had to be. Besides, she'd been the one to call my downfall before it happened.

Someone laughed near the bar and I jumped. Harding. His deep voice boomed off the rafters and I sunk further into the wall. My face burned with the adrenaline rush of potentially being recognized, but he didn't seem to have noticed me standing there.

A burly friend of his, Dormand, poked a finger in Harding's face, the ale in his other hand swishing in his glass precariously close to spilling. "And the king is 'sick'? Do they really think we are all that stupid? There's something going on in there and it's only a matter of time before we all find out what it is."

"Easy, buddy. You don't know anybody's lying." Harding slapped his hand on Dormand's shoulder and chuckled. "At least not yet."

Nice. I'd never lied to him. Not once. But clearly, he didn't have any issue pretending to support me. And I was the liar?

My feet moved toward the door, my brain still processing the deception to make the decision itself.

I jerked it open, the low creak in the hinges suddenly deafening.

"If it isn't Prince Fallon, coming to grace us with his presence," Dormand's voice said behind me.

My shoulders tensed, but storming out would only look weak. I forced my regal smile and turned as all the stares in the room landed at my feet. "Good evening, gentlemen."

Harding slid back into the crowd, likely knowing I might have heard him but smart enough not to find out.

"Now that the prince is here we can get the party started." Dormand pumped his thick fist in the air and a hearty cheer echoed through the tavern. The familiar clink of glasses behind the bar started as Mr. Takka starting lining them up beside the ale tap. Hunched over the bar, Kalmin sat staring at the bottom of his glass, his head not daring to turn toward me.

A pinching sensation tugged in my stomach. They all saw the Party Prince, but no one respected me. Maybe Veda was right. Maybe the party needed to stop.

"Not tonight everyone." I waved my hand in the air as I shook my head and tried to get the words out without sounding hurt. "I think I'm going to call it an early night."

A disappointed groan swirled around me and the pain in my stomach squeezed harder.

"No surprise. Probably have to get back to the castle and feed the monster," someone yelled.

Laughter erupted around me as I searched the faces for whoever had the gall to say the words to my face.

"Excuse me?"

Dormand stood up, his tree-trunk arms flexed tight at his sides. "What is it, Your Highness? You didn't think we bought that story you tried to feed us today, did you?"

"It's not--"

"Isn't it though? The servants are talking. They've heard the screams and the growls in the castle. They've said entire wings have been locked down." His fingers curled one after another into fists, then released and clenched again. "And no one has actually seen the king in days. How do you explain that?"

"My father is sick. And I'd watch your tone, or I could have you charged with treason."

Mr. Takka leaned over the bar, his finger pointed sharp at Dormand then me. "I don't want any trouble in here, gentlemen."

Dormand's eyes looked past me, a deeper level of disgust creeping into his stare. "Charge me if you want, but everyone else will know the truth--you're hiding something. We deserve a real king who doesn't lie to us."

"Enough!" Kalmin kicked the stool back and stood, his hand slamming into the Dormand's chest.

Finally. I knew I could always count on him. We'd been friends for too long, too many years for him to abandon me completely. I'm sure he'd just been scared like everyone else. I'd forgive him.

"Falls--" he crossed his arms over his chest and widened his stance, his eyes raking over me, "--I think it would be best if you left."

Every nasty word I'd ever heard collected like venom at the end of my tongue, but Kalmin's crestfallen stare sliced through me, cutting me into pieces until I could only nod in response.

I turned and left, a few mumbled comments following me out into the night. I slammed the door behind me and threw myself against the wall beside the entrance. My head banged against the stone and I actually invited the pain. Maybe the ache in my head could smother the one burning in my chest making it hard to breathe.

"Bad day?"

My head fell to the right. Veda stood next to me in her somber gray tunic, a book clutched tight to her chest.

"Yeah. Not my best."

"I heard."

Of course, she had. I'm sure everyone from here to Skyla had heard about it by now. I sighed, letting all the tension out of my body and collapsing flatter against the stone wall. "I looked for you at the castle today, but you weren't there."

"You did?" Her voice lilted up. "Why?"

I closed my eyes and tipped my head up, letting the night breeze wash over my skin, wishing the sky would open up and swallow me.

"I figured you would want to be there to watch me fall on my face. Apparently, you've always known I was bound to fail."

"Ouch. Sounds like it was worse than the gossip around town is saying." She slid her book into the bag across her shoulder and crossed her arms. "Besides, I wouldn't want to see you fail. I might be critical, but it's because I think you have potential."

"Can you please not use that word? I'm starting to hate it."

She nodded and mimicked my defeated posture against the wall.

"What are you--" I glanced over and she smiled.

"Looks ridiculous, doesn't it?"

"Are you seriously making fun of me right now?"

"No." She straightened up. "It's just that it's not the end of the world. I'm sure it was awful, but if you spend all your time worrying about what you've done, you'll never have the energy to do better in the future. So stop feeling sorry for yourself, and get over it."

"I..." I peeled myself off the wall and jabbed my finger in the air toward her, but the rest my argument caught in my throat, denying me the satisfaction but watering down my anger. "Why is it that you get to say these things to me and I keep letting you?"

She shrugged, a mischievous grin cracked upon her face as she raised her thick left eyebrow. "Because deep down you probably already know it's what you need to hear."

"Maybe."

Or maybe I enjoyed the punishment. Either way, the tension in my muscles eased and I took a deep breath. Veda nodded, seemingly satisfied at dragging me out of my pit of self-loathing, and I couldn't help being drawn in by her shrewd knowing smile until I grinned back. Her hair whipped in the wind and she pulled her arms tighter against her body. I reached to remove the few stray strands that fell across her face, but she beat me to them and tucked them behind her ear. I looked down the street, trying to drop my awkward floating hand with some sort of grace, but she chuckled low and I knew I'd failed. Apparently, I'd lost all my charm along with my reputation.

And then I laughed. Hard and loud, from deep in my gut. The whole evening blurred into a ridiculous kaleidoscope of scenes and snippets that had all culminated into a hopeless prince cowering under a streetlamp.

"See. Isn't that better than smashing your head against a wall?"

"Yeah. Thank you, Miss Macario."

The door creaked in its frame behind us. I jumped and wrapped my arm around Veda's waist, rolling us both around the side of the building. I peeked around the corner, the voices of the jerks from the bar echoing stupid and drunk into the night, but fortunately in the other direction. I exhaled and glanced down. Veda's eyes widened and her mouth hung open, my body pinning her against the wall, her heart drumming hard against my sleeve.

Taking a step back, the levity between us disappeared in the dark.

"I'm sorry." I grabbed the back of my head and looked at the ground, kicking the uneven cobblestones. "I just...I just couldn't deal with them right now."

She twisted her head to the side to meet my cast down eyes. "I had a feeling. Maybe you should go home?"

"I can't. Not right now."

I glanced around the corner again--all clear-- then paced in the small space between the buildings. Going back to the castle would remind me of all the obligations I couldn't meet. Staying here wasn't safe. The heavy darkness returned to my thoughts dragging me under, drowning me.

"I know a place. Did you want to get out of here?"

I closed my eyes. "Please."

She slipped her hand in mine, her cool skin melting against my flaming palm. My head jerked her direction and locked on her dark eyes, two mysterious shadows under the moonlit sky. A stillness radiated from her touch. A calm I hadn't felt in days ran through me and eased the constriction around my lungs. A hush. Veda gasped as her breath caught in her chest. Did she feel it too? She cast a glare at our hands twined together and slid her fingers up to grab my forearm instead, pulling us back under the lantern lights.

We ran silently through the streets, up the hill toward the dark forest. As we neared the edge she tucked two fingers between her lips and whistled. Above a black cloud appeared and sped toward us, growing larger and larger until it landed in front of us with a gust of wind and a deep throaty squawk.

"Your Highness, meet Alizeh."

The giant bird lowered its head as Veda ran her hand over its glossy bronze feathers, the massive beak sharp and inches from being able to snap at her arm and break it in two.

I stepped back taking in the full wonder of the massive creature. I'd seen these birds before. A means of transportation between the highest mountain ranges and the valleys, but never one this close. Royalty needed to travel using the safest means possible, and an unsaddled, untrained bird did not fit in that category.

The bird nuzzled next to Veda's face until she tapped it gently between the eyes and it bowed its front legs and lowered its body closer to the ground. I stared at the bird's talons carving deep trenches through the dirt, each one as tall as my hip.

I shuddered. "Are you sure this is safe?"

Veda grabbed at the creature's neck and swung her leg over its feathered back, mounting the gigantic bird as if she were a stable horse, straddling between its wings. "Of course. I've had her since she was a hatchling and she's never let me down. Have you girl?" She stroked the feathers on top of the bird's head. It closed its eyes and leaned into her touch. "Why? Are you scared?"

"Of course not." I crept slowly along the side of the creature, its burrowing stare following my every step.

Veda held out her hand and I grabbed on, pulling

myself up behind her on top of the great bird. Its lungs expanded and contracted beneath my thighs and I leaned closer to Veda. Hibiscus and eucalyptus diffused between us from her hair, and the scents calmed my pounding pulse.

"Alizeh, up," Veda called and the bird stood, our heads edging near the tops of the trees.

I swallowed hard and gripped handfuls of silky feathers, as the bird spread its gigantic wings.

"Hold on. It takes some getting used to." Veda emitted a whistle and the bird darted skyward nearly tossing me back down to the cobblestones.

My stomach rose into my throat as we lifted higher and higher, the lines of Mosa townhouses shrinking to doll-sized toys.

"I've never done this before," I admitted as we passed over Takka's Tavern, the image of Kalmin's betrayal stabbing me one last time.

"You'll love it." Veda rested her hand on my leg. "I just hope you're not afraid of heights."

24TH MAY

The stars hung big and bright in front of us as we soared past the moon through the mountains. I dared to reach my hand over my head and tried to grab a fistful of starlight as it slipped between my fingers, but I didn't care if I caught it, just the simple thought that I could try seemed amazing. I'd never been this high before, never flown through the clouds one wrong move away from plummeting to the ground, and as much as my stomach twisted with fear I'd also never felt this joy of weightless freedom.

Alizeh glided east and a small rocky peak came into view. She circled, bringing us closer and slowed until she touched down on the cliff edge with a jolt. I jerked backward and yanked on Alizeh's feathers to keep upright. She let out a loud caw but leaned down to help me regain balance.

Veda slid off of Alizeh's back and patted the bird's side before looking back at me. "Looks like you made it, Your Highness."

I swung my right leg over and jumped down to the ground.

Whoa. My knees wavered and buckled being back on steady ground and squeezing my thighs so hard to hang on during the ride. I fell forward.

Veda grabbed my arm and slid herself under my shoulder. "Don't worry, you get used to that after a while."

"I hope so because I definitely want to do that again."

She laughed, the notes echoing through the bottomless ravines around us. "Good. Cause I think Alizeh likes you."

I looked up at the giant bird and she stared back, then blinked.

Veda walked forward, easing me back to holding my own weight until I stood straight again.

"There you go. Now I'll go make some tea, can you give Ali a snack? I'll meet you inside."

"What?" I watched Alizeh's enormous beak and gulped. "Are you kidding?"

"Of course not. Carrying both of us must have been exhausting for her." She ran toward the cottage before I could protest any more. When she needed the door, her arm swung out to the left. "There's some fish in the bin over there."

Veda disappeared into the cottage and lights illuminated the windows. I stood under the dark, starry sky and watched her move around the kitchen.

"I guess it's just the two of us now, Alizeh."

The bird clucked and scratched at the ground.

I walked over to a large wooden bin near the lone umbrella-shaped tree in the small yard. If it could be considered a yard. The cottage sat in the middle surrounded by patches of wild grasses until the ground just fell away on all sides into nothing. In early morning darkness, I couldn't see far, but once the sun rose the precarious location of this place would probably hit me hard.

Pulling back the lid, I threw my arm over my nose as the briny stench of the pile of dead fish blasted at my face. I lurched forward then thrust my hand in, pulling out the first fish I could find and slamming the lid closed.

Alizeh squawked as I marched back with the fish, her beak snapping in anticipation. She lowered down to the ground and leaned slightly forward. I tossed the fish in the air and she caught it, swallowing it down in one big gulp. I wiped the slimy film from the fish scales across my pant leg, instantly regretting the lingering scent it would leave.

"I guess you were hungry."

She pressed her beak into my chest and I froze.

"Easy." I pushed my hand on her beak and she nuzzled into my palm, a contented coo coming from deep in her belly. "Good girl."

I ruffled the feathers near her face and she closed her eyes, leaning in. "Oh, you like that, huh?" I rubbed a bit lower near her neck.

"I told you she liked you."

I jumped and turned around.

Veda walked toward us from the cottage. She'd changed out of her shapeless tunic into a casual dress of the deepest green like the forest with tiny white flowers embroidered along the edges that glowed in the fading moonlight. She lacked the obvious beauty girls like Sophia held in spades, as well as the refinement and grace they'd been trained in since they could walk—proper ladies of the court. But at that moment, on the mountain at the top of the world, the way her loose hair fluttered around her shoulders and her deep red lips smiled with a kindness that shone from her core, all my words piled up in my throat rendering me speechless and short of breath.

I shook my head and swallowed. Must just be the thinner mountain air.

"The tea will be ready soon," she said and nodded her head toward the cottage, now alive with flickering light streaming from the windows.

I gave Alizeh one last pat on her head, then cleared my throat and followed behind.

Inside, Veda glided around the kitchen placing out cups on the counter while a metal teapot sat on the stove. I shoved my hands in my pockets and leaned against the closed door watching her fuss with the details and taking in the rest of the cottage. It didn't appear to be more than a few small rooms cobbled together with a thick wooden ladder in the far corner leading to what appeared to be a low loft. A bedroom maybe? Everything seemed neat and clean but in a relaxed kind of way that would've passed for a mess in the castle. Griswold's head would explode if he had to manage this place, even if it were only half the size of the royal stables.

"You live up here all by yourself?"

"Generally, yeah. My father comes home now and again, but he's been studying to be a wise man at the temple further up the mountain range and seems to be spending more and more time at the retreat there."

I scanned the cottage again, the thought of the quiet overwhelming. The castle always had people, any time of day or night I could always find someone. "That must get lonely?"

She laughed. An airy light chuckle that seemed a complete contradiction to her normal serious self. "I do have friends, you know. It's not like I am cursed to hide in my tower forever like they do in the west."

Steam billowed from the teapot and she poured the steaming water into two delicate red cups. "Besides, I kind of like the quiet. It helps me with my writing."

She handed me the tea, the clay cup warm on my fingertips and soothing my cold hands. I hadn't realized the chill that had crawled under my skin from the flight, but suddenly I shivered. "Writing? Wait, you don't work for one of those newspapers camped outside the castle, do you?"

I placed the cup on the counter and slowly began to back towards the door. No wonder she'd taken such an interest in me all of a sudden.

"No." She grabbed her own cup of tea and moved into the sitting room, then flopped down in a grand armchair next to an old dim lamp made of rough pieces of iron. "Maybe one day, but for now I just make up stories. I kind of feel like I have all these things to say, and writing lets me get them out of my head before all the voices drive me insane."

I relaxed a bit, the threat of being interviewed falling away. "Do you let people read them?"

She laughed but stared into the bottom of her teacup. "No. Or at least not yet. But I'm trying to get there. There's a competition coming up in Mosa where the winner gets a huge cash prize. I'm hoping it could be my ticket out of here. See the world, you know?"

"It's not as exciting as you make it sound. The world I mean. Sometimes home is way better than being away."

"Says the spoiled prince who has seen it all before."

I cringed. "Maybe. But that would make me an expert on the subject, now wouldn't it?"

I wandered to the back of the cottage to the wall of books carefully arranged in rows according to height and shade of the cover. I'd have to show her my mother's collection one day. She'd probably love it. I grabbed a familiar purple-covered volume and thumbed through the pages.

"I think we have this one in the castle library too. My mother used to read it to me when I was young. I loved the thought of there maybe being another world out there."

"I think I've read that one a hundred times. It's one of my favorites." Veda sat up and perched at the edge of the chair. "And I'd love to see the castle one day. I've always imagined what it might look like in there. I think I even wrote a story about it once."

"How come you've never been there? There are always open court days and my parent's annual Fall Ball. I'm pretty sure everyone in the kingdom has seen the inside at least once."

She placed her tea on the rickety table beside her and crossed her hands in her lap. "My father never let me go, and I guess as I got older I just assumed I shouldn't. That I wouldn't be welcome there."

I put the book back then wandered around the couch to kneel in front of her, her gaze still cast down to the floor. "That's nonsense, everyone is welcome at the castle. Once my father is better I will bring you there myself. I'll let you go anywhere you want."

"Are you sure? I don't want to cause any problems."

She finally met my eyes, a ghost of something passing through them that I couldn't identify. I had to be missing something here.

"Of course. Besides, you've invited me into your home, I should at least return the favor."

"Thank you. That's very kind, but we'll see."

A red line painted across the wall behind her. I turned and squinted as the first rays of sunrise burst through the window. I stood and followed the light, as if pulled on an invisible string, the sun tugging me towards it like a smelly fish on a fisherman's hook.

A strip of red fire smoldered across the skyline, burning away the darkness, a new day rising from its ashes. I took the well-worn path to the edge of the cliff and stared over the mountaintops out to the entire kingdom. My kingdom.

Veda joined me at the edge, her hand held over her eyes shielding some of the glare of the sun. "You should see this view in full daylight. You can almost see all the way to Urbis."

"Is that how you knew about the darkness? Because you could see it coming?"

Veda crossed her arms and jut her hip to the side, her green dress hugging the curves at her waist. "So, you believe me now?"

The fairy's words whispered in my head. *You might be our last hope.*

"I think I might. It seems like you're not the only one who's been noticing what's been going on around here. I'm starting to pay more attention."

"At least you're trying, that's an improvement."

My spine straightened and my chest puffed out at her words even though they likely weren't meant as a compliment. "Maybe. But I ran into a gale force of a girl who said I should probably take note of these things. I think that maybe she was right."

A soft pink tinged her cheeks as she cast her eyes to the ground and fiddled with the flowers on her dress.

"There may just be hope for you yet, Your Highness."

"Please, you can stop with the pleasantries. My friends, at least the ones I thought were my friends, just call me Fallon or Falls sometimes."

"Okay...er... Fallon." The words looked like they hurt as they rolled across her lips, but then she smiled, the melodic inflection of her voice on the double l's oddly charming.

"Much better."

Pink light bathed her face and highlighted the strands of red that weaved through her dark locks. I rested my hand on her cheek, my fingertips burying in her hair, and she stiffened under my touch.

"Sorry," I snapped my hand away. What was happening? I hadn't planned this, instinct pushing me instead of calculation. "I shouldn't have done that."

She turned her head to the horizon, curls falling over her neck. "It's okay. It's just...I've seen you in the tavern, with all those other fancy girls. That's not why I brought you up here. I think there's much more to you than that."

"Veda...I never thought..." I stepped back giving her space and letting my thoughts clear, her proximity messing with my head. "Why do you have so much faith in me?"

"Because I know how it feels. Having responsibility on your shoulders that you don't want, that you're too young to understand." Her eyes welled up, but she bit her lip and pushed down the tears. "My mother died before I could even remember her, and it's clear my father never wanted a daughter. I don't doubt he loves me, but I was a burden that took him away from his other projects. I grew up fast and on my own. Then I saw this prince. One who had the loving family I never did but had so many responsibilities on his head. I knew what that felt like. I knew what it would mean for you one day. That you'd be lost. I wanted to help."

Her story socked me in the stomach. No one should feel like they weren't wanted. I wanted to pull her close, but stopped myself, my fingers itching to try and make her feel better. "But you don't need to. I'm not a puppy that needs to be taken care of."

"But you will be king one day. My king. And I would do anything to make sure that you lead Aboria with strength and courage."

I rubbed my hands over my face and paced between Veda and the cliff, the height making me suddenly dizzy. "Please don't do that. Don't imagine me as some great leader. I'm not. I want to be, but I will never be the leader that my father is. And what if I end up—"

"Cursed just like him?"

My head snapped toward her. "What did you say?"

"Cursed like your father. You don't have to worry about that. Even if it is a family curse, you aren't in the bloodline so it probably wouldn't affect you."

"How do you know about my father's curse? Who told you?"

"I've always known." She laced her fingers together in front of her, concentrating on her hands as a deep 'v' dug in between her eyes. "But I didn't know it would happen again."

I grabbed a handful of my hair and pulled, hoping this would be a dream and I'd suddenly wake up in my own bed with Griswold knocking on the door, but

I didn't. She knew about the curse. She knew it had happened before. Until just a few days ago, I didn't even know that.

"And what do you mean I'm not in the bloodline. I'm the only child of the king and queen, of course, I'm in the bloodline."

She shook her head, pink bursting into deep crimson in her cheeks. "You really have no idea, do you?"

She grabbed my hand. The jolt from when her skin connected with mine ripped up my arm and I swore I saw it spark in the last drops of darkness before the sunrise. "Come on. I have something to show you."

She led me back into the house and dropped me by the faded worn couch then walked over to the bookcase. She stood on her tiptoes and reached toward the highest shelf, the hem of her dress inching up the back of her thigh. I forced my eyes to look away and stood to help, but she'd already grabbed a well-worn journal from the shelf and had started unwinding the narrow leather cord wrapped around the pages to keep them closed. She flipped the journal open. "I think you should see this."

"Is it your writing?"

She shook her head her full lips pursed tight. "No, it's my father's."

"I don't see..."

She thrust the open journal in front of me, a detailed hand-drawn image of a feral beast splashed across the page. The beast so terrifying, even the drawing made me shudder, or maybe because I'd seen that beast before. Hiding in the west wing. It was my dad.

My blood bubbled, the room heating up around me. "Where did you get this?"

"I told you, it was my father's. Everyone else may

have forgotten about the curse, but my father wrote down everything that happened so he could remember." She jiggled the journal closer to me. "Read it."

I lay the loosely bound pages across my lap and read the impeccably neat scroll beneath the drawing of the beast. Veda crossed her arms, popping her hip to the side as she watched my finger traced over the indentations on the page as I read. Each word collected in my brain as I struggled to make sense of them. Bright and sharp puzzle pieces but with no full picture to follow.

"It says he kidnapped my mother. Held her prisoner. But that can't be true? They love each other. I've seen it, this is a mistake."

She shrugged. "Maybe you're right, but it seems like there are a lot of things your parents have kept from you. Do you think it's possible that it really happened this way? Maybe they love each other now, but do you really know how they met?"

I slammed the journal shut, dust moats erupting from the pages.

"I don't believe it. This is a book of lies."

"Fine. But what about the rest of the story? The part about the baby boy with golden rings in his eyes left on the doorstep of the castle?"

I jumped up and Veda retreated a step giving me more space for my anger to grow. "Enough. Why are you telling this to me?"

"Don't you think someone should? You've lived your whole life in the dark, Fallon. If these people truly loved you, why wouldn't they just tell you the truth?"

She pulled the book from my hands and flipped quickly through the pages, the spine opening on her perfect page like she'd read this a thousand times before.

Maybe she had. Maybe my life was the story her father told her before bed, instead of the tales of dragons and far away lands like everyone else. But from the deep scowl carved across her face, I'd clearly been painted as the villain in this story.

"Right here." She stabbed her finger into the middle of the page. "And in the twilight on the fortnight, after the curse had been broken, the babe arrived wrapped in a golden cloak, his eyes the color of the sun. And the king and queen claimed the boy as their own and raised a bastard prince to one day claim the throne he did not deserve."

The world began to spin. The dim lantern light swirled into the night and back again, as my stomach contracted and this morning's breakfast teased a return.

I grabbed the arm of the ratty couch trying to make the world stay still for even just a second. This couldn't be true. Could it? There was no way. My parents loved me. They never said anything or even hinted that I wasn't theirs. I even looked like my parents. My wavy chestnut hair was just like my mother's, and the angle of my jaw and build were unmistakably my dad. I even had my mother's lone dimple on my left cheek. If I were someone else's child how could I ever look like them? Like they could change me to match the family portraits that hung in the grand ballroom.

"So you really didn't know?" Veda placed her palm on my shoulder and I blinked but cringed, the warmth of her hand bleeding through my shirt.

"No. But I don't how any of it could be true. My father is a good man. A noble king. He would never... would never hurt my mother. I can't be adopted. There's no way they would have kept something like that from me. This is probably just somebody's idea of causing trouble. Sell this story to the newspaper and discredit my family's order. It can't be true."

She pulled her hand away and wound the leather cord back around the fictional pages, then rested the journal on the small kitchen table.

"You could ask him if you wanted to."

I shook my head, the carousel of crazy still spinning in my brain, then narrowed my stare and looked at her, the words not sinking in.

"My father, I mean. If you wanted to know why he wrote those things. How he knows them. I can take you there."

"Of course. Let's go." I stomped out of the cottage toward the edge of the mountain searching the sky for her magnificent bird. I put my fingers in my mouth and whistled, but Alizeh didn't come.

"Fallon. I didn't mean right now. My father is traveling from the Emerald City and it's barely even daylight. You're going to have to wait." I turned around. Veda gripped her bare arms, contracting her body close, smaller than I'd ever seen her. "I didn't mean to upset you. I thought you already knew."

I dropped to the ground and held my head in my hands. My father was a monster. Not just a beast, but a kidnapper. And my parents, my real parents, they didn't even want me. Let me on a doorstep to be raised by strangers. This couldn't be true. If this were true... "You should hate me. Me and my family, and everything we stand for."

"Why would I hate you?" She sat next to me in the dirt, her knees pulled to her chest. "You haven't done anything wrong, and you still have the chance to make it right. Be better."

She placed her hand on my leg, but this time her touch didn't soothe the demons in my mind. "But what if I can't?"

25TH MAY

"Are you coming, Fallon?" Veda called from the front yard.

I peered out the kitchen window. Alizeh had arrived, strutting around the mountaintop her bronze wings shimmering in the morning sun. Veda faced the edge of the cliff, her hands on her hips as she leaned back and let the sun warm her face. Strands of her hair blew in the morning breeze and I caught myself wishing to tangle my fingers in it, but shook my head to erase the thought.

"Just a minute." I wound the leather coil back around the journal and slid it into its place on the shelf. It's not like I even needed to read the pages anymore, I'd scoured over them so many times in the last twenty-four hours that all the words were committed to memory. Every horrible thing my father had done. Every detail of how I didn't belong.

I raced out of the cottage, closed the door behind me and took one last look. The quaintness of Veda's cottage had started to grow on me, the quiet allowing thoughts to blossom like flowers of truth in the thorny garden of my mind.

"If you're having second thoughts, I can just take you back to the castle."

"No. I need this." I joined Veda and Alizeh near the edge of the cliff and stroked Alizeh's feathers on her wing. The whole world lay before us as the sunlight glittered off the tops of forests and cities in the distance. "Unless you don't want to go?"

She shuddered and turned away, staring off the mountainside. "I'm just not sure if my father will be angry. He's never said I couldn't share his journals, but again, I've never really asked either. I haven't even read them all myself."

I took her hand and rubbed my thumb along her bony knuckles and she softened, then gave me a half-hearted crooked smile. We'd reached an understanding—a closeness—built in the midnight hours of poring over books and stories searching for answers. A cause for the darkness and anything to back up the words her father had written so many years ago. We'd talked through a full day and most of a night until we both fell asleep beside each other on the cottage floor. When morning came, I still hadn't figured out if I was happy to be leaving.

She squeezed my hand. "I'm sure it will be fine. Besides, you deserve to know where you came from. What your future may hold."

She let me go and mounted Alizeh's back. The bird

dipped lower to the ground so I could fumble my way up behind her.

She spread her majestic wings and I risked taking a glance down into the depths of the ravine. Veda didn't move, sitting stick straight in front of me. The urge to wrap my arms around her waist and make her feel better pulled strong, but I forced it down, instead I savored in the sweet scent of her as the early morning breeze swept through her hair and her dark strands danced in the upstream.

The muscles in Alizeh's back moved and I dug my hands into her feathers as she took a running start toward the edge of the cliff. We plummeted over the side before swooping back up through the sky again, the weightless sensation of freedom reigniting in my veins, except this time something didn't feel right. I closed my eyes, my stomach slowly starting to twist into knots as we flew closer and closer to the truth.

Morning bled into afternoon, the sun rising high on the horizon as Alizeh crested the tops of the highest peaks in the Aborian mountain range. The splashes of green from the small patches of forest disappeared as we soared beyond the clouds, the elevation too great for much vegetation to grow.

"Almost there," Veda shouted.

She hadn't said a word in hours, the silence prickling up my spine for the entire journey.

Alizeh leaned right and I shielded my eyes as a blinding glow appeared in front of us. In the distance a temple rose, the sun gleaming off the sloped golden rooftop. I peeked through my fingers and watched as

Alizeh circled and landed across the mountain from the building.

I'd heard stories of the temples high in the Aboria sky, but I'd never actually seen one. They said the wisest of wise men lived and worked there, devoting their lives to the study of peace and higher ascendance. Once in a while, some of these wise men arrived in court with messages for my father, always so calm and centered compared to the city-dwellers of Mosa.

As soon as we stopped moving, I launched off Alizeh's back and stared at the temple as it glistened, my soul feeling calmer already.

I held my hand out to help Veda down. She gave me a nervous smile and accepted then jumped the rest of the way to the ground in front of me.

"Ready?" she asked.

"Yeah. Of course."

She nodded and started off toward the temple. I reached my hand around her waist and tugged her back.

"Before we go though, I wanted to say thank you. You could've left me, miserable on the side of the street, but you didn't."

"I haven't done much yet. We'll see what my father has to say first." She tapped me playfully in the chest, her hand lingering just below my neck. The warmth of her touch burned against my skin.

I peeled her hand away and held it by our sides linking my fingers between hers. "I'm serious. I owe you a lot."

"We'll work out a way for you to pay me back later. Let's just deal with one problem at a time."

"Okay, but I always pay my debts."

She laughed, light and playful and I laughed along

with her, letting the feeling take over and ease some of the dark thoughts still running through my brain.

"You're a prince, remember? I doubt you have many debts."

"Which means I have no reason not to make good on them."

Her head leaned slightly to the side and I suddenly saw nothing but her deep, red lips. The way they curled when she laughed and quivered when she breathed. I ran the tip of my finger across the bottom one. The softness tickled against my skin. She gasped and I tried to pull my hand away, but I couldn't, I just froze wondering how those lips might taste.

She puckered and placed a kiss on the end of my finger, then tugged my hand away. "Not here."

I shook my head, the spell finally broken, although my hand still burned from her touch.

"I'm sorry."

"Don't apologize." She slipped out of my arms and headed towards the temple. "I'm not sorry."

I followed behind her as the magnificent temple came into better view. Intricate markings etched the outer walls, an ancient language or maybe a magical protection of sorts, while statues of golden eagles perched proud on all four corners of the building. A babbling waterfall ran from beside the grand staircase, surrounding the temple with a small creek of brightly colored fish. Pinks and greens and blues of the most vibrant shades slithered through the cool clear water, and I had to fight the hypnotic call to stare at them all afternoon.

"I wasn't expecting company. Veda, why didn't you tell me you were coming? I would've planned time for you." A man in a long, sweeping robe appeared at the top of the staircase and started to descend. He seemed much taller than I expected. Broader. But maybe Veda resembled her mother more.

“Sorry, Father, it was a last-minute trip. I know you’re busy, but there is someone I want you to meet.”

He reached the bottom of the staircase, and scanned us over, absorbing every detail and making me feel very exposed.

Veda nudged me forward. “Fallon, please meet my father, Edwin Macario.”

He marched toward us, his crimson red robe dragging just above the ground. For a stranger, he seemed familiar. The bold line of his jaw or the haphazardness of his salt-and-pepper hair maybe? Or maybe the calm serenity of the temple played tricks on the mind?

I folded one arm behind my back and bent forward, extending my open hand. “Hello, sir. I’m--”

“I know who you are, Prince Fallon. Few people in Aboria live their lives without knowing of you and the royal family.” He took my hand and shook it, abrupt and tough, his grip pinching my knuckles together.

“I’ve never been to the temples before. It’s an amazing view, it must be very relaxing.”

“Few people have, especially those of noble blood.” He headed back toward the temple and sat in a large wicker chair his hands crossed in front of him, hidden by the wide sleeves of his robe. “So why would someone like you venture this far to see me? I doubted the castle even thought of me anymore.”

Veda ducked around me and stood by her father’s side, the resemblance between the two immediate. The same thin nose and thickness in their cheeks. “I told him that you might be able to tell him about before he was born. About the curse. About where he came from.”

The man's face soured. "And why do you think I would know about those things?"

"Because of your journal," I said. "The one you left at your cottage. I want to know if the things you wrote were true."

"No," he said.

I waited for a minute, two, maybe three, the silence doing little to help the confusion.

"No, it's not true?" I asked.

"No. I don't want to talk about it. That was many years ago, many long years that I would much rather forget. I've devoted my life now to wisdom and quiet contemplation, I don't need to raise such demons." He shook his head, fierce as if convincing himself instead of just me. "Besides, the curse has long passed. There is no reason to speak of such things. Unless--" he raised a steady finger across his lips and the tip of his nose, "--it is no longer in the past."

His stare narrowed, reading my face, waiting for a sign to confirm his suspicions.

I breathed deep. "And if it isn't?"

The man's eyes widened again and he shifted in his seat as he put his hands together in front of his face as if in prayer. "Very interesting. Very interesting indeed."

"So you'll help him, father?"

"No. Absolutely not." The fascination disappeared into a glare of stone.

"Please, sir. I need to know what happened so I can try to fix things now."

He pushed on the arms of the chair, standing before me again. "I owe you nothing, prince. Fix your own problems. Now go."

He flicked his hand at me twice, then started toward the steps into the temple.

Veda looked at me, and our eyes locked in a silent plea. She frowned and charged after him stopping just before the creek.

"Don't you always say 'truth is the path to freedom', Father? Who are you to deny someone on their search for enlightenment?"

Veda's father froze, a proud grin breaking across his harsh expression. "My daughter, how am I to become a wise man when you are more clever than I? But what if the truth leads to further suffering? Is it not my duty to protect others?"

She stepped forward. "Only if he chooses to be protected. You've warned him. If he still seeks the truth, you must oblige his wishes as you are not the master of his destiny."

Edwin turned around at the base to the staircase and leaned against the railing. He grabbed his chin and brushed the thick stubble as he pondered his daughter's request.

"If he accepts the consequences of his request, then I guess I am not doing my duty as a wise man not to provide answers."

"Thank you," I whispered and Veda looked away, the simple gratitude blooming pink across her skin.

"It's simple really. Once upon a time, as the storytellers say, there was an evil king. Selfish, ill-tempered, and generally a complete brute. One day he irritated the wrong person and suddenly he was cursed to become a beast--not much of a difference from his normal self, to be honest, just a bit hairier."

My fingers curled into fists, my arms tensing as he painted a dark picture of my father. Maybe coming to talk to him wasn't the best idea. Maybe I should've just gone home and asked my mother.

"And then one day an old man happened across his castle and he held him hostage. His daughter offered herself in his place, and the evil beast took her as his captive. He crushed that smart and beautiful girl until she foolishly believed she could change him and broke the curse with her love. Makes me sick to even think about it."

He scoffed and started back toward us. Veda returned to my side, hanging on every word.

"That can't be true. My father is a good man. He loves my mother more than anything. He'd never do something like that."

"Oh really? It's nice to know this nightmare has a happy ending. And then I guess that's where you come in. The golden boy with the golden eyes who sits on the throne of lies."

My pulse pounded in my temples, spots of light and dark flashed in my vision. A wise man? Or just a self-important jerk? "And why should I believe you?"

The man stopped and sneered, sensing my anger and from the delighted smile broad across his face, reveling in it.

"Because I was there, you fool," he laughed. "I used to spend my time at the castle. Attending court. The glamorous, ridiculous balls. A wasted existence kissing the feet of a tyrant who kidnapped a girl and made her his bride. A girl who should've never been a queen."

"If you were so important, why aren't you there now? How come I've never heard of you?"

He splayed a hand across his chest and feigned devastation as his jaw dropped almost comically. I grit my teeth so hard they threatened to shatter. How could this guy and Veda be family? Her mother must be where she received her compassion as Edwin had none.

"Because I finally saw the light. I told him to let the girl go, but he wouldn't listen, so I walked away from your father's sick and twisted game."

"You left, or did he send you away?"

I shouldn't have said it. As soon as the words rolled off my tongue, regret pooled in my mouth, salty and warm like blood from a fresh wound. Veda's father laughed. A disturbing cackle not of humor but of vengeance. He stormed toward us.

"Do not speak of things you don't understand. You were not there to watch the entire kingdom fall apart at the hands of a maniacal king. You did not spend your days cleaning up one mess after another. You've never had the sulphuric breath of a beast on your face as you begged for your life, one clawed hand wrapped around your neck the other positioned to shred the skin from your bones."

The memories flashed through the man's eyes, everything red and sinister. The scar on my hand throbbed, his image reminding me of my own near-death at the hands of the beast--the beast who was not my father, just a curse that needed to be stopped.

"So what do I do? My father has changed and even if he was the awful person you say he was, he's not anymore. How can I break the curse if I don't know what caused it?"

Veda leaned closer, her body shivering in the afternoon heat as she wrapped icy fingers around my bicep, gripping tight. I pulled my free arm across my chest and enveloped her hand with mine, tension draining from her grasp as my palm melted the chill pulsing through her and I bent to rest my chin on her head.

"What exactly is going on here?" Veda's father

bellowed and she twitched beside me, pulling her hand away and straightening her stance.

"Nothing, Father. Just tell us what to do now."

He ignored her and stepped in front of me, a finger pointed in the center of my chest.

"You are no better than him, are you?" The hatred in his snarl emerged from a deep, dark place inside him. "Take, take, take! That's all you do. That's all you know how to do, isn't it? And then you expect me to help you after you swoop in and try to steal my daughter from right in front of me."

"I've done nothing wrong, sir. I wouldn't hurt Veda. I wouldn't hurt anyone."

"Yet." His stare glazed over, my words falling empty to the ground. "You're just like your father, and you'll destroy everyone around you. If you want to know all about it, go ask him yourself. Let them tell you all about their toxic relationship, but keep your family's poison away from my daughter."

"He's telling the truth," Veda said, tugging on her father's arm. "Fallon hasn't done anything to me. I was the one who brought him here. I was the one who told him about the curse. If you are going to be angry with anyone, be angry with me."

"Well, that was your bad judgment, but I'll bet he's the one who orchestrated the whole thing."

"I did not," I yelled, stepping up to the man.

He inched closer, but I stood tall, biting down on the inside of my cheek. My words had caused enough trouble for one week, even though they collected in my mouth ready to fire.

"You'll not get another thing from me." A spray of spit escaped his twisted mouth and landed on my cheek. "Get out of this sacred place, you don't deserve to breathe its air."

I stared back with as much fury as I could muster. He already expected nothing but royal privilege and my narrowed eyes gave it to him. "Gladly."

I turned on my heel, his hot breath against my neck as Veda took my hand and we started to walk away.

"Don't think I'm going to let you leave with him."

She glanced up at me, then glared at her father her hands shooting to her hips. "When did my choices become yours?"

"You've always been my smart, strong, girl Veda, but right now you are acting like a petulant child."

She ground her heel into the dirt, her eyes still locked on her father's angry expression. "As are you."

His face exploded into one hundred shades of red, his robes billowing around him as he stuck his arm out and pointed. "You are not leaving this mountain, and that's final."

Veda sighed and her head dropped to her chest, quick and sharp like a guillotine blade. Her father spun around and stomped off toward the temple. Not a bird chirped, not a breeze rustled through the air, the world silent as if he'd condemned the universe instead of his daughter.

With a deep breath, life reanimated in Veda and she burst past me toward Alizeh resting on the far end of the temple grounds. I tripped after her, her small frame determined and focused like an arrow loosed from a bow until she stopped abruptly and I nearly fell over her trying to slow my own feet.

"Just tell Ali where you want to go and she'll take you there. Call her name first, and then give directions so she understands, and remember to speak loud enough for her to hear if it's windy."

“Wait, you’re not coming?”

She crossed her arms and looked away, water pooling in her stare but she blinked and pushed it down. “You heard my father. I’m not to leave this mountain.”

“But he can’t stop you. We could be gone before he’d even realize you’d left.” I placed my hand on her chin and turned her face to look at me. “Come with me.”

“It’s not that simple. Besides if anyone should understand about having to stand by their father when they don’t want to, it would be you.”

“I don’t want to leave you here.”

She placed a hand on my chest and pushed me toward Alizeh. “I’ll be fine. He’s angry with you, but once you’re gone he’ll calm down. Plus, if I stay around a while I might be able to convince him to talk to you again, or at least find out if he knows anything else. Now get going before he decides to come back and argue with you again.”

“But how will you get back home?”

She kept pushing me to go, but I held my stance.

“Ali will come for me. I’ll call her and she’ll come.”

I placed my hand over hers and held tight. The look of determination melted and the strength in her stare wavered. I put on my best face. The one Mosa city girls went wild for. But Veda didn’t surrender. “Are you sure you won’t leave with me?”

She shook her head, the lost look in her sad frown stinging in my chest. I pulled her to me and she rested her hands at the base of my neck as I held my arms tight around her waist. I let myself breathe her in. Taking every last opportunity to create a memory to carry back home.

“When this is over, come to the castle and look for me.”

Veda unclasped her fingers and twisted out of my grip. She took my hand and walked away, her skin lingering against mine until the last second before the link broke to let her go. The small smile she offered me dying as the space between us widened.

I pulled myself up on Alizeh's back and watched Veda shrink in the distance, a piece of me following behind and leaving me painfully hollow.

~

Moonlight cut through the valley illuminating the castle like a beacon calling me home. As we approached, the city grew larger, spreading out beneath us with its shops and taverns and familiar smells. But the closer Alizeh flew toward the castle grounds, the less I wanted to get there.

"Alizeh, the ridge on the left."

The bird obeyed sweeping around the city to a flat peak, just big enough for us to land. She ground her talons into the earth as dust spit up around us kicking in my lungs. She lowered her head and I slid off assessing the blissfully vacant ridge. A stand of trees lurked dark ahead of us, but without a proper pathway up the mountain, I doubted any danger hid beneath the foliage. I looked down at the castle again. The brightly colored flags flapped lazily from the tops of the turrets in the calm night. The gardens twirled in loops and curls among the flowers, a labyrinth to get lost in, which I'd done so many times. My chest tightened, the familiarity of home luring me there, but the fear of the unknown driving me away.

If it was even really my home. Veda's father didn't give me the answers I wanted but even after the hours of flight I still didn't know how to put words to the questions I needed to ask. Or maybe I really wasn't ready to hear the truth.

"Looks like will be camping here tonight, girl."

I pet her beak and she cooed softly as she lowered herself closer to the ground and pulled her wings in close. I lay on the dusty ground and stared up at the sky and its speckling of stars. Home lay just below me, and the truth lived at a temple on the highest of peaks, but I sat stuck in the middle, terrified of either option. As I closed my eyes, the stars smeared and I wondered if somewhere up there Veda was looking at them and thinking of me.

26TH MAY

"Did Dad kidnap you when he was cursed the first time, Mom? Oh, and did someone abandon me on your doorstep as a baby? Just wanted to check. Okay. Thanks."

I shook my head. No. Not like that. I had to ease in to the concept gently. If I came at her like a firing squad she'd never tell me the truth. She'd probably just get defensive and shut herself up in her library. Maybe Griswold knew? He'd been around the castle the longest out of anyone, I'm sure he knew things that he'd been sworn to keep quiet in exchange for a notable position.

Alizeh landed with effortless grace in the front courtyard of the castle just beyond the gates of the city. Seamlessly, she slid in between the gardens and the fountains. An impressive talent for a bird her size.

Guards immediately flanked her, not like they would be any match for a creature of her size although they were paid to try.

"Stand down," I called as I dismounted Alizeh and stroked the feathers near her beak.

Each of the guards dropped to one knee, their heads bowed. I approached the closest guard, a well-decorated soldier, and he rose to his feet, his head still tilted toward the ground.

"Send someone to the stables and get something for my friend to eat."

He nodded. "Yes, sir."

"And tell them, she is not to be harmed or mishandled in any way. She may also come and go as she pleases. This bird is a guest in our kingdom and should be treated as such. Understood?"

He nodded again. "Yes, sir. Permission to address His Majesty?"

"Of course, speak freely."

He finally dared to look at me, the heaviness of my position weighing down between my shoulders. "The queen has been looking for you, sir. She has been worried."

"I'll see to her right away. Thank you."

I gave Alizeh's wings one last stroke. "Take care of yourself."

Alizeh clucked and nuzzled her beak against my chest. I leaned into her. "And take care of Veda too."

Straightening my hair and tugging my shirt into place, I let out a deep breath and headed toward the castle. Time for the truth.

As I approached, the castle doors flung open, the locks thundering as they unbolted and the hinges squealing to let me through. Mom rushed into the courtyard, nearly barreling over me in her haste, a row of guards parading behind her. Slim pants covered her legs, her hair pulled tight behind her head in a thick braid. Odd. She didn't even wander around the castle without at least a casual dress. Something had happened.

"Fallon." Her glare widened, eyes dark and watery from crying, and then she flung herself at me squeezing her arms tight around my chest until I could barely breathe. "Where have you been?"

I studied the row of guards and dropped my voice. "I've been up in the mountains. But I really need to talk to you."

"Not right now. Your father—" her eyes welled up and tears streamed down her scarlet face, "He's escaped. I left to get him something to eat and when I returned, he was gone."

"Are you sure? Maybe he's just hiding inside." I darted around her, scanning the foyer just beyond the doors.

She grabbed my arm. "He's not in there. We've searched the entire castle. He's gone."

Adrenaline flooded my veins. The words of Veda's father rushed at me again. He didn't know my father like I did. Didn't know how he'd changed if he was ever the devil Edwin believed he'd been. But what if there was some truth to his story? What would that mean if he were set free? I pulled out of Mom's grip and grabbed the back of my head, pacing across the impeccable tile work of the courtyard.

"And it's worse," she continued, "he isn't himself anymore. The curse has taken over completely and I don't know if he'll listen to me anymore."

"Why didn't you tell me?"

"I didn't know where you were. And we'll discuss

that later, but right now I have to find him. Stay here in case he comes back."

"Are you kidding? I can't just wait here. I'm coming with you."

"Thank you, Fallon." The shadow of a smile crossed her lips and died. "Griswold."

The old man rushed out the open castle door to my mother's side. "Yes, my queen."

"Keep watch in case the king returns. He may simply be lost and then try to find his way back."

"Of course, madam."

She pointed at a group of guards on the left. "You six, stay here at the castle and make sure if the king returns that I am notified immediately. Do not try to stop him, just guide him back to the west wing and wait for further instructions. Do you understand?"

The nodded in unison and turned sharp, marching to their posts within the castle walls.

She took my hand, her quivering fingers betraying the display of strength and control she put on for everyone else. "Now, we should split up. You take half the guards and head towards the center of town and I'll take the rest towards the forest and the outskirts of the city. I think he'll try to avoid a scene so I doubt you'll come across him. If you see anything, send someone for me."

"Are you sure this is safe for you to be chasing after a beast?"

"Probably not, but I won't let anyone else handle something this important." She gripped tighter. "He's my heart, Fallon. I can't let just anyone take care of it."

I hugged her, giving her a second to compose herself before leading her army into the unknown. "Don't worry, Mom. We'll find him."

She raised a hand above her head and pointed toward the thick trees leading up the mountain range. The guards fell in line and followed her out, the rest staying back waiting for my instructions.

I jumped up on the edge of a fountain and scanned the guards' faces. Every one of them hung on my words. Every one of them willing to go into battle for me and my family. If only they knew the real truth, would they still be so honorable? However, this wasn't the time to cast doubt in their calling.

"Search every place, no matter if you think you won't find him," I called out to my team. "And try to avoid alarming the civilians. They are not to know what we are looking for."

"Yes, sir." They bellowed in unison.

I jerked my head toward the city and crested the golden bridge to Mosa, wishing with every ounce of strength I had that we weren't the ones to find him.

The sun beat down on my back, my shirt clinging to my chest as I searched every back alley and public place in all of Mosa. The people stared, but I didn't care. They didn't know they were all in danger, and I needed to keep it that way until we found my father. *If* we found my father.

I wiped my sleeve across my brow, the salty taste of sweat on my lips. We'd turned over every inch of this city, and hadn't uncovered one clue as to where my father might be hiding. Mom was likely right, he'd avoid the crowded streets and head for the cover of the trees. Maybe she was having better luck.

I pushed my way between two buildings into a small

secluded courtyard but found nothing. The light didn't penetrate the high walls of the Mosa buildings back here and the shadows hung long and dark upon the walls. I fell against the cool brick wall and let the darkness soothe the burn in my skin. This mission started to seem hopeless.

A hand grabbed my arm and I jumped as my pulse quickened.

"Sorry, sir." The guard let go of my arm and put his hands behind his back, widening his stance at attention. "We've finished sweeping the north side of the city, sir. No sign of the king."

"Thank you. I'm starting to think we won't be the ones to find him."

"Keep strong, sir."

I patted him on the shoulder. A good soldier.

"Tell your men to do one last look in the south then head back to the castle. I'll have the cook prepare something special for your efforts."

"Of course, sir."

So this was it. We'd searched everywhere and he'd just disappeared. Maybe he didn't want to be found? Maybe somewhere deep down he understood what he'd become, even if he wasn't able to communicate it back? If it had happened to me, I don't know what I'd do. Would I run too? Or would I just hide like a coward waiting for it all to be over?

A single scream ripped through the sky. I jerked my head in its direction and slid back out of the courtyard into the street. People rushed toward us, clambering up the hill as fast as they could.

More screams echoed, bouncing between the buildings. I closed my eyes and listened for the source. They seemed to be coming from the center of the city.

The market. *No.* Too many people who could get hurt. Too many people who might see my father for what he'd become.

"The market. Go. Now."

I thrust my arm down the main street and the guards rushed past me, swords drawn and prepared to fight. I chased downhill after them, citizens running against us, like salmon swimming upstream. Their shrieks resounded in my head as they ran. Windows and doors shuttered around us. Children were yanked from the streets, their parents shielding their eyes to avoid the horror.

Grrr!

A loud growl pierced through the crowd. My legs pushed harder, faster, trying to get to my father before he caused any damage.

I reached the market. Dad stood in the center of the square, his arms outstretched to the sky, with a row of guards surrounding him a circle. Citizens hid behind the market stalls and watched the drama unfold. My father reared his head back and let out a guttural roar. The guards shuddered then doubled down for an attack.

At the far end of the circle, one of the guards took charge. He pulled his sword back behind his shoulder and yelled, charging toward my father. My stomach clenched, bile burning its way up my throat. He wasn't just some monster to slay. Somewhere in there was my father.

"Stop!" I shouted as I lurched forward past the line of guards, but my warning came too late.

The guard swung the sword at my father. He dodged, the blade barely missing his torso. The guard swung again. Missed. But my father didn't. He grabbed the guard's arm in his clawed hand and dragged him off the ground, his feet kicking wildly as he screamed in fear. My father growled again and flashed his teeth, then tossed the guard across the square like a toy that no longer pleased him. People ducked as the guard's body smashed into a fruit cart. Crates splintered with a crack. Melons and dragon fruits splattered across the cobblestones.

The next guard in line took his turn, running at my father screaming his battle cry. His body landed two stalls away, spilling bolts of fabric into the street.

"Attack!"

The guards inched closer around my father tightening the circle. He spun around, the fur along his back rippling as his shoulders hunched preparing for a fight. They charged. All at once and from every angle.

"Stop," I screamed again but no one heard me over the noise of the battle. My knees weakened. All the strength in my body drained as I watched the havoc. Helpless to stop the battle that had already begun.

Swords clanged as they clattered to the ground. More bodies flew, blood poisoning the fountains and staining the square. My father yelped as the guards clambered over him, dragging him down. His massive arms swung out, swatting at them like bees. Guards fell, one after the other, none strong enough to take down the beast.

My insides twisted beneath my skin. Each blow hitting me hard, but also providing relief that this nightmare might end soon. The image Veda's father painted in my mind of the ferocious malevolent beast took form in front of me, but he didn't know him like I did. His kindness. His strength. His ability to care about his people. This was not the ending for a king, no matter what his form.

I pushed my way through the onlookers onto the

battlefield. Pieces of armor lay sprinkled between the aching guards, writhing on the hot stony ground. I picked up a sword, the weight of it heavier than I expected, or maybe the responsibility of it simply weighed more than the iron to make it?

My father jabbed his elbow out sending the last of the guards crashing into the crowd, then howled loud at the sun. I gripped the sword with both hands, bringing the blade up in front of me, and took a cautious step forward.

"King Ezra," I shouted, as I eased another step closer. "Look at me."

The beast ignored my plea, stomping around and scratching the claws on his feet across the ground.

"Ezra Balthazar Aldric. Look at me." No response. It'd worked for my mother, but maybe he was too far gone to recognize himself anymore. Maybe he was now more beast than man. Which meant that only one thing left for me to do.

I tightened my grip on the hilt of the sword. All those lessons in fencing and combat better not fail me now. Lessons the man I poised to kill, had paid for. Lessons he'd invested time in helping me perfect, spending hours going over the ideal form and stance. Lessons I'd never be able to thank him for.

A thickness built in my throat as the world blended into a watery haze. I swallowed, nearly choking on my own guilt as tears spilled to the bloody ground. I mumbled a prayer under my breath as I inched closer.

"Don't make me do this, Dad."

The beast cocked his head my direction and stilled, his stare moving from me to the sword and back again. He let out a pained roar, stumbling back a few feet.

"Dad, can you hear me in there?"

I lowered the weapon to my side, his eyes following my every movement. He grabbed the sides of his head and moaned, surveying the carnage throughout the square.

"It's okay. It's going to be okay, Dad. Just come back to the castle. We'll figure out a way to break the curse and everything will be okay again. I promise." I held out my hand, my arm shaking.

He hung his head, a sad whimper emitted from deep in his throat. He looked at me, his eyes soft. Deepest brown, warm and familiar, his eyes, my father's, not the beast's. He took a lumbering step toward me. Voices gasped in my periphery, but I forced myself to stand tall and tried to steady my hand.

"That's it. You can do this. Let's go home."

Argh! Metal glinted in the sun, the flash hitting me before my ears registered the scream. The heel of a fist slammed into my chest pushing me down onto my back, my head nearly smacking against the cobblestones. A guard, already bloodied from the first round of the fight, rose up and slashed at my father. An agonizing yelp rang out as the blade sliced my father near his shoulder. The fur darkened and he howled louder, throwing his paw over the wound. The guard struck again, cutting across my father's thigh, the silver sword marked by my father's red blood.

I pushed to my feet and reached for my fallen sword, but my father struck first, digging his claws into the guard's shoulder and lifting him off the ground. The guard screamed. I froze.

"Dad, stop! Don't!"

My father shook him like a doll and threw him down. The hollow sound of bones cracking as they shattered pulsed through me, moving through the crowd, everyone around taking a fraction of the guard's pain. His eyes closed, the light in them already gone.

I buckled over, gripping my knees, as I retched, the devastating terror too much to contain any longer. I wiped the back of my sleeve over my mouth and stood shaky on my feet, my father's cries calling to me.

He'd stumbled across the square and fallen into a heap on my mother's chessboard, the pieces scattered like the wrecked guards around him. Thick pools of blood gathered near his leg and his shoulder painting the white squares of the board a sickening shade of death.

I rushed to his side and fell to my knees, laying my hands on his leg wound. The sword had cut deep, strips of fur completely gone where the skin beneath lay sliced open. He winced beneath my touch, but let me apply pressure to try and slow the bleeding.

"I need guards," I yelled to anyone who dared to move. My voice cracked. "We need to bring the king back to the castle."

He rolled away from me and sat up, pulling his legs into his chest.

"You need to stop moving. Lay still until we can get you stitched up."

He shook his head and started to rock back and forth on his toes. Tears poured from my eyes. The broken beast before me splintering my heart into pieces with his mammoth paws.

"Please, Dad. I can't lose you. I need you."

I put my hand on his shoulder, but he jerked away, his stiff fur passing through my fingers.

"Please."

He grabbed the white knight from beside him and smashed it into the ground, shards spraying out in all directions. He grabbed the black queen and pulled it into his lap.

"Enough, Ezra," a voice called.

He stared past me and I glanced over my shoulder. Mom appeared in the square, with a squadron of guards following close behind. She clamped her hand over her mouth as she inspected the aftermath of the chaos my father had caused. She closed her eyes and clenched fists at her sides.

"It's time to go home," she continued, but the fear in her voice shadowed the command.

My father's body slumped, his massive frame compacting as small as he could make himself, a glaze of shame washing over his face.

I held my hand out to him again. "Let's go."

His face hardened, the last whisper of his humanity draining from his expression and replaced with a stare of cold granite. He ripped the queen from his lap and ground it into the chessboard, it's pieces mixing with the destroyed knight. He rolled his head back, mouth wide open in a growl as his pointed teeth glistened in the sun. I retracted my hand and he pushed me onto my back, pinning me beneath him. My heart pounded as I searched for any part of him I could hang on to and pull him back, but there was nothing left. He roared again. I covered my face with my arms and waited for the pain the sink in, hoping he'd make death come quick and not make me suffer.

His burning breath brushed across my skin, and I screamed, my vocal cords shredding as the sound ripped up my throat. But the shadow of him faded, as he pushed up on his hind legs. I glanced through my fingers as he gnashed his teeth and stared down at me. I pushed myself up on my arms, but they trembled and

I fell back down to the stone.

"Dad," I whispered.

He roared. My hair blew back from his breath. But then he turned away from me and ran toward the street and up the hill.

Guards tried to block his path but he whipped them out of the way. More casualties. More bodies cast aside. He bounded faster, falling to all fours and picking up speed until no human would be able to catch him.

Mom rushed to my side and helped me up. Her glassy eyes wept, as she shivered and wrapped her arms around me. "I'm so sorry, Fallon. You know it wasn't him. Don't you?"

I pulled her closer, the familiar scent of home rolling from her hair, but not giving me the serenity it usually did.

"We've lost him, Your Majesty." The decorated guard who'd greeted me with Alizeh marched up beside us, his jaw tighter and more dire than he'd been in the hopeful glow of morning. "He disappeared into the forest and headed up towards the mountains. I've sent men in after him, but it will be difficult to find him in that terrain."

Mom's body collapsed in my arms. "Keep looking. Don't stop until you find him."

I rubbed my knuckles along her spine as her tears bled through my shirt, soaking my skin. "They'll find him."

"Maybe." She looked up at me, completely shattered, her heart broken. "But what will happen if they do?"

She wiped her hands over her face and pulled away from me, then slipped off to address the remaining guards. Always the strong one.

I gazed out over the mess in the square. The broken

market stalls. Banners tattered, benches splintered, and the mass of injured bodies barely moving on the ground. The chessboard splashed with my father's blood already drying and seeping into the concrete. Every emotion hit me at once. Rage. Despair. Hopelessness. Until they burned so hot in my veins I boiled over into numbness. I kicked the black king still standing on its stained square. A jolt of pain shot up my leg as it tumbled over and lay among the other casualties.

Behind me someone clapped, slow and mocking. I whirled around, Harding and Kalmin stood with Dormand and the others from Takka's, their faces haunted and stark.

Dormand stopped clapping and stepped out from the rest of the group.

"Are you going to try and tell us there's no beast now, prince?"

HEIR OF BEAUTY

27TH MAY

Dusky moonlight filtered through the high library window painting lines across the shelves of books. When did night fall? I rubbed my hands over my face and blinked my tired eyes as the words in the open book across my lap began to blur. I slammed it shut then chucked it onto the pile of ones I'd already read and lay back on the floor. Another dead end. Another waste of time.

My father still hadn't come home and no one seemed to have any idea where to look. No rumors had surfaced from the neighboring kingdoms. No news or gossip on where he'd gone in the morning paper. Just embellished recounts of the 'market massacre' accompanied by a blurry image of him splashed across the front page, his teeth bared and stained with blood. The guards took turns in an endless loop of search parties, each one returning empty-handed, my mother's heart breaking piece by tiny piece with every failed attempt.

The last few days played over in my mind. Every time I wasn't concentrating on something else, the memories crept in. Like insects that buzzed around my head and nipped at my skin when I least expected it. Tiny pinpricks to keep me from forgetting. The stench of blood and sweat on my clothes. The sharp grit of rocks cutting into my back as I begged for my life. The hollow, cracking sound of the guard's bones snapping so easily, like brittle twigs in the forest. Each image haunted my thoughts and poisoned my dreams until sleep wouldn't come at all. Every time I closed my eyes I relived the horror again and again.

I grabbed another book from the never-ending pile and cracked it open. If only I'd taken the time to read most of these when I been assigned them by my tutors, instead of skipping out to find something more fun to do, I might not be stuck scouring over them now. Searching for answers to questions I hadn't even figured out to ask yet.

I thought of Veda. Her charming crooked smile, and the way she bit down on her thumb when she concentrated hard on something. The way her amazing brain spun faster than I could ever expect to catch up to. She would be great at this research. She read fast and everything always seems to make more sense with her around. I'd asked her to look for me at the castle when her father finally let her go, but she still hadn't arrived. Or maybe she'd heard about the chaos in the marketplace and stayed as far away from me as she could get. Whatever the reason, I wished I had a chance to explain. Maybe then I could focus instead of trying to think about what I'd done wrong.

The door creaked and a sliver of light from the hall grew larger as Mom entered the library. Her stare narrowed at the burning lantern on her desk then popped wide again as she spied me sitting amongst piles of books on the floor.

"Fallon, here you are. No one has seen you for hours, but I just assumed you'd gone out for a while. I never expected to find you in here."

She clicked the door closed behind her, then rested against the wooden frame. Her normally glowing face seemed dull, even in the flickering firelight. The toll of my father's condition slowly sucking the life out of her beautiful looks.

"I can leave if you wanted some time alone." I brushed the dust off my knees and grabbed a few more books from the pile, clutching them tightly in my arm, then stood next to the desk.

"Of course not, stay as long as you like. I just needed to get something quick anyway."

The stiffness in my back and shoulders ached now that I'd stood upright again. I stretched my arms over my head, a relieved squeal escaping my lips.

"Been a long time since I've seen you reading in here," Mom said as she cast her glassy eyes to the ceiling. "I remember when you were small, you used to hide in the corner every evening and wait for me to come look for you. I'd sit in my chair, then you would climb up on my lap and we would read stories together for hours. Just you and me and all the magic in the world."

She gave a quick nostalgic smile, then scurried from the door and pulled open a long thin drawer on the desk. She rummaged through the pens and papers until she found a small blue envelope and tucked it into her palm.

She closed the drawer and tapped her fingertips on the desktop. "It would be nice to have some of that magic right now, don't you think?"

I sighed. "Yeah, it sure would."

"But I guess those days are long past now. I'll let you back to your reading."

"Mom—" I reached my hand out toward her then grabbed the air and let it drop to my side. Another opportunity to ask her about Edwin Macario's journal and the lies he claimed my parents had told me. But I couldn't do it now. My father's disappearance already forced her to endure so much pain, I couldn't add to her struggle. Once they found my father I could try again.

"What is it, dear?"

"Never mind." I grabbed the back of my head and stretched my neck toward the skylight. Maybe I should just take a chance and ask her.

"Okay." She looked me over as if waiting for me to continue, then her questioning stare hardened and pierced through my skull. "There is something I need to tell you though."

I pulled my head right again as she crossed her hands politely in front of her, the true queen commanding my attention.

"The Council has asked to see you. With your father's disappearance, the kingdom is vulnerable and we need you to step up and take a more active role in the day to day operations."

An ache burned in the bottom of my stomach and I winced forward. "Shouldn't we wait a bit longer? He's only been gone a few days."

"The kingdom needs stability now. He's been battling the curse for a while and even if we did find him soon…

I mean...when we find him soon, no one knows how long it will be before he is himself again. Or how long it will take to reclaim the trust of the Aborians."

I huffed, the low sound of my breath echoing through the tall room.

"Fine. If that's what I need to do." The ache twisted. Deeper. Sharper. The red splatter of pomegranates on my white gloves flashed in my brain. "But I don't think it's a good idea. I mean, I doubt anyone is going to listen to me. I might just make things worse."

Mom crossed the room and sandwiched my face in her delicate hands. "You'll do just fine. And I'll be there to help. I know this isn't how you might have envisioned taking over the throne, but I really need you to step up and take on the challenge. Not only me, but Aboria desperately needs a leader right now. The kingdom needs you."

I tugged her hands from my face and clasped them tight in my own. "The kingdom needs you too, Mom."

She sighed and turned away. "I am afraid the demands of your father's search are taking up more of my time and energy then I expected. Besides, deep down I am just a village girl, when times get rough, the kingdom is quick to remind me of that fact."

"Well, just tell them all to take a flying leap off a cliff. You're one of the strongest, smartest women in all the kingdom, probably even further than that. Anyone who doesn't see that is blind."

"You're sweet, but I'm afraid that's not always how things work. Fair and politics rarely mix well. Now don't let me interrupt you any longer.“ She pulled her hands away and hurried out the door before I could continue to argue. Arboria needed someone like her on the throne, not someone like me who could barely keep their head when controversy struck. I didn't have her strength or conviction. The kingdom didn't want me. They had already made that very clear the last time.

I collapsed back down on the floor and turned up the lantern light. I had no idea what time it was, but it didn't matter, the pile of books wouldn't get any smaller until I finished going through them. If a tiny library on the side of a mountain had one journal holding the secrets of my entire family, there had to be something in this museum of literature that could help break the curse or at least give me some answers as to who I really was and what happened all those years ago.

I scanned the pages of the book in my lap, my eyes already hazy from the dusty books and the hours of strain, but I blinked and kept going. It was going to be a long night.

~

Click. Click. Click.

The clack of my dress shoes against the stone echoed through the corridor as I paced just outside of the war room. The rhythmic, repetitive sound helped slow my racing pulse, but even it couldn't fully take the nervous edge off.

Didn't the Council realize what a mistake it would be for me to take more responsibility right now? I didn't have the respect of the kingdom, how would anyone expect me to have their loyalty?

"I say, Your Majesty, you're looking very regal today." Griswold appeared at the end of the hall, as a proud smile beamed across his lips. "Your father would be so impressed to see you like this, sir." He brushed his hands over the embellished shoulders of my coat and tugged near the golden buttons so it sat properly against my chest.

"Trust me, I'd rather my father was here in general. That way I wouldn't even need to consider being king."

Griswold chuckled, the light knowing sound tugged my mouth into a frown.

"Just nerves, my prince. Don't you think your father was nervous the first time he met with the Council too?"

My pulse started to quicken again. I wiped my hand across my face and continued pacing. "No. I bet my father was leading armies before he could even climb into the throne."

"Oh sir, you still have such wit even when your focus is elsewhere."

I shrugged. I'm glad he found that humorous since I fully believed it to be true. Dad, at least as a human, commanded attention. The subtle way he stood taller, straighter than the average man. The tranquilizing, yet demanding cadence in his voice that charmed anyone into bowing to his will. I clearly didn't inherit those skills.

Griswold laughed and shook his head. "Your father was as nervous as a pig bound for slaughter as he stood outside this door. I think he may have even vomited a few times that morning as well. But in true Aldric fashion, he collected himself and dazzled the Council. Just as I'm sure you will." He fussed with my collar once more. "It's like looking into a mirror beyond time, seeing you stand here reminds me so much of that day. Like a painting. A moment captured in history."

I tried to let his words sink in. Tried to take comfort in the sentiment, but the logical part of my brain wouldn't let me. "Thank you, Griswold. I'm glad to have you here with me, as I'm sure my father was grateful for you as well."

The old man's wrinkled skin blossomed a pale pink. "Just doing my job, sir."

I stopped pacing and held the wall as I steadied myself against the dizzying sensation in limbs. "How long have you worked at the castle exactly?"

His eyes rolled towards the ceiling as he tapped his index finger over his lips, contemplating the question. "It's been a very long time sir. Thirty-eight or forty years maybe?"

"So you were here the first time that my father...you know?"

"Yes. But that was a long time ago." His posture stiffened and he inconspicuously slid back a step. "A dark time."

"But isn't it a dark time now too?"

He stared over my shoulder down the hall, refusing to meet my questioning stare or maybe reliving the past in his mind. "Fair point. But with each new year, we receive the opportunity to rewrite our own stories. This is now, and not then. We need to move forward and find a new solution. Besides, I'm afraid I don't have anything that will help with your father's curse. If I did I would be sure to share it with you and bring him home."

"I'm sure you would. But I wish I knew more about my father when he was younger, about what kind of leader he was, and even about how he met my mother."

"I am afraid I don't have much to tell." Griswold dropped his hands and stepped back again without trying to hide it this time. A chill infused the air between us. "And even then, it's not my story. I suggest posing any questions to your mother first. If she would like me to discuss it further, that will be up to her."

"You have always been discreet, haven't you?"

"Of course, sir. It's all part of the job. Now if you will excuse me, I have other duties to attend to."

He turned on his heel, precise and sharp, then hurried back the direction he came.

"One more thing, Griswold," He stopped and glanced over his shoulder, his blank expression clear that he didn't want to get involved with my line of questions.

"Have you ever heard of someone at the castle named Ed—"

The war room door thundered open and Mom slipped through the doorway, stepping in front of me. "Darling, you look wonderful."

I tilted my head around her, but Griswold had already disappeared. "Thanks."

"They're ready to see you now." She tapped my shoulder then pulled the door open again guiding me through in front of her.

I walked into the center of the room, and took my place before the Council, my hands crossed politely behind my back and my shoulders rolled high to compensate for the weakness in my knees. Around the outer walls of the room hung luxurious red and gold tapestries that depicted battles won in times long past, and I chose to examine them, hoping it would be viewed as reverence and not just a stall to swallow down the dry bread-like lump in my throat. Mom strode around me to the far end of the long oak table that spread across the front of the room. Lord Covington, Lord Marchand, and Lord Anwar stood at attention as they adjusted their cuffs and engraved buttons on their jackets until my mother sat down and they could resume their seats.

"Your Majesty," Lord Anwar said. "It is a pleasure to finally see you in this context. I feel like it were mere moments ago that you were running through the castle halls brandishing a wooden sword in search of dragons."

The Council laughed, almost in unison. I gripped my right hand tighter with my left, still feeling ever the boy with the useless weapon.

He continued, "Let us first begin by assuring you that the Council operates to provide wisdom and guidance in the best interest of the crown and the kingdom. We will always be at your full disposal as king and—"

"I'm afraid you must have mistaken me for my father, the true king of Aboria."

The gentlemen looked quickly at each other, their wide stares flitting between the other faces at the table.

"Perhaps Lord Anwar misspoke, Prince Fallon," Lord Marchand interjected from the middle of the table, his hands crossed politely on top of the oak. "As acting king, the Council will be at your full disposal with whatever you may need."

"Yes, exactly. Thank you." Lord Anwar cleared his throat. "However, we must address the fact that the longer your father remains in his condition, the quicker we need to solidify your claim with a full coronation. The turbulent times at the castle are a call to any other parties who wish to seek the throne for themselves."

"What other parties? With my father still alive, and both my mother and me at the castle, no one would be able to make such a claim."

A grave shadow cast over their faces, as Lord Anwar stroked his hand over the lower half of his face and the dark stubble that grew there. "Without a competent king in place, the entire kingdom is vulnerable for takeover."

I dug my fingernails into my palm, the sharp pain soothing the humiliation building in my cheeks. I should already know this. I should've paid more attention.

I stretched up on my toes, trying to force myself

taller, maybe channel some of my father's charisma. "Then I am willing to do whatever it takes to maintain the throne for my father's eventual return."

"And we hope that he will be returned to us swiftly as well, but our job is to be practical," Lord Covington said.

"So what do I need to do?"

"We would like you to hold a conference at the town hall. The people need to know that the castle has the situation under control and we are willing to continue business as usual."

I darted my eyes toward my mother who smiled back with the confidence I didn't have.

"I don't think that is the best idea. The last time I addressed the public it did not go well. They all think I am a liar, I doubt they will even listen to anything that I say."

The Council began a low rumble as they shifted in their chairs, my words hitting their mark. They didn't want me as their leader as much as I didn't want to be a leader. They were simply out of options and I was the best they could find on short notice. Fantastic.

"Yes, that was indeed a disaster, however, the city is unstable at the moment. No one knows who is in charge anymore. The marketplace has been destroyed causing huge problems for our merchants trying to earn an income, and we received word this morning that many of our neighboring trade partners are refusing to do business with us. They feel that the economy is at risk the longer the castle fails to regain control. If this continues, the word will reach all the way to Draconis, and we will have no suppliers for gold." Lord Marchand glanced over at my mother, pleading to her best interests, but with a heavy glare telling her to fall in line. "Of course, you are free to do as you please even if it goes against the Council's wishes, however, we feel this is a necessary step to cleaning up the mess."

My mother sat up straighter in her chair, clearly not willing to be talked down to by anyone. "I don't think that will be an issue, Bruno. I'm sure my son will do a phenomenal job. I doubt any of you would not have apprehensions with delivering news as delicate as this. Isn't that right, Fallon?"

My chest tightened, the reality that I was not getting out of this settling in. "Of course. I'll do whatever you need."

"Splendid." Lord Marchand clapped his hands and nodded until the other lords joined him. "I will make the necessary arrangements as soon as we have adjourned."

"Is that all you require?" I asked, hoping the answer would be yes and knowing it likely wouldn't be.

"For now," Lord Anwar said.

I exhaled and let the tension slide out through my mouth then rushed toward the door. As my hand gripped the doorknob, Lord Covington spoke again.

"Before you go, can I just provide one word of caution. We know you have quite the reputation around the kingdom, specifically in regards to the taverns and some of the young ladies in the city. Stepping into the role as king requires an image of flawless decorum to help maintain the respect of your people. Anything less should be handled as discreetly as possible to avoid any more controversy. I'm not sure how much the kingdom would be willing to forgive during the Aldric reign."

"Noted." I nodded and twisted the handle, the air already lighter on the other side of the door as it wafted in from the hallway. I rushed out of the room and clicked the door closed behind me, then rested my head against the wall, the cool stone helping to bring my temperature down. I shook out the tension in my arms and shuddered as each of the new truths landed on my shoulders. The Council had already given up on finding my father and they confirmed the one thing I dreaded — I would be the king now. The kingdom would look to me and I would need to devote everything to them. My life would never be my own again.

28TH MAY

"And I'm certain that through working together we'll be able to overcome the recent events and build a stronger community in spite of it."

I ran the speech over again for about the thousandth time since yesterday. My palms still sweating every time I said the words, but the rest of my nerves seemed to be held at bay. Somewhere between midnight and dawn, I'd accepted my new reality. Either that or practicing my speech put me under some kind of hypnosis as I repeated the same monotone words over and over again.

Voices boomed on the other side of the curtain as the citizens of Mosa and likely half of the neighboring villages piled into the theatre. My mother thought the theatre may feel more non-threatening than another speech in front of the castle or the town hall that was suggested before. The large stone structure of the castle looming over them would serve as a reminder of the anger and resentment building through the people instead of fostering hope as we'd planned.

Lord Marchand appeared around the corner, a glossy black walking stick in his hand and his long hair tied low at the back of his neck. Polished. Proper. All the things I tried to be. Needed to be.

"Remember what we discussed," he said, "Your job is to promote calm and order. The rest can be dealt with another day."

I nodded and rubbed my open palms over my thighs.

"Thank you. I'll do my best."

"I'm sure you will, son, but remember the future of the monarchy rests with you." He cuffed his thick fingers around my shoulder and pat twice before heading back into the theatre.

I closed my eyes and dropped my head to my chest, my breath struggling against the tightness in my lungs. I concentrated harder. Oxygen flowed in through my nose slowly and out my mouth. In. Out. Over and over until my pulse finally eased. Showtime.

I jerked my head toward the stage and the guards waiting for my entrance assembled into their predetermined formation to escort me. Disgruntled and unamused stares followed me to the podium from every seat in the theatre. Additional rows of chairs flanked the sides and aisles for the excess attendees, but even then people stood along the walls, arms crossed. A sudden hush fell over the room as I cleared my throat and forced my back straighter. The guards positioned next to nearly every row and at every exit glared at the patrons, but at least they provided for a more solemn and captive audience as my last speech attempt.

“Good afternoon my fellow Aborians.” The rehearsed words rolled easily off my tongue. One small victory. I gripped the podium tighter and dared to look out over the audience. “Thank you all for taking the time to assemble here today. I know the last time we spoke it was not under the best terms, but I have come here today to ask for your forgiveness on the past and your cooperation for enhancing the future.”

A loud snicker echoed in the hall. The nearest guard stomped at attention and snuffed it out, leaving an awkward silence.

“As you have all seen or heard, the king is not well and has taken on the unfortunate form of a beast. I understand this is upsetting news as my father, King Ezra, meant a lot to this kingdom and was… I mean, is, loved by many of you. The details of his transformation were kept quiet as a concern for public safety and to provide some privacy for His Majesty during this difficult time. Unfortunately, that decision has led to tragedy and for that, all of us in the royal family are deeply sorry.”

A few people wrestled in their seats, and I tensed, expecting some sort of assault but they remained sitting. Another deep breath. So far, so good.

“Today I’ve come to assure you that we will do everything possible to bring my father home, and rebuild the things we have broken. The—“

A hand jut into the air about four rows away from the stage. The practiced speech reeling in my head halted, distracted by the five fingers gesturing desperately for attention.

“You have a question?” I pointed at the older

gentleman waving his hand in the audience, the silver flecks of his hair picking up under the theatre lights.

"Yes, Your Majesty. My question is simple; after you have already lied to us and put us in danger, why should we believe you now?"

Bile rose in the back of my throat, just as I'd anticipated, yet it still came as a shock as the burn raged against my vocal cords.

A noblewoman in a fancy green dress stood in the front left row. "And what about our children? Are they not still in danger with a monster on the loose? What about them?"

Third row from the back, right side. "Who will fix the marketplace? I'm losing money every day I can't sell my produce."

"How do we know there are no other monsters that you're hiding?" Fifth-row centre.

By the back door. "What good is the monarchy anyway? Maybe it's time for something new."

The questions kept coming, each one smacking me in the face and forcing me back in defeat. I wasn't finished yet. Why hadn't they let me finish? My knuckles flashed white as I held onto the podium, using it as a crutch to keep from crumbling to the floor.

Towards the back of the room, a small hand flew in the air as the body attached tried to make its way forward. Two guards immediately surrounded the asker with their hands poised on the hilts of their swords.

"I also have a question for the prince." The voice cut through the rest of the noise, familiar and calming, like a stillness running through my blood. Veda, her hair pulled back and her unmistakable gray on gray uniform.

"Yes, ma'am." I waved my hand and made a shushing

noise, some of the chaos ending with the gesture. "Please let the lady speak."

The soldiers eased back, still in attack mode if necessary. Veda straightened her stance.

"I wanted to know how deeply difficult is it for you to deal with your family's pain and still try to address the kingdom with decorum and a smile? How traumatic has this whole ordeal been, and yet you've still managed to come here trying to help all of those who might be affected, without having the chance to grieve your own misfortune?"

The crowd silenced, all of my contenders dangling from her every word. Strength reignited in my shaky legs. Her confidence providing bricks of courage, each one stacking on each other to build my platform.

"Thank you, miss. It has been exceptionally hard, traumatic even, but I understand that being royalty comes with certain sacrifices, even if my own happiness and well-being are some of them."

"Thank you, Your Majesty. I've often wondered how many times the people in this room have been helped by your family without any concern for what it may cost you. King Ezra was a strong leader and there is hope for him to leave a good legacy behind."

The rest of the horde lay silent, but it didn't matter. Even through the flood of people, all I could see was her and her kind face cheering me on. Standing behind me, even though she too had her doubts about my family and their rule. But instead of joining the burgeoning rebellion, she gave me a chance. The one I needed if I was going to make things right.

"As I started to tell you all, there are plans in place to address all of your concerns."

Those who remained standing finally took their seats

as order fell back over the theatre.

"Security has been increased in the castle, the woods, and all of the surrounding areas of the city and nearby countryside to ensure there are no more casualties from the beast. Funds have been diverted from the castle's operating expenses to cover the restoration of the marketplace. We want to ensure that it is up and running as soon as possible, but we are taking suggestions for improvements in a special session of court later this week so we can remain the prosperous pride of the kingdom."

A few cheers and positive comments rippled through the crowd. Not the overwhelming response I'd hoped for, but definitely better than the alternative.

"And for those who fear that the castle is still harboring threats to your safety, we are opening our doors to everyone for guided tours whenever you feel the need. We want to show you that although we know we have made a mistake, that it will be our last and all decisions are made to make this kingdom the strongest in all the land."

Feeble applause echoed through the theatre. Veda locked eyes with me through the sea of faces and smiled, my lips curling upwards in response.

"I might not be my father, but I intend to make you all proud to be Aborians. Together we will rebuild and be stronger than ever." I nodded and released my grip on the podium. An ache rippled through my fingers from the strain of holding on so tight, but I welcomed the release. "Thank you."

The guard to my left nodded his head toward the curtain and I quickly rushed offstage before things could swing out of my favor. A rumble of voices flowed behind me, but without the sharp contempt of my last speech.

It wasn't perfect, but it was a start. A new beginning.

As the noise of the crowd fell away, I loosened the two coat buttons near my neck and breathed deeply as the oxygen sparked life in my veins. I'd done it. I'd given my speech and without anything being thrown. No fruit juice, or worse, staining my dress clothes. No mob of angry citizens waiting by the door. Maybe I did stand a chance at this after all. Except, of course, I hadn't done it all on my own.

I signaled to one of the guards and he came at my command. "The girl from the theatre, the one who stuck up for me during the question period, I need you to rush out front and find her. Tell her, no ask her, to wait for me near the entrance after everyone else has cleared out."

"Of course, sir." He nodded and quickly disappeared, weaving through the remaining guards and out the side door into the sun.

A lone steady clap echoed beside me.

Lord Marchand appeared with a smile beaming across his face. "Well done, Your Majesty. We all had faith that you would rise to your new station. I'm glad we were not wrong."

I grabbed the back of my neck and gazed down at the scuffed and peeling boards of the backstage area. "I'm glad things worked out well. But I'm still afraid that I may not be ready for such a large undertaking. Maybe we should employ more forces to search for my father. I'm sure the people would be pleased to know he wasn't running loose."

Lord Marchand narrowed his stare and grasped tighter onto the top of his walking stick, twisting it against the floor. "Perhaps. Or perhaps you should get better at taking a compliment and stop being so modest. Being king is your birthright, and by refusing you are risking everything your parents have built."

"I'll try harder." The last of the voices died in the main theatre. I glanced at the side door, but Lord Marchand stood still.

"Now if you could please excuse me, I have another meeting to attend to."

"Of course. However, before you go I would like to remind you about how important appearances are in your position." He pointed his index finger at me as his pleased grin dropped to a grim line. "I'm not sure how you bewitched that girl to come to your defense, or if you even know her at all, but she doesn't seem like the kind of girl befitting a future king. A little too plain. A little too...vocal."

I smiled back, my teeth grit tight enough to shatter. "Thank you. I'll have to remember that."

I rushed around to the front of the theatre. A few remaining guards still stood by the doors, but no Veda. My shoulders dropped along with my spirit.

"That should be all gentlemen." I waved my hand. "Thank you for your service and feel free to take the rest of the afternoon off."

The guards nodded and then marched in perfect time into the city. As the last guard passed, he jerked his head backward. "Maybe try the fountain, sir."

I rushed across the open square toward the large fountain. Cool droplets splashed my skin as I approached, a nice relief in the early afternoon heat. On the far side, Veda sat on the edge, just below the goddess of the fountain and her ever full jug of water, twiddling her fingers along the surface of the pool. I stood back and watched the serene look on her face as she splashed in the cool blue. I ached to feel that kind of peace. The last week bore down on my shoulders, sometimes like the universe was holding my head under that fountain water and I couldn't fight my way out. Eventually, the dark shadow of me lurking in the corner disrupted the air around her. Her nose scrunched up as she scanned the empty square, her eyes finally falling on my face. The sour look dissolved into a warm smile and she stood, flicking the last few drops of water from her fingertips.

"I thought we were meeting by the entrance?"

She shrugged. "You took so long that I got bored. Besides, it's such a beautiful day I figured I'd cool off a bit."

She flicked her hand toward me, and I flinched, except no water hit me and she laughed.

"Sorry for making you wait, but I needed to make sure that everyone had already left."

"Oh, I get it. Meeting me in secret?" She arched her eyebrow, playful, but the words stung in my chest like darts.

"No. Of course not." I snapped. Lord Marchand's warning burned bright in my head. Veda may not have the poise or upbringing as the noble girls, but what she lacked in grace she gave back in fire.

"Easy, prince. Plus it probably took you forever to change out of all that royal garb."

"Yeah. I couldn't wait to get it off. It's so hot and constricting."

"You mean you didn't want to keep the crown?" She ruffled her hand through my hair, the skin of her fingertips still cool from the fountain. I closed my eyes for a second, reveling in her touch and using it to try to push down my toxic thoughts.

"The crown is what I hate the most." I shoved my hands in my pockets and jumped up on the edge of the fountain walking around, one foot directly in front of the other and my arms outstretched for balance. "Are you hungry? Because I'm absolutely starving."

"I could be."

I jumped down from the fountain stomping my feet in front of her and she giggled, a playful smirk breaking across my own face. "Great. I know a place that makes the best hand pies in the kingdom."

She slid her arm to the crook of my elbow. "Then let's go. I can't miss out on the best hand pies in all of the kingdom, now can I?"

We turned the corner, leaving the theatre grounds and back into the narrow streets of Mosa. People in their colorful dresses and perfect jackets scurried down the narrow sidewalks. Lines of candy-colored window shutters stood open to let the fresh air in. The beauty of a typical day in the city under the warm heat of the afternoon sun, but something seemed off, broken, as it lacked the same buzz and magic it used to. The incident in the marketplace had fractured the spirit of the city and even though they tried to continue on, as usual, the dark cloud of my father's sins hung over them.

"Thank you for your help in there. You really have a way with words, don't you?"

She flexed her arm against mine. "Well, I am a writer. Or at least trying to be. But I'm sure you would've handled it without me. I just moved things along a little faster."

"Maybe." I struggled with her faith in me as I doubt I would have the same if our situations were reversed.

"I didn't know you'd even be there. When I hadn't heard from you, I just assumed you were still at the temple or had just gone home."

"Well, I stayed there for a while, but it's not like it was that bad. My father has quite the temper, but once he calms down he typically realizes his ways."

"So he didn't punish you for bringing me up there?"

"Unless you mean beating me in eight straight games of checkers as punishment, then no. However, he did make me clean up after the chickens."

She laughed and the muscles in my back and shoulders relaxed.

"But, I did have a long talk with him about your situation. He wouldn't tell me anything, said it really wasn't my business, but he has agreed to speak with you again if you want to?"

I peeled out of her clutch and stepped in front of her with my hands on her shoulders. I gazed into her deep green eyes as they sparkled in the sunshine, like the lush mystery of the forest at the top of the hill. "Of course, I do. I can have someone from the capital bring him here right away."

"Hold up." She slipped her arms between mine and pushed outward, breaking my hold on her then slipping her arm back in mine. "He will only talk to you on the contingent that you go back up to the temple. He has things to attend to there and since this is your issue, he feels you need to make sacrifices for the information."

"I guess that's fair, but I have no idea how I'll get back there. I don't know my way up the sides of the mountain, at least not that high. Maybe Griswold or someone else might have an idea of how to get there."

"Just borrow Alizeh. If you call her, I'm sure she would come. If she doesn't have time, she won't. You'll just have to wait, maybe, that's all." She nodded her head as she spoke, subliminally coaxing me to agree. "Besides, since you are a king now I guess everything belongs to you anyway."

"I could never do that. I'm not like that, you should know."

I pulled my arm back, but she squeezed it tighter.

"Wow. Does that crown suck out all of your sense of humor? Not that you are a sparkling wit, to begin with, but it was just a joke."

"Sorry. It's been a rough few days." I tugged her over to the right side of the street and the door of a small two-room shop with a dark blue awning to match its navy shutters. A rough hand-painted sign sat in the window, Madame Madeleine's Perfect Pies, it read with an oddly-shaped pie drawn in the corner.

The sweet, buttery smell of the shop wafted outside and I let my nose guide us to the entrance.

I held open the door, letting Veda pass. "You'll love this place."

She glanced up at me, her eyes twinkling with wonder. "I guess we'll see."

I followed behind and joined the long line that weaved between the tiny tables scattered through the front room of the shop. Madame Madeleine and her staff rushed behind the counter, back and forth, taking orders and serving food as quickly as they could. Sweat dripped from their foreheads and with the unbearable heat suffocating the room most of the customers too.

I pointed at the menu, no more than a list of flavors scrawled on a piece of butcher paper tacked on the wall with a nail. "I'm sure the savory ones are excellent, but I can never come here without buying something sweet."

"Why does that not surprise me? I'm pretty sure you

know how to indulge yourself."

"Maybe." I glared down at her with a mocking smirk, trying to hold back my laughter. "Or maybe I just know what I like."

She raised her left eyebrow and met my gaze. "Really? I'd love to hear more about that sometime."

We bumped along the line, the smells thickening in my nose and my mouth watering like a starving sheepdog until we finally reached the front. Madame Madeleine herself met us at the counter, straightening the already dirty apron covering her blue dress. A rainbow of shades from splattered fruit painted the front, but she didn't seem to care.

"It's been a while, Your Majesty."

"Too long, Madame. But I can't stop dreaming about your cherry lemon pie."

She blushed, the red showing through her cheeks even over the intense heat, and she hooted a deep belly laugh. She flicked her hand toward me and rolled her eyes. "Quit your flattery, my prince. You know you eat for free already anyway."

"Not today, Madame." I slipped my hand in my pocket and pulled out a Baht, leaving it on the counter. "How can I expect you to keep making your wonderful pies if your own cupboards go bare. This should cover mine and whatever the lady would like. I don't need any change."

She scanned my face, critical as if expecting some sort of joke, then took the bill, her eyes widening when she realized it would cover more than double our order.

"Why yes, I think it will. Now, where is your lucky lady?" She scanned over our faces, then pushed up on her toes looking towards the back of the shop.

I tugged Veda closer to the counter, however, there

wasn't much room left. "Right here."

Madame gave an unsettling chuckle. "My opulent stars, it must be busier than I thought. My apologies, miss. What can I get for you?"

"I'll have the same. Apparently, they are the best."

Madame nodded and disappeared into the kitchen, returning with two piping hot pies, steam billowing off the perfect golden crust.

We maneuvered around the rest of the line and snagged a small table near the window. I tried to be polite pulling out Veda's chair, even as the rumble in my stomach wanted to sit and devour my lunch. I raced into my seat and took a huge bite. The juicy cherry cut with the tart lemon slid down my throat in the most joyful way. I groaned and took another big bite, the sauce smudging on the side of my mouth. I ran my hand over the mess and licked it off my knuckles not willing to risk losing one taste.

"You weren't kidding about knowing what you like, were you?" Veda laughed, as she watched me gorge myself on fruit and pastry. She picked up her own pie and finally took a dainty bite from the corner. Her eyes rolled toward the ceiling and she collapsed against the back of the chair. "Okay, maybe you are right on this one. It's really good."

"Told you." I cast her a quick grin before returning to demolish the rest of my pie.

We ate in silence, except for the few tight-lipped *mmmm* sounds that were unavoidable with food this good. Once I finished and convinced myself not to get back in line for another serving, I leaned back in my chair and watched Veda enjoy hers. The blissful glaze that fell over her expression as the world slipped away leaving just her and the pie made me chuckle as I'm sure everyone else saw me in the same way. Except her enjoyment wasn't the only thing in the room. I glanced around at the other tables. Prying eyes watched our every move, scrutinizing me and evaluating her. I guess my speech did not go over as well as I had hoped, or maybe with my new position people were more interested in me than ever before. I tried to shrug off the uncomfortable feeling but as more people entered the shop, more stares fell on us. Tables close by leaned in toward each other, whispering under closed hands held over their mouths. The gossip had already begun, except I had no idea what it was about.

"I'll have to remember this place," Veda said snapping me out of my paranoid daze. She reached across the table and grabbed my hand. "Or maybe I'll have to convince you to bring me here again." The whispers around us grew louder, like hushed screams calling my attention.

I slipped my fingers into hers and stood, coaxing her from the table. "Maybe we should get going."

She followed behind me until we reach the door. I propped it open with my forearm and swept my arm to signal her to lead the way.

A bright flash. Black dots blurred my vision and I shook my head.

"Excuse me, Your Majesty, how are you feeling after your speech today?" A voice blared at me before I could cross the threshold into the street.

More voices.

"Prince Fallon, now that you're king, what does that mean for your father?"

"Prince Fallon, who are you with?"

The questions came rapid-fire like fists in a street fight and pummeled us back through the door.

Reporters, enough for every small town paper and city gazette for the next six kingdoms, hovered in the doorway refusing to let us leave without a quote. Each query fast and sharp, relentless, launching one after the other. Personal, political, mental, and none that I was prepared to answer. Veda stood her ground, bracing her stance although her eyes danced wild like a trapped animal with a hurt paw.

"Prince Fallon, is this your girlfriend?"

"Where is she from?"

"Does she really seem like the best choice for our next queen?"

I yanked Veda's arm pulling her to my chest and slamming the door shut behind her. The loud thud as it closed in the frame commanded the attention of everyone in the room. Madame Madeleine waved her arm, beckoning us. "Out the back, darlings. It'll buy you a few minutes peace."

I tugged Veda's hand and rushed into the kitchen, nearly falling as my shoes hit the greasy floor, but I slid across to the rear door and burst into the alley. The voices around the front of the building echoed through the narrow passageway, but no one thought to chase us back here. At least not yet.

"This way." I jerked my head up the hill, toward the forest and ran down the alleyway, trying to keep our heads in the shadows. We rushed a few blocks and came out on the main street, but the nagging, questioning voices appeared behind us. Predators who'd caught the smell of fear and blood. Flashbulbs from cameras lit up the sky. I dashed into the next alley, Veda quick behind, her foot clipping my back heel as we ran, but I had no time to stop. We meandered through the streets rushing uphill, the added strain from the incline clear in Veda's labored breath on in my neck.

Finally, we reached the edge of the city, the dark green leaves of the forest, full and beckoning. Miles of grounds where we could hide.

"Hold on." Veda ripped her hand from mine and bent over gripping her knees. Her breath came hard as her chest heaved in and out, her face blazing fire-red. I leaned against the stone wall of the last building in town and closed my eyes, listening for the reporters or anyone else who had decided to chase us, but the shouts seemed to have fallen away.

Veda's breath slowed and she slid her arm around my waist. "I didn't know that lunch could be such an adventure."

I opened my eyes and stared right into hers, the emerald glow drawing me in like the forest. Cool. Safe. Mysterious. I rested my forehead against her brow as our breaths mingled together and came to a slow even rhythm that spiked my pulse to pick up its pace.

"I'm sorry about all this." I swooped the few strands blowing across her face behind her ear. "They're normally not this bad, but with everything going on I guess everything I do will be public now."

She cast her eyes downward, breaking the connection between us and lowered her voice." It's fine. But I believe you still owe me a debt, Fallon."

I watched the words roll off her soft red lips as my memory took me back to the temple, the last time we'd been this close. The last time I almost kissed her. I struggled to swallow, my throat desert dry. "Not here."

Her arm slipped from my waist and the sweet familiar smell of her faded as she stepped away.

"Don't worry about it."

I wiped my hands over my face, the cherry lemon

scent still heavy on my skin. "It's not that I don't want to, but what if someone saw?"

She crossed her arms, her sad expression hardening faster than clay and more rigid than granite. "Oh. I get it. You're only interested if no one knows."

"No, not at all." I tried to take her hand but she backed up further. "It's just that being king has certain obligations and I need to be very careful with how I act and what ends up in the newspaper."

"So, let me make this simple. You're king now and I'm not good enough, if I ever was. I understand."

She stuck her thumb and forefinger in her mouth and let out a high-pitched whistle.

"That's not what I said."

"But it's what you meant."

She slammed her hands on her hips. I tried to form words, but the guilty flame of my face spoke first.

"No, I...it's just..."

She shook her head and cast her glassy stare toward the trees. I took her hand, but she jerked it from my grasp.

"Don't."

Alizeh appeared in the sky barreling toward the one open patch of ground before the forest treetops.

"Don't go. Please, let me explain. The Council...and my new responsibilities...I don't want to mess things up."

"Then I'll make it easy for you." She tossed her hands in the air and backed up a few steps, a seething anger building in her pointed stare, then she ran towards Alizeh without looking back.

"Veda!" I screamed after her, but she'd already mounted the great bird and started off toward the sky. I smacked my head against the stone wall, the pain a punishment for my stupid mouth. One too light for what I deserved.

29TH MAY

The gold-handled switchblade came from Draconis. My father always took me with him for his fall trade trip on the chance that we'd get to see a real live dragon. We never did, so he bought me the knife instead. The first addition to my collection. The straight blade with the ivory roses inset on the crimson leather-wrapped hilt came from our family trip to the Floris flower festival when I was twelve. The swords that stood tall in their showcases along the wall, each of them glittering with rubies, emeralds, sapphires, or even just the rarest crystals, each had their own stories to tell. Every blade a memory of my father and somewhere we'd gone together, or an adventure we had shared. Now they just reminded me of how much I missed him.

I pulled my favorite Kaiken blade out of its holder and gripped the velvety ray skin handle. I scratched the sharp metal against my forefinger. It tickled, but one small slip could slice the tip off at the knuckle. I'd been around weapons all my life, as artifacts in the castle or for sport, but I never actually thought I'd need to use one, especially not against my own father. I shuddered as I remembered the weight of the guard's sword in my hand, the shaking in my knees as I brandished it high, and the terrifying sound as it clanged on the cobblestones leaving me defenseless.

I dug the tip of the dagger into the top of my dresser, the wood curling under the thin sharp blade. This one would hurt if it made contact with someone's skin, likely slicing through before the victim even felt it. But a thousand cuts with this assassin's blade wouldn't come close to the feeling as I watched Veda run away from me. I'd screwed up. I knew I had. All I needed to do was kiss the girl, the one thing I'd never hesitated to do before. I'd probably kissed more girls then some people would even meet in a lifetime, but in that second with her lips almost touching mine, I froze.

My stomach cramped at the memory and I winced as my pained face mocked me in the mirror. What was it about this girl that messed with my head? Why couldn't I simply move past her like I'd done with every other girl before her? Why did I not want to?

A soft knock wrapped on my bedroom door and dragged me out of my self-pity.

"Come in," I called, still running the dagger over in my hands and wishing my father would be the one to come barging in.

Instead, my mother floated into the room. "I didn't see you at breakfast. I had the kitchen prepare all your favorites."

"Thanks, but I wasn't hungry."

"Too busy planning your next great speech, are you?"

"Not exactly." I slid the dagger back into its case and turned around to lean against the dresser. "I've just been doing a lot of thinking, that's all."

"About what? Maybe I can help."

"I doubt it. I just had an argument with a friend."

"Just a friend huh?" She flopped down in my armchair resting her hands on the sides. A little too comfortable to be leaving soon.

"Have the press already gotten to you?"

"The press? This must have been some argument." She picked lint off her skirt and flicked it in the air watching it slip down to the ground. "But no, I just know that when you've fought with your other friends you tend to throw yourself into physical things. Fencing, riding, even tennis on occasion, but this is the first time you have resorted to sulking, so something must be up."

"I'm not sulking, I'm just... fine, I'm sulking. But it doesn't matter anyway because I messed it up and she's gone."

"Gone? Are you going international again with your exploits?" She rolled her eyes, as a bored look settled over her face. "I know I don't normally mention it, but you need to start thinking, my son."

"What are you talking about?"

"How is it that young people never think their parents know half the things they do? I was young and foolish too, you know?"

I rubbed my hands over my face, partly to hide the embarrassment but also to get the image of my mother acting like one of the girls at the tavern out of my head.

"But that changed when you met Dad, right? You fell in love with him?"

The humor in her eyes dropped to the floor and shattered like glass. "Of course I fell in love with him. I'm still in love with him and always will be, no matter what happens."

"So he didn't force you to fall in love with him?"

"Force me?" She laughed and tossed her head back against the chair. "Where would you get a crazy idea like that? No, your father would never do such a thing, and besides, you can't force someone to fall in love with you, it just happens. Even if it's not ideal or even when others don't agree, it doesn't matter. The heart will choose and the brain must accept or find a way to deal."

I left the dresser and sat down on the bed with my back to her as I chose my words carefully. "But I've heard he kidnapped you. That doesn't sound like love to me."

Her skirts rustled behind me, as I pictured her sitting up straighter, her posture likely offended at my brashness.

"There are many things about your father and me that were not perfect. But how we met and how we fell in love are two different stories combined by common characters. Why didn't you just ask me about this before?"

"I'm asking you now."

My stomach turned as I dared to face her. Across the room, her eyebrows knitted together as she thought hard, her fingers laced in a pile in her lap.

"This girl, the one you argued with. Do you think you might be in love with her? Is that where the questions are coming from?"

Love? I never really thought about it like that, not in terms of a word or a status anyway. It was just this thing. This feeling I couldn't shake since...I didn't really know when it started, but it kept growing each time I saw her.

"I don't know. I just know that I think of her when she's not around and I can't wait to see her again. I want to know what she's thinking. Want to see her smile. And when I'm around her I feel more like myself then I ever have before, even if being around her scares me a little bit."

Mom sat beside me on the bed and ran her hand gently up and down my spine. "Then maybe you are. But I can't tell you that for sure, only you will know. But, whether you are or you are not, you need to make things right with her. She clearly means a lot to you to bring about this change, so even if she's just a friend, you should hang on to her. People can be cruel sometimes, make sure you hold on to the good ones."

I hugged her tight. A weight started to lift even though my problems still hadn't been solved. "Now what did you want to know about your father and me?"

Another knock sounded at the door, this one harder and rougher. I rushed over as my mother straightened herself, then whipped open the door to greet the captain of the guard standing outside in the hallway.

"Permission to speak to the queen, Your Majesty?" he said, his expression unreadable. All business in his perfect uniform.

I swept my arm back. "Of course."

"What is it, Amir?" She asked meeting him halfway across the room.

"I've received word from the last unit at the border. There is no sign of the king anywhere."

"Have you checked every forest? Every river bank and creek? He can't have disappeared into the air?"

"I'm sorry, my queen. We have looked everywhere, twice. Our only thought is that he's escaped to the mountain peaks or has left the kingdom. We've alerted all the neighboring kingdoms and they are all on watch with strict orders to return him home alive. I've enlisted the best falconers to search the mountain peaks, but nothing has surfaced yet. A full search would be difficult at best with our current resources."

Tears welled in my mother's eyes, but she quickly wiped them away as her strong mask of the warrior slid back into place. "Then we must find additional resources. Gather your men and we will devise a new plan. He can't be far without food or shelter."

"Yes, ma'am." He nodded.

"That will be all, Amir. Thank you for your diligence and your information. As always you are an asset to this kingdom."

The captain gave her a quick salute then marched out of the room closing the door behind him. The second the handle clicked in the frame my mother's eyes flooded with tears. I pulled her close and she buried her head in my chest, as my arms struggled to hold her tight against her gasping sobs. Her whole body shook, the strength in her legs to hold her up evaporating with each painful cry. I rested my chin on her head and closed my eyes as my own tears began to fall.

Eventually, the sobbing slowed and she peeled herself out of my embrace. Make-up smeared down her blotchy cheeks and red spiderwebs spun in her watery eyes.

"Fallon, the guards told me you appeared out of the sky on a giant bird the other day. Do you still have access to it?"

"I don't think so." Veda's offer to borrow Alizeh came before I hurt her. I doubted it still stood. But as my mother's face drooped, her heart smashing into yet another jagged piece, I didn't care. "But I can definitely try."

A brief spark of hope glinted in her stare. "Do whatever you need to, but please, Fallon, go find your father."

~

The light glowed at the end of the tunnel. The dark green leaves fluttered in the golden sun as I finally emerged from the underground passage that led from the castle. I could've tried calling Alizeh from the courtyard inside the gates, but I didn't want to attract any more attention to myself this week. Discretion had become a precious commodity that I wasn't willing to give up.

I shortened the strap on the leather shoulder bag to ease the load and stop it from banging against my leg. Mom insisted I bring half a year's worth of provisions, but I managed to put some back in the cupboard before she saw. I didn't need to be adding any more weight to the journey than I needed to.

Stopping at the entrance of the cave, I propped my foot on the rocky wall and let the peaceful breeze wash over me. Birds chirped in the distance as leaves rustled and added percussion to their happy song. I forced my shoulders down and closed my eyes, my neck stretched up toward the sky trying to relax, but the knot of guilt tying tighter in my stomach wouldn't let me let go.

I stumbled down the pathway towards the edge

of town and the only clear space I could land a giant bird without immediately alerting everyone in a five-mile radius. Shielding my eyes from the sun, I stuck my fingers in my mouth and blew, just as Veda had done before. A breathy half-whistle came out along with a shower of saliva. Gross. I wiped my hand on my pant leg and tried again. A low whistling sound emitted this time, but not nearly as melodic as she would have done. I watched the horizon, waiting for the giant cloud of feathers to come, but nothing dared dot the perfect blue sky.

I whistled again, this attempt much better and a lot less wet. But still nothing moved overhead. I tossed my hand through the air and sat down on a pile of dry leaves. I figured it probably wouldn't work anyway. Veda said I could borrow Alizeh anytime, but she'd probably changed her mind. Not that I blamed her for that decision, but I hoped she'd understand why I needed the bird when she finally spoke to me again. If she ever spoke to me again.

I propped my elbows on my knees and rested my head in my hands. Mom would be so disappointed. The one favor I might be able to do for her, to help ease her sorrow, and I let her down too. I clearly didn't have any luck with the ladies this week. Becoming king had been an even bigger burden than I'd imagined.

The sun faded behind a cloud, the warmth of it falling into shadow. I took a deep breath of the cool, new air and hoped it didn't mean rain on the way. Except, when I'd looked before there hadn't been any clouds in the sky.

The earth shook and I jumped to my feet as Alizeh's bronze wings dusted the treetops and her sword-like talons plowed the dirt upon landing. She clucked, snapping her beak in the air then gazed over at me with her oversized eyes.

"You came." I rushed to her side and leaned into the downy softness of her right wing.

I moved to the front of her and she lowered her head to me. I held the sides of her beak and locked my stare with hers, hoping she'd understand me. "I need you to do me a favor, girl. My father has gone missing in the mountains and I really need to find him. He is not himself, and he might be dangerous, but I need your help."

Alizeh nodded in my grip, whether understanding my plea or just responding to the attention.

"I know you belong to Veda, but I really need you. I care about her and I think she cares about me. At least I hope she does. Would you be able to help me?"

She snapped her beak and I stepped back. Maybe she hated me too? But instead of ripping off my arms she nudged the bag at my hip pushing it back.

"Are you hungry, girl?" I pat her head and pulled a dark pink and green dragonfruit from the bag. She clucked happily, and I tossed it in the air, the entire piece disappearing in one gulp.

"Is that a yes?"

She pulled her talons back and lowered herself to the ground, her head laying low on the dirt. I mounted her back as fast as I could, in case she decided to change her mind and tried to buck me off. Instead, she stood tall and proud with her enormous wings spread out in a perfect line, waiting for my directions.

"Let's go."

I jerked forward as Alizeh climbed higher into the sky. I scanned between the trees, looking for any movement, any sign that my father may still be in the forest. But as we ascended higher and higher, the hope that I would find him disappeared in the open air.

~

The silvery moonlight twisted through the mountain peaks. The cool evening air helped soothe the sunburn etched into my skin, but still didn't stop the burn completely. I rubbed my tired eyes, the dust of flight and the intense concentration from surveying every movement below itched under my eyelids.

Unfortunately, I hadn't found one clue as to where my father may have gone. I'd searched all of the lower peaks, every one that was accessible by road or pathway, moving into the ones that required actual mountain climbing experience, but they both seemed untouched. The window for finding him kept closing and I needed to find a way to prop it open a little while longer. My stomach growled, battling hunger and the dread of telling my mother that I'd found nothing, just like the captain had warned her.

But no matter where I flew, I couldn't lose the awful feeling of hurting Veda. Mom said to make it right, but lately every time I opened my mouth I offended someone. Or could I have been making excuses to avoid owning up to my mistakes?

I leaned forward and gathered a fistful of feathers near Alizeh's neck. "Alizeh, bring me to Veda's mountain."

The giant bird turned in a wide arc and the wind whipped through my hair as we soared straight into the current. I settled back and watched the stars float by above our heads, trying to figure out what I could say that might convince her to forgive me. But how would I explain that I let the Council get into my head, or worse, that the thought of kissing her meant more to me than any other kiss I'd ever had?

Alizeh circled the familiar peak, slowing down to land, as the tiny cottage appeared below us like a dot on a map. The windows stood dark as the surrounding night, so she might have already gone to bed. Was it even that late? Or maybe it was early tomorrow already? Flying all day had messed with my concept of time. Alizeh landed as smooth and graceful as always, and I slid off her back as the odd feeling of the stable ground beneath my feet buckled my knees.

"Thank you," I said, as I rushed across the yard. I grabbed a fish from the box by the tree and tossed it toward the bird, her sharp beak shredding it almost instantly. I owed her so much more than a partially rotting fish, but it would have to do for now. Once I returned to the castle I would have the kitchen prepare a feast deserving of the most decorated knight.

"Good girl." I tapped her beak and she closed her eyes with a contented cooing sound. "I'll be right back."

I took the narrow winding path toward the dim cottage. No lights were visible from the ground either. The flowers in the tiny garden flopped over on their stems waiting for the morning sun to wake them again from slumber. Maybe it was a lot later than I thought.

By the time I reached the door, a thickness had already built in my throat. I swallowed, trying to force it down as my fist hovered beside the wooden door. I'd come all this way and still had no clue what I would say to her, but I hoped the right words would come when I saw her face. I clenched my teeth and knocked.

The sound echoed between the peaks, but inside the house remained silent.

I knocked again, louder but trying not to sound too

aggressive.

Nothing.

I looked at Alizeh out in the yard and shrugged. She turned her head to the side watching me with upended eyes.

One last try.

I banged my fist harder and longer, the sound reverberating through the mountains. “Veda, it’s Fallon. If you are in there please come to the door. I’m sorry it’s so late, but I really need to talk to you.”

I leaned against the wall next to the door, one foot crossed over the other and waited.

Still nothing.

“Veda,” I called again, “I just need five minutes, then I promise I’ll leave if you want me to.”

The moon moved miles across the sky while I stood there by myself, holding up the wall. I’d never had to chase a girl before. Any time I did something to offend one of the tavern girls, I simply continued on with my life and they came back the next day pretending like nothing happened. The thought stung in my chest. I hadn’t exactly been the most upstanding guy. Maybe I deserved this. I’d done so many people wrong that now I had to pay the price. Except, I never knew karma would be so all-consuming. Veda deserved to be mad at me. I deserved to be standing out in the dark begging for her forgiveness. But who knew that it would sting this bad?

“She’s either not home, or I screwed up even worse than I thought,” I said to Alizeh as I snaked back down the path. She’d already made herself in a comfortable pile, but as I approached she laid her massive head on the ground, her eyelids drooping as she fought sleep.

I sat beside her and leaned against her wing as the

slow rhythmic rise and fall of her lungs provided a warm cushion behind my back. It wouldn't be the most comfortable sleep, but I'd had worse over the last few days. Besides, even though Veda's comfy old couch lay only fifty feet away, I couldn't risk violating her trust again by breaking into her house. If she'd found me sleeping there in the morning, she'd likely throw me off the mountain and deserved the right too. I pulled the shoulder bag onto my lap and dug through the contents. Mainly fruit peels and scraps remained, but I found a squished sandwich along with a couple of bright orange clementines near the bottom. I peeled back the rind and took a bite of clementine. The sweet juice exploded in my mouth as I closed my eyes and let the weight of the day pin me down.

Slowly my mind sunk into the emptiness of sleep. The future king, the Crown Prince of Aboria, laying in the dirt, waiting on a girl.

30TH MAY

My body ached. Every inch of flesh pressed against the hard ground as I tossed and turned the night away, my subconscious shouting at me for being so cruel. Anything else not beaten by my restless sleep burned deep with the scars of sunburn, and I still had who knows how many days of searching I had left.

I stretched my arms above my head and finally opened my eyes.

Ahhh!

Two massive yellow eyes hovered just above me. I screamed again and clawed myself backward, ripping the tops of my fingers as I pulled myself away.

Alizeh squawked and shook her head. Small bits of

fluff from her feathers billowed around her, like bronze snow.

"Don't do that when I'm sleeping."

She tilted her head and stared for a moment, then ignored my panic and tried to rummage through the bag I'd been using as a pillow.

I let go and fell back to the ground digging the heels of my hands into my eye sockets and letting my heartbeat go back to a normal rhythm. Alizeh had a point though. Time for breakfast.

I staggered over to the side of the yard and pulled the last fish from the box. I tossed it in the air for Alizeh, then stared up at the lone tree and its shady branches. Small apple-like fruits grew in several clumps within the blanket of leaves and hung just low enough that I might be able to reach. I jumped up and swiped with my arm, dragging down a few branches and shaking a few little green orbs to the ground. I scooped them up, wiped off the dust, then wolfed them down and choked on their tartness. I bit into another and my lips puckered tight. Awful. But the contents of my mother's care package had run low after last night's dinner so unless Veda came to the door this was all I had. I flopped down beneath the tree and enjoyed the cool shadow the leaves overhead provided. Nothing seemed to move in the cottage, no silhouettes in the windows or open doors to let in the morning breeze.

I rolled my neck in a circle, still trying to stretch out the stiffness from sleeping on the ground. Maybe Veda really wasn't home, or maybe she'd tiptoed around me this morning and already disappeared. But unless she had another bird, which could be possible, she wouldn't have left Alizeh here. A giant thing like her would be hard to miss, and definitely made the worst alarm clock.

But leaving here without trying again would be foolish. I stumbled toward the cottage and knocked on the door, each pound slow and solemn as it echoed through the wooden panels.

Nothing.

I slumped against the door frame. What now? I still had the higher peaks to search, but the probability that my father could've climbed that high seemed unreasonable. Maybe I should just sweep back over the valley, go home and refresh before going out again? Besides, what if Captain Amir already had news of a sighting? Or maybe, I stood up straighter as the faint glimmer of hope sparked in my veins, maybe he'd already come home. If that were true, then wasting another day searching would be useless.

Except, since I'd already spent nearly a whole day flying all the way up here, I could always go the rest of the way up to the temple. I could give one last quick check through the mountain peaks for my father, I'd get a chance to talk to Veda's father again and finally get the truth, and possibly, Veda would be there and I could try to explain. I launched off the wall and ran down the path.

"Alizeh, time to go." I scooped up my bag from the ground and launched myself between her shoulders. "Take me to Edwin Macario."

The spire of golden light rose into the sky as we soared closer to the temple. Below us, the gilded statues and babbling waterfalls glittered in the afternoon sun. I scanned the yard, hoping to see Veda standing in the garden or sitting on the grand staircase, but they both sat empty. The entire yard lay quiet, just like the first time Veda brought me here.

Except as we circled closer, something seemed different. A large box loomed at the end of the yard in the farthest spot from the temple. Something moved inside the box, back and forth, its shadow darkening the ground beside it but barely distinguishable through the series of bars that constructed the top and sides. As we neared closer it looked more like a cage, one fit for a tiger or a bear, or maybe worse. I shuddered and steered Alizeh to the opposite side of the yard, away from the box. She reared her head back at me as she touched down and I shrugged. She scratched her feet along the ground, refusing to stay still as I stroked her feathers and nearly tossing me off as I tried to dismount.

Snarls and growls emanated from the cage. Alizeh bucked, her head tilted toward the sky.

"Easy, girl." I shushed and tried to calm her, but she wasn't interested in my comfort.

The inhabitant of the cage roared again, and I froze, the terrifying sound too familiar to be a coincidence. It smacked its large hairy paws against the cage bars, and its razor-sharp claws clicked against the metal. A rough and tangled mane framed its enraged face as it bared a row of lethal teeth.

"Dad? Is that you?"

The beast growled and rammed the side of the cage with his shoulder. The bars rattled but still held him captive.

"Dad, it's me, Fallon." I ran across the yard, nausea building in my gut. "Don't you remember?"

He growled again and tossed his head back, then slammed the cage again. I jerked away, keeping my hands far from the bars. Who knew how long he'd been locked up here? Had he eaten? Did he think I did this to him on purpose? The questions flooded my brain, but only one answer rang through the noise--I needed to get him out.

I walked around the outside of the cage until I found the door and the iron lock holding it in place. My father followed my every movement and mimicked my steps. Stalking me like a lion does its prey. I examined the lock. Pretty standard from what I could tell, but once it came off, how would I get my father off this mountain? I grabbed the side of my head as my mind reeled. Only one problem at a time.

"Don't worry, Dad, I'll get you out of here"

I gripped the side of my shoulder bag and yanked the metal buckle from the front. My fingers ached as I stretched out the metal to a long strip with a pointed end. I stuck the end in the lock and fished around trying to move the tumblers, but it wouldn't work. My father paced inside his cell growling and banging on the bars, the lock shaking in my hands every time he smacked the wall.

I dug deeper trying to find the sunken spot where I could pop the lock. The number of doors and private cabinets I'd invaded should have made this an easy task, but the lock wouldn't budge. Either it had some other mechanism or the adrenaline coursing through my limbs scrambled my technique.

I pressed harder then heard a snap as the thin metal buckle broke off in the iron lock.

Banging my hands on the bars I tried pulling again rattling the bars of the cage and the door, but the lock stayed shut tight.

From the ground, I grabbed a sharp rock and

smashed it as hard as I could against the latch. Sparks flew on contact, but I reared my arm back and smashed it again. Barely a scratch showed on the metal.

"What do you think you're doing?"

I smashed the rock one last time against the cage. More sparks flew. I whirled around, the rock clasped in my fist, and came face to face with Edwin Macario.

"I'm trying to break the lock on this cage. What does it look like? You can't just lock up my father like this."

His face exploded in a rainbow of colors, each one angrier than the last. "Of course I can. And I should."

He grabbed the rock from my hand and chucked it over the side of the mountain. "Your father is dangerous. A danger to me, to everyone else, and most likely himself. The cage is for everyone's safety. Do you honestly not think before you act?"

The purple fury crept up the sides of his face from his neck, and he pushed me away from the cage. I regained my balance and tried to circle around him, but he stood directly in front of the door.

"You expect me to believe that you're trying to keep him safe? He's been missing for days. My mother has the entire royal guard searching for him. She is sick with worry. If you were protecting him, why wouldn't you tell someone that he was here?"

"Because he asked me not to and I wouldn't betray his trust like that," Edwin shouted and my head jerked back as the words smacked across my cheek. "Your father came to me, I didn't find him. If he wanted me to tell the castle, I would've, but he wanted to be left alone."

I tossed my hands through the air, the anger rising from the bottoms of my feet and I trembled as it started to take hold of my limbs. "You're telling me he scaled the highest mountain to the tallest peak without any help just to find you? How stupid do you think I am?"

"From where I'm standing, pretty damn dumb since you tried to let a dangerous beast run free without a backup plan. I don't know how he got here. I know it sounds unbelievable, but I woke up the other morning and he was sprawled half-dead across my doorstep. I fed him and took care of him and now I've locked him up until we find a way to reverse whatever spell he's under." Edwin gazed into the cage at my father, his chest rising as he took a deep breath then exhaled loudly. "I want to help him as much as you do. But my way will be a lot safer for everyone. Plus it was his choice to come to find me instead of going home."

I shook out my hands, every part of me afire and my brain completely unable to get it under control. I glanced at my snarling father in the cage. What would I have done with him if I'd set him free? He might have killed me and ran off again so that we'd never find him. But Edwin? Something twinged deep in my muscles when I saw his smug face. Things didn't add up.

"Why you?" I grabbed the sides of my head and tried to sort out my thoughts as I paced in circles. "Out of every place he could have gone, in the state he's in, why would he risk coming all the way up here just to see you?"

Edwin crossed his hands behind his back and widened his stance. "Because out of everyone in the entire kingdom he trusts me. He knows I might be the only one that can help him."

"Really?" I met his stare, not willing to back down so easily. Last time I'd been here he didn't have the highest opinion of my family, but all of a sudden he was going to help? "Then how come he's never spoken of you?"

A dark shadow cast over his face as his proud smile deflated to an angry frown. "Because we had a falling out many years ago and I'll bet he never intended on seeing me again. Besides, from what my daughter tells me you've been left in the dark about a lot of things. It's no wonder you hadn't heard of me."

I crossed my arms to protect myself while doubting every line he threw my way. He was right, someone had been lying to me, but was it really my parents or was it him?

Edwin softened his tone and stepped away from the cage. I stared after his every move, but stayed in one spot, still unsure how to react now. His ability to flip from angry to calm tossed me off guard. Maybe all the years of training to be a wise man helped control his emotions. Or maybe he didn't really care that much at all.

"Your father and I used to be very close, and I worked for him at the castle. I was his confidante. A consultant of sorts."

"So, you were on the Council?"

"Not exactly, the Council can't provide the same type of assistance that I can. In fact, the Council and I didn't get along very well."

"It sounds like there were a lot of people at the castle that you did not get along well with."

He laughed, "You're right. People hate what they fear. They ostracize what scares them."

I looked him over. Nothing about him, other than his self-righteous sneer, screamed menace. His bulky frame could easily be overtaken by the most inexperienced guard, even though his wider shoulders looked like he might have been muscular back in his younger days.

"You don't look that intimidating to me."

"Because you're an arrogant know-it-all. Plus, you haven't seen what I can do." An odd, mischievous twinkle flashed in his eyes and a chill pulsed through me.

"Watch that statue over there." He pointed at the brilliant golden eagle perched on the right corner of the temple.

He closed his eyes for a moment and brought his hands together in front of him as if in prayer. The mountain fell into silence. Even the breeze stopped blowing while he postured in front of me.

Suddenly, Edwin whipped his right hand over his head and flexed his fingers into a claw shape. A strange blue light emanated from his fingertips and snaked through the air like smoke. It billowed higher and higher in the air as it snaked toward the eagle statue. A loud crack echoed through the peaks and the golden figure spread its metal wings as the blue light wrapped itself around the metal bird. The statue's head turned and stared at us, then it pitched into the air and glided off the side of the building.

The eagle statue circled above our heads, flapping its wings occasionally to keep momentum. The sun reflected off its body, and I shielded my eyes, still not believing what I saw. Alizeh jumped to her feet and squawked at the gilded bird, chasing at it, her beak snapping loud and angry behind us.

"How did you..." But the words stuck in my throat as I kept staring into the sky, wonder and dread mixing a strange cocktail in my blood as my heart pounded a warning my chest.

"Magic," Edwin said, "I can do a lot of things that you probably haven't even dreamed of."

I'd heard of people who could do things like this, but never met one, especially not in Aboria. Enchanted creatures walked all over these lands, but humans who could wield magical powers, that was something only people in far off lands could do. Places like Enchantia or maybe even in Oz. But not here. Never here.

Edwin snapped his fingers and the blue smoke cloaking the eagle dissipated. Immediately, the metal bird's wings fused back to its sides and it plummeted from the sky smashing into the earth between us. I stumbled backward from the aftershock and tripped over a rock falling down as well, the stones grating my elbows and sending a jolt of pain through my body.

From my spot on the ground, I examined the bird, but it no longer moved. No chest heaving with breath. No feathers blowing in the breeze. Just hard, precious gold.

"I think it might be time to tell you more of my story." Edwin extended his hand, and I eyed it with caution, refusing the assistance. "Except, I think you need to be in a better frame of mind for this tale. A little less hostile, perhaps. Why don't you spend a few more minutes with your father, then come meet me inside? I'll prepare you something to eat and you can take a rest before we talk. From the black rings under your eyes, I'm assuming you haven't slept in days."

"Thanks." I scrambled to my feet, still refusing his offer of help, and brushed the dirt from my clothes. "And are you going to tell me what you just did there?"

He smirked, then retracted his hand with a vile snort. "Depends. We'll see how the rest of the story goes first."

I bit down on my cheek wanting to say so much more, many of those things not very appropriate for royalty, but arguing with him likely wouldn't help my cause--even if it looked like he would've enjoyed matching wits with me.

He straightened the high collar of his robe and tapped the eagle on its head, the metal clanging against the golden rings on his fingers. He cast me one last glare and shook his head, then started to meander slowly back towards the temple.

I swallowed down the list of insults I wanted to spew behind his back and conjured my most cordial tone.

"Is Veda here?" I called after him. "I've been looking for her but she seems to have disappeared."

He halted and stood in silence for a moment. Maybe considering if he really wanted to answer me.

"I'm afraid not. Women can be quite crafty when they don't want to be found." He chuckled to himself but I struggled to find the humor. "She said she needed a few days to think. You must have done something pretty stupid for her to be that angry with you."

"Maybe," I muttered under my breath, but from the sneer on his lips, he likely heard.

He turned and continued his strut back to the temple. "But at least that means she's no longer with someone of your type. Your squabbles are of no consequence to me."

I groaned, the prospect of spending any more time with that arrogant man caused my stomach to churn. But if he was finally willing to talk, I needed to take him up on it while I had the chance.

"However, I must tell you, a real prince would never toss out a diamond because it needed a bit of shine."

Ouch.

So Veda had told her father what happened. Who knows how many details, but it sounded like enough.

He already had my past and my father to dangle over my head, now he had my bad behavior to add to his collection of torture implements. Great.

The breeze picked up again and I pulled my coat closer to my chest. My father sat in the corner of his cage staring out into the distance as it ruffled the fur around his face. His rabid fit had subsided, replaced by a sad glaze in his dark chocolate eyes. A deep pain.

I inched closer to the bars, each movement long and drawn to avoid throwing him back into a frenzy. He swung his head my direction his lip stuck out, but without any fight.

"Dad, I don't know if you can hear me in there, but I wanted you to know that I'm here to help. Mom is beyond worried and we both can't wait to have you home."

I wrapped my hands around the metal bars and he jumped but stayed on the far side of the cage.

"I love you, Dad. I don't even remember the last time I told you that, but it's true. I wished I'd spent more time with you, learning and just being around you. I took for granted how hard your job is. How hard you have to work to you make the kingdom run and still maintain the respect of your followers. We're going to fix this. I know we are."

My father glared at me then took his head in his paws and let out a crestfallen whimper. The high-pitched whine stabbed right through my chest burrowing straight through to the other side and leaving a hole I didn't think I'd ever fill until the curse was finally broken.

I ran my hand across the bars as I walked towards the temple, each one playing its own mournful tune as I delayed letting go.

31ST MAY

Metal bars surrounded me. Above. Below. On every side. An iron lock the size of my fist sealed me into my cell, stole my freedom. I grabbed ahold of the bars clanging and rattling them, screaming for help, but only the echo of my own voice came back. Nothing existed beyond the bars, just darkness, deep and hollow. I smashed my fist against the lock until my knuckles bled. Dark red blood poured down my fingers and stained my clothes. I retreated to the center of the cage and sat on the floor with my knees pulled to my chest. A wintry chill prickled up the back of my spine, the hair on my neck standing on end, waiting for something that I didn't know but feared anyway. Suddenly a strange blue smoke started to fill the cell wrapping and twisting around me. It filled my mouth. My nose. I coughed and choked against the unknown substance. My lungs burned, my breath shallower as I struggled against the smoke. The cell filled until I could no longer see. Just blue magic smothering me. Wrapping tight around my neck. The burning in my lungs deepened, scalding my throat. I coughed and coughed and coughed and...

I bolted upright in the tiny metal cot as sweat dripped from my forehead and across my chest. Just a dream. Or was it? And where was I?

The tiny room slowly came into focus. The peaked roof loomed above my head and the stark white walls stood bare except for a small hand-stitched sign that read *'to know one's mind is to know one's self'*. The temple. I rubbed my face with my hands, the memories of the last few days and my nightmare swirled and merged into a dark play, acting out over and over in my mind. But I was safe here. Wasn't I?

I lay back on the cot and rested my head on the soft pillow. The lumpy mattress beat sleeping on the ground, even though being closer to Alizeh would have soothed my nerves a bit more. Even with the serene peacefulness of the temple surrounding me, I still didn't completely trust Edwin. He seemed to be hiding something from me. But everyone was hiding something from me. Maybe I just didn't like him much? Either way, the faster I heard his story, the faster I could get off this mountain and go home to send the guards to my father's rescue.

I rolled onto my side and stared at the pyramid of light cutting through the narrow opening of the nearly closed door. Sun or lantern light? I couldn't tell. A tiny ornately-carved table sat across from my face with a glass of water and two stalks of prickly aloe vera placed neatly on top. A note written in meticulous handwriting read '*for the sunburn*'.

I swung my feet to the floor and sat up, letting my mind recalibrate for a moment before grabbing the glass. The water went down in one gulp, my dry throat craving more as soon as the last drop disappeared, the search mission taking its toll. I squeezed the sticky ointment from the aloe and rubbed it over my arms and face, the coolness instantly feeling better against my scorched skin. Finally, I dared to stand up, but my head ached and the room spun. I grabbed the side of the table until the dizziness faded, then took a deep breath before staggering out of the room.

Outside, the rich scent of baking bread wafted from down the hall. My stomach rumbled and saliva built on my tongue, as my feet followed my nose.

"Good morning, Your Majesty. Sleep well?" Edwin asked as I entered the quaint and simple kitchen of the temple.

I blinked. The clean starkness of the room too bright for my half-asleep brain to process.

"Already morning?" I rustled my hand through my hair as a yawn stretched my face. I'd only intended to sleep an hour, maybe two, but clearly my body had other ideas.

"Not quite. It's nearly two in the afternoon." Edwin grabbed a metal teapot from the stove and set it on the small dining table, already set for two. "Jasmine tea? It'll help clear your mind."

I lumbered across the kitchen, nearly collapsing in the empty chair across from him. He offered a basket of fresh buns, my mouth already salivating from the delicious smell. I gazed at Edwin carefully, scanning his face and looking for a hidden agenda. He caught my scrutiny and grinned as if he would've done the same in my position, then nudged the breadbasket closer. I kept my eyes locked on him, but accepted the soft bun and let the fresh from the oven warmth seep into my palm.

"So I hear you want to know the full story. How I ended up leaving the castle, and the real truth about your parents," Edwin said.

"Yes, please," I mumbled through a mouthful of bread and fresh blackberry jam. The tart fruit melted against my tongue. Maybe Edwin wasn't so bad.

"Well, I guess the best place to start is the beginning. I've known your father since we were children. I grew up in the castle by his side and we were the best of friends. Until, of course, we weren't. He always had a charmed life. Handsome. Wealthy. The ladies loved him. But he was often selfish and stubborn if he didn't get his way. His father was a harsh and stubborn man, who fortunately wasn't around much, but he loved his mother with all his heart. She doted on him and spoiled him every way she could until she died when he was just a young boy. After that, his arrogance grew worse. Ezra grew up in the castle raised mainly by servants and given any of his heart's desire, which changed almost daily. With no one around to keep him in line, he had no consequences for anything he did. No responsibility or ownership of his actions."

I cringed, the story sounding more like mine then my father's, except I was lucky to have two wonderful parents. "But he isn't like that."

Edwin smirked and tented his fingers on the table.

"Not now. But it wasn't always so. And unfortunately, as with most things, major changes do not come easily. One day a forest fairy visited your father in disguise. Disgusted at what she saw of the future king, she placed a curse on him and the rest of the castle, so that his unreasonable obsession with beauty and perfection became his downfall. The fairy's curse insisted that until he learned to see past the material and obvious aesthetics, he would remain hideous to everyone else. He would be a —"

"Beast." I took a sip of the hot tea, the warm flow of it down my throat soothing against the horrible image in my brain. I shook my head. The story sounded so fantastic, if I didn't know my father was locked up outside I'd think it was a hoax.

"Exactly. He stayed that way for a few years as he watched his kingdom fall into ruin and his own father pass away. He became a king that couldn't rule. One day an old man happened upon the castle and your ill-tempered father took him prisoner for trespassing. His daughter came searching for him and when your father wouldn't let the old man go, she offered herself as a replacement."

I pictured Mom at the gates of the castle, her long chestnut curls blowing behind her, ready to face the beast. Always the beauty with the warrior soul. "It sounds like my mother was quite the brave girl back then."

Edwin laughed and pounded his fist on the table. The sugar bowl and cream jumped. "You call that bravery? She wasn't brave, she was foolish. Giving herself up with little chance of survival. Martyrdom is not a virtuous path, it just means she didn't try hard enough to find a solution."

I bit down on my tongue, the coppery taste of my own blood filled my mouth. How dare he speak of my mother that way? If I didn't need his help I would launch across the table right now.

"And where do you fit into all of this?" I tried to hide the bitterness in my tone, but it shone through.

Edwin narrowed his gaze. "As I said before, I'd been around the castle for years and at that time was still a friend to your father. As much as his arrogance and stubbornness plagued him, he was also a hell of a lot of fun. During his time as king I became more useful as I knew the ins and outs of royalty and my other skills —" he twisted his palm through the air and rolled each of his fingers in towards his hand, "— became useful to your father. Especially when it came to disputes. I had a knack for making problems disappear in the most creative ways."

I gulped and choked on a mouthful of tea. I coughed and leaned over the tabletop until my airway cleared. Gasping for air, I pictured the blue magic wrapping around my throat like in my nightmare. Maybe it wasn't just a dream?

"Are you alright?" Edwin reached across the table and gave a firm pat on my back until I stopped hacking.

"Yes, of course. Please continue."

He eyed me carefully, then sat back down, his hands laced in front of him. "However, when your father kidnapped that girl I realized he'd crossed a line he would never return from. The fairy had paid him back for his obvious flaws, but this was reprehensible. One night we argued about her in the garden. He insisted that the girl would be the one to break the curse and he would keep her captive until she did. I told him it was wrong, and that I'd had enough of watching him mess with other people's lives and that I was going to free her. He became enraged and threw me across the courtyard then held me up against the wall and threatened to kill me if I even considered messing with his plan. I begged him to let me go and instead he banished me from the castle. That night was the last time I ever saw him, until now."

I sat and stared at Edwin, letting all of the details simmer in my brain, picturing that final flight and knowing the terror he must've felt when cornered by my father in his monster form. I'd been there twice in the last week as well. However, Edwin's story didn't sound like the happy fairytale everyone in the castle made things out to be. Everyone loved my father. My mother likely most of all. Was there romance really this dark or were there pieces of the story still missing?

"If my father hadn't spoken to you in years, how did he know where to find you? Why did he come here?"

"I'm not sure how he found me, but he is the king after all and I doubt he'd let me get far without keeping an eye on me. Especially, knowing what I could do. I'm one of the few people who even remember what happened. When the curse broke, everyone's memory was wiped clean. Everyone except those living in the castle. I wrote everything down, which you have already read, without my permission I'd like to add, to make sure if the memory ever faded I would still know what happened."

"That still doesn't answer why he's here now?"

"It's the magic, dear prince. Your father was cursed by magic, so he sought out someone who could do magic to help him."

It made sense, in a weird twisted kind of way. "But if you are truly that powerful, why didn't you just end the curse last time?"

A bright red burn started at the tips of Edwin's ears and stained across his cheeks then into his nose. For someone considered to be wise, his pride sure got in his enlightened path. "I tried, but I wasn't able to. However, I'm a lot stronger than I used to be. I haven't figured out how to stop it yet but I'm sure I will with a bit of time. You should be careful when judging someone who could toss you off this mountain without using his hands."

Except, he never would. A dead prince would be questioned and combined with the king in a cage it would likely end in his own execution. Either way, angering him again didn't serve much purpose either. "The magic, where did it come from? Why are you so powerful?"

"The magic runs through the Macario family tree. My father was a wizard, as was his father before him and his mother before that all the way back as far as anyone can remember. I've had these abilities since I learned to read the spells they came from. Now it simply courses through my blood. It's who I am."

"And Veda? Would that make her a wizard as well?"

"A witch. A female wizard is called a witch. But no, she's not. I typically try to avoid using it around her." Edwin took the teapot off the table and placed it back on the stove then cleared the plates into a large basin sink. "She never developed the gift. Must take after her mother more than me, but she is likely better off as having power like this tends to attract more trouble and attention than it's worth."

I grabbed the sugar bowl and cream from the table, following Edwin's example, then swiped the crumbs off the table into my hand and brushed them into the garbage."But there's still one thing that doesn't make any sense. If the original curse was triggered because of my father's vanity, what would have triggered it this time? He's not the same person he was before. He's kind, gracious, and altruistic. Plus, it sounds as though this time is worse. That last time he was still more man than monster, when now he barely knows who he is."

"That is a good question. Unfortunately, until I find a way to lift this curse there will be no way of knowing how it came back."

I took the rest of the dishes and placed them in the sink. Above the basin, a large window faced the edge of the cliff. Dark clouds rolled on the horizon.

"Do you think it might have something to do with the other bad things happening around the world? That maybe somehow the same dark magic was released back into the air and is stirring up all the old curses?"

Edwin stroked his chin and tapped his index finger against his lips. The darks of his eyes darted back and forth as if he were running through a list of options and checking them off in his mind. "Perhaps. Or perhaps we shouldn't jump to the end of the world quite yet. The answer may be simpler than we think."

I paced around the small kitchen then rested my arm on the counter, staring out into the distance again. Maybe Edwin was right, and we'd all been trying too hard. Maybe we just needed to calm down and figure it out? Or maybe, he wasn't as powerful as he thought he was and his arrogance would waste whatever time my father had left? Either way, the urgency of the situation seemed to ramp up even in this tranquil place. Something had changed. An energy sparked and the only way to snuff it would be to finish the puzzle before the hourglass ran empty. A mystical chess game waiting for me to make the next move. If only I knew what it was.

"So, have I answered all of your questions?"

I snapped out of my thoughts and returned to the table. I sat face-to-face with Edwin, one question still looming heavy in my mind. "Am I really adopted?"

His face lit up, a beaming smile crested his lips as if he'd finally made it to the main event. "Absolutely."

I hung my head to my chest. "Are you sure? You said you'd already left the castle before the curse was broken, is it possible you don't remember as clearly as you say?"

"Just because your father wasn't speaking to me doesn't mean I didn't still have my sources on the ground. News of a baby boy abandoned on the castle doorstep travels very fast in certain circles. Besides, what would be the point of lying to you about this? I have nothing to lose or anything to gain at this point."

"Then where did I come from? I'm sure I must have parents somewhere, and how come I look just like my mother and father?"

Edwin shrugged. "I can't say much for the appearance, maybe since your mother is a simple commoner you share a similar look with the other common city folk. But who you are and where you come from is a mystery I have yet to solve. No one saw anyone coming or going from the castle that night. Nothing appeared unusual about the basket you were left in. It's as if you appeared out of thin air at the exact right place and time. Besides, what's better to smooth over a rough patch in the kingdom than a lavish wedding and a male heir."

The weight of the truth bore down on my ribs and crushed my lungs. The taste of the Jasmine tea burned in my throat as it threatened to return. I wasn't really an Aldric. My parents weren't my parents, and at least a handful of people at the castle had helped them lie to me for eighteen years. The betrayal squirmed and twisted through my stomach as if I'd swallowed the lie and let it grow into a full-sized demon now struggling to claw its way out.

"If you don't believe me, you can ask them yourself. You live in a kingdom of secrets, dear prince. You'd be wise to learn that truth now."

I grabbed my forehead and rubbed my temples, a sharp pain stinging behind my eyes. "I think I should go. Thank you for everything."

I thrust the chair back and started for the exit, the world spinning and hazy.

Edwin's chair screeched across the floor as he flew to his feet and grabbed tight on my right bicep. "You can't just leave."

"And why not?" I stared Edwin down, but his expression wasn't harsh as I would've expected. The fight faded from his snarl and was replaced by a wide-eyed, gaping mouth stare. He ripped his hand from my skin and staggered back, falling into his chair without taking his eyes off of me.

"What are you trying to pull with me, boy?"

I shook my head, the fog of confusion getting thicker by the second. "What are you talking about?"

"Don't mess with me. I felt it, coursing through you. Who sent you here?"

"Veda. Veda sent me to talk to you, but what are you babbling about? Felt what?"

He held up his hands, palms apart like holding an imaginary ball as he leaned toward me. "You can't feel it? That electricity charging through your blood. Feel it in your marrow?"

His words jumbled in my already crowded brain. I

tossed my hand into the air and headed for the door again. "I have no idea what you're talking about, but I need to go."

"Your Highness, you can't leave here. Not yet. If you go now before I can stop the curse, the guards will come for him and I may never get the chance to help him."

"My mother would do anything to save him. I know you said their love was built on hate and tragedy, but no matter what has happened in their past she loves him more than anything and he —" I pointed toward the cage in the yard "— loves her more than his own life. She would let you help him any way you could. She would even let you come back to the castle if she thought it would make things easier."

Edwin shook his hands in front of himself. "Oh no. The temples are a sacred place for the guardians of the light. I do my best work in the peace and quiet of the mountains. Besides, if we returned your father to the castle the entire kingdom would be looking at the gate night and day. It would be a disaster."

The pulse of a memory. Running through the streets as the reporters chased Veda and me. Hunting us down like wild dogs. Trapping us in the corner. Her lips so close to my lips. The longing look in her clear eyes. The last time I saw Veda smile. "You're right. But I need to tell her that he's alive. She deserves to know what's going on."

"Just like she told you the truth?"

I charged towards Edwin, my patience non-existent, but he cowered his arms up covering his head. "Fine. I'll let you go, but you are only to tell your mother that he's here. She's welcome to come to visit if it makes her feel better, but I can't have anyone else charging up on my mountain. You understand?"

I nodded. Whatever nonsense Edwin spewed before seemed to change his opinion of me in a hurry. Either that or he'd lost a grip on his sanity. Or maybe I did?

"I'm serious. If you dare to tell anyone else I will open the cage and let your father run forever if he would even make it down this peak alive."

"I've got it."

I ran down the gilded steps and through the yard to the cage. My father sat in the corner, the same spot I'd left him last night. He looked up for a second and saw me standing by the bars, then hung his head again and stomped his large feet against the floor.

"We are going to find a way to break this curse, I promise. And I'm going to tell Mom to come."

I cringed as the word 'mom' came out of my mouth because if what Edwin said was true she really wasn't. I didn't even have one.

I stuck my fingers in my mouth and whistled, and the looming shape of Alizeh quickly emerged over the early evening sun.

A restless feeling overcame my body, a sudden urge to be off this peak, or to scream, or even just to fall to the ground and curl up in a ball, but I needed to do something and I needed it fast.

Alizeh landed and I tossed myself on top of her back. "Alizeh, to the castle."

1ST JUNE

Red and yellow bubbled on the horizon as dawn threatened to boil over and flood the night. Keeping my eyes open proved harder every mile as we descended through the sky toward the castle, but the obligation to tell my mother that I found my father helped me battle on.

Alizeh circled the city then gently landed in the front courtyard of the castle. The eerie stillness of morning clung to my skin like the early dew clung to the blades of grass beneath my feet. Two guards rushed from the main castle door, swords drawn and ready to fight.

"We weren't expecting you, Your Majesty," the first guard said as he stopped in his tracks after recognizing me as the intruder.

"Not to worry. All is well. But I will need someone to

take care of my friend."

Alizeh nuzzled her head into my shoulder and made a gentle cooing noise. The mouths of the guards dropped to their feet but took their orders like the professionals they were.

"Yes, sir. What exactly do we do, sir?"

"Talk to the kitchen about some food, meat or fish and any other scraps they can spare. Then show her to the ponds in the garden to cool off. I don't want her going far right now as she will be needed again shortly." I leaned into Alizeh and smiled. She'd been my truest companion over the last few days. And not once had she let me down.

The second guard sheathed his sword and circled around Alizeh, his arms outstretched and his brow furrowed. "Excuse me, sir? Do we get a leash, or..."

I cuddled Alizeh closer to me. "Absolutely not. This magnificent animal is a guest at the castle and will be treated as such."

They both nodded although the uncertainty of my request cut puzzled looks into their faces.

"If you treat her well she will follow your commands without any complaint. Trust me, you'll love her."

I rushed across the courtyard and through the front castle entrance as Alizeh clucked at her new handlers. The sweet smell of home flooded toward me and eased some of the tension in my shoulders, except it also left more questions that I needed to have answered. The trip to Edwin's had left an unresolved feeling itching in the back of my brain, but my happiness would have to wait.

"You're back, Your Majesty." Griswold greeted me in the foyer with a beaming grin. He helped me slip off my coat and brushed my shoulders off. "We weren't sure when to expect you. I'll alert the kitchen of your arrival and have them prepare breakfast."

"Thank you, I'm starving. But tell them to hold off for a little while, first I need to speak with the queen."

Griswold clasped his hands together as the beginning of a frown started across his lips. "I'm afraid your mother did not make it to her chambers last night. She has been working late into the night in her library, and has asked not to be disturbed."

I smacked him on the shoulder blade and he lurched forward from the force. "Trust me, she will want to see me. And I promise if she gets me in any trouble I'll be sure to tell her that you did everything you could to stop me."

"Very good, sir. Is there anything else I can do for you? Do you have a plan for your feathered friend outside?"

"The guards will take care of Alizeh, but if you could put together a few of my mother's favorite snacks and put them in a bag that would be wonderful."

"Planning a picnic to cheer her up? That would be lovely. She's been extra dreary with your father still missing and you disappearing for so long."

"Not exactly. But I do hope it will make her feel better."

I ran for the stairs and stopped short where the rug met the tile. "One more thing, Griswold, has anyone come to the castle looking for me?"

Griswold shook his head. "No, sir. Should I be expecting someone?"

My shoulders dropped as a sharp pain of disappointment stabbed into my gut. "Apparently not."

~

Lantern light flickered from under the library door and painted pictures with spark and shadow across the stone floor. I wrapped my knuckles against the wood. No one answered.

Instead of waiting, I turned the knob and slowly pushed the door inward so as not to frighten my mother if she were lost in thought. The last time I'd accidentally done that, she knocked over the lantern and nearly burned down an entire half of the castle.

But this time she sat upright in her ornate armchair, rather than hunched over her desk. Her head had fallen back against the chair, and an open book still sat clutched at her waist. I watched her chest rise and fall as the slow, steady breaths of sleep escaped from her open mouth. Dark blue tired skin ringed her closed eyes.

I shimmied the book from her grasp and her hands flopped limp into her lap. I glanced at the pages. A spellbook written in an ancient text. Symbols and primitive line drawings edged the margins of the pages and I shivered at what some of these writings might mean. What evil they might intend to conjure. I'd had enough of magic for a while.

I pulled a quilt from the large trunk near the shelves of picture books I used to scan through as a kid, and laid it gently over her chair tucking the edges around her shoulders. She looked small curled up in the blanket. Fragile in a way she never let show in daylight. Wouldn't show if she knew these moments even existed.

"Sweet dreams." I kissed her forehead and lowered the lantern light. Shadows darkened across her face and I tiptoed toward the door.

A soft murmur stopped me at the threshold.

"Fallon, honey, is that you skulking away in the

dark?"

My hand hovered over the door handle. "Yeah, it's me. You were sleeping so soundly, I didn't want to wake you."

"Well, hopefully not too soundly. I've heard I snore when I'm exhausted."

She shifted in the chair, positioning herself more upright as the quilt fell loose into her lap. She grabbed the hem and twisted her fingers through the multi-colored squares of cotton. "Did you just get back? What time is it anyway?"

I walked back across the room to her side. "It's not long after dawn, and yes, I got home about fifteen minutes ago then came straight to see you." I took her hand and enveloped it with my own, her fingers cold as ice against my skin. "And by the way, Griswold wanted me to tell you that disturbing you in here was completely against his instructions."

She chuckled, a glimpse of her old light shining for a brief second. "Of course, he did. I'll be sure to commend him for his obedience, as always."

"But I couldn't wait. I have news."

She turned her body toward me, every part of her tuned into my announcement.

"I found Dad. He's still in his beast form, but he's okay."

"Oh my gosh, Fallon. You have no idea how much relief that brings me." She dove forward wrapping her arms around my neck and squeezing tight. I struggled to breathe against her grip but rested my head in the crook of her arm, the familiar rarity of it giving me a sense of calm that I so desperately needed.

"So is he here?" She tried to let go and jumped to her feet, but I held her steady in her chair.

"No. I found him on one of the highest mountain peaks. He'd gone to visit one of the wise men of the temples and he's still up there with him."

"Oh," her excitement dialed back several notches. "But he is safe, right?"

"Yes. He's locked in a cage —"

She jerked forward again. "A cage? He's not an animal, he's..."

"I know. But as long as he is still not responding to his human side he is a threat to himself and everyone else. At least in the cage, we will know where to find him when we find a way to break the curse. Have you had any luck with that?" I nodded toward the open book on the desk.

She rubbed her hands over her face and stood, stretching her arms above her head with a tiny squeal. "No. I've been searching, and I've enlisted help from some of the oldest witches in Enchantia, but no one seems to know anything yet."

"I'm sorry. I'm sure we'll find something soon, but in the meantime did you want to see him?"

"Of course, absolutely." She rushed toward the door. "Let me tell Captain Amir, and he will arrange for a full unit to accompany me. We can bring him back here, and even if we need to put him in the dungeon for a little while, I can stay with him until it's all over."

I waved my hands in front of me. "Wait. You can't tell the captain. I promised that I would only tell *you* where Dad is. If I go back on that, I'm worried that they may let him go again."

"That sounds absurd. Why wouldn't I be able to take my guard with me?"

"The temples are a sacred place. Plus, if Dad gets overly excited we might lose him again. At least on the mountain, he is safe, and there won't be anyone trying at the castle to catch a glimpse while we deal with this nightmare."

She shook her head, her hands on her hips, but slowly it seemed the logic started to make sense. Edwin's words coming out of my mouth tasted strange, especially since he'd used them to calm me and now I'd turned around and used them on my mother for the same reason.

"Fine. I'll do whatever I need to get your father home. But he needs to be here with his family, in his home."

Family? Is that really what we were?

She opened the door and the dim light from down the hall filtered into the room.

"Can I talk to you about something first, before you go?"

She paused with her hand on the doorknob, a deep 'v' forming between her eyes as her eyes narrowed. "Of course, you can always ask me anything."

"As I've been researching the curse and my duties as king I've come across some information that doesn't seem to make any sense."

She closed the door and leaned against the wall, the seriousness of my voice likely setting her off. I sat on the edge of the desk and rubbed my sweaty palms together, staring at them as they generated heat between my hands.

"I've heard that it's possible, I might be adopted."

She crossed her arms and let out a huge breath deflating into the wall as her head tipped toward the ceiling. "Oh, Fallon. Your father and I honestly hoped you'd never find out, or at least that we'd to be the ones to tell you. I'm so sorry."

"So it's true?" I jumped up from the desk and she

rushed over placing her hands on the sides of my face.

"Please don't be angry. We never wanted to hurt you so we decided to keep it a secret until you were old enough to understand. Then as the years went by we realized that you were always ours and we never wanted you to doubt that."

I took her hands and pulled them away, as my own began to shake and heat rippled through my blood. If they never wanted to hurt me, keeping secrets was not the way to do it. "Then tell me now. Where did I come from?"

"I don't know." She clutched her arm over her stomach and rested the other hand on her forehead as she paced between the bookshelves. "It was the night your father proposed. It was late at night and there was a knock at the door. Griswold answered, but there was no one else there, just you lying in a basket wrapped in a thin blanket. The guards never saw anyone. Whoever it was managed to slip past the gate and disappeared into the night. We searched for whoever left you with us, but no one turned up. Not one clue as to where you came from. Your father and I so wanted to have children, but he always worried that his curse might one day affect his own children so we decided to raise you as our own. Only you. We'd never even dreamed of having another child."

"You adopted me because I was convenient?"

She paused, her brain spinning in her eyes. Maybe trying to find the right words. Or maybe hiding more of the truth. "Of course not. We both loved you from the second we saw your little face. During the time spent looking for your parents, we grew into a family, even before we knew it was even a possibility. There was no question that you belonged with us."

“How many people know?” I knocked my fist against the desk and a cup of pencils fell to the floor with a crash.

She winced and watched them roll along the floor, but didn’t dare lose her connection with me to gather them up.

“A few of our trusted people in the castle, most of them have already long passed on.

From what I know, the only ones left to know the truth are Griswold, your father and I, and the Council.”

“The Council knows? No wonder they hate me.” I grabbed fistfuls of hair and tugged, spinning in a slow circle on the floor, the thoughts in my head spinning even faster.

“They don’t hate you, Fallon, they just need to do what is best for the crown without being emotional. None of them were even around when the adoption happened, but we needed to tell them and provide the documents that you had been appropriately claimed and legitimized as heir to the Aldric line to avoid any possible issues.”

The room fell silent, her pacing on the left and me reeling on the right, neither of us knowing what to say next. Eventually, her strides came closer and she pulled me into a hug, squeezing as tight as her petite arms could. I hugged her back, still the only mother I’d ever known and even if we weren’t blood she’d always treated me as though I was. Like she’d lay down and die for me if the choice ever came. And in that moment, her tight embrace mixed with the familiar rose scent of her perfume and I knew that I would do the same.

“I love you, Fallon. I always have and I always will, no matter what happens. And your father, even with everything going on, I know he loves you more than anything."

"I know."

"How long have you known?"

"I heard the rumors a while ago, but until you told me I didn't believe that they were true."

"Never hold anything like this in again, please. We may have kept this is secret, but had you asked we would have always told you the truth. I'm sorry you had to find out this way, but I hope you can forgive me? Forgive us."

I pulled her tighter, no words required.

"And thank you for finding your father, but I can't go see him just yet."

"Why not?" I let her go and she dropped her arms to her sides. "He needs you."

She patted my cheek. "And you need me too. It's not fair for me to leave you. Not like this. Not right now."

"I'll be okay. When you get back we can talk about this more, but I know he's lost without you."

She clamped my chin in her hand and forced me to look at her. To see the warmth in her wide eyes. To witness the love. "You have a bigger heart than you realize. For that, and so many other reasons I will always be proud to call you my son."

I hugged her again, as new tears escaped my eyes and landed in her hair.

"I won't be gone long. And when all of this is over, all three of us can clear the air."

"Sounds good. Now pack light and meet me in the castle courtyard. It's time for the queen to go get her king."

~

Just beyond the iron castle gates the golden bridge to Mosa gleamed in the midday sun. I wandered through the courtyard, appreciating the beautiful scarlet petals on the rose bushes that lined the miles of metal fence and kept the rest of the world outside. Three bushes from the gate I found the most perfect rose and plucked it, grazing my knuckles against the thick pointy thorns.

"Are you stealing my flowers, dear prince?"

I held the rose out to my mother and gave a sweeping bow. "No. Someone taught me to always bring a gift when you stay at a guest's home. Maybe it will remind Dad of the castle and his life here."

Her cheeks blushed the color of the flower's petals as she took it from my hand and tucked it in the bag around her shoulder. She raised the hood of her dark purple cloak over her head and scanned the courtyard.

"How exactly am I going to get to the temple?"

I whistled and almost immediately Alizeh appeared in the sky before landing in the courtyard. A gust of wind from her arrival rustled the leaves of the trees and plants around us.

My mother stared in awe but took a few steps back.

I took her hand and pulled her next to Alizeh's wing.

"There's no reason to be scared. She's the most gentle creature you'll ever meet," I said as I stroked her long feathers. "Aren't you, Alizeh? Just a big baby bird."

My mother held out her hand, hesitant at first, but eventually taking the risk to pet her. Her fingers slipped gently across the feathers and her lips curled into a smile.

"She'll do all the work. But if you need to change course, say her name and then give your directions. Just make sure you are loud enough for her to hear you."

"She's so soft," my mother said as she continued to stroke her wing. "Do you think she'll listen to me?"

"Of course. Just be firm. I know you know how to do that."

Mom shot me a harsh glare. "Thanks a lot."

I laughed, then wandered back to the fountain in the middle of the yard and scooped up the bag of fish I'd stolen from the kitchen. The bag reeked and I lurched forward, holding my breath, but still much fresher than what Alizeh had been used to. Silvery-green scales chafed my hand as I pulled one out.

"Alizeh."

She turned and clucked as I tossed the fish through the air, and she caught it with one gulp.

I held the bag out to my mother. "Here, you try. She'll love you forever for it."

My mother turned up her nose at the smell, but scrunched back the sleeve of her cloak and reached in. She glanced at me again, uncertainty in her eyes, but didn't waver and threw the fish toward Alizeh with perfect aim. The bird caught the snack and cooed as she devoured the treat, then nudged her beak toward my mother, gently pushing her backward. My mother brushed the soft feathers between her big eyes.

"See. I told you she'd love you."

"Speaking of love, have you figured out if you're in love with that girl yet?"

I stared at our feet on the cobblestones, answering with my silence.

"And did you resolve your problems?"

"No. I haven't seen her since we last spoke. But I will. Next time I see her I'll make things right."

She clutched my arm near my shoulder and drew small circles with her thumb. "I don't doubt you will."

"Maybe you'll meet her soon. The wise man at the temple is her father."

"Ah." She smiled, a warm knowing smile. "Maybe the rose wasn't really for your father."

"Alright, Mom, time to go."

I helped her climb onto Alizeh's back, her confidence growing slowly as she shifted and moved into position.

"I'll be back soon. Running the kingdom will be difficult for one person. Remember to ask the Council if you need anything."

"Everything will be fine. I've got this."

I stepped back to give them more space and yelled, "Alizeh, take her to the temple."

Alizeh spread her wings and within seconds they were soaring above the tops of the castle towers. I waved as they flew by, even though I doubted my mother would dare look down to see it.

The courtyard fell silent, just the babbling of the small garden fountains and the spring song of the birds in the trees. I took a deep breath, letting the fresh air in and felt it circulate through my veins. As I exhaled, some of the weight on my chest lifted, disappearing in the open breeze. I took my time heading back into the castle, but Griswold still met me at the door, as expected. He looked different to me now, knowing that he knew my secret for all these years and never once told me. Part of me was grateful for keeping things quiet, but another part still felt partly betrayed.

"My mother had to leave for a little while. If anyone needs anything, they can run it through me."

"Very good, sir." Griswold crossed his arms behind his back and nodded. "Is there anything I can do for you?"

"Not right now." I yawned, the entire morning

suddenly feeling like it had taken weeks. "I think I'm going to get some rest."

I stumbled to my room, stripped off my jacket and collapsed onto my bed. My body sunk into the thick mattress as the soft sheets brushed against my skin. Shadows danced along the far wall as the afternoon sun peeked in and out of the clouds through my window. Each shape cast triggered a different thought in my brain. My father's cage. The abandoned baby in the basket. The crown. My mother. Then just as my eyes closed and the light disappeared, a warm rush flowed through me. Emerald eyes sparkled in my mind. A sarcastic smile on the reddest lips. Curves my hands ached to touch and follow wherever they might lead. One face above the rest.

Veda.

2ND JUNE

Bang. Bang. Bang.

I rolled over and groaned.

"Who is it?" I called toward the closed door, not bothering to even sit up. Yesterday's clothes still clung to my body, now wrinkled after what appeared to be a full night's sleep by the way the red dawn shone a line of fire on my wall.

The door swung open without a response. Griswold hurried in and held the doorknob for the parade of servants to enter behind him.

I shot up, my hand landing in a wet puddle of drool on the duvet. Gross.

"What's going on here?" I asked as the servants

rummaged through my wardrobe and arranged my father's crown along with a collection of jeweled rings and brooches on my dresser.

"With the queen unavailable, you must hold court in her absence." Griswold clapped his hands and a couple of the servants bowed and took their leave. Two servants remained and stood in a row with their heads cast down toward the floor, waiting to complete their duty of dressing me. "And you must hurry, I'd been knocking for nearly twenty minutes."

He pulled back the covers and clapped his hands until I slid from the bed and stood next to the dresser adorned with jewels.

"Court? You must be kidding, Griswold? I'm not prepared."

Griswold nodded at the two remaining servants and they quickly started buzzing around me like worker bees. One of the servants, a pretty dark-haired girl, unbuttoned my shirt and slipped it off my shoulders, while the other older woman slid on a clean one. Both wrinkled their noses, as the sharp smell of sweat hung off my body like a cheap cologne, but both of them had been trained well enough not to mention it.

Griswold grinned, pleased to be moving forward or just content to see me uncomfortable. "I'm afraid so, sir. The Council is expecting you, and the line of complainants began early this morning."

I groaned as the servants continued to primp and polish me into something that would be presentable for the public. The younger servant gazed up at me through her impossibly long black lashes and I smiled, teasing a pink blossom in her cheeks. However, it didn't have the same satisfaction that flirting with a beautiful girl usually did. Something in my head must be broken.

In record time, they'd morphed me into a proper royal, all pomp and circumstance and clean clothes then disappeared with sweeping curtsies out the door.

"Much better." Griswold adjusted the cape at my shoulders and carefully picked up the crown off the dresser and placed it on my head. "Now you're perfect."

I glanced in the mirror. The bright and shiny version of me stared back with an uncertain glare. I forced a wide smile but didn't feel it.

"I'm definitely far from perfect, Griswold."

"Well, it will have to do, Your Majesty." He swept his hand through the air toward the door. "Now off to greet your subjects. Quickly now. Everyone is waiting."

I rushed out the door and down the hall towards the throne room, my shoes clicking as I lugged the heavy costume of the king on my back. Lord Covington, Lord Anwar, and Lord Marchand stood outside the door waiting and dressed top to toe in black as if expecting a funeral.

"A pleasure to see you, Your Majesty," Lord Anwar said as the three bent their knees and bowed in unison. "It is a shame the queen could not be with us today."

"Indeed." If they thought her absence was merely a shame than for me it was a tragedy.

"Then this shall be another rite of passage for you on your way to claiming the crown. The people will want to see your face and know you have the ability to lead them in a fair and just way," Lord Covington added.

"Well, I will do my best. Although this is my first time."

"Of course, we will be right there to assist you." Lord Marchand stepped forward. "It's a shame we haven't seen you at more of these, it would have been an education for you. May I?" He nodded at my head then straightened the crown, the weight dragging it crooked.

"Thank you."

Lord Covington pushed open the door to the throne room and a trumpeter sounded our arrival.

"All hail his Majesty, Prince Fallon of Aldric," the Herald rang.

The lords scrambled in ahead of me and took their seats beside the raised platform holding my parent's thrones. I stared at the ornately carved chairs of dark wood, inlaid with a lighter carving of our family crest, the lion in the center seeming to mock me with his dangerous claws and tongue stuck out. The largest chair sat empty for my father, and the smaller one empty and waiting for his queen, neither ready for me. I glanced over at Lord Marchand and he motioned for me to sit. I shrugged, unsure of my place, but chose the smaller throne as a sign of respect, and to show the kingdom I still believed the true king would return to rule them.

A crowd of faces stared up at me. Of the few courts I'd attended recently, none had a turnout like this. Maybe they had been delayed due to my father's condition, or maybe the citizens had come out in droves just to see if I would fail.

"The court welcomes Duke Reynaud of Baudelaire versus his neighbor Duke Ormand of Ibalos," the Herald called.

Both men stepped forward towards the platform, dripping of gold and jewels in their tailored finest. They bowed before me, each one eyeing the other and attempting to bend lower than his rival until both nearly collapsed in piles on the floor.

I placed a heavy ringed hand over my mouth to stifle a laugh. "You may stand, gentlemen. What is your dispute?"

As Duke Ormand began his testimony, I looked over at the lords and their beaming pleased smiles. I guess I must have done one thing right, but as I examined the line that snaked through the center of the front room and into the Great Hall I knew the smiles wouldn't last long. I leaned back in the uncomfortable throne, the rigid wood already bruising my backside, and tried to listen to the words coming out of the decorated Duke's mouth.

Alright. Here we go.

~

"And I decree that the tree growing between your two properties to be cut down and two identical trees planted firmly within the property lines for each landowner."

I collapsed back into my mother's throne and tried to keep a pleasant smile on my face, even though all I wanted was to run out of the room screaming.

"Thank you, Your Majesty."

Both men bowed and took their leave. Finally, the end of the never-ending line. The sun had moved through all the windows of the throne room, passing me by. My stomach growled, aching to be fed. How long had I been trapped in here?

"Thank you, but that will be all for today," the Herald said, his chipper voice now faded into a hoarse murmur.

I stood and the rest of the attendees filed out the oversized doors at the end of the hall. Two guards flanked the throne and ushered me and the lords back out into the hallway from the royal entrance.

"That seemed to go okay," Lord Anwar said as the door clicked closed behind him.

"Are they always so long?" I asked rubbing my fingers under the edges of the crown, a low-grade headache beginning at the back of my skull.

"Sometimes even longer."

I tried my hardest to avoid making an irritated face, the trained royal smile coming in to save me. "Would anyone care to join me for lunch?"

The three men chuckled and looked at each other, then me again.

"We've still plenty of work to do, Your Majesty," Lord Covington said. "There are contracts and treaties that require your signature and attention.

They all turned and headed left towards the war room and I reluctantly followed behind, my head still turned right towards the kitchen. My stomach churned again and I gripped my waist.

Inside the war room, documents sat piled high on the table. I perched in the chair in front of the papers and ran my hand over the stack. Going through each of these would take days, and that's if I even understood them with the first read. How did my father know what was right and what to do? Was it something that came with practice, or did I just have no hope of blending well into this role?

I sat down and pulled the first one from the top.

"This is a trade agreement for gold from Draconis. I suggest reading that one carefully as they like to hide tricky clauses in their contracts." Lord Marchand sat down in the chair beside me and read over my shoulder.

The words quickly jumbled together, too much formality mixed with an already long day and an empty stomach, but I kept trying. Why couldn't they write these things in language people would understand?

Around the twentieth page, a knock echoed on the

door. My shoulders dropped, hoping maybe someone brought a snack. The door opened and Griswold entered from the hall, unfortunately empty-handed.

"Sorry for the intrusion, gentlemen, but we have a foreign guest asking for an audience with the king. I told her that I would bring the prince."

"We can go through these later this evening," Lord Covington said as he snatched the document from my hands and added it back to the pile.

"Or tomorrow?" I offered. "Tomorrow would be good."

He rolled his eyes then quickly halting when he seemed to realize I was no longer just the prince, but at this moment I was his ruler. I followed Griswold back to the throne room, dread building in my blood as flashbacks of the endless line of complaints circled in my memory. I took my mother's seat again and faced the red-cloaked visitor.

She removed her hood and dark curls dangled over her shoulders, the front of her locks pinned back behind her head. She appeared older than me, but younger than my mother, and definitely not someone I'd seen around the city before. Her striking beauty rivaled the noblest ladies of the court, but she stood with the stance of a soldier and the proud stare of a prized fighter. I sat tall at attention as her presence pushed me to stay strong. If this woman decided she didn't like my face I expected she could easily ascend the platform and change it with the blade strapped to her hip before the guards would even know she'd moved.

"May I present the High Chieftainess of Elder, known in Elder as the Red." Griswold said and scurried from the room.

"Welcome to Aboria," I started. "I hear you have asked to speak with the king. He is indisposed at the moment, is there anything I can be of service as the Crown Prince?"

She placed her hands on her hips, increasing the intimidating look she already had working for her. "Do not lie to me, prince. I am no fool. I know what is happening to your father, the king."

I stiffened in my seat. The room temperature plummeted to match the chill in her tone and I shivered.

"Fair enough. Then tell me why you have come?"

"I represent the wolf packs of the Kingdom of Elder. We've noticed that something strange has been happening in our woods. I've come to investigate whether this unknown force has spread to your cities?"

"We've heard no such thing," Lord Anwar said. "Other than the issues with the king, that you claim to already know about, our kingdom is peaceful and content."

"Then I guess I've come a long way for nothing. Thank you for your time." She nodded toward Lord Anwar then tugged the hood back over her head and turned to go.

I bit down on my tongue. Hard enough to draw blood as I tried to force down the words begging to come out my mouth. My leg tapped the platform as she sashayed toward the exit. Then as she reached the door, a guard holding it open for her, I jumped to my feet. There was something she was holding back.

"Stop. Please. I've heard things about which you speak."

The lords looked at me as their mouths hung open and the Chieftainess halted her steps.

"Some call it the darkness, and I've been told it's been spreading east. I don't know what's causing it or how to stop it, but I think it has something to do with my father's condition."

She turned around her arms crossed over her chest. "If you can't stop it then you are no help to me. But thank you for your honesty." She glared at Lord Anwar, her dagger stare sharp even on the periphery. "I'll keep to tracking it on my own. Should I need it, would you be willing to offer guards?"

"Absolutely," I said as I stepped to the edge of the platform.

Lord Covington cleared his throat and I looked over as he made a gesture with his hands. I didn't quite understand what he meant but I had the feeling it wasn't in line with what I just promised.

"Good." She jerked her head up and stormed toward the door. "You'll hear from me soon."

The guards cleared a path for her to continue, probably more from fear than duty.

As she walked to the door, something bothered me. She was still holding something back. Something she didn't want to speak about in front of an audience. I ran to her, catching up when she was just outside.

"The darkness. That's not the reason you came is it?"

She inhaled a sharp breath, then after a quick look around to see there was no one in ear shot, she spoke. "Have you seen my son? His name is Castiel."

I wracked my brains for the name, but came up empty.

"I have not had the pleasure."

"Then I shall be on my way." She turned to walk away again.

"Should I have met your son?"

"He has eyes just like yours, although I see no other similarity. Only the gold circle around your iris."

My hand instinctively went to my face.

"He set out to come see you. He should have been here by now. I don't know where he is."

And then I understood the sadness behind the strength. She too had lost someone.

"If I see him, I'll make sure to send word to Elder."

"Thank you," she said, and this time she walked away.

"Do you know what you've just done?" Lord Covington asked, his disappointed scowl answering his question without waiting for my response.

"No, not exactly. But if this darkness is as bad as I think it is she'll need every resource we've got."

My eyes threatened to close so many times that I nearly fell asleep face down in my soup. I knew being king would be busy, but I never imagined how physically and mentally draining. The silence that echoed through the oversized dining room didn't help. Being king was tough, but being lonely seemed unbearable. The chandeliers lost some of their luster, and the gilded candlesticks didn't seem to shine as bright without people to share them with. I stared through my haze down the long dining room table and ached for someone to talk to.

A soft knock sounded on the door.

"Come in."

Griswold appeared beside me at the table. "Sorry to interrupt your dinner, Your Majesty."

"No problem at all. Why don't you sit down with me for a while?"

I gestured to a large chair where my mother usually sat. Griswold shook his head, but I nodded still pointing.

He grimaced then pulled the chair back with the tips of his fingers and sat at the very edge of the seat, his face scrunched between the years of wrinkles.

"Your bird has returned, sir. She's waiting for you in front of the castle."

"My mother has returned already?" I jumped to my feet and wiped my face with the napkin then tossed it onto the tabletop.

Griswold didn't move.

"No, but the bird has a message for you and refuses to let anyone else have it. One of the guards almost lost an arm trying to pry it from her."

"Thank you, Griswold."

We rushed from the dining room. A sense of relief stretched across Griswold's face as he put my mother's chair back into its perfect spot and dusted the ornate carvings on the back. Out in the courtyard, Alizeh's feathers glinted in the evening sun setting over the horizon. A group of guards, swords drawn circled her, each one in lockstep with her every movement.

"Stand down," I called as I rushed into the circle. Alizeh brought her head to my chest and clucked softly, an envelope tucked tight in her beak. I tugged at the paper and she released it without hesitation as the guards behind me whispered.

I pet her cheek. "Thank you, my friend."

She bobbed her head, as if to nod, then snapped her beak at one of the guards to her left. He retreated and tripped over his own feet, landing with a thud on the ground. Alizeh cooed in victory then launched off into the sky.

"The next time Alizeh returns, I expect to be contacted immediately." I held the letter behind my back and marched in front of the line of guards. "No weapons are to be drawn on her ever again. Do you understand?"

"Yes, sir," the guards answered in unison and charged back to their posts.

"What is it, Your Majesty?" Griswold asked, peering over my shoulder.

I slid my finger under the royal seal and ripped open the top of the envelope. Three rose petals slipped out and fluttered to the ground.

"It's from my mother. I think I'll take this in my room and turn in for the night."

Griswold raised his finger, his weight shifting to the tips of his toes.

"If there's anything you need to know, I'll call on you right away," I added, and he relaxed, or what looked like relaxed for Griswold.

He nodded. "Goodnight, sir."

"One more thing" I halted and punched my fist in the air as my memory poked at my brain. "Have you seen Captain Amir today?"

"Yes, sir. No word on the young lady you'd asked him to find, but they will let me know if she turns up."

Again my heart sank. I promised my mother I would try to make it right with Veda. I needed to make things right with Veda, but with the demands of the kingdom and my parents away I had no idea when I would get the chance to look for her again. If only she'd just come to me. But after the way I acted, she never would.

I gripped the letter in my fist, and rushed off, staring at the floor to ensure I didn't make eye contact with anyone. I had enough of being king for one day. Maybe after a good night's sleep, I'd be ready to go again. Somehow I doubted it though.

As soon as my own door came into view in the hall, I sprinted the rest of the way and slammed it shut behind me. I flopped across my bed and ran my finger along the perfect loopy scrawl of my name across the front. On the back, I inspected the green wax seal with the Aldric coat of arms impressed from my mother's ring and pulled the letter open.

My dearest Fallon,

Thank you for finding your father and lending me Alizeh to go see him. It's been tough seeing him in this condition, but I feel much better knowing that he's alive and safe in one place. I will be forever grateful for your willingness to find him against the horrible odds.

Edwin has been kind and extremely helpful dealing with your father's condition. I'm so glad he is the one looking after this situation.

I will be staying here at the temple for a while to make sure that he's okay. I hope things are going well, but if not, please send me a note and I will come back to help.

I love you with all my heart.

Always,

Mom

I refolded the letter and tucked it back into the envelope then clutched it to my chest. It would be so much easier to have her here, but I couldn't take her away now. Dad needed her and his affliction was thousands of times worse than a rough day at the castle. Besides, I think she needed Dad too.

The weight of the day dragged on me, everything getting heavier and hazy. I chuckled to myself. I'd started to sound like an old man, constantly tired and lacking energy. I should be in the prime of my life, partying with my friends at the tavern until the early hours, but it was barely twilight and all I wanted was sleep.

Slowly, I stood up and slipped my jacket off, then pulled my shirt over my head. The sunburn on my skin had started to fade but left behind an irritating itch. I fought myself to avoid scratching, even though I had to clench my teeth at times to do so.

I tossed the letter on my dresser and flipped my belt out of its buckle. Then I stopped cold, my hand gripped on the piece of leather as I glimpsed a new face in the mirror. It wore my shoulders and naked torso, but instead of my youthful features and strong jaw were strands of thinning silver hair and thick bushy eyebrows. I leapt toward the mirror and ran my fingers down my face, but soft wrinkled skin hung limp from my cheekbones. My heart pumped loud in my chest, the sound echoed through my room as the blood rushed to my aged complexion. What was happening? This couldn't be real. I closed my eyes tight hoping for this to be a dream, or more accurately a nightmare. Except when I opened them again the face of the old man stared back at me.

No. No. No.

I smashed my fists against the dresser, the mirror shimmied, but the image didn't get any better. I grabbed the sides of my head, gripping grey hair in my hands, and paced the floor of my room. I felt like I'd aged, but I didn't really mean it. At least not like this. I rushed to the door and my hand hovered over the door knob, but I didn't turn it because where would I go? Mom and Dad were gone, and no one else would understand. I closed my eyes as wet tears formed in the corners. Anyone else with think I was some sort of monster.

A strange tingling sensation rushed over my skin. My

face burned, My hands raged with fire. I looked down as fur and claws appeared on my nails and knuckles. I rushed back to the mirror as a thick furry mane and a beast-like face stared back at me. I screamed, but it came out as a roar. I slammed my mouth shut, my heart pounding even louder, banging against my ribs as if it's tried to escape me. The curse. I hadn't escaped it after all.

My arms trembled. This couldn't be happening. Not to me. Not now. I grabbed the mirror from the top of the dresser and tossed it to the ground with a growl. The wooden frame splintered as the mirrored glass smashed into shards. But no relief came. Instead, the destruction only fueled my rage. Heat coursed through me, electric and strong. I bit my tongue and tasted blood, trying to calm the beast inside aching to be set free. I didn't want this. I wanted to be me again. I needed to be me.

The strange itching tingle started again, but this time when I looked at my hands they were mine again. I touched my face. Smooth young skin spread out beneath my fingertips. I knelt down beside the broken mirror and my own face, my real face, reflected in every single shard, staring back in fractures like a spider's eye.

Relief washed over me, but only for a moment as pieces started to fall in place, even though big gaps in the puzzle still remained. Edwin said he felt something in my blood. I arrived right after the curse was broken, and no one knows where I came from. Maybe I wasn't their miracle baby after all. Maybe I was phase two. I fell back onto the floor as the idea rammed my chest like a flock of arrows, each one piercing my skin and leaking poison into my blood. Could this be because of the darkness? Or maybe the curse never really went away. Or, the one thing that made sense of all this; maybe everything was my fault. Maybe the problem in the castle was me.

THRONE OF BETRAYAL

3RD JUNE

"Make me the beast."

I gripped the sides of my dresser as the tingling burn started in my chest and radiated through my limbs. I no longer feared the feeling but embraced it, so now it almost tickled as it surged through my bloodstream. Coarse, brown fur sprouted along my arms then down across my hands before growing thick and wild around my face. I smiled at my reflection in my brand-new mirror, except the sharp canine teeth gave my satisfied expression a darker, menacing look.

Perfect.

I closed my eyes and concentrated again.

"Now go back to normal."

The familiar rush of power trickled through me. I

glanced at my reflection again and my own beautiful face stared back. No sign of the monster I was only seconds before, except the deep blue-black circles that hung around my eyes that seemed to grow darker every time I forced a change.

I lay back on my plush bed and stared up at the ceiling. The soft bedding attempted to lure me in, but even though my body would gladly comply, my mind kept running like an amateur thief with a fear of getting caught.

Last night, I'd been afraid. When my reflection changed to an old man before my eyes it punched me in the gut and left me weak in my knees. But as the panic grew my reflection kept changing. Replaced each time by someone or something until I begged it to stop.

When I finally calmed and was able to think somewhat clearly, I sat on the floor with a shard of my broken mirror and intentionally willed myself to change. I grew my hair then shortened it again. I colored it blond, red, green, even blue. The golden rings around my eyes disappeared as they took on the form of everyone and anyone else. By morning, all I had to do was wish for it and my entire body instantly morphed into a completely different person.

If this curse turned out to be the same as my father's, maybe he just needed to focus hard enough to bring himself back. Except it didn't seem right that this would be the same thing. This thing, this power or curse, or whatever it was seemed to manifest differently between the two of us. When I became the beast, I still had full control of myself. Like I'd dressed in a costume that I could take off and be myself again. So maybe these two things weren't the same, or maybe Dad had become the beast for too long and it started changing his insides too?

I shuddered, the thought of becoming a beast forever seemed like a death sentence. I needed to make sure I didn't stay in one form for too long. Or perhaps work on not changing at all to avoid the risk.

Another challenge also arose. I had to keep this curse, or power, or magic, or whatever it was in check when I wasn't using it. After spending the entire last night experimenting with my powers, I wanted nothing more than to try it out in the real world, except my duties as king came before any of my own extracurricular activities. Attending court, and being on stage in front of hundreds of people caused my palms to sweat. What if my mind wandered during yet another boring account of feuding neighbors and I turned into something else? The extra energy required to make sure I didn't accidentally turn on another face didn't help the exhaustion from my busy days.

But now, even though sleep would be the smartest choice, I needed to go out and play. I craved it. An obsession with what I could do with this new trick consumed me until I could think of nothing else. I jumped up and headed to the mirror again. Who could I be tonight? An old man? With the thought my skin began to wrinkle, my hair graying before my eyes. A beautiful woman? The gray hair took a blonder tone growing long and flowing from my scalp. Long curly eyelashes framed a sultry stare as full lips puckered at my reflection. I shuddered, suddenly attracted to myself and disturbed by the thought. I flipped out of the gorgeous face. Probably safer if I blended in anyway.

I changed into a dark pair of pants and a heavily worn shirt. From my wardrobe, I selected a hunter green cloak, plain and simple without any embroidery around the hems or hints of the royal crest, and fastened it at my neck.

Tiptoeing into the hallway, it appeared that most of the servants had left the castle proper for the night. I hurried down the corridors, winding closer toward the front door and freedom.

"Good evening, Your Majesty. Is there anything I can assist you with this evening?"

I skidded to a stop, my heart pounding hard as Griswold appeared beside me. I grabbed my chest and fell against the wall.

"I swear sometimes I think you might be a ghost. Why do you need to sneak up on me like that?"

"Why did you need to try to sneak past me, sir?" He folded his hands politely in front of him as a proud smug grin curled across his mouth.

I straightened my stance and splayed a hand across my chest, willing my breath to slow. "I wasn't sneaking. I have every right to come and go as I please."

"Of course you do. But that doesn't mean I didn't just see you creeping through the foyer like a felon."

"Fair enough. I've decided to go out for the evening and didn't want to have anyone pull me into another matter. I am getting tired of being cooped up in this castle all day."

"And you should leave the castle, sir. Balance is an important factor in maintaining your health for a long, successful reign. Would you like me to order some guards to accompany you?"

"No, thank you. I'd rather try to be inconspicuous." And I knew I could be if I could just get past his watchful eye.

He shook his head. "You do know that as king you are even more of a target than as the prince. Especially since you have yet to claim the crown. I would feel better knowing that you were safely guarded. The Council and your parents would likely agree."

I shifted my weight from foot to foot and Griswold's movements mimicked mine. Loyalty was his greatest virtue, but right now it was also the biggest pain.

I tossed my hands up in the air and dropped my shoulders in defeat. "All right, go fetch some guards. I guess things around here need to change."

"Very well, sir. I think that is most wise." He scurried down the hall, his head tweaked over his shoulder to watch me until he couldn't any longer. The second Griswold broke contact I ran for the door and slid out into the night. I nodded at the two guards by the main door, slowing my steps to avoid suspicion, then slipped off into the garden.

The moon hung full and bright and cast an eerie blue glow over the slumbering flowers. Not a whisper of wind blew through the trees. Even the stars hid their faces to avoid seeing too much. A perfect night for a perfect plan.

I sat on the edge of the lion fountain and stared down into the water. My handsome features stared back, a hint of apprehension in their glare. I closed my eyes.

"Be inconspicuous."

Looking back down into the pool I watched the change overtake my face. My hair grew three inches, straighter, stringier and hanging limp in my near-black eyes. My nose developed a small upturn as my thick jaw slimmed in the rippled reflection below. In the water, stood a different person. An exciting newcomer. One I might pass on the street without even noticing. The ultimate disguise.

I fidgeted with my cloak, the operation of the clasp

odd with my recently adopted more slender fingers then took one last look at my new self. The large white moon ringed this stranger's head like a halo and I chuckled, the sound falling dead in the calm night. I wasn't anything close to an angel, and a feeling twitched in my bones that tonight would be anything but good.

~

As I crossed the golden bridge to Mosa, the entire city lay out in front of me, shiny and new through my stranger's eyes. The lantern lights blazed brighter. The colorful shutters and awnings popped against the rows of stone buildings in a fresh way, the simplistic beauty sinking into my borrowed skin and leaving a tingling sense of awe in my blood.

I walked down the cobblestone streets with my head held high, and not one person cared. Other then the occasional polite wave or nod of recognition, everyone went about their way unfazed by the acting king walking among them.

No one moved out of their way for me to pass or stared when I walked by. Even the reporters, standing vigil near the castle for any glimpse of potential gossip, ignored my presence. This strange magic turned me into a ghost, haunting the city with only a select few able to see me as I floated past. The pressure lifted from my shoulders. A relief. A freedom. A glorious vacation from myself--even if it only lasted one night.

Eventually, my feet led me down a familiar road. The sign for Takka's Tavern swung above the door as the sounds of music and laughter poured out into the street. I hesitated with my hand on the door handle. The last time I'd cross this threshold I'd run away like a coward. This time needed to be different.

I held my breath and swung the door open, the smell of hops and smoke twisting around me like a charmer's snake. Bodies packed around the bar, the room already more than half full with still so many hours of night left to drown. It seemed a bit early for the crowd this size, but maybe I'd been roaming the streets longer than I thought. Veda's regular corner table sat empty. My shoulders dropped a bit as even though she'd gone into hiding part of me hoped I'd look over and see her face scrunched in concentration, pouring over her books. But I didn't know why I bothered hoping anymore. She wouldn't appear again until she wanted to be found. Until then, I'd just have to wait.

I squeezed my way up to the bar and waited my turn as Mr. Takka raced around slinging glass mugs to the impatient patrons. Eventually, he made his way to my side of the bar. He pointed at my face, his shirt already rolled up to his elbows with spots of water or ale dotted on the front.

"What can I get you?"

I smiled. The unamused look on his face meant my disguise was still in place and working exactly as it should.

"A pint of ale, please, kind sir."

He raced away before I barely finished my order, his hands working quickly to pour the drink from the tap and slide it back down toward me. I slipped a bill on the bar and he quickly stuffed it into his pocket then moved down the line. I lifted my glass and took a deep swig in celebration. I'd become a nobody and it felt amazing.

"Haven't seen you around here before?"

I froze, glass in hand, hovering it just above the wooden bartop. An all-too-familiar voice. Kalmin.

I ran my hand through my long hair and let it fall over my features, masking any possible chinks in my magical armor. “Pardon me?”

Kalmin nudged up next to me at the bar and stuck out his hand. “I don’t ever remember seeing you around. Are you new in town or just trying out a new place?”

I took his hand and shook it. No reaction met his face as our skin touched.

“I’ve been around. I guess I just like to keep to myself.”

“Very well. You do look a little bit familiar now that I look at you closer.” His face scrunched up as he placed his hand on his chin and narrowed his stare.

I took another drink, masking as much of my face as I could, and stole the last inch of space behind me that I could in these close quarters. “Maybe. But you’re always hanging around with that flashy Prince Fallon. When you have friends like that, it’s probably harder to notice the other people on the outside.”

Kalmin took a step back creating some much-needed space between us, his arms crossed tight over his chest and a faraway look in his eyes. “Yeah. But I don’t see the prince very often anymore.”

“Oh. Did something happen?”

I bit the inside of my cheek and fought the urge to yell ‘of course, you turned your back on me when I needed you.’ But why would I risk blowing an opportunity like this? This sudden strike of coincidence far too delicious to let it pass by.

“I’m not quite sure. People just change, I guess.”

“I see. But was he the one who changed or was it you?”

Kalmin angled his head down, his stare becoming hooded. “Maybe a bit of both. Where did you say you were from again?"

"I didn't." I grabbed my mug from the bar and bolted into the crowd, leaving Kalmin standing alone with the thought of the real me left to plague him. He didn't seem to care as confusion twisted with the red anger building over his face.

I took a huge gulp of frosty ale and savored the sensation as it slid down my throat. It'd been too long and I missed the taste, but unless I planned to build a tavern in the castle, I needed to find a new regular spot. I pulled my arms in closer and squeezed through the bodies, heading for the open air on the far side of the tavern.

Oomph!

My arm holding the glass bumped someone beside me. Liquid sloshed over the side of my mug and splashed on my victim's shirt. Veda's emerald eyes sparkled up at me, even through her wicked irritated frown.

"I'm sorry, miss," I said as I stabilized my glass and attempted to brush the spot off her shoulder.

She jerked back out of my reach and rolled her eyes, her attitude about tavern guys still unchanged. "It's fine. Just be more careful next time."

"Of course, I'm sincerely sorry."

She flipped her hand in dismissal and shook her head, then retreated to her usual corner then arranged her books in her ritualistic way.

I squeezed back into line at the bar and ordered another drink, then slowly, carefully, I maneuvered my way across the crowded tavern. Her head hung down deep in thought already as her left hand scribbled away and she twirled a thick strand of dark hair around her right index finger.

I slid the drink onto her table and she glanced up

through her inky black eyelashes.

"What's this?" she asked flatly. No expression to read and see if I'd played things right.

"I wanted you to know that I really am sorry for spilling on you. The people here can be so rude sometimes and I didn't want you to get that impression of me."

Her lips curved into a smile, but I didn't know whether it be the peace offering, the snipe, or a reflexive reaction to the beaming grin my borrowed mouth gave her.

"Well, in that case, thank you. You're forgiven."

She turned back to her notebook, all the lines perfectly spaced with a rhythmic slanting cursive. As I stood by waiting for her to say anything else, I glanced back toward the bar. No one seemed to notice us. Glorious.

I slid into the chair opposite her.

She closed the cover of her book and leaned forward on her elbows. "Can I help you with something?"

"No. I was just wondering what you're working on?"

She glanced down at the notebook, then back to me, then the book again. "You might think it's dumb, but there is a writing competition coming up and I'm hoping to enter."

"Why would that be dumb?" I stretched my legs out and tried to make myself comfortable in the hard wooden chair. "If it's something you want, then I say you need to go for it before you talk yourself out of it. Do you think you stand a chance of winning?"

She sighed, her posture curving forward as her body deflated. "I don't know. Some days I do, but I've been really distracted lately. Too many things going on in my head to get words down on the page."

"I get that."

She perked up and her voice raised an octave. "Are you a writer too?"

"No," I stared down at the beer in my hand. Maybe that's what she needed, a smarter, more intellectual type to challenge her. "I just know what it's like for other things to get in the way of what you want. Kind of feels like you're trapped in a cage, but too afraid to check the lock."

Her left eyebrow crooked up, as if it triggered her brain to process my words, then she wrinkled her nose and took a drink of her ale. "Kind of. Yeah."

I leaned back and watched. Every insignificant movement stirred something within me. The way her fingers laced through the handle of the mug, made me want to tangle them in mine. Her hair falling over her shoulder ached for me to brush it back and trace the sensitive skin around her ear. Her neck stretched so my lips could kiss the delicate spot where it met her shoulder. And as her eyes blinked slow and slack, I pictured us in the dark, dreaming beside each other.

"...and you are?"

I shook my head as her voice cut through my imagination. "Sorry, what?"

"I said, my name is Veda, and you are? Did you just drift off on me?"

"No...I...just thinking about something. My name's--" Think. Think. Think. "--Amir."

Hopefully, the Captain wouldn't be too upset that I stole his name. I tipped my head forward and my hair fell over my face. I tucked it behind my ear, but it dropped down again. Next time I picked a new face I'd have to remember to conjure a shorter hairstyle, or at least tie it back.

"Well, Amir, what are you doing here in Mosa?"

"Living life." I laughed. "But what do you mean. I'm an Aborian. I've always been here."

"Oh." She jerked up straighter and wrinkled her nose. " I just don't think I've ever seen you in here. I have a bad habit of watching people and I don't think I've ever crossed your path before."

"You watch people?"

She leaned back in her chair and shrugged. "Nothing creepy. I just prefer to observe rather than participate. Maybe it's the writer in me."

"Maybe. But I'm not surprised. It happens a lot where people don't know who I am. I kind of like it. It's freeing. Being a mystery. Being a nobody."

"Yeah, I'm a nobody too." Her voice dropped low as a pained expression clouded her face.

"Did I say something wrong?"

"No," she sighed. "I understand what you mean. The anonymity of it all. But I never realized what being a nobody meant until recently. That apparently it does matter. I wish I'd paid more attention to that earlier."

I leaned across the table and tried to hold her gaze, but she looked away. "Why? I don't know you all that well, but you seem like you're above all that nonsense."

"It's nothing. There was just someone...this guy."

Me. She was talking about me and how stupid I'd been to open my mouth that day by the forest. The hurt pinched at her smile and stabbed me in the gut. That uncertainty. That pain. It was all my fault.

"Hey. Look at me."

She listened as miles of distance unfolded in her eyes.

"Whoever this guy is, he probably didn't mean it or he'd quickly learn that he'd made a huge mistake. Anyone who really knows you at all wouldn't ask you to change who you were. He'd be a fool to do that, and I'm sure wherever he is he's beating himself up over hurting you."

"Maybe." She nodded then rested her elbow on the table, her chin in her hand. "You're very sweet, Amir. Very insightful too. Thank you."

"No problem. You're a very easy person to just be yourself around." Even if I didn't really look like myself she still drew it out of me. Like cracking open an oyster and pulling out the pearl inside. "Besides, you're smart, you're beautiful--"

Veda tipped her head back and laughed. Hard enough to shake the table, the ale shimmying in our glasses.

"What?"

"Um. Nice line, but you should take a look around. If you came here looking for beautiful, I'm definitely not it. Why don't you try her?" She pointed toward a gorgeous redhead near the bar. "Or her?" A mysterious brunette a few tables over.

"But I didn't come here looking for anything, I just found you by a stroke of luck."

She rolled her eyes.

"And you're wrong about them. They look beautiful, but I have no idea if they are beautiful."

"Really? Don't they mean the same thing?"

"I thought so too, but they don't." I pulled my chair forward, the legs scraping on the tavern floor as I closed the gap between us. "A gorgeous face doesn't make a smile beautiful, it's the warmth and spirit of the person that gives it a glow. True beauty makes others beautiful. It grabs ahold of you and attracts the positive like a magnet, pulling it to the surface. Beautiful people are a force of nature, not just pretty pictures to hang on a wall."

"Oh." Her lips parted and I thought I heard her gasp over the noise of the room, but maybe I was being hopeful. I watched her lips move. The deep, red lips I regretted not kissing so many times over the last few days.

"How did a nobody like you get so perceptive, Amir?"

The world stopped moving, no other sounds but her and me.

I inched closer, my hands trembling and threatening to drop me onto the tabletop. "Because one day I found a true beauty and I've never been the same."

My lips grazed hers. A second. A whisper. Then she pulled back and I fell forward. Her books knocked to the floor with a loud thud.

People stared. The world spun again, faster than before. I dropped back into my chair and swept up the books in my left hand, then stacked them on the table. Veda's face flushed bright red.

"I'm sorry. But we've just met. I'm not--"

"No. I'm sorry. I just got into the moment and I thought, that you thought, that...never mind. I'm sorry."

I grabbed the back of my neck and tipped my head to stare at the ceiling. I'd blown it. Of course, I did. She had no idea who I really was. I considered dropping the mask, but in the room of crowded people, it would not go unnoticed. Besides, even though I hadn't planned on coming here to trick her, she'd likely feel even more betrayed if she knew the truth.

She slid her books toward her and started piling them in her bag. "I think I should probably go."

"No." I stood up and pushed in my chair. "It's my fault. I should go."

She continued collecting her books. "No really. This

whole thing just reminded me of something else, and now I just want to leave."

"Of someone, you mean?"

She nodded.

"Do you love him? This someone?"

She stopped and wrapped her hand into a fist, knocking it on the tabletop. "I don't know. I might. I'm still mad at him, but I think I might."

I stepped around the side of the table, closer, but with as much personal space as I could manage. "Then if he were here right now, standing in front of you instead of me, what would you say to him?"

"I'd tell him...I'd tell him he's an idiot." She laughed, even though her eyes started to fill with tears. "And then I'd tell him that I miss him, and I can't stop thinking about him even though I try so hard not to. And that I understand what happened, but it doesn't mean it still didn't hurt."

She wiped her eyes and tried to smile, the glassy tears still falling down her cheeks.

"I think you need to find this guy and talk to him. I'm sure he feels awful too."

She blinked and looked up to the ceiling. "I'll think about it."

"Can you do me one favor though? Can you please just wait here for a few minutes? Keep working on your writing, pretend I was never here, but just wait."

She collapsed back into her chair. "Fine."

I ran for the door. No more games. She needed to know how I felt. That I was sorry. That I felt the same way about her. I disappeared into the dark alleyway and faced the wall.

"Be me again."

The tingle rose through my body as the fringe of hair

covering my eyes disappeared from view. I looked at my hands and felt around my face. Seemed right. No time to check, but no time to lose either. I pulled my hood over my head and bolted back into the tavern.

Veda's table sat empty except for a small folded piece of paper.

Amir,

I'm sorry, I had to go. It was great to meet you.

-Veda

I crumpled the page and rushed into the street. Behind me, someone called out for the prince, but I didn't stop.

"Veda," I yelled, but the name echoed down the street and died without a response.

Above me, the light of the moon disappeared. I stared up at the sky and watched Alizeh carry Veda away—again.

4TH JUNE

Heat prickled my skin as sunlight pierced the treetop canopy and sparkled along the surface of the water ahead. I held back the wall of branches and trekked deeper into the forest, following the sound of the babbling creek that wound into the pond.

Veda smiled as I approached. She sat at the rocky edge, swiping her fingers through the water and creating ripples that widened into the larger pool.

"You came," I said, as I extended my hand, a wave of relief flooding over me.

She grabbed hold and I pulled her to her feet, wrapping

my arms around her waist.

"Of course."

She stretched onto her tiptoes and clasped her hands behind my neck, her fingers twisting in the short strands of hair there.

"I'm so sorry about what happened. It's all my fault. Will you please forgive me?"

Veda tossed her head back and laughed. A light and breezy chuckle echoed through the clearing and stirred up the trees. Leaves drifted through the sky. Hundreds of green confetti filled the air and rained down on us. They caught in her chestnut hair and created a haphazard crown. A fairy goddess. My forest queen.

I pulled her closer and the heat of her breath fell on my jaw. "I regret not kissing you before. Letting everyone else's voices in my head."

She smirked as the golden rays of sunshine danced in her eyes. "Smart men don't make the same mistake twice."

I slid my hand beneath her hair and held the nape of her neck, tilting her head toward mine. "I don't intend to."

Her lips inched towards my lips, slow as if time stopped so it could watch. This one perfect moment I didn't know I'd been waiting all my life for. Didn't know it was what I needed. I closed my eyes.

"Prince Fallon," she said.

"What is it?"

"Prince Fallon," she repeated, her voice drifting away. A soft whisper on the wind.

"What?"

"Prince Fallon."

A gruff voice. Gravel and grit. I whipped my eyes open. Griswold loomed over me as he snapped his fingers in front of my face. I screamed and he jumped back. My chair teetered beneath me and I gripped the edge of the table to avoid tumbling to the floor.

"Wake up, sir. You nearly fell asleep face down in your breakfast."

I wiped my face with my hand and looked down at the plate of eggs staring back up at me. "Sorry, Griswold. I didn't sleep well last night. I had a lot of things on my mind."

"It appears so. The guards noted that you didn't return from your evening out until near dawn."

I hung my head. After Veda left I couldn't bring myself to climb into bed and spend the rest of the night thinking about how I'd messed up again. Instead, I roamed the streets of Mosa until I felt better. Except, I never did. Just watched the shadows of the night grow along the narrow cobblestone streets and then shorten again as the threat of morning hovered on the horizon. Eventually, my feet ached and my legs grew tired, so I gave up and went home.

"And don't think I'm not disappointed that you disregarded my instructions about bringing guards with you." His stern voice developed an extra sharp edge this morning that sliced through my eardrums and scored lines across my heart.

"I'm sorry, Griswold. I just needed some time away from the castle and all its protocols."

He rested his hand on my shoulder, his warm touch soothing the pain of my disobedience. I'd never crossed Griswold without a reason, and in the daylight, I wasn't sure if it had been worth it. Except, that Veda said she loved me. Or at least she thought she did. My leg tapped under the table, the anticipation of seeing her again too much to contain to the dining room table.

“What does my day look like today anyway?”

Griswold puttered with the sugar bowl, then refilled my cold cup of tea. “Actually sir, today has a rather light schedule. The Council is off and other then a small afternoon meeting with the organizer for the upcoming Fall Ball, your time is your own.”

The prospect of freedom sparked in my brain. “Any chance we can postpone the meeting? The ball is still several months away. I’m sure I could make it up with an extra-long appointment next week.”

Griswold tensed, his body rigid like the iron posts that made up the castle gates. He pointed his favorite lecture finger in the air, but then withdrew it and let out a sigh. ”I guess it wouldn’t hurt too much to delay planning a bit, especially under the circumstances. As long as we don’t leave it too long. Then, in that case, your day is wide open.”

“Really? Nothing to answer to?”

Griswold’s silver brows clenched together.

“Other than you, of course.”

“No, my prince. Enjoy the day. Or perhaps you should catch up on your sleep, as it seems like you have been lacking a full night.”

“No need.” I swallowed the cup of tea in two swift gulps. The heat burned down the sides of my throat, but I didn’t care. I tossed my napkin onto the table and headed for the door. “I actually feel more awake then I have in a long time. Don’t wait up.”

Griswold shook his head as he gathered up my dirty dishes. “Please be careful, Your Majesty. The kingdom still needs you to return in one piece.”

I gave him a quick salute and bolted into the hallway before he could change his mind about letting me go. One whole day free of obligation. I figured I’d need to wait until nightfall to sneak out again and try to talk to Veda, but this would be much better. No hiding. No sneaking at all. I could simply walk right out the front door. I raced through the castle corridors, nearly spilling over my own feet as I turned sharp into the foyer. The guards at the door eyed me with caution.

I slowed down to a leisurely strut and crossed my hands behind my back. "Lovely day, gentlemen."

"Yes, Your Majesty."

They nodded and chuckled to each other as the smile on my face beamed brighter than it had in ages. I quickened my pace again and burst out the oversized doors into the sunshine.

I put my fingers in my mouth but stopped short before whistling. Just because she said she loved me didn't mean that she would forgive me that easily. I'd been awful to her and that hurt was something I would need to pay for. However, I fully intended on making sure she understood how sorry I really was, and that I would never betray her like that again.

I doubled back towards the garden. Flowers may not be enough, but it would be a start. If I could win her forgiveness, I could give her anything she wanted. A whole kingdom of treasures. But grand gestures didn't seem to be her style. I'd have to win this battle with sticks over swords.

The thick, sweet smell of my mother's prized roses blanketed the air as I walked the rows of bushes near the castle gate. Only the finest blooms would do to help say all those things I'm sure I'd mess up once Veda and I stood face to face. Talking with her as someone else came easily. But only because I struggled to put words to how I truly felt when wearing my own face. But it's a challenge I needed to confront as I missed talking to her. The day and nights I'd stayed with her at her cottage replayed in my head. Telling her things I'd never been able to tell anyone else. Listening to the soft click of the wood-carved clock on her wall as we passed time in silence, just enjoying each other's company. Hearing her low breathy voice as she helped the world make sense. She grounded me in a way no one else had ever done. Dared me to want to be more.

I stopped in the middle of the densest bush, the rich crimson petals of the most exquisite flowers hid beneath the hunter green leaves. I gathered a bouquet of roses in my hand, the thorns scratching against my palm and took a deep breath in of their scent. The gorgeous spring had been generous to my mother's collection, the blooms bordering on unearthly perfection. Hopefully, they would help.

"I didn't expect gifts," a voice boomed behind me. "How did you know I was coming?"

I whirled around and stared at the salt and pepper head of the last man I expected in the queen's garden.

Edwin Macario.

He'd foregone his typical crimson robe in exchange for a vibrant purple jacket that swept just above the ground and heavy leather boots. Less the wise man, and more of a renegade general.

The flowers tumbled from my hands, the petals splashing across the ground on impact. "What are you doing here?"

He smirked and eyed the mess of roses at his feet. Red petals on his black toes. "I think we need to talk."

~

"I hope I didn't interrupt your plans. You didn't have

anything going on today, did you?"

Edwin crossed his left leg over his right as he stretched out in my father's favorite armchair. The drawing room seemed smaller with him in it. Maybe the way he made himself at home, or the large beaming grin that didn't seem to match his face. Or maybe I just hoped that the next person sitting in that chair would be my father.

I conjured my most diplomatic smile. "Not at all. I'll just run my errand later."

"Perfect. Your bouquet of roses made me think you were running off to meet a lady friend or something. But we both know a young king, like yourself, can't afford any distractions at the moment."

"Of course." I gritted my teeth and started to pace behind the antique sofa near the fireplace. His presence in my personal space crept uneasily down my spine. Except, I didn't really know why. He'd been the one to tell me the truth about my parents. He'd been the one to take my father in when he needed a safe place to stay. He'd allowed my mother to stay at his temple by my father's side. I should be grateful. I was grateful. But maybe it's that he knew too much that stood the hair on my arms. Plus, he'd been the one to identify the strange power within me, did he know what it meant? Did he know what I was capable of?

He leaned his head back gazing at the peaked rafters of the cathedral ceiling, then rolled his longing stare over the rest of the room leaving nothing unseen. "I forgot how luxurious this place was. I've been gone a long time, but every detail brings me back like I'd only been gone a few days."

"You said you had news about my father. I've found you the privacy you requested, can you please tell me what's going on?"

"All in due time, my prince. But maybe we should start with a drink. I've been traveling quite a ways to see you. Is it no longer customary to offer guests refreshments?"

He crossed his hands politely on his knee and eased deeper into the chair. A fixture, not to be removed easily.

"You're right. I must've forgotten my manners —" *when you barged into my castle unannounced.* "— I'll see what I can do."

I crept into the hallway and the creak of the drawing room doors echoed down the corridor. Just ahead, one of the servants dusted the frames of painted landscapes that lined the wall.

"Excuse me," I said.

He stopped his cleaning and immediately bowed in my direction. "Yes, Your Majesty."

"Could you please get Griswold for me and send him into the drawing room."

He nodded and quickly scurried away. I returned to Edwin, as he picked at the bronze tacks that embellished the leather armchair. My hand shook as I fought the urge to smack his fingers away, refusing to let him taint my father's things.

"Someone should be here shortly. Now can you tell me what is happening?"

"I'm afraid, things have not been going well."

My shoulders sunk, my stomach tense and ill at his words.

"We've been doing all that we can to find a cure for the curse, but none of our research has produced anything viable. Your mother—"

A knock sounded on the door as Griswold entered, his hands tucked together behind him.

"You called for me, sir?"

"Yes, Griswold. We have a guest." I swooped my hand in Edwin's direction. "I was hoping you'd be able to get him a beverage. Edwin, please meet my oldest companion, Griswold. Griswold, please meet—"

Griswold's eyes popped open, then quickly narrowed to slits. "Edwin Macario."

"Ah Gris, you haven't forgotten me." Edwin clapped his hands then clasped them together in his lap. The amusement at being recognized painted streaks of joy across his face.

"It would be difficult to forget, sir. You certainly left your mark on the kingdom with your departure."

"All in the past, my good man. Now, it's time to celebrate the achievements of our young prince here. Could you please fetch me your best bottle of Florian Shiraz?"

"I'm afraid we don't keep that on hand," Griswold said. "Perhaps I could interest you in a cool glass of water."

Edwin tapped his middle finger over his lips as his eyes rolled toward the ceiling. "Perhaps, it might be available in the bottlery. Florian grapes are by far the best in all the kingdoms so I suspect it would be kept out of the normal stocks."

Griswold cast me a suspicious glance. "I will see what I can find, sir."

He hurried from the room as if the conversation had set his pants aflame.

"I feel like you two don't quite get along?"

Edwin glanced at the closed door then flicked his hand through the air. "Oh Gris? He's always been far too uptight. He'll relax after a few days of me, I'm sure."

I froze and gripped the edge of the sofa, digging my

fingers into the plush upholstery. “A few days? How long do you expect to be visiting?”

“I haven’t quite decided yet. But as I was saying, we have yet to find a cure for the curse. Your mother has been working night and day to find an answer, the poor thing, but she is quite distracted worrying about how you are managing the kingdom. She considered coming back and trying to work remotely, but your father needs her with him. He is much calmer with her around, and I think that she feels better knowing he is safe.”

“That still doesn’t explain why you’re here?”

He brought his index finger to his lips and made a shushing sound. “Patience. You royals and your lack of serenity. You’d all benefit from a few weeks of meditation and personal reflection.”

The door opened, and the coquettish brunette I had flirted with the other day entered with a wine bottle and two glasses. Edwin stood from his seat and gave her a lecherous smile that my skin crawled from watching, then scooped up the open bottle in his hand and read the label.

“Draconis Rose. Not quite what I had in mind, but at least it’s something. He poured himself a generous glass and downed it in one gulp. “As I thought, still tastes like dragon piss.”

He refilled the glass then nodded toward me. I waved him off and he shrugged, retiring back to my father’s chair with his drink and the rest of the bottle.

“All right, now can you explain your visit?”

“Of course. Your mother didn’t want to leave your father but was plagued with guilt for leaving you on your own. I offered to come down in her place to act as an advisor on your behalf. Plus, it will give me a chance to utilize the castle’s extensive collection of texts in our search."

He took another deep swig, his face scrunching at what I expected to be a bitter flavor. Griswold rarely made mistakes and the castle prided itself on serving Florian wine. Besides, we'd started importing stocks for the Fall Ball and there should be at least four crates stowed away already.

"Thank you, that is extremely kind of you to help, but I think I'm doing just fine. If anything comes up, I can be sure to send word and you or my mother can come if needed. However, the Council is very capable and I've already started settling into the role."

Plus, with Veda's father lurking around, I'd never be able to see her. If he truly worried about distractions, not letting me see her would be the worst distraction of all.

"I'm glad to hear that things have been going well, but I think she would feel better if she knew you were being looked after. She's quite the incredible woman, your mother. So selfless, so ambitious."

The words rolled off his tongue with honey but resonated in his eyes as if stung by bees.

"That's very kind. I'm sure if she's concerned, I could write a letter or possibly come up and visit to make her feel better."

Edwin sat straighter in his chair. "That wouldn't be necessary. Your parents are dealing with a lot right now, knowing that you abandoned your post in the castle, even just for the day, would likely cause more stress then it would be worth. If you'd prefer, I could simply stay a couple of days, do you my research and then leave. I'd be no more than a ghost haunting the halls and very little trouble. To be honest, we are running out of leads with my limited resources. If we want to find a real solution, we need to start looking elsewhere. Maybe, while I'm in the city, I can meet with some of the other kingdoms to see if they've encountered anything similar?"

I turned away, my furrowed eyebrows and blank stare betraying me. Did Edwin know of the darkness? Veda did, and it is possible she told her father, but did he know if they were truly connected? Besides, I thought he'd said he had immense magical abilities. Either he'd exaggerated, or this curse was much bigger than him. Bigger than anyone had ever seen.

I ground my fist into the back of the sofa, the silky fabric soft against my taut knuckles. "Then I guess you should stay."

"Fantastic." Edwin polished off the rest of his glass of wine, then swiped the bottle and tucked it into the crook of his elbow. "I'll find an empty suite in the east wing. I doubt you'll even hear from me except to say goodbye. Unless, of course, I find the solution we've all been searching for."

Edwin nodded, his bottom lip sticking out slightly. He lifted his empty glass above his head. "Long may you reign, my king."

"Yes. Thank you."

He spun around and quickly exited the room, letting the door slam shut behind him.

I circled the sofa a few more times, everything jumbling in my brain, then flopped down on the cushions and stared at the fireplace. A large family portrait hung above the mantle. My father, in his human form, my mother smiling sweetly by his side. A small dark-haired boy bounced on my father's knee. The perfect royal family. Now a perfect disaster.

The last thing I needed was to be under Edwin's

watch. I'd nearly learned to control the strange power I found, but with someone who knew about magic in the castle, I'd probably be found out quick. I could, of course, ask him about the magic. Maybe he could teach me what it meant and how I could use it. But something deep inside grew darker the longer we were in the same room. I let out a deep breath and concentrated on the rise and fall of my chest. I needed to get over this mistrust of him. Just because he wasn't my favorite person didn't mean he deserved to be treated like lesser than, especially after all he'd done for my family. With no gain for himself.

My mother's gentle face appeared in my mind. She always worried far too much. If letting him stay would bring her peace, I guess I could stand a few days. However, my trip up the mountain to see Veda was out, for today at least. Maybe if Edwin kept his word and stayed out of the way I could try the tavern again tonight. Except, this time I wouldn't mess it up.

I dragged myself from the sofa and down the hall into the grand foyer.

I approached the two guards at the door. "Have either of you seen Griswold?"

"No, sir. He stormed through about an hour ago mumbling something about unwanted pests, but we haven't seen him since. Maybe the kitchen has a rat problem?"

"Maybe. Thank you, gentlemen." Or maybe the rat had made himself at home in the east wing.

5TH JUNE

The glorious morning spilled through my bedroom window. I rolled over and stretched, the bed sheets tangled around me in knots. From the brief flashes of wakefulness I remembered, the tossing and turning made sense as my brain tried to fight the negative thought monsters raining havoc in my mind.

Edwin said he'd be nothing more than a ghost, and he'd held to his word. Except instead of disappearing into the shadows of the castle, he lurked and loomed over my shoulder like my own personal poltergeist. I didn't even get the chance to go to the tavern and see if Veda had come to the city again. Edwin met me in the foyer and thwarted my plans with talk of my obligation to the kingdom and how proper kings should behave. And, of course, I fell for it, hoping he wouldn't report back to my mother that I'd made a mess of things. If only I'd be able to show Edwin I didn't need him, maybe he would run back to the temple before I lost my mind.

I scrambled from my bed and dressed quickly, then headed into the casual dining room for breakfast. My stomach growled as the delicious smells of fresh-cut fruit mixed with spicy notes of cinnamon spilled out the doorway. One of the servants typically woke me to eat, but either I'd awoken early or possibly slept right through their knock of warning. I grabbed my forehead and tried to shake out the remaining fog that cloaked my tired brain, but it didn't help.

"Good morning, Your Majesty." Edwin folded the newspaper closed and slid it onto the table, his breakfast already half-eaten and mine waiting on the table across from him. I stifled a groan and slid into my seat. The old meal had already grown cold and my hunger suddenly flitted away.

"Did you have a restful sleep?" I asked, wondering if he'd battled his own demons as I had.

"Absolutely. The east wing is so quiet at night. It's amazing how peaceful it can be."

One of the kitchen staff entered the room with a steaming pot. He refilled Edwin's cup of coffee, the rich smell taking over the room. Edwin placed his hand on the servant's shoulder and stared at him in the eyes. "Thank you. Now please bring me more of the cook's delicious jam."

The servant bowed. "Yes, sir. Whatever you'd like, sir."

I watched the servant march from the room, his feet nearly dragging on the floor as he lumbered off to do

Edwin's bidding.

"I see you've already made acquaintances with the staff."

"It's best to make sure they know their place and yours." He winked then spooned some sugar into his cup and blew across the top before taking a small sip. "Besides, I'm a bit of an early riser and wanted to get a head start."

Good. The faster he found what he was looking for, the faster he could send my parents home and get out of my space.

"Have you already found my father's study? My mother has a library as well, but the study is where I would start. I can show you after breakfast if you would like."

"No, not at all. I noticed some tasks around the castle that needed to be handled. Some small orders needed to be taken for the kitchen. I addressed the guards about their security posts. Oh, and I also arranged for a luncheon with the delegates from The Forge."

I choked on his words and coughed up my tea. Hot liquid spilled down my chin and puddled on the tabletop. Edwin passed me a napkin. I snatched it from his grip and wiped my mouth.

"I thought we discussed that you would be staying out of castle matters."

He stuck out his pink bottom lip. "We did, but I just feel so terrible for not helping after I promised your dear mother. I didn't think it would be a problem if I lent an experienced hand. It's only the small things anyway, I'll leave the important stuff to you. Allow you to concentrate on the big things."

I collapsed back in my chair, no words to respond to his blatant overstep of my authority. Did he not realize that I was king now and no matter what his position had been with my father, it no longer stood?

"Actually, Griswold takes care of the small things for me." I glanced around the open room and frowned. "We usually meet over breakfast to discuss the needs for the day. Have you seen him around this morning?"

Edwin shrugged and took another dainty sip of his coffee before placing it back down on the table. "Maybe it's time to reevaluate that position as well? He's been very loyal to your family, but he is getting on in years and might not be up to performing his tasks as he should."

"I'm afraid staffing decisions would fall under the category of big things the king should handle, and therefore up to me."

He stood and walked around the table then knelt beside my chair. He rested his palm on my shoulder and moved his head to meet my gaze. "Very well. But maybe it would be easier if I just handled those matters?"

I shirked my shoulder out of his grip, and his eyes widened. "And maybe it would be easier if you obeyed the wishes of your king?"

The chair legs screeched across the floor as I pushed against the table and stood up, then stormed from the room.

How dare he go back on his word? I understood that he might have been trying to help, but he needed to follow proper protocol with this. And where was Griswold?

I returned to my room, the only place in the castle I assumed even Edwin would have the courtesy not to breach. I propped my arms on the dresser and stared into the mirror. All of his touchy wise man theatrics, what was that about? I rolled my left shoulder back, still feeling his heavy hand on my skin. If he wanted to irritate me, it worked. Maybe next time I should give him a demonstration of what I could do. I stared down at my hands and whispered

"Make me the —"

"Your Majesty."

I jumped and knocked the dresser with my knee. Several rings and a hairbrush fell to the floor. Behind me, Griswold stood wringing his hands as he hid between my wardrobe and my armchair.

"Griswold. Don't scare me like that." I leaned back against the dresser and laid a hand over my pounding heart. Just two more seconds and I would've exposed myself and my power. Was nowhere in the castle safe anymore?

"I'm extremely sorry, sir. I know I have no right to be in your chambers without your permission, but I feel that this is an urgent matter and I fully accept any form of punishment I may receive for it."

I extended my arm and motioned for Griswold to sit, then sat down on the bed across from him. "There is no need for your apologies, Griswold. I know you'd never betrayed mine or my family's trust without cause."

His trembling hands seemed to still as he settled into the plush of the armchair, his posture still stick straight as always.

"Now, tell me what has you so upset?"

He glanced at the closed door, then leaned forward and lowered his voice. "I need to warn you about your guest, Edwin Macario. I was working here in the castle before he was banished. There are a lot of things that you don't know about that time. Things were very dark, and I'm afraid many of them were because of Edwin."

"If you mean the magic, I already know."

Griswold's jaw fell open. "How did you?"

"He showed me. He told me a lot about the things that happened. About his banishment and my father's curse. He told me they fought about my mother and then my father banished him. Is that correct?"

Griswold nodded as his head hung to his chest.

"I understand your concern, he irritates me as well. However, he is also working to help bring back my father back from this new curse."

Griswold perked up and slid to the edge of the seat, leaning closer. "They've found your father, sir?"

"Yes. However, it is a secret. Only Edwin, myself, and my mother know where he is hiding and we want to keep it that way. To keep him safe."

"I will not breathe a word. You know how much your family and its safety means to me."

I cuffed my hand on his shoulder and squeezed. "Absolutely. And your safety means the world to us as well."

"I'm sorry for having disturbed you." Griswold stood and straightened his uniform before heading toward the door. He paused as his hand hovered over the knob. "I'm glad you're guest is helping to save your father, but as someone who spent more time around him than most in the castle, please be careful of what you believe. He had a way of tempting your father into things and I would hate to see a young man with promise led down the same disastrous path."

I rubbed my palms down my thighs. I knew I didn't trust Edwin, but part of me expected that was because we had gotten off on the wrong foot and, of course, because he was Veda's father and wanted me far away from her. However, maybe my gut instincts weren't wrong?

"I know of someone who might be able to tell me if he's changed. However, it will take some time for me to reach her. Do you think you would be able to keep Edwin off my trail long enough for me to get some more information?"

"Of course, sir. But please hurry. If he is still the same as he was back then, then we all may be in danger the longer he stays under this roof."

Griswold poked his head out the door and looked both ways before hurrying out and closing the door behind him. If Edwin had really changed then I had nothing to worry about, but if he hadn't, who knew what he could do and how much stronger his magic had grown over the years. If my mother and father trusted him to help, Edwin was likely harmless and Griswold was just being his overly cautious self. But the bad vibes I felt around him at breakfast, or any time we talked, still slithered under my skin. Being on top of the mountain for years meant no one would really know the truth, except maybe one. The one person closest to him. The one girl I desperately needed to find.

I fastened the cloak around my neck and looked in the mirror. My borrowed stringy hair dangled in front of my eyes and I swept it to the side as I double checked my disguise. I could've chosen anyone else, but I kind of liked fake Amir. In a weird way, being him comforted me. His dark eyes an ocean to lose myself in and step out of my own world for a while. Besides, to pull off a deception like this in front of a legitimate wizard, I'd need all the confidence I could muster so sticking with the familiar was the safest bet.

In my shoulder bag, I placed some fruit and sausage that I'd stolen from the kitchen, then tossed it over my arm and took a deep breath.

I slipped out of my room and down the hall racing through the twists and turns until I hit the grand foyer. I nodded at the two guards on the inside of the door, and they didn't seem concerned. Unknown faces sneaking into the castle were a much bigger threat than those sneaking out. They opened the doors and sunlight streamed in. Inches from freedom.

"Thank you," I said as I nodded at the guards politely then headed out into the courtyard.

"Stop right there." Edwin's voice rattled around the foyer. I increased my pace and glanced over my shoulder. No mistake, his demand was directed at me.

"I'm not sure we've met," Edwin said as he huffed and puffed from racing through the castle. "Where are you going?"

I kept as much distance between us as possible, as if he could somehow sense the magic coming off of me and cast my eyes to the cobblestones.

"Out running a few errands, sir. I'm just a lowly castle servant. No cause for alarm."

His shadow loomed closer as his hands fell to his hips. "I thought I'd met all the servants this morning?"

"I only work in the afternoons, sir. I'm here early to assist the prince."

He crossed his arms. "And what exactly are you doing for the prince?"

I stared at his gloating face as he lorded over what he thought was yet another peasant. "He insisted that I go to the city and find some Florian wine."

Edwin's smile burst brighter, his ego inflating even bigger. "Well, in that case, please run along."

"Thank you, sir." I rushed to go.

"Just one second," he called.

I halted in my tracks and winced. "Yes, sir."

Edwin scurried in front of me and stared into my eyes as he reached his hand toward my shoulder. I bowed quickly, his hand whisking over my head as I turned and ran for the castle gate. Even if Edwin couldn't see through my disguise, one touch would expose me immediately.

I breezed past the guards and over the golden bridge as I head through the streets and up the hill. People parted out of my way as I ran. A mad man on a mission. Edwin likely wouldn't bother sending guards after me, but I refused to take the chance.

I pushed harder until I neared the end of the city and the glowing green edge of the forest ahead. As I raced down the main path, Mosa and the castle disappeared behind the curtain of foliage and I took a sharp left then collapsed among the leaves. That was too close. Hopefully, a flighty servant wasn't enough to send him searching for the real prince, or maybe Griswold could keep him off my scent for a little while. I'd planned to have a few hours grace before Edwin started to become suspicious, but I'd lost that advantage now.

After I forced my breathing to slow back to a normal pace, I conjured the tingling sensation to change my face back to normal, then whistled for Alizeh. Within minutes, she appeared on the horizon and landed at my feet.

"I missed you, girl," I said as I rested my head against her cheek, my arms around her neck.

She clucked and lowered to the ground as I mounted her back. "Alizeh, take me to Veda's cottage."

~

The sun turned a violent red as it started to dip down over the mountains. The tiny cottage appeared in the distance and my body shook. When I considered this a mission for the castle, I'd almost forgot the other reason I needed to come here. The breath before that almost kiss. The glassy tears as she said out loud the words I wanted to hear her say to me. The real me.

Alizeh landed and I tossed her the packet of sausage from my bag. She curled up on the ground and tucked her wings into her sides, her beak quickly demolishing the treat.

"Good girl." I scratched under her neck then swallowed hard as I stood at the end of the path leading to Veda's front step. No roses this time. No chance to memorize some grand apology. Just me, as plain and honest as I could get. Hopefully, it was enough.

I knocked on the door and the booming sound echoed off the nearby mountains.

No answer.

I waited a few minutes and tried again, but still, Veda didn't answer the door. Without Alizeh, I doubted she'd just run into the city, but maybe she had another way to travel. Or maybe her meeting with Amir had sent her back into hiding and there would be no way for me to find her now? I slunk down on the steps, my knees at my chest, and gripped my head in my hands. If I couldn't talk to Veda, how would I ever find out about Edwin? She'd known him her entire life, even if he'd spent most nights at the temple, she still knew him better than anyone. She'd also read his diaries several times, and probably knew more than people who worked at the castle back then.

The diaries.

I shot to my feet and tiptoed through her garden, careful not to trample her violets and daisies. I peered through the front window into the dark front room, squinting to see the floor-ceiling bookshelves on the far wall. On the top shelf, the collection of leather-bound diaries sat in their regular place. If Veda couldn't tell me what I needed to know, maybe Edwin had written it down for me already. From the volume I read, he didn't seem to hold anything back, likely not expecting anyone to ever find them. I'm sure Veda would understand. If she were here, she would likely let me borrow them. After all, she'd been the one who'd pushed me to find the truth.

I rushed to the door and searched through my bag to find anything that might pick the flimsy door lock. Nothing came from the search so I pulled the pin that clasped on my cloak. I pushed it into the lock and grabbed the doorknob. As I knelt to look closer the knob turned and the door flew open and I fell, sprawling onto her kitchen floor. Not locked. When you lived miles above everyone else, security must not be an issue.

I refastened my cloak, then rushed over to the shelf. I pulled volumes down one by one checking the dates on the first and last pages. Three journals seem to coincide with the time of the curse. I shoved them in my bag then spaced the remaining journals in the empty slot on the shelf, hopefully masking my theft until I could return them, or at least get an opportunity to explain.

As I rushed toward the door, I ground to a stop near the kitchen counter. Veda's notebook sat open next to a half-filled cup of cold green tea. I glanced out the open door. No one but Alizeh lurked in the yard. Maybe Veda wouldn't want me to look, but before I could reason with my hands they'd already started flipping pages. Pages of lines of stories and thoughts. Entire sections scribbled out or crossed with slashes. But the ones I could read caught my heart in my throat. Elegant thoughts and images spelled out along the notebook in ways I never imagined. Veda wasn't a writer, she was an artist who painted pictures with her words. I kept flipping, entranced by her polished script until I reached the last written page. In the margin sat two words. True beauty?!!? With three underlines. So what I said had affected her. But even if she had run away again, I doubted she would've left her notebook here. I hadn't seen her without it since we met, and with her competition drawing closer it seemed unreasonable for her to forget it. Unless she'd given up. I clenched my fists. If I hurt her enough to quit then I didn't deserve for her to hear my apology. But that conversation would need to wait.

I clicked the door closed behind me and ran down the path, then launched myself onto Alizeh's back. I scanned the yard again, hoping to find Veda hiding in the pending shadows of the coming night, but nothing stirred on the peaceful mountaintop. I exhaled a deep breath and clutched my bag closer to my chest. Alizeh stood and spread her wings. I gripped the feathers near her head and clenched my knees to her sides.

"Alizeh, take me to the forest."

~

As the bookcase slid open, I peeked my head inside my mother's library.

Darkness. Perfect.

At least my entry back into the castle seemed to be going better than my exit.

I slid my thumb under the strap of my bag and adjusted it across my shoulder. The diaries hidden inside should tell me more about what happened all those years ago, because between the stories from Edwin, my mother, and Griswold the plot holes kept getting bigger. Things didn't quite click together as they should. Was Edwin dangerous? Was my father? What really happened the night Edwin was banished? The questions flooded my brain on the flight home as they tried to sort themselves out, but nothing made sense.

If only Veda had been home she could've saved a ton of time and work. She could probably recite all her father's stories by heart and help piece together the clues. Plus, then I would know where I stood with her instead of this stinging ache in my heart pulling my concentration from my other tasks

I closed the secret passage behind me and slipped open the door to the hall.

"What do you mean no one has seen the prince?" Edwin's voice boomed from down the hall.

Busted. I eased the door back in place and leaned against the wall. I couldn't just wander back through the castle now. Perhaps, if I slipped out to the forest and came through the front door I could explain my absence as a trip into the city. But, if I did that Edwin would probably tell my mother I wasn't fit to rule. I didn't need him to plant the seeds of doubt in my parents' minds.

I yanked off my cloak and stuffed it in the trunk in the corner along with my shoulder bag, and closed the lid without a sound. I paused, then pulled the trunk open again and removed the diaries from the bag. Edwin already operated with a paranoid agenda, if he suspected anything it wouldn't be long for him to find me out.

I glanced at the bookshelves, any one of them a possible read if Edwin truly was doing research here. The diaries needed to go somewhere he wouldn't bother to look. I pulled out a row of children's picture books, then slid each of the diaries flat against the back of the shelf and replaced the books. That would have to do until I had the chance to come back and move them to a better spot.

I quickly lit and extinguished the lantern. The sulphuric smell from the flame filled the enclosed space and I closed my eyes as I breathed in my escape plan. I grabbed some books from the shelves and placed them on the desk, some open, face down, and others stacked in neat piles near the corner.

When the scene was finally set, I rushed out the door and slammed it closed with a loud bang.

Footsteps pounded on the stone, growing louder as they approached.

I clasped my hands behind my back and marched slowly away from the sound.

"Prince Fallon, there you are," Edwin's voice carried down the hall.

I stretched my arms out over my head and faked a wide yawn. "Of course, is something the matter?"

"I went to speak with you this evening and you were nowhere to be found. None of your so-called guards knew where you were or when you had left."

He stared down the two guards that followed behind him. Both men felt the accusations and stared at the floor.

"That's absurd. I've been in the castle all day." I patted Edwin on his shoulder and chuckled. "You seemed to enjoy my daily tasks so I retreated to my mother's library to help with your research. I think I might've even dozed off for a while."

"Really, Your Highness? I thought every room had been checked."

Another burning glare at the guards. I cringed. They didn't deserve this, but it would be worth it. I'd make it up to them later.

"Don't blame the guards. I would never bother with the library under normal circumstances. The odds of finding me there on a regular day are likely the same as finding me on the far side of the moon. Now, if you'll excuse me, I'm feeling quite tired. Whatever you wanted to discuss, can it wait until morning?"

Edwin nodded, still distracted by the jagged pieces of puzzle I'd thrown at him. "Goodnight, Your Majesty. I hope you sleep well."

I continued down the hall and, as expected, the library door clicked closed behind me. I smiled to myself. Clearly, Edwin had become suspicious of me as I had of him, except maybe now I had the evidence I needed to prove that I'd been right. Two adversaries locked in a chess game. Although in this match, no matter what moves Edwin made, I couldn't let him overthrow my king. Especially since in this match, that king was me.

6TH JUNE

Knock. Knock. Knock.

"Just a minute." I slicked my hands through my hair and straightened my shirt in the mirror. My bloodshot eyes screamed from lack of sleep, the golden rings outside the hazel irises muted and nearly unnoticeable. "Come in."

The door opened slowly as Griswold stood on the threshold. "The Council has requested to see you immediately, Your Highness."

The Council? Between trying to keep my new magic in check and keeping Edwin at bay, I didn't have much capacity for the important matters. My mother had been the right to worry about the kingdom's affairs, but sending Edwin here only made things worse, not better.

"Of course. I will head there immediately."

Griswold nodded, then turned to leave but I lunged across the room and took his arm then jerked my head to the left, silently inviting him to come inside.

I closed the door behind him and ushered him to the chair in the corner.

"Just so you know, I'm still working on finding out the truth about Edwin. The contact I mentioned hasn't been seen much lately, but I do have another plan to find out more." I paced the rug in front of him. The repetition helped the plan develop into full form in my brain. "Hopefully, I will know more soon."

"No need, Your Majesty." Griswold rose from the chair and quickly dashed toward the exit. "Please forget anything I said to you the other day. This quest of yours is just a waste of time."

I sidled up close to him and scanned every available corner in the room. I shivered. Was someone hiding in here listening to our conversation? Did he know? "Wait a second, Griswold. I don't understand why you've had such a change. You told me to be careful, and I am, but now you're saying not to worry. This isn't like you."

He tried to open the door again, but I slammed my hand down and held it closed.

"It's probably just my advanced age. My memory isn't what it used to be, but I'm sorted out now."

I leaned closer and stared into his soft eyes. "Is someone threatening you? You were so determined the other day that I don't understand why you would tell me to forget this now."

"Nothing that sordid, my prince. I've simply spent more time with your guest and it appears that he has changed from the foolish young man I remember. He is kind and helpful and we'd all benefit from listening to his guidance. Especially you, sir."

I stepped back and Griswold took a deep breath.

"Are you sure?"

"Yes. Please forget we even talked. Now, it would be best if you didn't leave the Council waiting."

He shut the door with a loud thud and left me alone in my confusion. Not even two days ago he'd come to me borderline terrified to have Edwin in the castle, and now everything was suddenly fine? It didn't make sense. Griswold never lied. He'd shown his loyalty to our family time and again without fear for his own life. Could he be right and Edwin really had changed? Or could it be what I feared—that I was the monster with a grudge and not him?

The door to the war room stood ajar, the lights inside bleeding out onto the stone floor in the hall. I leaned against the wall and took a breath, my hand splayed over my ribs to concentrate on the rise and fall. Griswold's face flashed through my mind as he lied to my face. That was the only explanation for his behavior. It had to be. He never made mistakes. He'd always been an excellent judge of character. Besides, to risk his life and position to warn me about Edwin wasn't something he would have done if he didn't honestly believe it. Another fact that didn't make sense in this whole story.

I tried to push the confusion from my brain and focus on my breathing. In. Out. In. Out. Until finally a calm started to take hold. I straightened my posture and adjusted my jacket, then strode into the room, my head held high.

"Ah, Prince Fallon, we've been expecting you," Lord Covington said, his lips clenched in a tight line.

"Of course, gentlemen. I came as soon as I received word." I took the empty chair at the far end of the table and clasped my hands in front of me. Shifting in the seat, I focused on sitting taller, another attempt to exude the confidence I didn't have. "Your service to the kingdom is crucial to its survival."

Lord Marchand nodded. "Why thank you, Your Highness. We always have the crown's interests in mind."

And I intended on making sure it stayed that way. Edwin might have charmed the servants, but if I really wanted him gone I had to prove I could manage without him. I'd have to step up my efforts as ruler.

"The crown is exactly why we asked you to speak with us today," Lord Anwar added. "We are all growing concerned about how things have been going since you took over the throne."

I flinched. "Well, it would be expected there would be some issues while I got used to the position."

Lord Covington looked at his companions, a concerned crease digging deep across his forehead. "Yes, Your Highness, but we are very concerned about the decisions you've been making. Who you've been choosing to make alliances with."

"How so?"

"For one," Lord Convington continued, 'the promise of forces to the High Chieftainess of Elder. We haven't even had a full assessment of whether a threat exists and what it could mean to our own resources. You can't be sacrificing your people on a whim."

"That wasn't a whim. There are many things going on outside of these castle walls. That choice was for the protection of the people of Aboria, not their destruction. If the High Chieftainess believes that something is coming, I believe her. Besides, I know that something is happening. I've seen signs of it too."

The men began to mumble and assess each other. Each of them shrugged and shook their heads, likely none having left the city or its comforts to see what might be going on.

"Fair enough. But could you please consult us before making such commitments in the future. We deserve to know what is happening and show a united front to our foreign allies instead of just an impetuous young king playing war. This brings up the concern that you are not fit to rule."

"I didn't mean to overstep. I saw an opportunity to protect the kingdom and I took it." My hands started to shake. I couldn't lose the crown. Not now. I slammed my fist on the table and stood up. The lords flinched in their seats. "This my kingdom and I will do whatever it takes to maintain the Aldric line."

"But, Your Highness--" Lord Covington raised his finger in the air, his face scrunched up as an uncomfortable feeling seemed to overtake him.

"Yes, I know. I'm not an Aldric, not by blood. And I know you have all known and kept it from me, but I also know that I've been claimed and legitimized by the true king and as such have the strongest succession claim."

Lord Covington dropped his hand to the tabletop, the words of his argument now stolen. "Then what we are trying to tell you is that you need to take it. Claim the throne. To maintain the safety of the kingdom, we need to have your coronation and assert you as Aboria's leader. People are unsteady with the monarchy in flux."

I settled back in my chair. “I can’t.”

“You must. The longer a kingdom exists without a king the more dangerous things become.”

“But Aboria has a king. My father is still alive and when he returns he will want his throne.”

“The king is alive?’ Lord Anwar asked, his jaw falling to the tabletop. “How do you know this?”

Heat built in my cheek. So much for secrets. “I just do. My mother is still investigating, but we have a strong reason to believe he is still alive.”

Lord Anwar’s expression turned dark and he stood, squaring off against me. “You need to tell us, Prince Fallon. We need to know what is happening in the kingdom.”

“Fine,” I shouted. “Edwin Macario found my father and they are trying to find a cure for his condition right now. He’s asked me not to tell anyone as it might risk my father’s safety.”

I pushed the chair back and paced the room in front of the table. Tears pricked at my eyes, but I held them back. My show of confidence disappeared in the silence between us all. Maybe they were right and I wasn’t fit to rule.

“Your Highness,” Lord Anwar’s tone softened and he settled back in his seat. “I know this is a difficult time for you and your family, but Edwin Macario is not someone you should be putting your legacy’s future in the hands of. With his history, we don’t think it would be smart to keep him involved in castle operations. He needs to leave.”

“I know. I know. But he doesn’t seem to understand that. I’ve asked him to go, but he claims he’s here on my mother’s behalf to ensure that the castle is running smoothly. If he tells her that I’ve let the kingdom suffer she'll leave my father alone and who knows what will happen then." I swallowed hard, trying to slow my breathing. Hot blood pumped through me, beaming in my cheeks and burning at the tops of my ears. I gripped my head in my hands, my steps speeding up as my path shortened. "I don't know how to get rid of him without risking my father's life."

Chair legs shrieked across the floor and the thump of Lord Marchand's walking stick thudded toward me. "Calm down. It's going to be fine. We'll arrange for a few guards to escort him home and they can take care of your father. No harm will come to him, you have our full support on this."

I pulled my head up, genuine concern marking Lord Marchand's face as he tried to force a smile for me.

"Except, we can't do that. Guards would never be a match for Edwin. He's a wizard."

"What?" Lord Marchand's eyes widened, his concern morphing into full out terror. "This changes things. We need to take care of this threat immediately. Are you certain?"

A knock rapped on the door.

"Yes, I've seen him use magic before. He changed a gold statue into an eagle and made it fly. But I don't know what else he's capable of. Griswold told me he's known about this for years. He said Edwin's always had his powers."

The knock echoed again.

"Who's there?" Lord Marchand called.

A male servant with hair the color of fire opened the door. "I'm sorry to interrupt, but Griswold needs to see His Royal Highness right away."

I turned my head away from the door, hiding my weakness. "Tell him I'm still busy, but I will come as soon as I'm free."

The servant bowed his head, but didn't retreat. "I'm sorry, but he insists that you come at once. He said it's an emergency."

"Go," Lord Marchand said. "If Edwin Macario is as powerful as you say, you need to show that everything is normal until we take action. Plus, it will give you a minute to collect yourself before we continue."

"Thank you." I raced toward the open door, my body tingling. Hopefully, not in the magical way. "I just hope we can deal with this quickly."

The portraits on the wall blurred together. Reds, blues, and greens all muddled as I rushed to the foyer, my head still back in the war room plotting.

"Griswold," I called, my voice bouncing off the tall ceilings.

"Yes, my prince. Is there something you need?" Griswold appeared at the top of the east staircase, guiding himself down the steps slowly.

"You summoned me. The servant said it was an emergency."

He paused and furrowed his thick silver eyebrows, then chuckled. "No emergency, sir. Unless, of course, a shortage of plums in the kitchen qualifies as a crisis these days."

"Are you sure, Griswold?" I eyed him carefully.

"Absolutely, Your Highness."

I grabbed the back of my neck and shook my head, the first pangs of a headache building between my shoulders and up the back of my spine. Had I woke up in some backwards universe this morning?

Taking my time, I walked back looking for the red-haired servant to find out what went wrong. Laughter echoed in the hall and I picked up my pace to follow the sound, leading me back to the war room. I peeked around the corner. The three lords sat in their chairs, amused with a new guest standing in the middle of the room. A tall man in a sweeping purple jacket and thick black boots.

Edwin.

I ran my hands over my face trying to destroy any last sign of frailty, then marched into the room. "Sorry for the delay, gentlemen, but everything has been taken care of now. Should we now continue with our discussions?"

I brushed my hands together and pushed my nose into the air. "Edwin, it's nice to see you, but if you could please excuse us we have important matters that need to be addressed right away. I'm sure you understand."

"Of course." He bent his left knee and made a dramatic bow, sweeping an arm out in front of him. "I'm glad to see that you are taking your role so seriously. I'll show myself out."

He paraded past, his stare full of fire and holding tight to my face until he had to let go to close the door behind him. I exhaled, the air lighter again, then returned to my seat at the table.

"Now, how exactly do you propose we remove Edwin from the castle without incident?"

Lord Anwar looked over his notes, then at his two cohorts and then down again. "We discussed the issue while you were away and we've decided that maybe we need to hold off making any rash actions while there isn't a king in place."

I fell back in my seat, the weight of what I needed to do pressing me down. The relief of having Edwin gone fluttering away. "Okay then. I'll go through with the coronation, assume the crown, and then we can get rid of Edwin."

"I'm sorry, my prince," Lord Marchand continued. "I don't think you quite understand. We've decided not to do anything right now. No coronation. No hasty decisions. Besides, isn't that what you said you wanted when you came in here? To hold off until your father returns to power?"

"Yes, I did, but don't you think Edwin is a threat?"

"Or maybe he's the experienced hand you need to guide your rule," Lord Covington said as he tapped the arm of my chair. His soft eyes rested on my face along with the combined stares of the rest of the Council. Pity stares.

The three of them rose from their chairs, in sync like cavalry. The meeting now over.

Lord Covington glanced at me again before heading toward the door. "Give Edwin a chance and see if he can't help make a difference. He may surprise you."

I stared at the ceiling as I lay awake and waited for the night noises of the castle to fall away. Today's encounters with Edwin seemed stranger and stranger, or maybe I did have him all wrong after all. He'd swooped in and managed to win over the staff, the Council, and even Griswold after his stern warning about the potential threat Edwin presented to the kingdom. Maybe the problem just rested with me. My own ego getting in the way, or maybe just frustration over the fact that he'd promised to help my father and it had yet to be done.

But I still had the diaries. Who knew what kind of secrets those may still hold? Edwin had exploded when he knew I'd read one, but was that just invasion of his privacy or something more? How could everyone change their opinion of him so quickly, when his obnoxious behavior nagged at me? Pulled me as if tied by invisible strings. Didn't they see it, or did I make it all up in my own head? This was it. If the diaries didn't have anything incriminating, I'd have to admit I was wrong and finally accept his help.

I crept from my bed and slid into the empty hallway, my bare feet moving silently across the stone floor. Dark shadows lingered in the corners and the portraits of past kings and queens of Aboria seemed to stare as I moved past.

My blood pumped fast in my temples, the sound echoing in my head and hopefully not for anyone else to hear. I looked left then right, then sprinted for the staircase.

"Couldn't sleep, Your Highness?"

I stopped on the first stair and grabbed the railing to keep from toppling over.

"Good evening Edwin. Yes, I've been feeling a bit off lately. But I'm sure I could ask you the same question since you're wandering about just before midnight."

I straightened myself and casually stepped toward him as he entered the hall from the opposite end.

"I'm not a very good sleeper. Clarity of the mind can sometimes be a lonely and terrifying place."

"I see." Except, I didn't. His lurking about the castle irked me. "I was just hungry."

Edwin laughed. "Your hunger must be ravishing since the kitchen is the other way."

Not again. If he could just stay out of my business I wouldn't need to lie. Clearly, I wasn't very good at it.

"I know. I heard a noise and decided to investigate. I must've heard you coming down the hall."

He nodded as his left eyebrow shot toward the ceiling. “Possibly. And I’m feeling a bit peckish myself, mind if I join you?”

Yes. “Not at all.”

“Excellent.”

I tried not to grumble as we walked back the way I’d already come toward the kitchen. So much for getting to the library. Did this man really never sleep or was it his personal mission to keep his eye on me at all times? Maybe someone was spying on me in my chambers.

The kitchen stood pitch black in the night. No windows or outside doors were in this room to let any of the natural moonlight in. I fumbled near the door but managed to light a lantern and lead us in deeper as the flame began to grow.

“Craving anything in particular, Your Highness?” Edwin puttered around investigating every shelf and counter he could reach, popping anything small or loose into his mouth. Grapes, nuts, small pieces of cheese, whatever might be around. A scavenger, like a raven hopping around the kitchen.

“Not particularly. Just a little something to put me back to sleep.”

Edwin leaned against the counter and held palm out in front of him. A path of blue smoke emanated from his hand. “If it’s sleep you need, I have other ways to help with that.”

I jerked back nearly dropping the lantern in my awkward retreat. “No thank you. I’m sure some fruit will be fine.”

Edwin closed his fist and the smoke disappeared. “Suit yourself. However, if you ever need you can always ask.”

I crept slowly to the table in the middle of the room

and pulled back the stool, keeping my eyes on Edwin. He gathered up apples and some pears then rolled them out onto the table in front of me. I reached for an apple but Edwin snatched it from my grip as he pulled a large knife from the counter. "Allow me. You've been more than kind with your hospitality. It's only fitting that a king be served."

He sliced the apple into quarters, working with the precision of a professional with the sharp blade, then offered them back to me.

I cleared my throat, a sudden dryness itching at my vocal cords. "Thank you."

Edwin chopped himself a pear and pulled a stool across from me. For a moment we sat quiet, the snap of bites and grind of chewing the only noises between us. I settled on my stool and enjoyed the calm rhythm of the lull. A rare instance of silence in an otherwise cacophonic week.

Once the pear and apple disappeared, Edwin chopped the remaining fruit and arranged the pieces into concentric circles on the table. He stared at me as he ran the side of his forefinger down the side of the blade collecting the juice, then licked it off his finger. I swallowed in time with him, but for different reasons, one foot already flexed and ready on the floor. Finally, he rested the knife on the tabletop and my muscles relaxed.

"Your father always used to sneak into the kitchen late at night too, you know? An insatiable appetite, that man."

I grabbed a piece of apple and took a large chomp. "Really? I've never seen that."

"Maybe he stopped. People change. Or maybe he's more stealthy than you?" Edwin flashed a mischievous smile.

I cringed. "Maybe."

His eyes rolled toward the ceiling, glassy in the lantern light. "I have so many memories sitting around this table. Nights we talked for hours about anything and everything. About the pressure of the crown. About beautiful women and far off places. About his visions for the future of the kingdom. So many grand plans."

"Like what?"

"Nothing important. We're both in different places now. Grown up and moved past boyish dreams." He shook his head and the haze of nostalgia floated out of his expression. "Do you have mates that you rely on?"

"I used to. But I don't think so anymore."

"That's unfortunate. It's a tough road you're walking, it helps to have people on your side."

I dug my fingernail underneath the apple skin and peeled it away from the crisp, white flesh.

Edwin leaned further across the table and lowered his voice as if someone might hear in this late hour. "Don't you have anyone you can rely on? Outside the castle, that is."

I shook my head, then pictured Kalmin. I missed him but thinking of him stung a deep pain through my body. It kind of felt like a knife in the back. "Not really. As soon as my father fell under the curse again, my friends didn't want anything to do with me. Turns out when I'm the Party Prince, I'm everyone's best friend, but as soon as things turn rough they disappear."

"It happens. Just remember to be thankful for what you have. Your world can change quickly and without your consent, and just because it happened once doesn't mean it won't happen again. In the end, you need to look out for yourself and you'd be wise to keep your circle small and closed."

"Thanks." I took another bite and concentrated on the tart juice as it washed down my throat. My circle couldn't get any smaller. Other than Veda, this was the most meaningful conversation I'd had in forever. Veda. Her face flashed in my mind. Where was she?

I polished off the last of the apple and my jaw stretched into a deep yawn. "I think the food is starting to set in. I'm going to head off to bed."

"No problem. I'll clean up."

I nodded and slid off my stool.

"Wait, one more thing." Edwin met me at the door before I could turn the handle. He placed his hand on my shoulder and locked his stare with mine. "You should let me get more involved in the running of the kingdom, save you the stress."

I tapped his hand then removed it and let it drop back down by his side. "I'll think about it."

Pulling open the door, Edwin kept his eyes on me watching as I headed back toward my chambers but further away from the library, and potentially the truth.

7TH JUNE

"Make me a servant."

I gripped the sides of my dresser. The tingling started in my hands and flowed up toward my face. Crystal blue eyes and dark wavy hair. Short in the front, at least that was a relief, but longer in the back tied with a leather strap at the neck. A thin white scar jut through my new right eyebrow. The face looked sort of familiar, but not entirely. Was this face even based on a real person or just a combination of several of the servants in the castle? Once things calmed down, I needed to do some more experimenting to figure out exactly this power could do.

Late-night missions didn't end well with Edwin patrolling the halls and pre-dawn probably had the same luck. Time for a new plan. Instead, of trying to sneak up to the library unnoticed, I'd go during the busiest part of the day and just hope that no one cared.

I peeked out the door and slid into the hallway casually walking through the maze of corridors. I concentrated on my feet. Would this person walk just like me? Or maybe they would have a swagger, a bit of attitude that people would notice? So many things I still needed to uncover.

I quickly made my way to the east staircase. Many of the other servants were busy scrubbing floors, dusting, or moving items from one room to another. Edwin had kept everyone hopping with a list of chores longer than the West Mosa river. But busy people were distracted people.

I took the steps two at a time until I reached the top, waving at everyone as I passed and smiling at them. At the top and to the right of the staircase, Edwin addressed one of the guards, his face red and showing his temper. They couldn't already be looking for me. I'd barely been gone ten whole minutes. I walked down the hall and slipped behind the guard. Neither of the men even noticed as I continued on down the hallway. Success. Finally. I hurried the rest of the way, not wanting to risk my luck when I was so close to my goal. I double-checked behind me again and disappeared behind the library door.

"Make me myself again," I whispered in the dark.

I grabbed the thick trunk from the corner and slid it across the door. It wouldn't hold a strong guard for long, but it might be enough to hide the journals or hide in the secret passageway before someone made it through. Inside the trunk still sat my cloak and bag, except they'd clearly been rummaged through, the bag

I'd left tucked in the corner now across the top with all the pockets pulled out.

I grabbed the lantern and slid it underneath the desk, without lighting it. The skylight would be enough for a while, but if this took too long I'd need it later and I couldn't chance the glow under the library door.

After one last check of the room, as if maybe someone or something could be hiding in the corner, I reached behind the picture books and sighed with relief when my fingers grazed the aged leather diaries in the back. The three books weighed like bricks in my hands. This may be my last chance to find the truth, whether it be about Edwin or my own prejudices. No wonder my mother obsessed about her books--they held powers even a wizard couldn't defeat.

I laid the books in a line across the desktop and sat down in my mother's chair. The velvety upholstery slid soft against my arms, immediately stirring up images of late nights curled in my mother's lap listening to her angelic voice tell me tales of pirates and knights and lands beyond my imagination. A sudden ache to hear her voice again spread through my chest. I allowed myself to wallow in the feeling for a few brief moments, then cleared my tightening throat. I had work to do.

I flipped through the middle diary, the one I had read over and over that night in Veda's cottage. The story stayed the same, a ferocious beast, a kidnapped girl, and a mysterious baby boy on the doorstep. I followed each line and analyzed every word as if somehow the story had changed since the last time I read it. With context, however, the story filled in with color. The harsh brutal encounters with my father and an unknown disdain for my mother. Edwin clearly didn't like having her in the castle, whether due to the circumstances of her supposed kidnapping, or maybe something else, but I would've expected more sympathy for a prisoner.

I closed the book and rested my hands on the cover. My fingertips picked at the edges of the pages while my mind drifted and tried to piece together what I knew, what I'd read, and what I thought I knew. A lot of the story linked with my mother's, but something still felt unsaid.

The diary to the left predated the other two and started back to just before the curse. Lines and lines of my father and Edwin's exploits filled the pages. Late nights at the tavern, pointless duels with civilians for sport, lists of women that came and went. A roster of names eclipsing my own experience. But underneath the stories, a common theme arose. An emotion laid bare in script. Edwin, my father's closest companion, needed him. His long flowing monologues describing how handsome my father was, how gifted, how charming, and how spoiled. Edwin wanted to be just like him but resented him for it in equal measure. My father was Edwin's best friend and his worst enemy.

Midway through the diary, the story began to change. My father's father, the king, fell ill and his condition worsened. As my grandfather slowly passed on, my father took on more responsibility in the castle. He struggled between his playboy lifestyle and taking on the responsibility of the crown. On a night in cold January, Edwin wrote:

I've had it. Ezra treats this kingdom like his own personal playground. His vain and womanizing ways have to change or we are all doomed. He simply takes as he pleases and I can't stand by and watch anymore.

Samara was the last straw. Watching her tangled in his arms gut me like a fish, my insides torn apart and strewn along the coast. I loved her. He knew I loved her, yet he didn't think twice before taking her for himself.

He doesn't deserve this life. Just because his father was born first doesn't make him a better ruler. My father would have made the better king. He's always been the better man. Then even more insulting, the awful tyrant passed his turncoat ways to my despicable cousin and now he's not only taken the crown but what's left of my bleeding heart.

The throne should be mine and Samara should be at my side as my queen. Ezra is unfit to rule Aboria. I just need to prove it.

A chill coursed through me. His cousin? Does that mean...was Edwin a prince of the blood? If his father was my grandfather's brother, that meant he would have been in line for the throne behind my father. Could he really be my uncle? The familiarity when we first met. Maybe it wasn't in my head. Maybe he reminded me of my father more than I realized. Maybe they were family.

I continued flipping pages reading how Edwin's anger and contempt for my father grew. The lady, Samara, didn't last long in my father's orbit, and that seemed to make Edwin's anger grow as she rejected him for my father's mistakes. The writing itself changed. Letters sharper, tees crossed with deep slashes that cut through the paper. And symbols, ones like I had never seen drawn in the margins. Circles and stars and ancient-looking drawings, maybe runic or some other foreign alphabet.

I shifted in the chair and leaned closer to the book,

Edwin's anger grew paragraph by paragraph, page by page. It drew me in, like a fabricated tale from a fictional land. The evil wizard descending into rage and madness.

And as Edwin's frustration with my father increased, it changed his magic. Darker and harder to control, nearly killing a servant at its peak by magically tossing him off the castle tower. According to the story, my father fought with him often about what it would mean if the kingdom found out about his powers, until one hot July morning.

I don't know how much longer I can control it. Every day Ezra grows more suspicious of me. More intent on keeping me close and under his watchful eye. He sends guards to follow me around the city. I've seen them, skulking in the alleyways, thinking I don't notice them there. But I do. I always do.

But last night he crossed a line. He stumbled home late, after the rest of the castle was long asleep, and found me in the courtyard practicing my craft. He called me a monster. An abomination. A danger to myself and the rest of 'his' kingdom. My dear cousin has no concept of how powerful my magic has become. How adept and capable I'm getting each day. Why doesn't he understand that the kingdom should've been mine?

We fought. Fists to fists. I could've killed him if I'd used magic. I know I would've. I wanted to. But being that close to the king I'd be hanged for sure. If only there was a way to let him destroy himself? Let his beloved kingdom see him for who he really is. I'm not the monster. He is. He just needs to see it for himself.

I read the passage several times, each time sending a new chill through my body. I flipped to the final page. Only three words were written in dark black ink. Thick and thrice underlined.

I am done.

I slammed the book shut, and looks around the room, tiny spots from concentrating so hard encroached on my vision. After all, they had been through, Edwin and my father were not friends. Maybe they never were. But one thing did come clear through the journal, Edwin wanted to be king and without my father, he could have it. That also meant one other terrifying truth, without me, he still could.

I held my hand over the final diary, unsure if I really wanted to know more. I'd been uneasy around him for days, but never once had I considered he might be plotting my death. I flipped open the cover. No words. No symbols. Just a hand-drawn picture of the beast and a figure wearing a dress and a crown, both with their eyes slashed out. I slammed the book shut and chucked it against the wall, then let it fall to the floor with a thud.

The room spun. I grabbed my head in my hands and stared at the desktop, trying to make it stop. My stomach churned, this morning's breakfast threatening to come back up.

Things finally started making sense. Edwin hated my father and wanted the crown for himself. When he turned into the beast he thought he had his chance, but instead, my mother came and saved my father thwarting

Edwin's opportunity. Now with the curse back again, Edwin had a second chance at taking the throne. He tricked my mother, pretending to be helpful when all he really wanted was to get me alone and vulnerable before he could take what was rightfully mine. And I'd played right into his trap. In fact, I was the one who told him everything. I sent my mother to him. I left myself alone. I opened every window to pay my father back for the pain he'd cost him so many years ago. I needed to get him out of the castle. Fast.

I collected the diaries and hid them back in my original spot behind the picture book, then slid the trunk into the corner.

The sun through the skylight had already started to fade, which meant Edwin was probably already looking for me. Plotting against me. I checked the hall and fortunately found it empty, then slid out the door and casually walked down the hall trying to pretend that nothing happened. Now for the biggest problem, who could I get to believe me?

People buzzed around the grand foyer like bees working hard at the hive. Any other moment it would've been empty, but as my tongue bled to tell someone what I'd found, fate decided to play games.

"There you are, my prince," Griswold said clasping his hands together as a joyful smile burst across his face. "We've all been looking for you."

I started down the grand staircase as my mind tried to come up with a reasonable answer that would prompt any more questions.

"Yes, dear prince. Where have you been?" Edwin

stalked out from the corner, always where I least expected and least wanted him to appear.

I bit the inside of my cheek trying to hold in the hatred building inside me. "Just roaming around the castle. Sometimes I miss my father, the true king of Aboria, so much I just want to be near his things and remember all the goodness he's given me and his loyal subjects."

Edwin's face twisted sour. "Yes, your father will be missed by many."

"Griswold, I'm feeling out of sorts right now. Could you get the kitchen to make me some soup and bring it by my room? I have some other tasks to be taken care of, so if you can handle it personally I would be ever grateful." I descended the rest of the staircase and forced myself to near tears. "And Edwin, you've done such an amazing job handling things, I hope you don't mind taking my place for the rest of the afternoon. I just don't feel up to the job right now."

"Of course, Your Highness. Anything that I can do to help." He gave a grand bow, the delight practically rolling from his smile in double rainbows. "I just hope it's nothing serious."

"I'm so fortunate to have such an ally right now." I tapped him on the shoulder and bit the inside of my cheek to keep a smirk from sneaking onto my lips. "I'm sure I'll be fine. I just need some time alone. Forgive me for this display of weakness, but it's been rough these past few weeks."

"Anything for you, my prince. Don't worry about a thing."

I held my hand to my chest, gave a dramatic heaving sigh, then headed down the hall toward my room. I peeked back over my shoulder, Edwin's stare followed my heels as he vibrated with joy. Maybe I was getting better at lying.

Once my door had clicked closed behind me, I started to pace. I twisted my fingers together. I grabbed at my hair. Anything to keep my hands busy and away from wringing Edwin's neck. Even though the diaries were dated long ago, I didn't doubt that his desires remained the same. No one with that much vengeance gave it up so easily without some sort of payoff.

Finally, a hollow knock landed on my door. I let Griswold in, ushering him quickly as he tried to avoid upending the steaming bowl of chicken soup. I grabbed the tray from his careful hands and deposited it on the dresser.

"Thank you, Griswold. I'm so glad you're here."

"Yes, sir. I'll do whatever you ask, that's my job."

"I needed to speak to you in private and this was the only way I could think to do it. I have the proof I need to show that Edwin isn't what he seems."

Griswold tossed his hands in the air and scrambled for the door. "I've told you before, my comments were out of line and everything has been a misunderstanding. There is nothing going on with Edwin Macario and I was foolish to say otherwise."

He yanked the door open but I slammed my hand between the panel in the frame keeping it shut.

Griswold glared at me.

"I don't know what happened to you or who is behind this, but you don't have to worry anymore. I can prove that Edwin is a threat to the crown, a threat to my reign, and a threat to everyone in Aboria."

"What kind of proof, sir? That would be a lot to demonstrate."

"Edwin wrote everything down. He kept diaries from

his life at the castle and beyond. He tells everything that happened and even talked about himself. If written proof is not enough, I'll bring my mother back to support the story. You don't need to be afraid of him anymore."

"Well done, sir." Griswold relaxed and removed his hand from the doorknob. "These diaries? Where did you find him?"

"I found them in his old cottage. But I have them here, hidden away in the castle, just waiting for the right moment to present what I've found."

Griswold eased back into the room as a strange shadow cast over his face. A dark look. Not his typical level-headed self. "I hope you have them hidden somewhere safe. Maybe I should move them to the vault where the guards can keep an eye on them?"

The vault? The only thing we kept in the vault were jewels, and Griswold never had access to that space. Only the family and Captain Amir could enter the vault. He knew this, but something still seemed wrong. Griswold wasn't himself.

"You're probably right." I stroked my chin and scrunched up my face to appear lost in thought. "If you really think the vault would be better then maybe you should go get them. I left them in the throne room, behind my father's throne. I piled them in a gap between it and the wall. No one would ever think to look there."

"I'll be sure to deal with that straight away, sir."

"Thank you. You may go."

Griswold rushed to the door and quickly sped out of the room. I watched him from the threshold then silently followed him out. Something twinged at the back of my brain. I'd never seen Griswold that jumpy before, and he knew better to accuse anyone without being certain. If no one had threatened him, then what could he be hiding? Maybe I needed to read further in the diaries to see if he made a guest appearance?

I raced down the corridor and headed for the throne room, except from the public entrance side. The oversized door creaked and the sound echoed through the giant room, but it looked as though it was still empty. Three large metal suits of armor lined the throne room entrance on each side, reminding the citizens of the grandeur of the castle while still hinting at security to keep everyone on their best behavior. I tiptoed to the left and slid in behind the middle suit to wait.

Colored shapes like puzzle pieces projected on the floor from the stained-glass and moved down the aisle as time ticked on. Maybe my intuition wasn't as strong as I thought. My stomach growled. Last night's dinner had worn off and I hadn't stopped today to refuel. I slipped out from behind the armor and headed for the kitchen, but as I reached the door I heard a creek on the other end. I doubled back behind the suit as Griswold crept in on the far side of the room. He bounded up the platform and stuffed his hand behind my father's throne. Finding nothing, he reached further, falling down to his knees for a better grip.

The door creaked again as Edwin entered the throne room. I clasped my hand over my mouth, fearful that even my breath would get me noticed. The victory of being right landing like a brick in my stomach and felt more like defeat.

"They aren't here, sir," Griswold said as he rose from the floor.

Edwin skulked past him and placed his head on the wall trying to see behind the throne. He extended his arm fishing around, the angry tension in his face visible even from my position yards out of the way.

"You're certain he said behind his father's throne?"

"Of course. Perhaps, maybe he's already moved them."

Edwin marched past Griswold and exited the room. I relaxed against the cold stone wall.

Grrr.

My hungry stomach gurgled again. I slapped my hand over my abdomen as the blood rushed from my face.

Griswold stepped to the end of the platform and surveyed the room.

"Hello," he called, but only his own voice echoed back. He took one more step, scrutinizing every wall, then shrugged, finally satisfied, and followed Edwin's path out of the room.

I dropped to the floor, my knees to my chest. If Edwin had Griswold spying for him who else did he have working against me? He seemed to get along well with everyone, but I never thought he might be building his own internal army. He was readying himself for war, every calculated move attempting to overthrow me as king. I finally knew the stakes of the game, but was it already checkmate?

8TH JUNE

The castle had become a prison. Ever since Griswold betrayed me and told Edwin about the diaries, my entire world had become covertly locked down. Every hall had at least two guards on watch at all times, and even with my instructions to stand down there would be another less than five feet away to deal with. Even if I got past a few, they would've reported enough to Edwin that I'd never make it to either of the secret passage entrances without raising suspicion. He also had the Council completely on his side. No matter what I suggested or which of the lords I tried to reason with, they shut me down refusing to help me remove Edwin and telling me I should listen to his experience. Of course, he had experience, he'd been waiting for a chance to take the throne his entire life.

Changing my appearance did nothing either. Edwin had instructed that anyone coming or going from the castle needed to meet with him beforehand or not be allowed to pass. I'd fooled him once before, but with his paranoia on high, I doubt I'd make it halfway to the gate. One by one he severed my connections to the outside world. Soon I'd be nothing more than one of his puppets, or worse, I might be dead.

I continued my melancholy prince act and tried to manipulate his sympathies, but since my cover had already been blown it didn't seem to help. Every time I left a room someone came after me as if they needed to see what I was doing. Even my private chambers felt different every time I returned. A pillow out of place, a new footprint in the plush carpet, and even as blatant as my dresser drawers being left open. Whoever was doing Edwin's bidding wasn't even bothering to be discreet about it anymore. Or maybe he wanted me to feel the constricting squeeze he'd put on my life? If so, it worked.

Edwin knew that I knew his grand plan, the only thing I had going for me anymore was that he didn't know what, if anything, I planned to do about it. And unfortunately, that remained a mystery for both of us. Everyone in the castle had turned against me, or at the very least wasn't entirely under my command. Any contacts with the outside world had been shut off, not like I had many people in my corner to call on anyway. If I planned on getting any traction with this, I needed to know what exactly I was up against. He'd only given me a small sampling of his powers, what exactly could he do?

Plus, I needed to find my parents. They needed to know what was going on and be here to help me take him down. It seemed strange that my mother hadn't sent word to me again, but with Edwin's prison-like regime her letters might just have been confiscated before they reached me.

I sat alone in the casual dining room and finished my breakfast, the salty taste of smoked pig still burning on my tongue. But Edwin's eggs and bacon sat across from me untouched. His presence at meals ran like a perfectly wound clock, exactly on time. I assumed it gave him yet another way to keep me in line by knowing when I came and went, and raise the alarm if I decided to skip eating again. Or maybe, he'd already gotten used to indulging in the luxuries of the royal life. I dropped my napkin on the table and nodded for the servant to clear my dishes, then headed into the hallway. A steady stream of loud voices echoed through the hall. Laughter and pleasantries mixed with accents I didn't recognize.

I crept along the hall nodding to the guards on watch as I followed the sound toward the throne room. I eased the door back, the small opening enough to see eight strange people standing in the middle of the room, each one dressed in their prim and proper best. White gloves, petticoats and dapper suits adorned with bronze chains and brooches. The men had elegant top hats while the ladies wore intricate bonnets atop their heads.

The group carried on politely, their voices blending together in a delightful din. Except, one voice stood out amongst them all. Deep and menacing, coming from the front of the room. I shuddered as fury coursed through my blood and my fingernails dug into the flesh of my palms. I pulled the door open further, pushing my entire head in.

"You can't go in there." A guard slapped his hand down on my shoulder and wretched me back into the hallway.

I ripped his fingers from my shirt and tossed them back at him.

“Do you understand who you are talking to? As ruler of this kingdom, I may come and go as I please. You’d be best to remember that.”

His eyes widened then narrowed again hard as stone. “I’m on explicit orders from Edwin Macario that no one is to enter the throne room while he is with his guests.”

I clenched my hands tighter into fists and fought the urge to swing. “Edwin Macario is not a resident of this castle, therefore, he cannot possibly have guests.”

I smacked my hand into the door throwing it open and marched through the center of the throne room. Edwin bolted upright, his presumptuous buttocks sullying my father’s throne. The rage within me nearly bubbled over seeing him sitting there, although flames likely shot out my eyes as Edwin stood and inched away from the throne as I approached.

The foreign visitors gasped and looked back and forth between us. I took a deep breath and plastered on my royal smile. “Hello, welcome to my castle. I’m sorry to keep you waiting, but I hadn’t been informed that you had arrived. Prince Fallon Aldric.” I walked forward and extended my hand. The gentlemen took their turns at shaking and the ladies curtsied with an elegantly graceful motion.

“I’m sorry to hear no one passed on the message, Your Highness.” Edwin stood behind me the grind of his gritted teeth the most pleasant sound I’d heard all day. “However, I’m sure you have so many important matters to take care of that I can handle one simple meeting with the lovely delegates from The Forge.”

I clasped my hands together and pushed my grin

to nearly artificial levels. "Actually, I don't have much on my agenda for today. It appears that everyone else is watching everything else in the castle, so I am completely free to meet with these fine individuals."

Edwin's grimace deepened. "But you've also not been well over the last few days, I'm certain a day of rest would serve you and the kingdom the most."

"Thank you so much for your concern, Edwin. But I seem to be feeling much better today."

"That is wonderful news. Maybe we could meet in private for a moment and I can get you up to speed on what we've been discussing."

Edwin skulked into the hallway and I followed him, not before giving a cordial wave to The Forge delegates.

"How dare you barge into my meeting like that?" Edwin snarled as he wagged his plump index finger in my face.

"Your meeting? This is still my kingdom and any meeting that happens with any delegates must go through me."

"I'm afraid you're wrong, prince. This isn't your kingdom as your father still holds the crown, not you. And last time I checked he sat precariously on the side of a mountain."

"Because you put him there." I pushed past toward the throne room again and knocked Edwin with my shoulder. He snapped his fingers and my arms jerked back behind me as two guards lifted me off my feet.

"Let me go at once. You are under the command of the royal family of Aldric. You'll be arrested for treason if you do not stop immediately."

Edwin smirked as the guards pulled me away. "I think you should take my advice and rest, Your Majesty. It seems your condition is making you say feverish things."

I struggled in the guards' grip, throwing elbows and kicking at their shins. Except none of my efforts made any difference as they dragged me down the hall away from the throne room.

"Griswold," I screamed, my voice echoing then dying in the corridors. None of the other guards or servants stopped to help. Not one guard came to my rescue. It was as if Edwin had paid each and every one of them to pretend not to see me. I screamed louder, kicked harder, but nothing worked. Eventually, the guards rounded the final corner and tossed me into my chambers roughly like a thief in a dungeon. At least, he didn't choose to lock me away down there.

"You'd best stay in here, Your Highness," one of the guards said as he shut the door behind him. I kicked the bedpost and pain shot up my leg. What the hell was that? My own guards weren't even listening to me. Even at risk of death for treason they didn't seem to care. There was no way I'd ever be able to compete with that type of obedience. What had Edwin promised them to prompt such a suicide mission?

If everyone else in the castle started following Edwin's orders, he wouldn't even need to take me out himself, he could easily get one of the guards to do it and blame them instead. I needed out of this castle before Edwin tried to take my head. I glanced back into the hallway, but the guards were already gone. I ran back to the throne room, but the grabby guards had already resumed their posts and now blocked the door in its entirety. I followed around to the far side of the room, the public entrance, and a new set of guards stood watch there as well. The voices of the delegates inside continued to banter and chuckle. But maybe they could be my escape.

I bolted back to my room and ripped through the drawers of clothes, grabbing a pair of gloves and a dark brown pair of pants. From the wardrobe, I collected a plain white shirt and a dark grey jacket. I pulled the clothes on and grabbed some jewelry from the dresser. Gold instead of bronze, but it was the best that I could find. Then just before I left, I doubled back to my collection and selected a switchblade inlaid with mother of pearl then balanced the weight in my hand. It wouldn't take down an army, but it might give me a head start if I needed it. A gift I never thought I'd ever use. I closed my eyes and slid it in my pocket, holding it tight. After pulling a sword on my father I'd hoped I'd never need to brandish a weapon again, but this time it might my life I needed to fight for.

I made my way through the corridors refusing to make eye contact with any of the other guards or servants then waited in the shadow of the staircase in the grand foyer. Eventually, the voices of the delegates trailed into the main exit. "It has been a pleasure to meet you all. I look forward to more trade talks as our relationship develops over time," Edwin said in a saccharine voice.

A gentleman in a long cream and brown striped coat shook Edwin's hand clasping it between his own. "And we look forward to more discussions with you as well. It's unfortunate that the prince has fallen ill again, we hope it is nothing serious. It would be great to engage him as well."

"I will send your well wishes, but do not worry about the prince. I'm sure his condition will change very soon."

Likely. Instead of sick I'd just be dead.

"Make me a Forge gentleman," I whispered in my

hiding place. As the change took hold I slid into the larger group, keeping back behind the flashy head gear of the ladies.

"Safe travels to your kingdom, your excellencies," Edwin said then nodded towards the entrance guards who opened the main doors to the outside, letting the hopeful sunlight in. As the group walked out I weaseled myself into the center of their group keeping my head straight and focused on the castle gates ahead.

"Hold on a moment," Edwin called rushing after us.

I froze, refusing to make eye contact as he might sense something. He might be able to see past my disguise.

"I believe you haven't seen the lovely gardens yet. May I escort you."

I inched closer to the gates. More time spent with Edwin would be my own undoing.

"Thank you, Mr. Macario," one of the ladies responded with a graceful bow. "But we really should be getting back. Nightfall isn't the safest time to travel."

I exhaled as relief washed over me. At least someone was sensible.

"As you wish," Edwin took the lady's hand and kissed her knuckles as he caressed her fingers and held her gaze. She giggled at the attention but I gagged and tried not to bring up my breakfast.

The group moved to the gate waving politely at Edwin and the remaining guards. The iron groaned as it opened letting us pass into the city. The weight of my shoulders dropped as the gates clicked shut behind me. Finally, free.

~

The foam stuck to the sides of the glass as I swirled my ale around the bottom. Mr. Takka arranged stacks of cups and wiped down the bar anticipating the evening rush which would likely start at any moment. No one fussed with me as I sat along the bar rail still wearing my face from The Forge but without the heavy jacket.

The brutal sun bore down on my back all afternoon as I wandered the streets of Mosa and tried to develop a plan. After a while, the jacket became a burden and I left it in an alley for a lucky vagrant to find. Even though no one would recognize me, I needed to keep moving. The pacing helped my thoughts come together and I felt like I was moving forward even if I was no better off than when I skipped out of the castle.

The first step would be to find my parents, but I'd called Alizeh five times already and she never came. Without a way up to the mountains, I was stuck. I considered hiking the treacherous roads up to the summits, but without proper supplies, I might never make it.

So I wandered. Around and around the familiar streets until they almost became a loop. I had nowhere to go. No one to turn to for help or even just to hold me down for five minutes so my head could stop floating. The only place I had left was the tavern and without exposing who I really was, no one cared about me here either.

Veda's table sat empty in her usual corner. Maybe it was too early for her to show, or maybe she still hadn't come out of hiding yet. Either way, the depressing state I'd been falling into kept getting worse.

I chugged back the last few dregs from my glass and slipped a few baht on the bar. Mr. Takka grinned and quickly pocketed the bills, wiping down my spot for the next nameless patron.

The sun started to dip low in the windows. Might as well try to call Alizeh again, then if she didn't show, try to figure out where I'd spend the night. Edwin would have deduced that I'd escaped by now, but keeping a borrowed face would give me some extra time. I might have to switch up again soon so I didn't get too obvious, or worse, stayed in someone else's body forever. My experiments had only been for short periods of time. Even that one long night as the fake Amir, I'd never gone more than ten hours in disguise and I didn't have time to solve that problem if I couldn't change back.

The sounds of the tavern muffled as the door closed behind me and I walked out into the street. The lanterns burned in the half-light of the approaching night, the world around me glowing with hope. If only I could appreciate it while everything around me crumbled.

A group of men turned onto the street ahead as I started toward the forest, my head down as I passed them. They talked and joked without a care, light and easy, not seeming to notice the mysterious stranger walking right by. A sickening feeling spread underneath my skin, hot and electric. I used to be one of them. I wanted to be one of them. Being alone had left me defenseless with few people I could turn to. My life would never truly be my own once I fully claimed the crown, but closing myself off from everyone else punched a hole in my chest that royal obligations couldn't fill.

A familiar voice laughed among the crowd and I froze, my ears perked toward the sound. The ache to respond seared deep in my veins, paralyzed in nostalgia. He likely didn't deserve a second chance after the way he treated me, but one thing Edwin did get right was that I needed someone I could turn to. A true friend.

I'd thought he was it once, but maybe not. Either way, maybe I gave up too easily. Exposing myself would be a risk, but Edwin already knew I was gone. A few minutes wouldn't ruin my escape.

"Make me myself again," I whispered then turned back around. "Hey, Kalmin."

He stopped then looked over his shoulder, his eyes wide as soon as he recognized me. The rest of the group stopped with him, a few nudging each other with their elbows and snickering under their breath.

"Falls, what are you doing here?"

"Can I talk to you for a minute?"

The other guys seem to be even more amused.

"Alone."

Kalmin nodded and snapped his fingers. The rest of his crew simmered their laughter and disappeared into Takka's. I'd forgotten how much influence Kalmin had on his own. The son of a successful businessman; he was prince of his own empire. Maybe I should've paid more attention.

"Haven't seen you around much lately." Kalmin stepped forward, just a little, his hands pushed deep into his pockets.

"I've been busy. I have an entire kingdom to run and no one to talk about it with."

He hung his head as the moonlight cut shadows across his clenched jaw. "What about all your new important delegate friends? I'm sure they all keep you busy."

I swallowed and took a step closer. I hadn't really thought this conversation through before I decided to confront him so all the words jumbled on my tongue and caught around my tonsils. Kalmin and I didn't talk about how we felt, we were just friends. Great friends.

Playing around the castle as kids. Skipping lessons to cause havoc in the market. Sitting on Kalmin's rooftop under the stars and talking about the most useless random things. Then things changed. We changed. But now the memories plucked at my brain like guitar strings, each one striking their own note and creating a longing I couldn't put words to.

"A bit. But no one that I can just be around, you know? I always thought when the time came to be king, you'd be there beside me, but I guess you didn't think about it the same way I did."

"If you wanted a pet, you could've found anyone else." He huffed and glanced toward the tavern door, avoiding or simply refusing to make eye contact. "Can't you just demand someone to be your friend now? You don't need me. You never did."

"Like you really needed me? Except for bar tabs and party invitations, did you ever even like me?"

He narrowed his eyes but it wasn't anger that resonated from his stare. "'Course I did. But then all this bad stuff happens and you don't tell me anything. Your father turned into a beast, for pixie's sake, and I had to hear about it in the newspaper. Ignoring the fact that you put the entire city and possibly the kingdom in danger, you didn't tell me. You used to tell me everything. Then when I got angry, you just made it all about yourself. What you were going through. How hard it was for you. And it's not new. I've been nothing more than your sidekick for a long time now. Not once have you asked what I might be going through. The fights I've had with my father. My mother's sickness. The fact that they might ship me off to Skyla to live with my uncle and leave the only city I've ever known. You dropped out on me months ago, I'd just had enough."

I stared down at the cobblestones, following the maze of lines and trying to gather the courage to look up. Maybe this was coming longer than I'd thought? Had I really been that awful? I didn't know about any of the things he'd talked about, but from the tone of his voice he'd clearly made them known and I didn't even care.

"Then I never heard from you again. You showed up here once and picked a fight with one of your own subjects then disappeared. How do you expect me to be friends with that?"

"Well, I wished you would have tried."

"I wished you would have too."

The shouts echoed around us. The accusations coming at both of us from all sides. Shame stained Kalmin's cheeks or maybe it was the reflection of my own on his face.

"So," Kalmin pointed his toe and rubbed it along the ground, his head dropped low as he watched. "Did you want to come in for a drink. On me, and we can chat some more."

I looked behind my shoulder toward the forest, then Kalmin's remorseful face as a sharp pain poked in my chest. "I do. I really do. But I have something I need to do right now."

Kalmin tossed his hand and shook his head. "'Course. Go do what you need to do."

I turned around and started running down the street, then half a block away I froze. I couldn't make amends tonight, but every small step helped, right? I'd changed from the callous prince he remembered over the past little while. I clenched my fists at my sides and closed my eyes then yelled. "My evil uncle has taken over the castle and is trying to steal the throne. My parents have gone missing and I need to find them before I lose the crown. I don't want to go, but if I don't leave now, my uncle might have me killed."

"Geez Falls."

I spun around and Kalmin stood with his hand on the tavern door, watching me standing in the street.

"You wanted me to be honest, and that's about as honest as I can be right now until I figure this all out. Promise me you'll keep it quiet for now. I'm trusting you with this because I want you to trust me again."

He released the door handle and walked down the street to meet me. "I'm sorry things have been so awful. No wonder you've been in hiding. But I'll keep your secret, I'll do whatever you need. You can always count on me." A smile broke across his face. Not joy or pleasure, but understanding. A peace offering. "Is there anything else I can do?"

"Unless you happen to have a giant bird in your pocket or some way to get up on those mountain peaks, then not right now. But when this is all over, I might need a friend if you're willing?"

"Yeah. Come find me and I'll be there." He extended his hand and I took it then he pulled me close and tapped me on the back.

"I really missed you, Kal."

"Me too. Now do what you gotta do."

I peeled myself away and started to run again, but skidded to a stop after two steps. "Oh, one other thing. That girl that's always lurking in the corner of the tavern. The one with all the books."

"Yeah, the awkward-looking one? What about her?"

I cringed at the description but didn't have time to set it straight. "Have you seen her in the last few days?"

Kalmin looked toward the sky and tapped his lips

with his index finger. “Not really, not for the last few days. I hadn’t been looking for her either though.”

“Okay, thanks. “

“Why?”

“That’s another story for another night. But this time I’ll make sure to tell you. Only after you tell me what’s going on with you first.”

I raced off toward the forest and called Alizeh then hid in the shadows under the canopy of leaves. Within minutes, Alizeh bounded through the clouds.

Finally. Time to find some answers.

9TH JUNE

Alizeh glided through the stars, each one glimmering around me like a swarm of fireflies that I could reach out and trap in a jar to keep beside my bed. A beautiful night taunting me in my mission. Such a waste of perfection when my head seemed stuck in a dark cloud.

I'd headed straight for the temple, but as we flew I redirected Alizeh for a quick stop at Veda's cottage. We would pass her mountain on the way regardless, so I saw no harm in a small detour. Besides, maybe she could fill in some of the blanks still left in Edwin's story.

We landed in the usual spot and I jumped off Alizeh's back before she'd come to a full stop. Not a breeze blew tonight. The eerie stillness crept into my bones and drained the wetness from my throat. No lights. No sign of life anywhere on this peak. Again.

I swallowed against the growing thickness and headed to the door, the feeling of déjà vu hitting hard.

Like so many times before, I knocked and the noise of my fist echoed through the cottage, loud and booming.

I waited. No answer. Not like I actually expected one this time. If she'd wanted to disappear, she had perfected it into an art.

I glanced over my shoulder as if anyone could even see me here then tried the doorknob. The door pushed into the cottage and I followed into the kitchen.

Very little light streamed in through the window and I stumbled on the rug nearly crushing a small table near the couch. Nothing moved at the sound of my clumsiness. My own breath the only noise for miles. I flopped down in a chair, trying to avoid wrecking any more of her furniture and clasped my hands in front of me, my elbows on my knees. I soaked in the hush of the obscenely early morning and scanned the dark corners of the room for something I couldn't seem to place. What exactly did I expect to find? Either my head or my heart had drawn me here--maybe both--neither satisfied by the vacant cottage. Two very distinct and conflicting reasons.

The first time I had come here had been to escape, and now I wanted nothing more than to be found. I didn't know about the sins of the past and I didn't have this gnawing urge to be near her. And then everything changed. One night. The briefest passage of time and my world flipped upside down. If I had the chance to do it again, would I? Would it have altered everything that happened since?

I glanced up at the space where the diaries I'd stolen

once sat. For all the thinking about Veda I'd done, I'd forgotten one small detail. She was still her father's daughter. He said he kept the magic from her but did he keep his plans for usurping the throne to himself as well? Or had all this been a delicate ruse?

A thought grew in my brain. Slow and careful like soap expanded into a bubble, getting bigger and bigger until it released fully formed. I'd never considered if Veda's attention had been an act. Approaching me in the tavern. Taking me to see her father. Maybe she'd been playing me all along? If her father became king it would make her a princess, even though that didn't seem like something she cared about. At least not the Veda she showed to me if that person even existed. Maybe she'd been plotting to take the throne from me while I spent my time dreaming about handing it to her as my queen? Maybe I didn't know her at all?

I grabbed the hair at the back of my head and pulled, deserving every inch of pain as it shot through my scalp. I was so stupid. Fooled by both of them into believing a fairytale, then giving them complete access to everything that would assist in my family's downfall. Enough. No more being taken in by their lies.

I sprang up from the chair and marched toward the door. Items knocked and smashed on the floor, but I didn't care. I grabbed the door intent on slamming it and making myself feel better, except one stray beam of moonlight lit the counter in the kitchen illuminating the teacup and notebook still sitting there. I stormed back in and looked at the forgotten items. A black film of mold grew on the surface of the tea. The notebook no fuller than the last time I'd come here. She hadn't been back.

My emotions battled in my head until a red pulsing

light throbbed in my vision as my heart hammered to keep up. Worry. Anger. Regret. She wouldn't go anywhere without the notebook. It seemed strange for her not to have it before, but it had been days and she hadn't bothered to come back for it. What did this mean? Was the aspiring writer part of her role to play in gaining my sympathies, or was she also a pawn in Edwin's bigger game?

I growled and rushed out, the door banging shut behind me. As I passed the tree I snagged a few apples and tossed them toward Alizeh. My aim faltered, but she caught them midair even though it nearly sent her over the edge.

I held my breath until my pulse slowed. "Sorry, girl."

She nudged her beak into my chest until I relented and brushed her silky feathers with my fingers. The motion calmed me a little, but not nearly enough.

"If only you could talk. Maybe you could tell me where she went and if she tricked me." I leaned my head against her beak, the hard smoothness rubbed against my cheek. "If she really even loved me at all."

Alizeh clucked but provided no help.

I climbed up on her back and gripped her neck tight. "Alizeh, take me to Edwin's temple."

The blood-red dawn broke over the horizon as we crested the mountain peak to the temple. Scarlet light bathed the yard, a harbinger of dread as a new fixture appeared in the yard. Large and square. A dark blotch on the otherwise open temple yard. We sailed closer, circling in for a landing, and the bars from a second cage came into full view.

Alizeh landed and I raced to the twin prisons. My father lay on the ground his left arm ascended and his right crossed over his furry belly. His head lolled back and forth as a pathetic groan escaped his lips. Beside him, in her own cell sat my mother. She cowered in the corner, her knees to her chest and her head hung down between her crossed arms. Her skin burned red and blistered from the sun, her hands and knuckles torn open.

Warm saliva built in my mouth as my knees threatened to drop me to the ground.

"Mom," I yelled as I pushed my shaking legs to run faster.

She didn't move.

I looped around the backside of the cage and tried again. "Mom. It's me."

I thrust my hand into the cage and brushed her shoulder gently, her skin hard and ashy beneath my fingertips. She startled and shifted back on her hands, her eyes wide.

"Get away, you aren't real." Tears spilled from her bloodshot eyes as she covered her face. She shook her head as her matted hair whipped around her hands. "Nothing is real."

What had Edwin done to her? I'd kill him. Take the sharpest sword from my collection and pierce it through his chest where his heart should be. Except he didn't have one. He called my father the monster, but he was even worse.

"It's not a trick. It's me, Mom." My throat tightened as I said her name. Hurting her stung my entire body. My skin raw. Each nerve sparking under my flesh as I watched her suffer. "It's Fallon. I'm here to rescue you."

She softened and crawled back towards the bars.

"Fallon. It can't be. Is it really you, my son?"

"Yeah, it's me. I'm here."

She held up her left hand and slowly reached toward me as if I might disappear when our fingers touched, but I held still. A ghost of a smile drifted across her face as our hands connected. I wasn't the illusion she feared. She leaned closer. Her right arm shook holding up her weight. Our fingers twined. Her arm gave way.

"Mom," I screamed and reached further into the cage.

She fell forward smacking the bars with her forehead and collapsed on the floor.

My body trembled as I pushed my way into the cage as far as I could. "Mom."

She rolled onto her back and grabbed my arm cradling it near her chest. "Fallon. My boy. I've missed you so much."

"What has he done to you?" She flopped her head toward me, tears still welling in her broken eyes. "I haven't eaten for days. There's no water and the sun--" she blinked and cringed gripping my hand tighter, "--the sun burns hotter every day."

"I'm going to get you out of here." I pulled my arm away even though she tried to hold on, her nails carving white stripes on my skin. I grabbed the lock on the iron door. Thick and heavy just like the one my father's cell.

"Do you know where the key is?"

"No," she whispered. "I'm not sure."

I slid the switchblade out of my pocket and flipped it open. The sharp blade slid easily into the lock, but again I couldn't get the latch to open. I pushed harder wiggling the blade back and forth, but it stayed shut tight. My shoulders fell, deflating in towards my ribs.

"Is anyone else here?"

She shook her head. "I don't think so. I've only ever seen Edwin."

"Okay," I held my hands out and tried to keep her calm. "I'm going to go see if he has the key inside. But I won't leave. I promise I will not leave this mountain without you."

"Don't go," she cried. "Don't leave me here."

"I won't, I'm just going to find the key and see if there is any food inside."

I raced across the courtyard, my legs sailing over the patchy grass and dirt, but not nearly fast enough for my liking. Had he actually left them there to die or did Edwin plan on returning and the desire for power became too strong to care? But it's probably what he wanted. Not only would it get the king and queen out of the way, it would also strengthen his claim for the throne. The thought curdled in my mouth. The taste sick and rotten against my tongue. I'd been right, he would kill for the crown.

After bounding up the gilded stairs, the heat burning through the soles of my shoes, I thrust open the door of the temple with a bang. The sound echoed through the open concept rooms, reverberating off the walls and coming back to greet me and die in the otherwise silent building. I swung my head side to side looking for a place to start. A key could be anywhere, but even a saw or a hammer might work. If I couldn't break the lock, I might be able to take out enough bars to get my mother free.

I ran down the hall toward the kitchen at the back of the temple. The earthy, sweet smell of jasmine tea lingered in the air, but instead of calming my nerves it fueled my search. Edwin had sat in this room, in the now empty chair, and lied to me. Told me what he needed me to hear to betray my family and let him into our home. I'd been stupid. Foolish. Arrogant. And now I would pay the price unless I could find a way to get him out of the castle.

I yanked open the drawers, tossing dishcloths and cutlery aside for anything that might resemble a key or be of use in a jailbreak, but found nothing more dangerous than a bread knife. I slammed the last drawer and stopped, my hand hovering just over the handle. A rustle sounded somewhere deeper in the temple. I froze.

A voice. High-pitched and muffled down the hall to the right.

I glanced over my shoulder and slipped my switchblade back out of my pocket. Nothing moved. The voice stopped, but the rustle echoed again.

I slipped into the hallway, the noise increasing as I neared a closed mahogany-colored door at the far end of the hall. I held the switchblade near my thigh, the blade extended and at the ready, then pressed my back against the wall as I crept closer to the door. Had Edwin returned in the middle of the night when he realized I'd escaped the castle? Could he have sent someone else to wait for me? A guard or an assassin, maybe? No matter who it was, they wouldn't be able to stop me now. I'd never let them.

Pressing my ear against the wooden panels, the rustling noise grew louder. Definitely inside this room. I slowly turned the knob and peeked through the small opening. Books and papers spread across the floor like a large disheveled rug. A desk buried in even more paper stood behind the mess, but the chair sat empty. I pushed the door open further and took a cautious step inside.

My muscles tensed. Scalding adrenaline flooded my face and limbs. I took another step.

Bang!

The rustling broke into a rumble behind me. Metal clanging. Wood banging.

I jumped back and knocked the door completely open, my blade aimed in front of my face.

A grey and brown speckled dove fluttered in its golden cage, wings flapping. The cage swung on a hook from the ceiling, swooping back and forth and smashing against the nearby wall.

I slapped my hand over my chest as my heart pounded hard enough to hammer nails. Just a bird. I scanned the rest of the room. Nothing else moved. Nothing else alive. I gripped the top of the cage and slowed it to a stop. The dove thrashed harder, trying to escape. Another one of Edwin's pets, not meant to be confined. I unhooked the small golden latch and opened the cage door. The dove slowed and crept to the edge, poking its head out into freedom.

"It's okay. You can go."

The bird inched forward, slowly, then burst out the open cage door and disappeared into the hall. The cage swung empty and banged against the wall again.

I held up the switchblade and eased into the room, being careful not to trip over the library of material scattered on the floor. What a mess. Edwin must've left in a hurry to leave everything out like this. I scooped up one of the blue fabric covered books from the floor. *Protection Spells and Curses*. The words inside the pages jumbled together in a language I didn't understand. Something foreign, or maybe ancient with black ink drawings in the margins similar to the ones I'd seen in Edwin's diary. But he didn't only mark his books.

I glanced behind the desk. Black and red symbols covered the walls. Circles, crosses, arrows, stars, all painted bold and telling a story I didn't understand. Across the center, a row of pictures clipped from the newspaper hung on the wall. The lords from the Council. My mother. My father. And one last photo with an "x" drawn overtop in deep crimson--me.

A wave of dizziness knocked me back and I gripped the edge of the desk. It was true. I never doubted his plan once I uncovered it, but seeing it spelled out in front of me gave it a tangible reality I could taste and feel, but still didn't know how to fight.

I guided myself through the maze of books and crumpled into the desk chair, my arms dangling limp over the sides. He planned to kill me. Not an act of convenience or a casualty of getting in the way. It was premeditated. Preplanned. Had I not escaped I might already be dead.

The thought haunted me as I rummaged through the paper looking for a key. Every page blurred together as I chucked them onto the floor and continued to dig. Before I left I should set this room on fire. Destroy the hateful image of me, even though it would remain forever etched into my memory. Ruin his castle as he'd ruined mine.

Summoning Spell, one piece of paper read. I ripped it into pieces and let them flit to the floor. Levitation Spell. Crumpled into a ball and chucked at the window. Memory Spell. Shredded into strips. Mind Control Spell. Wait. What?

The instructions read simple and clear. To assert a mind control spell one must be in contact with the target and maintain eye contact during the conjuring. Of course. That had to be how Edwin had won over the entire castle. He spelled them all. Every single one. I flinched remembering his hand on my shoulder, his stare boring through my skull as he tried to talk me into giving him more responsibility. He'd tried to control me. Tried and failed. But why? How could a powerful wizard like Edwin Macario not be able to control a young stupid prince?

I stretched my hands in front of me, palms up, staring at the life and health lines crisscrossing my skin. Did my ability to change my face somehow block Edwin's power from affecting me? Maybe the power running through my veins was stronger than I even imagined. I folded the page into a square and shoved it into my pocket.

Blueprints for cages appeared as I cast aside the mountains of paper. More evidence. More sick, twisted schemes. Every piece of evidence piled up on each other and painted a clearer picture. The lies. The plotting. This wasn't just a crime of opportunity, it was something more. Something much bigger. Edwin had been hiding in the mountains plotting the downfall of the entire Aldric line.

I yanked at the desk drawers. The left one flew open easily revealing a supply of inks and a wax seal stamp cut into my mother's signet. The right one jiggled in the desk frame, but remained closed. I slid the switchblade along the top of the drawer and jerked hard. The flimsy lock gave way and I tumbled to the ground, the desk drawer still in my hand. Quills burst out in a circle around me and an iron key thunked against the floor next to my leg.

Finally.

With trembling fingers, I scooped up the key and rose to my feet as I took one last look at Edwin's den of horrors. Days and nights of work covering every surface. Each page cursing my family and plotting my end. Reams of hate unfurled from the brain of a madman, each item piling on each other until shivers of terror reverberated through my bones.

I kicked my way out of the room, sending loose pages into flight, and slammed the door behind me as I bolted out the front of the temple.

I tore back across the courtyard, the key searing into my palm as the cages grew larger and larger with every step.

"I found it," I yelled as I approached.

Mom met me at the cage door as the iron key slipped into the lock. The tumblers clicked as the shackle sprung free, the chains around my chest loosening too as I fumbled to remove the lock and swung the door open.

Mom fell into my arms, her head burrowing into my shoulder as her knees shook and wobbled barely holding her up. I squeezed her tighter, taking the weight of everything she'd experienced and trying to keep her upright. "It's going to be okay."

"Thank you, Fallon." She gasped, her tears soaking through my shirt. "We need to get out of here. If Edwin comes back, I don't know what he'll do."

She released my arms and grabbed the key in my hand then stumbled toward my father's cage. She tripped along the flat ground, desperate in her struggle, but I clamped my hand on her shoulder and turned her back into my grip.

"We can't leave yet. You need to get your strength back and we need to make a plan." I let my arms loosen around her and she pulled her head back, her watery eyes connecting with mine. "I think Edwin is the one who cursed Dad and is trying to steal the throne."

She glanced over at my father's cage, the barely breathing lump of fur on the ground breaking her heart, the fractures spreading from her chest to her anguished cheeks.

"Yes, I don't doubt he's behind your father's curse."

She sighed. Sun glistened against her wet face as she raised her head towards the sky.

"After all, Edwin is the one who cursed him the first time all those years ago."

GOD OF ILLUSION

10TH JUNE

"Are you sure it was Edwin who cursed Dad eighteen years ago? Do you really think he would've tried this twice?" I tipped the steaming teapot and poured the hot liquid into a cup. A few drops splashed on my arm and I flinched, but the pain reminded me that this was real. Every dangerous, disastrous thing I'd endured so far wasn't just a bad dream. Edwin Macario had really betrayed my family and set himself up in the castle while he plotted my downfall. My father was really a beast locked in a cage. And even my mother had been held prisoner, starved, and left for dead. These things were my new disturbing reality.

I wiped the water away with my sleeve, then carefully carried the cup on its saucer across the temple's kitchen floor and placed it in front of my mother.

Mom linked her finger through the teacup handle and rubbed the pad of her thumb across the burning porcelain as she stared at the floor, her long chestnut curls hanging limp over her sunburned shoulders. "I'm sure of it. Why do you think he's been living on this mountain all this time? Your father banished him, never to return to Mosa. We always suspected that he had been responsible for the curse, but we'd never been able to prove it. I think we can now."

She sipped the tea, her dull eyes glazing over as she disappeared into her own thoughts. From the moment I'd opened the cage, her focus wavered. Sometimes she stayed with me, answering my questions and assuring me that she would be okay, but other moments she faded into herself as if recounting a painful memory or maybe just trying to regain her strength from the inside out. The horrors of the past several days flit across her face, occasionally drawing a twitch or shiver from the rest of her body as if it struck a raw nerve. I sat in the chair across from her and gripped the fingers of her free hand, hoping that whatever haunted her might float away with me by her side, if even just for a few moments of peace.

I hung my head and studied the haphazard lines of the table's wood grain, as my emotions battled for what I felt the most; fear, anger, or maybe just shame. "I'm sorry I didn't tell you about what Edwin told me. I believed his lies because I didn't want to upset you. Or maybe I was worried that you'd confirm it as true and I couldn't question him anymore. If I could go back and change things I would. He never would've hurt you."

"Nonsense, Fallon. How were you to know that you were dealing with a narcissistic sociopath? Your kind heart would never let you see him for what he was. But maybe it's time I told you my side of the story." She shook her head and trembled as she lowered the cup to the table. Painful memories bubbled up in her distant stare, but she took a deep breath and rejoined me in the present. "Edwin used to live with us at the castle. Your father loved him. Trusted him. He was his favorite cousin and the one person he felt he could confide in. They were inseparable. And then I came along.

"Your father had already fallen under the curse by that time, but other than the beastly appearance and the grouchy disposition, he was still him, not like the animal he is now. He was always the man I fell in love with, just with more hair. As we grew closer, Edwin became jealous of the time I spent with him. He started acting hostile and aggressive toward both of us. He told your father to release me and send me away, but he didn't understand that I wasn't your father's prisoner. He'd already stolen my heart. Sending me away was pointless as I'd never leave him.

"One night Edwin's temper finally spilled over. Your father and I had spent the evening in the garden and I decided to sit outside under the stars for a few extra minutes while he went inside to deal with some kingdom business. Edwin cornered me beside the rose bushes and threatened me."

Tears welled, but she flicked them away and swallowed.

I slipped from my chair and knelt in front of her. "It's okay. You don't need to tell me."

"But you should know the truth." She wiped away the new tears coming faster and harder than before. "Hiding it from you hasn't done any of us any good."

She placed her palm against my cheek and I leaned

in as a broken smile cracked across her quivering lips. "He said if I didn't leave your father he would kill him. He said that the throne should have been his and he'd done everything he could to make that happen but I was ruining everything. As the curse took a stronger hold on your father, he'd eventually become a beast and never be suitable to rule, but if we broke the curse first everything he'd done would be for nothing. I tried to run away but he tossed me against the garden wall and started to cast some sort of spell. I fought back, but your father heard my screams and came running. He grabbed Edwin by the throat and if I hadn't pleaded for your father to spare him, he would've been dead. Instead, your father banished Edwin, never to return or face the death I'd spared him. A stay of execution that maybe I'd been too naive to grant. Edwin left but rallied the villagers to attack the castle and kill the beast on his behalf. That's the night we broke the curse. The night your father was given a second chance. And the night Edwin disappeared from our lives."

"Except instead of moving on, he's been hiding up on this mountain plotting his revenge."

She nodded. "Looks like it. I'm so sorry for involving you in all this. I could've ended it back then, but I thought he could change. That maybe over time he'd realize his mistakes. I failed both of you, you and your father."

"You did nothing wrong." I pulled her into a hug, her body shaking in my arms. "You granted him the kindness he isn't capable of understanding. You saved him, he chose not to take your grace. But after all he's done, he will get none from me."

"I'm so sorry, Fallon." My mother gasped as she cried, her breathing heaving hard against my shoulder.

"You shouldn't have been pulled into all of this. It's not your fight. It's our fault for not telling you about Edwin and the threat he posed. Our fault for trying to hide the truth from you."

A tightness built in my throat. Darkness seeped from my memories. "You didn't. Someone else brought me here. Someone I trusted. Someone I..."

"Loved, maybe?"

I dropped my embrace and walked over to the counter, gazing out the window to the cliffs beyond the temple. Sharp rocky drops into the nothingness below. "I don't know."

"That girl? The one that finally coaxed the joy out of my melancholy son?"

My head fell against my chest as I jabbed my knuckle into the countertop. "She manipulated me. Fed me into her father's jaws."

"Did she tell you that?"

"No. But how else can you explain it?"

Mom appeared by my side and covered my fist with her hand. "If it's true then, I support your decision to condemn her, but do you really think she would betray you?"

"I'm not sure."

"Then be sure. She might be as much a victim of her father's sins as you are. If there is anything I've learned it's to look beyond the obvious and to follow your heart, no matter where it leads you. If she did betray you, I will support whatever you decide, but if not, don't let my mistakes be your downfall."

I took a deep breath, inhaling her words and letting them swim through my bloodstream, starting small fires through my body. I wrapped my arm around her shoulder and kissed her on the top of her head. "Maybe.

But what do we do now?"

She leaned into my side, knocking me off balance. "We take back what is yours. Your kingdom. Our kingdom."

"But how are we supposed to do that? Edwin has the entire castle under his mind control spells. We wouldn't last half a second."

"Good point. That will be a problem." She retreated to the table and placed her head in her hands. "If only we could find a way to get him out of the castle and lure him away. He can't assert influence over anyone if he's not around to do it."

An eagle soared in the distance, the sun beating off its majestic wings. Blue sky and fluffy white clouds mocked me on the horizon. The castle seemed so far away. Someone else's problem. I crossed my arms and stood up straighter. My face hardened in the window's glare, a reflection of who I'd become, or maybe what was left of me. Eyes heavy and full of doubt. Jaw clenched and forehead furrowed. The reality of the world bore down and rooted me to the floor. I looked away, disgusted, my face blurring in the window's pane. Someone else's face. I sighed.

"There is one way we could get in."

I crossed the floor and sat across from my mother. She lowered her hands, the red from blood rushing to her cheeks faded as she looked at me and gnawed at the corner of her lip.

"Something is wrong with me. I'm not sure why or how, but..." Words jumbled in my brain and caught in my throat unsaid. Where could I even start? So many things had happened in such a short time they all whirled in my head, each tale begging to be told.

I shook my head and closed my eyes. I'd never find

the right way to explain, so why try? The familiar tingle rippled through my body and I let it take me over until my mother's gasp pulled me back to the kitchen. I looked up as her hands flew over her mouth and she scrambled up from her chair, her eyes locked on my face. I reached up and rubbed my chin, the soft stubble prickled under my wrinkly fingers.

"Griswold. How did you? What?" Mom stumbled backward toward the kitchen threshold.

"It's just me. Fallon." I stood from the table but didn't dare go after her. Instead, I lowered my head and let the tingle come again, resuming my original form.

She gasped again and fell to the floor. She pulled her skirt higher and sat cross-legged on the tile as her eyes flit back and forth, her brain processing what she'd just seen.

"So, you didn't know I could do this? Change myself?"

She shook her head, still silent.

"It only started after you left the castle, or at least that's when I think it started. Who knows?" I started to pace the kitchen floor. I doubted she knew about these powers, but having her confirm it made it worse. "Maybe I've always been able to do this and just didn't know, but I think I would've figured it out sooner. Or maybe not?"

She clasped her hands together and held them near her chin. "Does...does it hurt?"

"No. I can feel it happening, but it's not that bad. At first, I thought it was the curse, that I was going to end up like—" I jerked my head toward the yard and its draconian cages, "—but I don't think it's the same thing. I can control this, and from what I can tell I can be anyone I want."

She scanned me over again. "That's incredible.

Amazing."

I hung my head as my skin heated. Exposed. No going back now.

"I could change my appearance and get past the guards. It's probably our only chance."

"Yes, that might work." Her eyes started moving again as she'd probably started to formulate a plan. "And if you could get in, we'll just have to find a way to get Edwin out."

I crouched down in front of her and held out my hand. "Are you ready?"

She accepted and together we pulled her up from the floor. "Yes. But are you?"

~

I slid the last of the supplies through the cage bars and stepped back. Pitchers of water, blankets to block the sun and enough food to last at least a week—even for a beast. Above the cage, the canopy I created hung loose and looked like the sail of a ragtag pirate ship with its patchwork of sheets and tablecloths, but hopefully, it would keep some of the heat down.

"Are you sure you want to leave Dad here?"

Mom slid a stack of books into the cage. Her lips pressed together as lines creased along her forehead. She gazed at my father huddled in the corner of the cage, his thick furry legs crunched up to his broad chest and his large lower lip jutted out like a petulant child. "It's safer for him here. At least for now. Once we get Edwin out of the castle, we'll bring him back home."

Home. The word rang in the open air and echoed in my heart. Not really a place, but a feeling. One I ached for more than I'd admitted to myself up to now.

I slid the iron key into my pocket and tossed an apple at Alizeh. She reared her bronze head back and snapped it out of the air, scratching her talons across the ground and digging deep crevices in the dirt. Nothing left to do now, but go. I took a deep breath and let it out slow, mingling with the cooling evening air. The sun dipped lower on the horizon. A persimmon ball of light fading into the night, another day ending just as our clandestine plan began.

I closed my eyes then clenched and unclenched my fists, fanning my fingers out one after the other then curling them up again and falling into the lull of the repetition. I'd have to face Edwin alone, but if this plan worked there would be plenty of sunsets to see in my future. If not... I shook my head. Best not to think of those things.

Alizeh nudged her beak at my chest and I opened my eyes.

"Almost time to go, girl." I ruffled the feathers on her jaw then rubbed the red blistering skin on my index finger.

I couldn't leave without showing my mother Edwin's den of evil. She waded through the reams of paper and books as her jaw hung nearly to the floor. I wanted someone to bear witness to this. To know I wasn't the only one who saw the depths down that Edwin had planned to go. Except, walking through that room and seeing all the hateful things again didn't bring me any peace, it started a fire. Then, when I couldn't contain it any longer, so did I. Every scrap of paper. Every photo. Every random note that my mother didn't deem to be of use in searching for a cure ended up in a pile that I set ablaze. The red and orange flames ate through the pages one by one and as they disintegrated so did some of the anger pent up in my chest. Then when the pile finally became nothing but ash, I felt like I could move on. I left the burnt pieces in the middle of Edwin's desk to send a message in case he ever returned but caught the one glowing ember still burning in the center which branded my finger for the occasion.

I poked at my finger again. The heat of the burn still radiated almost a half-inch from the wound. It would probably scar. But that was fine. I wanted to remember it. I wanted to be reminded to never let myself be betrayed again. What hate and desperation could reduce powerful men into.

Alizeh cawed and scratched the ground as the night fell faster on the horizon.

I glanced back over my shoulder.

Mom had crept down the side of the cage and crouched just behind Dad. Her delicate fingers twined in the fur near his right ear as she leaned her head closer to his. The hiss of a whisper floated through the air, but I couldn't make out the words, just the calming flow of the syllables wafting on the breeze. My father leaned his head into my mother's touch and blinked, then swat his paw at her, his claws clanging against the cage bars. She yanked her hands away and backed up, her chest crumpling forward as she stared at what was left of my father. She trudged the rest of the way toward Alizeh, her index finger wiping away the tears she tried to hide.

"Are you going to be okay?" I asked as I rested my hand on her shoulder and guided her toward the back of the bird.

"Yeah, let's just end this and get back to our lives. I'm getting tired of it all."

Where I reveled in my dark emotions, she rose up

and let them make her stronger. Like a broken sword into a forge. I'd let myself get burned but she came out shiny and ready for battle.

"But what's going to happen if Edwin won't fix Dad? If he can't?"

She peeled my hand away and mounted Alizeh's back. She shifted in her seat, adjusting her position until she sat up pin-straight. "Then I'll find another way. Love is a very powerful thing, Fallon, and I'm willing to fight for it."

11TH JUNE

Night faded as we neared the city of Mosa. Ribbons of daylight wrapped around the shadows and tied them down until their nightly escape underneath the moon. The ritual dance between dark and light played out before us as Alizeh sailed over the lush green forests below. The thickness in my throat constricted as we glided closer to the ground. If this plan didn't work, I didn't know what else we could do. Edwin had already taken control over too much and breaking the hold he had on the Council and the castle staff grew harder the longer he maintained his seat on the throne.

I tugged on Alizeh's left-side feathers and she careened down to the valley just below the castle then landed with a jolt among the tall grass. My mother dismounted and pulled her skirt to her knee, marching toward the worn path up toward the gates.

After jumping off Alizeh's back, I raced after her as the grass whipped against my legs. "Slow down. We don't want to call too much attention."

She shrugged but stopped walking, the determined fire in her stare dimmed a bit at my caution. "We don't have much time to waste. Edwin has been in that castle far too long and it makes me sick. I need to defend the crown for the people I love—for your father, for you."

"Of course—" I placed my hand on her shoulder and held her gaze as I willed her to calm down. "—but we have to do this delicately. Edwin seemed to know my every move before I made it and we won't get a second chance to get this right."

"And you know that I'm still not pleased about you going in there alone. I get it. I really do, but I wish there was a way for me to know what's happening behind those walls. If you get yourself into trouble, how will I know you need help? What if this plan goes badly?"

I swallowed hard and looked off toward the rising hills that surrounded the valley. *Then I'd be doomed.* "You'll just have to wait. Watch for when Edwin leaves the castle, then fly into the courtyard and help me lock the castle down. Hopefully, he'll take a fleet of guards with him to give us a little more pull with the brainwashed staff. If I don't come back soon, take Alizeh and get out of here. Find an army and storm the gates, but for right now, just lay low and keep watch. If anything looks wrong from your view, don't hesitate to hide."

"You're right." Her body deflated, the possibility of failure growing thick and tangible between us. Suffocating. She headed back toward Alizeh and flopped down on the ground, her elbows propped on her knees with her skirt bunched up around her ankles. "But I can't stand the thought of not being able to help. I don't want my son having to be the one to save me."

I let out an airy chuckle. "Trust me. No one would ever mistake you for a damsel in distress. But you also can't solve all the world's problems on your own. It's not your job to be everything to everyone."

She narrowed her eyes with a harsh glare, but her lips curled up stripping the sentiment. "Just get going, Fallon. We have a kingdom to reclaim."

I nodded and tried to maintain my grip on her faith in me. I'd need it. "Fine. I'll be right back."

The tingle started in the bottoms of my feet and exploded up through my body like a fountain. Mom watched with wide eyes as my hair grew to dust my shoulders and my skin darkened from its typical hue. New blemishes, marks, and hairs decorated my arms and hands. Another successful disguise.

"Absolutely incredible," she whispered. Even Alizeh flapped her wings as the transformation took hold.

Would my mother ever get used to seeing me change? Would I?

She rose from her spot on the ground, then brushed the dust from the front of my jacket and straightened it to my waist. Her lower lip quivered and she hugged me tight. "Be safe, my son."

I nodded and peeled her arms away, then started the trek up the hill toward the castle gates. The wind whistled through the field as my hair blew back and tangled at my neck. For a moment, the strange breeze sounded like a warning. A whispered caution for what I was about to do. But it didn't matter, I was committed to this task, even if I failed.

Instead of heading straight up, I circled around the

castle grounds and chose to approach from over the golden city bridge. If I raised suspicion, my meandering path might give my mother the head start she needed to get away, plus it gave me a few more minutes to get my head together. No room for error.

As I neared the gates, two guards loomed tall and stoic. Their hands sat folded on the hilts of their swords, each deadly blade hanging like a harbinger from their waists. I swallowed and cleared my throat as my fingers trembled at my sides.

"Good morning," I said, trying to force my voice lower to mask the tremor.

The guards looked me over, but remained silent and sidled closer together in front of the gate sending a louder message.

"I'm here to bring a message to a Mr. Edwin Macario. It's of the utmost importance."

The left hand guard smirked. I'd seen him before. His job had been to keep me and my family safe but now his job was to keep me out. "You can leave the message with us and we will make sure His Excellency gets it."

His Excellency? My stomach heaved and I closed my mouth to keep from spitting. What kind of garbage was that? He'd never hold the throne if I could help it.

"That won't be necessary." I reached into my pocket and pulled out the crumpled letter with the royal red seal still intact. "It's from the prince and he insists that I'm to deliver his message in person."

The guard leaned forward and examined the seal. The family crest sat emblazoned crisp and clean in the red wax. He nodded to his partner. The second guard frowned but stepped back, giving me room to pass.

"Thank you, gentlemen." I grit my teeth and pushed

through the gates. One checkpoint cleared.

I gripped the letter tighter in my hand. Each step toward the grand entrance doors took more strength than I had to give. The walls of the castle loomed ahead. The same stone I'd always known, but with a different feeling now. Like a prison rising up where my home used to be. Snipers lurked on the turrets waiting to take out anyone who might threaten Edwin and his regime. Guards circled the normally unguarded gardens. A fortress that I was about to walk right into.

"What is your business here?" A castle door guard stepped in front of me and I jumped back a step, still wrapped up in my own head.

"I have a message for Edwin Macario. I was told by Prince Fallon to hand-deliver it."

"Prince Fallon?"

I nodded and held up the letter. He snatched it from my grip and looked it over just as the gate guard had done. The other guard glanced over his partner's shoulder and inspected the seal as well. His stare drifted past the page and pierced through my chest, examining me with even more scrutiny. I cast my eyes away, studying the vines that crept up the stone walls and avoided eye contact. Something in my left periphery moved. I blinked. The guards kept up their inspection. Another movement. My stare followed the motion to the tallest tower. The normally empty tower. It served as a hold for long-term or political prisoners, one's not quite guilty enough for the dungeon. Except, it hadn't been used as long as I'd been alive. At least I didn't think so.

Another movement in the tower window, then it swung open and a figure leaned out the frame, gazing all the way down to the ground. The stranger shook their head. Too far to jump. No escape, exactly as it was designed. Except, this wasn't the typical prisoner. A girl. Dark hair piled high on her head and a tough know-it-all stance that stung sharp even over the distance between us. The face I'd searched for, standing in my own house. My stomach hollowed.

Veda.

"Is something wrong with you?" the guard said.

"What?" I gripped my forehead and dragged my eyes back to the guard. "No. I'm fine. Just a little tired, I've been traveling all night to bring this message."

I glanced back. The tower window shut again and Veda disappeared. Or had I only imagined her there?

"Well, the prince isn't welcome here anymore. He's smart to send a messenger but I suggest getting in and getting out. Those who lurk around the castle end up in the dungeon or worse." He slid his thumb across the flesh of his throat.

"Understood." I nodded and ducked inside the castle as the double doors rumbled open then took a hard left and hid beside the grand foyer staircase. I pressed my body against the wall and listened to the rhythm of my heart pounding hard in my chest.

The whole plan looped over in my mind. Get the letter to Edwin and ensure he read it. Edwin would leave thinking I, the prince, would give him the throne in exchange for my father's safety. Wait in disguise for him to leave, then appear as Griswold and start locking things down while I signaled for my mother and Alizeh. Simple, and so far working flawlessly. First time's a charm.

But even though my head knew the steps to take, my feet itched to take the stairs to the tower and see Veda. To find out the truth of why she'd been hiding. To see if she'd actually betrayed me. I glanced around the edge of the staircase at the servants running to and fro through the halls. It wouldn't hurt to just check on her. I'd probably imagined it from the stress and blinding sun anyway.

I stuffed the letter in my pocket and shook out my remaining nerves, then raced up the stairs— away from the throne room and towards the one person who might be able to hurt me more than Edwin ever could.

Creeping through the corridors worked much better with a new face. No one bothered to look at me and simply let me walk by without a second glance. I ascended the final staircase to the tower and peeked around the corner. Not two, but four guards flanked the entrance to the tower room, each of them with bored stares on their faces and postures tight as wound clocks.

This didn't make any sense. Why would guards be watching over Veda? I understood if she wanted privacy, but armed guards usually meant a captive, not a guest. Plus, if she were under lockdown, four guards must mean she put up quite the fight. A jolt of pride flushed my skin as I remembered the mighty roar that came from her mouse-like body. A force unlike any other. It must definitely be Veda in there.

Extra guards also meant that the level of difficulty to enter the tower room increased substantially if it hadn't become completely impossible. I leaned against the staircase wall and rested my head against the cool stone, searching for inspiration. If she was a prisoner only a few people would be allowed to come and go, but what if I could be one of those people? After a few minutes, I raced back down the stairs and weaved through the castle again to the kitchen.

Steam and the delicious sweet smell of baking bread wafted out as I whipped open the kitchen door. My stomach growled and I clutched my abdomen as it drew the attention and suspicious glares of the other servants in the room.

I shrugged. “It smells amazing in here. Keep up the good work. Long live His Excellency.”

The head chef looked up from her pot-stirring at the stove and shook her head with annoyance. I grabbed an apron by the door and slipped it over my clothes, then strutted further into the room like I belonged there or at least like I had some idea what I was looking for. A few servants cast lingering stares, but after a few seconds resumed their tasks, chopping and prepping, without any more concern for me.

I stole a tray off one of the far counters then loaded a plate with bread and blackberry jam in the center. Pretty bare for a meal but for a true prisoner it would be a feast. I nodded and smiled as I made my way back through the prep area and slid back out the door. I glanced up and down the hall before shoving a small loaf end in my mouth and groaning. So good. The way it almost melted against my tongue. I wouldn’t last too long out in the wilderness if two days without proper cooking already distracted me this badly. I needed to end this quick.

Up the stairs again, my breath coming hard and fast as I hurried along until I reached the top of the tower again. I straightened my apron and turned the corner. All four guards jerked to attention.

“I have food for the tower prisoner.” I crossed my leg in front of the other and made a slight bow, my head dropping but my eyes still focused on the guards’ reactions.

They remained rigid, not one hint of smile or frown, as their stares darted between each other. My hands started to tremble and the dishes rattled. I gripped the tray tighter to the tray. The closest guard lifted the small bread plate and peered underneath then let it drop back down.

"Very well," he said then twirled his finger in the air.

The remaining guards parted like repelling magnets as one graciously held open the door for me. I nodded as I entered then the door slammed closed in its frame nearly clipping the back of my leg.

"I told them I wasn't hungry." Veda sat at the edge of a wide upholstered armchair, staring out the window without bothering to look up or acknowledge my entrance.

I rested the tray on the dresser. "Then I'll just leave it here for you for later. Do you mind if I ask why a young lady like yourself would be locked up here? You don't look like much harm."

She bolted to her feet, the insinuation fueling the fire that burned in her soul, unable to simply stand by and take abuse. The exact emotion I'd banked on.

"I'll have you know that I can be a lot more intimidating than I look. Besides, I'm not locked up here for what I've done, it's what I might do that scares your master."

"And what exactly is that?"

She shook her head. "It makes no difference, you would never see things the way I do, at least not while my father is in control."

Or under your father's control. Did she know about the spell Edwin had the castle under?

I sat down on the edge of the bed and crossed my hands in front of me. "You would be surprised at what

I believe. What I think."

"Aren't you a bit brash for a castle servant?"

"Well, aren't you a bit brash for a castle prisoner?"

She smiled. The rally of wills amusing her. Bringing out the spark in her emerald eyes.

"Let's just say that the royal family is in danger and I wanted to warn them."

"Yes." I stood and stepped toward her. She retracted in tandem. "I can see how your father might be upset about that. But since when does your allegiance stand with Prince Fallon and his family? Shouldn't you be loyal to your own blood?"

"Blood doesn't mean I need to side with his dangerous plans. We are still family even if we disagree, but what he's doing is wrong. " She sighed and flopped back down in the chair, her arms resting over the sides. "Besides, I know the prince, or at least I thought I knew him. He has his flaws, but his will is with his people and he should be the one sitting on the throne. He can be misguided sometimes but his heart is good."

My stomach clenched. "And your heart, miss? To me, it sounds like it might still be with the prince, wherever he is."

Veda's face flushed and she looked away, studying the intricate mosaics around the fireplace. "Thank you for the meal, but you should probably leave before I get you into trouble too."

"Very well, miss." I made a dramatic turn and headed for the door, still keeping watch over her. That instant reaction. That blush. It wasn't much, but maybe it was enough.

I closed my eyes. My skin tingled. A surge of power, then it stopped. I opened my eyes and glanced at my reflection in the Baroque mirror on the wall. My own face stared back. My real face. My true self.

"Veda, I've been looking all over for you."

She turned her head toward my voice. Her normally loud mouth dropped open in silence as her stare scanned me over in recognition. "Fallon? Is it really you?"

I held my breath then let it out in a gasp to create the illusion that I'd just run in the door. "Yeah, it really is."

She leaped from the chair and rushed toward me but stopped short as her widespread arms fell to her waist. "How did you get up here?"

"Help from a certain servant and a little bit of magic." I flashed a proper smile, full of teeth and charm. "Your father isn't the only one who can make the impossible happen."

"Great." She nodded, but the movement reeked of sorrow instead of surprise. "But I could actually do with less magic in my life."

"I wanted to tell you, but I couldn't find you anywhere. I figured you just didn't want to see me. Or that..."

The disappointment spread from her eyes as her shoulders slumped and she dropped her head to her chest. "I betrayed you to my father."

I didn't answer. I didn't need to. She knew my words before I needed to say them, but from her mouth, they sounded more eloquent and damning. She breathed deep, a heaviness building in the rise and fall of her chest before she dared to look up again.

"But I didn't. I wouldn't do that."

Her glassy stare punched straight into my gut and I struggled to stand. Less than inches between our toes on the floor but miles between my heart and hers.

"I didn't know everything. I knew my father had issues with the Aldrics, but I assumed those problems were ancient history. He's not really a bad man, Fallon. I brought you to him to help. To try to make things right, for both of you."

Her arms quivered as the shame bled through her guilty gaze. I should have been furious. I should have turned and stormed back out, taking Edwin down and relishing in the pain it would cause. But my vengeance didn't matter. Watching her hurt broke pieces inside my soul I never knew existed. Never felt before. I wrapped my arm around her shoulder and pulled her to my chest. She melted into my arms as if it were her place. That she belonged there.

"I'm so sorry. I didn't know." Her words muffled against my skin. "I left because I was upset, but then my father said you'd gone missing and thought I'd helped you hide so he tossed me in here. I tried to warn you, but I haven't been able to escape."

I rested my chin upon her head and inhaled this smell of her. Wildflowers in the wind, free and uncompromised. "I believe you. And I'm so sorry for everything that happened."

She wiped her eyes with her fist and pulled back. "What?"

"I should've kissed you. I wanted to kiss you. So many times, but I..."

That was the moment. The one to tell her exactly how I felt, but all my emotions swam through my bloodstream instead of formulating into words. Slippery fish who refused to be caught.

She slipped her index finger over my lips as she held my gaze with her soft eyes. "Let's get out of here first."

A loud thundering clap pounded behind us. I whirled around and stood in front of Veda, shielding her from the door.

“Very sweet, Your Majesty,” Edwin said, my father’s golden crown nestled in his dark hair. “But I suggest you stay far away from my daughter.”

Veda maneuvered around me, slick and quick like a fox. “You don’t decide my life.”

“That’s where you’re wrong. As King of Aboria, I decide everyone’s lives. And right now, I think the treasonous prince should die.”

Veda gripped my bicep and we slunk back further into the room, but there was no escape. The tower had one way in and one way out unless you were stupid enough to jump from the window to your death.

“Guards,” Edwin yelled.

Two of them appeared in the doorway, swords drawn as they raced toward us. Each one grabbed a wrist and twisted them together behind my back.

“No,” Veda screamed and raced at her father, pummeling him with her fists.

“Save your energy, dear. I’ll deal with you later.” He swatted her aside like a gnat then paraded out of the tower. The guards nudged me forward, one kicking behind my thigh to get my defiant legs moving.

I glanced over my shoulder as Veda’s tears tumbled down her red cheeks. “I’m sorry.”

The guards pushed harder on my back and pain shot through my spine as they led me out into the hall. The tower doors slammed shut behind us. I cringed. I’d blown my chance.

They pushed me down the stairs and through the rest of the hallways. The servants stopped their tasks and stared as the guards marched me through my own home like a felon. I fixed my eyes on the crown atop Edwin’s head as he bobbed along in front of us. I pictured ripping it from his skull and using it as a noose. Watching his last breath wane as a stillness fell over his treacherous body. A heinous act the kingdom would be better for. That might be worth dirtying my hands to carry out.

"Let me go," a voice shouted as we descended the grand staircase into the foyer.

"Mom," I yelled as I squirmed in my captor's grip.

She fought harder to free herself. "Fallon!"

The guard behind her pulled his blade and held it near her throat until she stopped moving. Instead, she rose up on her toes and stared him down with all the tenacity she had left.

"Don't ever pull a sword unless you have the guts to use it," she spat.

I lunged after Edwin, the skin on my wrist burning against the guard's hold. "What have you done to my mother?"

"We caught her lurking around just outside the castle grounds. You don't think we didn't have people watching for that massive bird, did you?" He lowered his forehead and let out a jovial laugh that echoed through the halls and bounced back even more evil then how it left. "I'm still not sure how you managed to get into the castle, but I will figure it out. Not like it will matter much where you're going."

The guards pushed me along and down the hallway as my mother fought against her own guards just in front. These fools would be executed for treating their queen in such a rough way. But as they shoved her down the hall, I tried to remember that Edwin was the villain here, not the guards. Instead, I bit my cheek and tasted blood, craving someone else's.

We filed down the narrow stone steps under the castle. No light penetrated the walls. The dank musty smell seeped into my clothes. We rarely used the dungeon, or at least I didn't think we did. My father's rule had been a peaceful one and real criminals were not kept here. That also meant, that no one would be able to hear us scream.

The steps beneath my feet disappeared into the inky black with no lanterns to light our way. The guards shuffled us deeper, as if from memory, between hallways until the high-pitched screech of long forgotten hinges echoed through the cavern.

"In you go," one of the guards said as they pushed my mother forward and she yelped in the dark.

My guards chucked me forward and released my hands. I skipped forward as my balance wavered and my toe smashed against the stone floor. An empty weightless bubble rose in my stomach as my body fell forward. The door slammed shut behind me as the lock clinked shut. I reached into the dark to cushion my fall. My head bobbed. Too close. The smack of my skull against stone pierced my eardrums. Sounds muffled and disappeared. My thoughts drifted away. Lost in the ether.

Then just dark.

Nothing.

Sleep.

12TH JUNE

My head ached. I rolled onto my back and grabbed my forehead waiting for the pain to cease. A checker-sized lump had erupted just below my hairline and it shot sparks of agony through my limbs if my hand even grazed it. No light. No heat. Just the endless dungeon and the soft cadence of a light hum. The tune seemed familiar, the heights and valleys registering somewhere in my broken head. Maybe a song I remembered as a boy, or maybe just a dream I'd had once upon a time. Maybe I was still dreaming?

I groaned and pulled myself to sitting, but waves of dizziness pounded at me, saved only because I couldn't see anything to tell if the world was spinning.

"You're awake." My mother's voice whispered.

"Barely. My brain feels like it might explode."

Her gentle hand pat my arm and kept tapping around until she found my face. "I'm sorry, but there's no time to rest. If we don't get out of here soon, we may never get another chance. I heard the guards talking about an execution, and I'm not going to sit and wait to see if it's ours."

Execution. Everything Edwin ever wanted, the prince and the queen given up for treason and then he'd have the throne all to himself.

"But how are we going to do that. I can't even see my own hands, I'm not sure I'd be able to fight my way out when I don't know what I'm looking for."

"That is something I can help with. Do you remember the rhyme we told you as a boy? The one to open the secret passage in the library?"

I nodded, pain pulsing through my head for nothing as she couldn't see me anyway. "Yes, you sang it to me every night for years."

"Good. We'll need to use it to get out of this place. A dungeon is always a dangerous place for a king to be so they connected the hidden passageway to the block of cells, except you need to know the combination to open the door."

She felt for my hand and gripped it tight then coaxed me to my feet. I stuck out my free arm and held the wall beside me to keep from falling over.

Three Aborian maidens fair,
with silvery voices and golden hair.
Wandered into the wood one day,
left the path and lost their way.
They met a group of goblins five,
then only two maidens came out alive.

She swayed back and forth as she followed the cryptic directions. When she finished, a soft clunk echoed through the cell.

"This way," she said and pulled me through the door.

I pushed it closed behind me and took a deep breath before following my mother up the stairs. We turned and weaved several times, the motion threatening to bring up my lunch but eventually, the steps felt familiar and a small spark of light appeared at the end of the path, growing brighter as we approached. Blankets of green leaves lay ahead. We'd made it.

We exited the cave into the forest and I crumpled to the ground, the pain in my head still not cured by freedom. My mother gasped and plunked down beside me, her hand splayed out just below her throat as her chest heaved.

"They took Alizeh, so we won't be able to call her," she said between her labored breaths.

A sickening sharp jolt jabbed at my stomach. Edwin better not hurt her. She'd helped me so much, and I'd let her fall prey to that madman. He'd captured virtually everyone in my life that mattered—the ones that were left anyway. Each one a trophy to dangle over my head and force me into line or to my own death. My limbs vibrated, the black thoughts dripping like poison into my bloodstream and coursing through my muscles. An image of Veda locked in the tower flashed through my brain accompanied by a sharp stab of pain in my skull. The gorgeous spark of fight still left in her eyes after all that she'd been through, that defending me had forced upon her. And that night in the tavern she said she thought she loved me. Could it still be true?

I smashed my fist into the ground and twisted my knuckles deep down in the dirt, reveling in the pain as pebbles scratched and tore my flesh.

Mom rubbed her hand across my shoulder blade,

her face trying to remain resigned, but the desperation cracked the facade and exposed her fear around the edges of her false calm. “We’re going to need some help. Hopefully, Edwin hasn’t spelled any of the other cities or the border guards. We can slip into Oz and beg for military assistance.”

“That voyage will take days, maybe even weeks without any supplies or a way to travel without being seen. We don’t have that kind of time. Edwin’s power will be too strong by then, and he’s always one step ahead of us.”

She dropped her hands in her lap and stared at her fingers as she twined them around themselves. “We don’t have much choice. We can’t overthrow him if we can’t get in the castle.”

“But we can get into the castle. I can disguise my face again. We can try again.”

“And last time you were captured. Don’t be foolish, Fallon. This isn’t a time to be proud.”

I leaped to my feet and paced the small patch of ground between my mother and the trees. The damp lushness of the forest wrapped around me, a blanket constricting tighter as my thoughts raced a million miles per second through my mind.

“Edwin has been inviting the neighboring nations to court. Delegates from The Forge were here just a few days ago. Who knows how far his influence has already spread? We’ll have to do something ourselves.”

Mom cast her stare up at me as the moonlight sparkled in her watery haze and clouded her vision. “Then we don’t have any resources left. No allies here. I’m afraid we might never regain the castle, but at least we can make it out of here with our lives.”

“No. I refuse to let that happen.” My footsteps

quickened, crushing the few blades of green grass that forced their way through the dirt and managed to grow.

There had to a way out of this. A way that wouldn't kill us all. Leaves rustled in the late-night breeze. Secrets whispered on the wind from the creatures hiding deep in the trees, or maybe just the voices in my head of everyone Edwin had hurt begging me to do something—to save them.

"C'mon." I halted my pacing and held my hand out to my mother. As soon as her delicate skin brushed mine I swooped her to her feet. "Help might be closer than we think."

I glanced down towards the sleeping city as we broke through the woods onto the main pathway. A few streetlamps still glowed in the darkness, but otherwise, it lay still, patiently waiting for the dawn. This was my city. My home. Edwin couldn't have those people. I wouldn't let him.

Branches crackled under our feet as we ran under the canopy of leaves and night, zigging and zagging deeper into the forest.

"Where are we going, Fallon? We'll get lost in here," Mom called from behind me, her voice unsteady as she gasped for air.

I looked back over my shoulder at the worry spidering over her face. "Trust me. We don't have many other options left."

My nose perked up as the familiar smell I'd been searching for wafted toward us. I pushed my legs faster as the strain burned in my calves. Ahead, the clouds of dainty white petals kissed the treetops and dusted their ends like winter snow. I trudged on further until the flowers surrounded us. I closed my eyes and inhaled. Memories flickered like sparking candlelight.

The intoxicating scent. The humidity of the greenery cloaking my skin. The gentle sound of the wind as it whisked through the forest and across my cheeks. This had to be the place.

I opened my eyes and spun around, letting my feet remember their steps and go off the path into the thicker brush.

"Come back here," Mom called from the path, but I couldn't stop.

She followed behind me, her irritated groans growing louder as she started to catch up through the denser bushes. The moon disappeared from above us, casting us into the shadows. In the distance, a wolf howled. Hungry. A shiver shot through my spine as my feet sped up, plunging us even deeper.

Soon the twisted branches of the ancient banyan tree spread out gnarled in front of us. A slight relief washed through me but it didn't cleanse all the fear bubbling through my veins. Better to be cautious anyway. I knelt down. An arced row of bulbous mushrooms grew near my boots in a strange circular formation. I slid my fingers over the top of the closest one. Smooth and slippery, but were they magic?

I rose again and stepped inside the circle, then raised my head toward the leaves above me. "It's me, Prince Fallon. I need to talk to the silver fairy. It's about the darkness."

Nothing responded. Nothing stirred. Just me in a circle of fungi with my mother looking on, her lips flat and thin as if she sensed I'd lost my sanity.

"You asked me to save you. Well, I accept. I'll be the hero you've been looking for. Defeat the darkness for you and whoever else needs saving, but I need you to help me first."

Still nothing.

I hung my head to my chest. Our one last hope vanished in the dark.

"I guess everyone has abandoned us." I exhaled and my shoulders fell forward as my body crumpled inward. "Better get going toward the border before Edwin finds us gone."

Mom jerked her head toward the path and held out her hand. A tiny light flickered in the tree above her head. Pink, then purple, then finally blue. It swayed for a second, then cascaded through the air like a fallen leaf, meandering until it landed on my mother's palm. She yelped and ripped her hand away, the tiny fairy suspending herself on her beating wings then flitting toward me.

I put my hand out for her to land, her tiny silver feet tickling my skin.

"You do know it's three in the morning, right? Fairies need sleep too." She slammed her hands to her hips and stuck her lip out in a pout, the drowsy look in her stare hardened into poisonous darts aimed straight at my forehead.

"Trust me, this isn't what I had planned on doing tonight either, but we're here now and we desperately need your help."

My mother inched closer until she hovered near us. Her eyes doubled in size examining the angry sprite.

"Greetings, Your Majesty," the fairy said and curtsied toward my mother. "I've never had the pleasure of meeting the mortal queen before."

"And I've never met a real fairy, at least not close enough to talk to one." She extended her index finger to the fairy. "Queen Abigail. It's a pleasure to make your acquaintance."

The silver fairy wrapped her hand around her fingertip and shook it. “I’m Natania. Ruler of the fairies in this forest. A blessing to meet you.”

My mother bowed her head.

“How come you are so much nicer to her?” I shook my hand and the fairy wobbled nearly losing her balance.

“Ah, Prince of Many Faces, if you need to ask, then you wouldn’t understand my answer anyway.” She crossed her silver arms and flexed her wings. “Now, you barge into my forest in the middle of the night demanding a favor. Please tell what you want so I can ignore you and go back to sleep.”

I held my breath and forced the story to come out even, lacking the edge of scorn and sarcasm that brewed around my tonsils. “An evil wizard cursed my father to turn into a beast and now he has taken over the castle with magical mind control and is trying to kill me and my mother so he can become king of all Aboria.”

Her saucy attitude flipped away as her arms fell back down to her sides. “Wow, that is a problem. But, this isn’t my fight. What do you think I’m going to be able to do about it?”

“I don’t know. Can’t you use some of your fairy magic to just—” I swung my free hand in a circle, “—poof away all his spells?”

She clutched her stomach and buckled over, the tinkling sound of her fairy laugh echoing through the forest. “Poof away his spells? You read too many fantasy books, my prince, and apparently really bad ones.”

“I thought fairies were these powerful beings. You can’t handle this?”

The laughter disappeared and she regained her serious stance. “Don’t test my patience, prince. I can’t do this because magic doesn’t work like that. Mind control requires a connection between the spellcaster and the target, I can't just poof that away, but if you can break the connection it'll eventually wear off."

I sighed. This was getting nowhere. "But that's the problem. We can't get him out of the castle. We've already tried and failed. If we show up there again, he'll have us beheaded for sure."

Mom leaned in closer as Natania's glow reflected off her skin. "Please help us. There aren't a lot of other options and if we don't move quickly I fear that my husband's kingdom—" she paused and patted my shoulder, "—my son's kingdom will be stolen from them and will never be the same. You don't want Edwin ruling Aboria either. If he thought you and your family were a threat he would try to wipe you out as well. I'm sure you understand, one queen to another."

"You flatter me, Your Highness, but I am no queen. However, I do understand that you will do whatever you need to if you feel that your family is being threatened. Unfortunately, that's why I need you so badly." She stomped her foot on my palm and I twitched. "The darkness threatens us all, but if this reluctant knight refuses to meet his destiny with this plague on his throne then I guess we might need to step in."

She tapped her tiny finger against her chin as she hummed a tune like chimes blowing in the wind. "Let me have time for consultation."

Her wings flickered as they vibrated and she hovered in the air then zoomed back to the protection of her tree.

"You didn't tell me about the fairies. What other secrets have you been keeping?" Mom winked and sidled in closer beside me.

I dropped my hand to my side and sighed. "Secrecy

seems to be my legacy."

Mom frowned.

"It's the truth." I shrugged and cocked my head to the side. "Let's make a promise that is we get through this, there will be no more secrets in their family. Okay?"

"Like it should've always been. Maybe if we'd all been more trusting we wouldn't be in this situation now."

Lights flickered in the treetops. Every color of the rainbow blinked in the night like stars speaking to each other in code. Eventually, Natania's blue light grew brighter as she flew back toward us. I held out my hand again and she landed on my palm, the last glint of shimmer falling from her wings as they closed behind her.

"Now, prince, my family and I have discussed the issue and we are willing to provide assistance, however, it is on the condition that we have your word about stopping the darkness."

"Of course," I nodded. "Anything."

Natania wagged a silver finger in my face. "Oh, be careful how you wield your words. Lesser creatures would take advantage of your desperation."

Then she clamped her thumb and forefinger between her lips and let out a high-pitched whistle. The wolf howled again in response and I shivered. Natania toppled over onto her behind.

She swept her rose gold locks out of her face and dusted off her dress as she stood back up. "Easy now. A hero must have stronger nerves than that. Besides, do you honestly think I can control the wolves? They respond to no one but their alphas."

The skin on my cheeks warmed, fortunately, hidden by the cloak of night to avoid more ridicule. A pair of green and yellow lights flitted toward us, wavering awkwardly up and down in their flight. As they flew closer, a small purple sack came into view, the contents weighing the two fairies down. My mother put out her hands and they both landed there, then dropped to their knees, huffing and puffing.

"Well, aren't you two darling?" Mom said, her face illuminated in the dark by their light.

The yellow fairy stood and grabbed the edges of her short dress to give a polite curtsy, while the green one bowed at the waist instead. "An honor to meet you, my queen," they greeted in unison.

"What is in the bag?" I asked.

Natania flitted over to my mother's hand and pulled the gold string on the sack. She stretched up on her tiptoes and peeked inside, then nodded to her helpers with a warm smile. They both saluted in response then burst into the sky, disappearing almost instantly in the treetops.

"This—" Natania swiped her hand into the sack and pulled out a handful of silver flecks, letting them cascade from her hand back into the bag, "—is fairy dust. Traveler's dust to be exact. When someone causes trouble in our forest we use it to send them far away. The bigger the dose the farther they go and the longer they stay lost before they can start making their way home."

"Do you have a bigger bag? I need Edwin as far away from here as I can get."

Natania flitted back up in front of my face and kicked the tip of my nose. "Don't be so flippant. A fairy handful of traveler's dust can lose someone for a week. A bag that size will send your enemies so far they may never find their way home."

I glanced over at my mother's open hands. That

much firepower in such a tiny bag. Impressive. And exactly what we needed.

She snapped her fingers drawing my attention back. “But it’s also all we’ve got left, so you’ll only get one chance. We can make more, but it will take months and it doesn’t sound like you have that much time.”

“We don’t.” I snatched the bag from my mother’s hands and shoved it in my pocket.

“Easy now, are you always so careless with weapons?”

I shrugged. “Probably.”

Natania scoffed then flew further away so her blue light tinged the dark forest around her. She turned to my mother. “Thank you for the visit, Your Majesty. You are welcome in our forest anytime, but hopefully, next time will be under less precarious circumstances.” Then flipped to me, her glare hardening as she thrust her hands on her hips. “And you. Be careful with the traveler’s dust and make sure you’ve locked down your mark before you use it.”

She fluttered higher in the sky until she became nothing more than a flashing light, then stopped. “And one more thing, Prince Fallon. Remember your promise to the fairies. To save the world from the darkness. We are all counting on you.”

Her light extinguished leaving us both in the dark as the shadows crept in again.

“Give me the bag,” Mom said as she reached for my coat pocket.

I pivoted away, just out of her grasp. “No. Why would I do that?”

“Stop being stubborn. You heard Natania. We only get one shot at this and then we’re done. If something goes wrong, you need to be around to rule Aboria. I’ll have to be the one to get rid of Edwin.”

She hiked her skirt to her knees and stormed through the brush toward the main path. I rushed behind her, careful not to step on the mushrooms and tripping on exposed roots. I caught her shoulder and spun her around.

"And how do you expect to get into the castle? If anyone sees you, it will be about five seconds before you end up back in the dungeon...or worse. At least I can disguise myself."

She stopped rushing and her shoulders dropped, her posture caving in and making her look small.

"You know I'm right." I stepped in front of her and held out my hand. "Besides, between me, you, and Dad, we all know you're the one most fit to rule."

"But it will never be my throne." She stretched her head back toward the sky, her breath puffing heavy in the air. "And what if he kills you. I'll never forgive myself."

"Then I guess I'll have to not die." I tugged at the bag and her fingers relaxed their grip. Giving up. Knowing she'd never win this argument even though she'd probably come up with ten other rebuttals to try. The thin slivers of white moonlight slid into the lines of worry cutting around her eyes. Even in sadness, her beauty transcended. She'd carried the weight of my family's secrets and still held her head high with a welcoming smile across her lips. No castle guard or wandering knight was half as strong as my mother and her wild heart. It may be true that I'd been adopted, but I hoped I'd grow up to be just like her.

I wrapped my arms around her and her head fell against my shoulder. "I'm going to survive this and we're going to be a family again."

"I hope so." She squeezed around my ribs so tight

my breath stayed trapped in my lungs. "You know I don't feel okay with any of this, right?"

"I do. But I also know that this is the only way. That I need to do this for all of us."

I wriggled out of her grip and looked back into the darker part of the forest as my mother's stare seemed heavier and more frightening. "You can't stay here either. Head into the city and go to Kalmin's house. Tell him I sent you to hide out there and he will keep you safe. Just stick to the shadows until you find him."

"You trust him, Kalmin?"

I took a deep breath. "Yeah." I had to. I didn't have any other options left.

"And then what? I can't just hide out forever. Edwin will eventually spread his influence to the people if he hasn't already."

I took her hand and clutched her soft fingers tight. "Give me a day. If you don't hear from me by tomorrow morning, run."

13TH JUNE

I fought to keep my eyes open as my head bobbed toward my chest again. Over twenty-four hours with no sleep weighed on the back of my neck and my body begged to rest. But dreams would come much easier when I claimed victory over the nightmare posing as a king.

Darkness blanketed the dank, narrow cave that led to the secret entrance to the castle. I considered curling up on the ground for a few glorious moments, just to get my strength back, except, if I missed my chance one may never come again. Edwin had to know by now that my mother and I had escaped the dungeon. He'd probably trotted down the stone steps first thing this morning to rub in our capture, just to find our cell empty. I pictured the explosive shades of rage as he probably slammed the dungeon door shut and ripped through the nearest guard that he could find. Sometime in the afternoon thick, heavy footsteps trampled through the forest, as deep male voices ricocheted off the trees. They'd been looking for us. They wouldn't stop until my mother and I were both dead. No longer a threat to Edwin and his potential reign. I cringed every time a twig snapped or a bush rustled in the wind, hoping that I wouldn't end this life in a musty cavern of rock.

After nightfall, the stomping stopped. The wind howled, or at least I convinced myself it was just the wind. The faint sliver of moonlight that appeared near the entrance of the cave had tip-toed across the dirt as it counted down the hours. Almost time.

I patted the pocket of my coat and checked for the pouch of fairy dust for the millionth time. Still there. At least Natania and her family hadn't chosen to trick me, or at least not yet.

My legs ached as I pushed off the ground and a sharp stiffness stung in my thighs from sitting all day. I muffled a groan and staggered to the entrance then peeked out carefully into the night. Nothing seemed to move outside the cave except for a few leaves too high for humans to disturb. Slowly, quietly, I emerged and took a sharp right heading farther away from the main path until I reached a small creek running down the forested hill.

I dropped to my knees and scooped the cool clear water in my hands then splashed it on my face. A reflection of who I was stared back through the ripples and the bluish light of the moon. I'd changed since the last time I'd looked at myself in the mirror. The angled cheekbones had hardened with anger and betrayal as deep lines of worry cut across my forehead. A few stray locks of my unkempt hair flopped across my brow but did little to hide the wear and tear on my expression. Except, each one of these new changes grew from strength. From taking charge and responsibility for my kingdom. Like chips and cracks in cobblestone, only enhancing their allure while holding strong under everyone's feet. Just a few weeks ago I would've cried at such deformity, but now I knew what every mark stood for and once I took Edwin down each one would be a source of pride, like each jewel in my father's crown. My crown.

I leaned my head back and closed my eyes letting the tingle surge from the top of my head to the soles of my feet. I looked back into the creek and gasped. The shifty menacing eyes. The thick jaw with its traitorous smile. The thin scar cutting through my left eyebrow. Perfect. An exact match to Edwin Macario, except without his cold, black heart.

Patting my coat pocket again, I rushed back to the cave and slipped inside rushing to the broken stone stairs that led me home. My brain focused on the task at hand as it ran over the plan's steps one by one in a vicious loop, while my feet guided me to my mother's library from muscle memory.

I pulled open the bookshelf door and crept into the silence, the skylight the only guide for me to follow. On my first step, I stumbled and teetered forward, but grabbed onto the shelf to avoid falling. A book. No, a pile of books. Tons of them littered on the floor ripped from their perfectly sorted rows and tossed aside like dirty handkerchiefs. I scooped one from the floor and ran my fingers along the letter spine. Each embossed letter stamped hard on my heart. Mom would be devastated, but if I did this right she would have an eternity to fix it. A new fire stoked in my soul and I cast the book onto my mother's desk as I headed out the door.

~

Silence filled the corridors. Each one empty save the occasional servant who bowed with reverence then scurried quick in the opposite direction. I crossed my hands behind my back and tried to hurry but still maintain a slow nonchalant pace. No need to alarm anyone, at least not yet.

On occasion, I'd catch a glimpse of myself in a hall mirror, except Edwin's eyes would look back. A guard caught me flinching at my own reflection and gave me a curious narrowed stare, but I held my head higher and he moved on.

As I neared the guest suite, my stomach twisted with every step. I slid my hand in my coat pocket gripping the fairy dust in my fist. One shot, that's all they gave me, and hopefully, that's all I would need.

I gripped the door handle and turned it slow as my head turned back to search the empty hall behind me. No light escaped through the crack between the door and the frame so I edged farther into the room. The air lay still. No breath. No sound, as I crept near the bedside. The thick silk comforter remained untouched from the last time a servant had cleaned in here. No personal objects lay on the dresser. No dirty clothes strewn on the floor. No sign of Edwin at all.

"Can I help you find something, sir?"

I jumped and emitted scared yelp as Griswold entered the room, his hands gently crossed in front of him and his know-it-all stare analyzing my every move.

I cleared my throat and forced my voice deeper.

"Griswold, don't ever sneak up on me like that."

He bowed his head at the harsh tone, enough that he couldn't see me cringe. Even though Edwin still had him under his spell, the empty hollow in my heart where he lived ached deep in my chest.

"Of course, sir. I just saw the door open and wanted to make sure no one was trespassing where they shouldn't be."

"Not to worry." I patted him on the back and he lurched forward. "I was just looking for something but I guess it's not here."

"The staff should've taken everything from this room when you moved to the king's chambers. If you'd like I can have someone re-search this room in the morning?"

The king's chambers? Of course, he'd be that arrogant. I'd probably barely left the grounds before they started moving his things.

"No need, my good man. I'm sure I just misplaced it."

Griswold narrowed his stare and raised the lantern near to his face as he scanned me over from brow to boots. "Are you feeling all right, Your Highness?"

I clenched my fists at my sides and fought the rage bubbling in my blood from showing across my cheeks. No one should ever refer to that villain as a royal.

"I'm fine. Just having a bit of trouble sleeping, that's all." I stretched my arms out and up as the yawn came naturally and on cue. "I think I'll head off to bed and look again tomorrow."

He nodded, but his sharp suspicion still pierced my flesh. He stepped aside and swept the lantern out to the side to guide me down the hall. "Would you like me to send up some warm milk or maybe some brandy to help you get some rest?"

"Thank you, but I think I'll stop by the kitchen on my way up. I'm sure you have plenty of work to keep you busy." I clasped my hands behind my back and paraded past him. "Goodnight, Griswold."

As soon as I hit the corner, I doubled my pace and headed for the grand staircase before anyone else could see me. My fraudulent face likely had him convinced, but his keen loyalty and years of silent observation made Griswold the most lethal enemy in games of deceit. He'd seen through almost every lie I'd ever told, even when my parents had fallen for my stories, but never overstepped his place. Except now he had a new master. One who needed me dead.

Up I ran, taking the steps two at a time and twisting through the hall until I reached the west wing. What little noise remained fell away as I turned into the dark stone corridor.

I gripped the pouch of traveler's dust in my pocket, then swallowed the rest of my fear. I crept down the hallway, each step slow and steady so no one came running. The lion statue guarding the secret passage loomed over my head. The bared teeth and readied claws dripped in shadow and turned the symbol of my family's pride into a thing of nightmares. An omen, perhaps. Or maybe just my brain warning me to turn back.

At the outer door, I gripped the handle and pushed in. A whiny creak echoed through the corridor and I froze. My heart thumped loud, almost louder than the door. I glanced back over my shoulder, but no one lurked behind me. Safe, at least for now. I gripped the door frame and breathed slow until my nerves settled again.

I pushed the door the rest of the way open and

slipped into the dark outer chamber. A large mirror stood across from me, and in the dark, it twisted the reflection of Edwin's face on my bones. Pale and deathly. A ghost or a phantom with an evil sneer. I forced my eyes away and continued deeper into the bedroom. The moon illuminated the far wall as it beamed through the grand window and cast a spotlight on my father's four-poster bed. A large lump rested in the middle of the mattress, tangled in the expensive silk sheets and hand-embroidered duvets.

Thick, warm saliva pooled in my mouth. I held the dust in my pocket as I tried to keep focused on my task, even though my mind wandered to the sword mounted over my father's mantle and the pure joy that plunging it through Edwin's heartless chest might bring. Except, what would that make me? The short-lived pleasure would not be worth knowing that I would be the murderer that even Edwin had yet to become.

I hovered beside the bed, one hand on my magic weapon the other gripping the edge of the duvet. The fairies gave no instructions, but logic seemed that the dust needed to at least hit the target's skin. Besides, a devious part of me wanted to see the shocked look on Edwin's face when he woke to see me standing over him before he disappeared into oblivion.

My hands trembled. A few seconds. One final uncertainty coursed through my bloodstream before a smooth calmness overtook the anxiety.

I ripped the covers back.

Pillows. Nothing but fancy pillows and crumpled clothing piled high in the center of the bed. I caught the bag of traveler's dust before it fell, my other arm still moving before my brain managed to process the deception. What?

"Do you think I'm stupid enough to lie around waiting for death?" a familiar deep voice bellowed from behind me.

I whirled around and shuddered as I stood face to face with Edwin Macario. His eyes lit. Flames danced in his dark irises as the heat of the fire rose up his clenched jawline.

"How dare you insult me by wearing that mask," he shouted.

I brushed my cheek, as I remembered what I looked like and backed up a step until my calves smacked the side of the bed. "How dare you insult the people of Aboria by pretending to be their king."

"Why you hateful devil." Edwin grabbed my arm. His furious expression faded as the color drained from his face. He released his grip and recoiled, as he slammed his open hand against his chest. He staggered back several paces, his stare locked on my face. "It's you! I should've known."

He clutched his forehead and stared harder as he absorbed my features. His thoughts flickered across his face as each one fell into place. Puzzle pieces firing together to create a clearer picture.

"You know nothing," I shouted back as I maneuvered the bag between my fingers and spilled the dust into my palm.

"Oh really, Prince Fallon. That energy within you. The power pulsing in your veins. I felt it before at the temple, but I never expected you to figure out how to wield it or what it might mean. I guess I underestimated you. But I won't again."

He reared his arm back as a purple light built between his fingers.

I flinched, trapped between the bed, Edwin, and the

wall. No escape. The purple light crackled and charged. It covered Edwin's hand until it wasn't clear where his body ended and the magic began. I pitched forward to strike first but lost the draw. Edwin's arm surged toward me, the purple magic flinging from his fingertips. I tucked my head into my arm. My body tensed until my muscles ached. My brain flit through the people I'd let down. My mother. My father. Veda. Griswold.

The purple magic grew brighter. I held my breath. It slammed into my forearm.

But nothing happened.

My arm stung. No more than a bee sting. The purple light dissipated and slithered into the darkness. A nuisance rather than a pain.

"What?" Edwin yelled, but left no chance for response. He pulled his arm back again as if throwing a ball and launched another purple strike. Another sting in my shoulder. I shrugged it off as another orb of light crashed into my abdomen. Then another at my knee.

"Enough," I shouted against the onslaught.

But he didn't stop. Magic pummeled me over and over, but nothing seemed to be doing anything. Each time the light sparked the fury grew in Edwin's face. Veins throbbed in his neck and forehead as he launched attack after attack and I swatted them away. I stepped toward him and he stepped back, a dance of distance where I might for once have the lead.

I needed to get closer to hit him with the traveler's dust. I stepped closer to the fireplace. Edwin stepped back as he tossed another attack of purple lights.

With a quick pivot, I ripped the sword down from my father's mantle and extended the tip of the blade underneath Edwin's chin.

He lowered his hands and the magic fizzled out. "You

don't have the guts, kid."

He grabbed the blade between his palms and thrust it back.

I strengthened my stance and nudged the tip forward, pushing Edwin backward to maintain his grip. "You have no idea what your vendetta has done to me."

He narrowed his stare and stood taller. A game of posturing. One he had more experience with playing than I did. "I'm far more powerful than you will ever be."

"Then how come your magic fails against me? You tried to control my mind, but it didn't work. You hit me over and over again and I'm the one with your life at the end of my blade. You will not win this fight, Edwin. You will not take my kingdom."

His head rolled back as a loud, hearty laugh escaped his throat. "Your kingdom? You're not even a real part of this family. My blood runs more royal than yours ever will. You were left on a doorstep, unloved and unwanted. I have more claim to the throne than you do."

"But I won't destroy the kingdom for my own gain. Even if I were the son of the lowliest beggar, I'd still have more honor and nobility than you."

"And that my boy, is what might just be your downfall." He shoved hard on the sword blade and pushed me back.

I stumbled but quickly regained my footing. Edwin swooped his right arm in the air and snapped his fingers with a loud pop. A puff of smoke billowed in front of him. Sharp smells of strongest incense and the last of the fireplace embers clouded around burning my nostrils. I coughed into my shoulder as I forced my arm to stay steady. I rubbed the dust in my palm. A perfect distraction. Now was my chance.

I dropped the sword to my side and held up my fist. The smoke thinned. A high-pitched voice shrieked.

"Let me go," Veda screamed as she wriggled against her father's forearm wedged underneath her neck. "What are you do—"

Veda's eyes widened as she stared at me, then twisted her head up to look at her father, then me again.

"Pretty incredible isn't it?" Edwin said, as he chuckled and his arm twitched beneath his daughter's chin. "Don't you recognize your friend, dear? Why don't you show her your true face so she can see the kind of monster that you really are?"

"What are you talking about? Who is that?" she argued. "What is that?"

Her words pierced my skin and sliced a thousand cuts in my soul. What was I? Good question. One I hadn't had a chance to answer. At least not yet. I leaned my head back as the tingle flowed through my bones and changed me again. Altered me. Maybe forever.

"Fallon," Veda called. "Is that really you? How did you? I mean, what is going on here?"

"Didn't you know? Or did he keep it a secret from you?" Edwin backed toward the bedroom door as he clamped Veda tight to him. "I thought you two were closer than that. You seemed to be when I interrupted you in the tower yesterday. After all, it seems like you are the only weakness this boy has. Relationships shouldn't be built on lies. It never ends well."

I mimicked Edwin's winding path looking for a clear shot. I should've taken my chance before. I may have missed but at least I wouldn't have to risk Veda getting hurt.

"Let me go," she yelled as she scratched at her father's arm. She struck her elbow back and made contact with his stomach, but he simply flinched and kept on his escape route. The look in her eyes. The glow of fight mixed with a dark edge of fear that bled around the edges. This girl. Edwin was right, she would be my undoing, but not like this. This wasn't her battle.

A sick feeling churned in my stomach. The solution formed in my brain and its darkness poisoned the rest of my body. The wrongness of it.

I raised the sword toward Veda. Her throat quivered as she swallowed, her stare locked on the shiny, silver blade. "Weakness? That would mean I actually cared." I forced a laugh, trying my hardest to make it sound light. "Look at me. A young, rich, prince like me could replace her before she had time to slink back to her mountain. It's not my fault if everyone falls in love with me."

Tears formed in her eyes as her lower lip began to tremble. "That's not true."

Her voice wavered, each break in cadence tearing gashes in my heart.

"It was fun, but you and your family are way too complicated for me. Besides—" I cleared my throat, the words hanging on, knowing I could never take them back, "—a plain mountain girl like you could never be good enough for someone like me."

The venomous arrow hit its mark. Her arms fell as her vigor faded. Her jaw dropped open as the tears she tried to hold back rushed down her cheeks. Each small tick, each defeated motion breaking another piece of her heart and flinging it at my feet. My eyes prickled watching her in pain. Knowing I'd done this to her. Even though hurting her might be the key to saving us all, I didn't know it would wreck her this much, or that I would be too cowardly to be able to watch it. What had

I done?

Edwin's grip relaxed around her throat. "Cold, prince. Maybe we could've gotten along after all."

He tossed Veda to the ground and sprinted for the open door to the outer chamber. I glanced down at her watery face and the broken glare she cast back up. I cringed. The sword in my hands less deadly than that look.

"I'm sorry," I called as I leaped over her and after Edwin.

I clamped my hand on his shoulder at the door and whirled him around. I opened my hand and threw the traveler's dust at him. The fairy magic glittered through the air, not nearly as impressive as his purple bolts of power. And then, nothing happened. The fairies tricked me. How could I have been so stupid?

He cackled and ran down the corridor, then stopped under the lion statue.

"Guards," he yelled, his booming voice reverberating off the stone. "Such an amateur. You can't stop—"

Edwin's body shook. His limbs vibrated in the dim light as a terrified scream rose from his gut and exploded out of his mouth. "What have you done?"

A sweeping funnel of silver glitter wrapped around Edwin's feet. It spun faster and faster, around and around, as it squeezed tighter around his body. All the light in the hall sucked into the column, dying into darkness as the cyclone sped up.

The pounding of footsteps echoed at the far end of the hall as a row of guards appeared and stopped short watching the spectacle. Edwin screamed again as the magic encased his head, his pain so loud it weighed on my chest.

"Stay far away from my family and this kingdom,

Edwin," I shouted as the column undulated ahead of me.

"I will kill you for this," he shouted.

His last threat resonated through the hall as the glitter lost its brilliance, then dropped dark and colorless to the floor. No more funnel cloud. No more screams. No more Edwin.

I let out a breath as a calm rushed through me, but only for a second. Veda's muffled sobs split the sudden silence. I spun around. She stood just inside the inner chamber and leaned against the doorframe, her soft cries disconnected from her cold, marble-like scowl.

I rushed toward her. "I'm so sorry. I didn't mean any of it."

"You don't need to apologize. I shouldn't have been so stupid." She held up her hands and backed into the room, retreating from my advance step for step.

"Don't say that. You know I don't think like that. I've told you before. In the tower. I just needed to get him to let you go."

"I get it. But it doesn't matter." She wiped the back of her arm against her face, a few stray tears dropping to the floor as she tilted her head toward the window. "You were right. Every word. I brought my father into your world and almost lost you your kingdom. Maybe it would be better if we never met. Guys like you don't belong with girls like me."

A fire sparked in my blood. Her words were a match, dangerous and deadly, burning away at the one true emotion I had for anyone outside my parents. My skin flushed as my brain screeched at me to do something. Maybe I would be better off without her in my life, but it didn't mean that's what I wanted. What I needed.

"Veda, meeting you was the best thing that could've

happened. You helped me uncover the truth about who I am. You pushed me to stand up for my kingdom and be the leader I never thought I could be. Never would've been without you. You made me see things so differently in these past few weeks, and that never would've happened if you didn't tell me off at the tavern that night."

Her expression softened and she turned to me again. The moonlight cast a glow around her and glinted in her emerald eyes. Like the night on the mountain. Just her and me. The most like myself I'd felt in my entire life. With tear-stained cheeks and messy hair, torn clothes, and a crooked grin, Veda was the most beautiful girl I'd ever seen.

I held up my hand and slowly moved closer, and this time she didn't pull away. "Veda. If you ignore everything else, that's fine, but please believe me when I tell you that I love—"

Veda flashed in front of me. Here one second then gone the next. Once. Twice.

"What's happening?" She reached for my hand.

My fingers slid through her palm.

She flashed again.

"Veda!" I yelled.

Then she disappeared.

14TH JUNE

Sunlight splashed against my window and puddled on the large rug beside my bed. I groaned and rolled over then shielded my eyes with a soft, fluffy pillow. It couldn't be morning. Not yet. My body ached and from the dizzy sensation in my head, I felt like I'd only slept about ten minutes.

I sighed and sat up, my hand clamped against my forehead. Images rolled through my mind on a loop. The same ones since yesterday. The same ones that might haunt me forever. Edwin disappearing into a cloud of glistening silver. Veda's hand disappearing as I reached out to touch her. The empty tower room I ripped apart to try and find her. If only I'd had the chance to tell her how I felt. That I loved her.

A soft knock wrapped on the door.

“Just a minute.” I dragged myself to standing and grabbed yesterday’s clothes that still lay crumpled on the floor. I slipped on the pants and pulled open the door as I tugged my shirt over my head.

“It’s almost afternoon, Fallon. Time to wake up sleepyhead.” Mom smiled and patted my cheek as she glided into the room. She wore one of her favorite gowns. A bright shade of pink with a field of hand-embroidered flowers around the bottom of the skirt and her signature deep crimson roses stitched up the bodice. My father bought it for her in Tulis years ago, but she always stood a bit straighter and smiled wider when she wore it. Today was no exception. The worry and weariness of the past few weeks still tattooed their marks on her face, but seemed more of a memory than a reality in the morning light. As if she woke up this morning and breathed fresh air for the first time in weeks.

Her skirt whisked across the floor and she stopped in front of my large mirror to fix her long curls that had twisted over her shoulder.

She glanced at my reflection next to hers and frowned. “Is today not a better day? You defeated the wizard. You’ve won back the throne. The castle staff have fallen out of Edwin’s spell. You should be happier, my son. Grim times are still upon us, but we have already come so far.”

I wiped my face with my hands and retreated to the armchair, my head turned toward the wall so the mirror couldn’t lay my emotions bare. “I don’t know. I just can’t figure out what to do now.”

Mom laughed. A lightness I hadn’t heard from her, or anyone in weeks. “Just because you’ve conquered one battle doesn’t mean the war is over. The kingdom needs you. Your family needs you. So many people are counting on you, Fallon. Don't tell me you're bored."

"Not bored, just lost. Dad still needs to be cured. I promised the fairies I'd help them with the darkness, but I have no idea where to even start. And..." I sighed and dropped my head to my chest as I twined my fingers together in my lap.

"You don't know what to do about that Veda girl you care so much about."

"If I can even find her. I said some really awful things, but I didn't get a chance to explain. I don't know where she is and if she'll ever even speak to me again."

Mom walked over and rubbed my shoulder. "I'm sure she'll come to her senses. You're a great catch, and not just because you are a prince. I have a feeling this girl doesn't care much about that anyway."

"She doesn't."

"Then if she's smart, she'll come around. And if you're smart, you'll hold onto her if she gives you another chance."

I nodded. "Thanks, Mom."

"Of course." She headed over the window and straightened the thick curtain flanking the sides as she gazed out to the courtyard below. "Plus, even if she doesn't, you have so many things to be grateful for in this life. You have a family who loves you, a good heart, and great friends who care about you. Kalmin said he misses you, by the way."

I flinched as a twinge of pain dug into my stomach. "Yeah, I miss him too. But I'm going to work on that as well."

"You should. He's a noble young man, a bit misguided at times it sounds like, but he's trying his best. Just like everyone else. And he honestly cares about you. Good, loyal friends are worth any sacrifice."

"How did you get to be so smart?" I asked, the weight finally lifting a little bit from my shoulders.

She turned around, the light glowing around her like a fairy queen or maybe even an angel. "Always. You're just mature enough now to notice."

A low knock reverberated on the open door. Griswold stood in the doorway, his arms crossed in front of him as his body closed in taking up as little space as possible.

"Sorry to interrupt, Your Majesties, but I have news for the queen."

I leaped from the chair and pulled Griswold into a hug. He let out a tiny gasp as I held tight but otherwise stayed stick-still in my arms. "I missed you, old man."

He looked at the ground. "My apologies, sir, but I don't deserve your kindness. I have much work to do before my debt to your family is repaid."

"Don't be silly, Griswold. You were under the spell of a mad man. Had you not tipped me off to him when he first arrived we all could still be in trouble."

The old man's cheeks tinged pink, but he kept his eyes locked on the ground. "Thank you, my prince."

"You said you had a message for me?" My mother cut in front of me and gave me a glare while she shook her head.

"Yes. Captain Amir has indicated that a fleet of guards was dispatched last night to the mountain temple with a full carriage of supplies. They will be taking the royal road and should arrive by nightfall."

She clapped her hands together, a joyful smile breaking across her lips. "Thank you, Griswold. That's wonderful news."

Griswold nodded and scurried down the hall, getting away as quick as he could. He deserved so much for all he'd done. Once everything was over I would need to see what my role as king could afford to grant him.

"Are the guards bringing Dad home?"

Mom shook her head as her smile disappeared. "No. The captain and I discussed it, but it would be dangerous to move him in his current state and after so many weeks of torture. We decided to station guards in rotating shifts to watch over him and keep him comfortable while we search for a cure. It's safest for your father, for the city, and for the guards."

I frowned. Having Dad home would make this feel more of a victory, but he'd still be suffering on the side of a mountain. Comfortable, but suffering. "Do you think we'll actually find a cure?"

"Now that we know how the spell was cast we have a lot more to work with. I also plan on getting the guards to bring back what's left of Edwin's notes so that we can go through them and see what he had planned, but the first concern is your father's safety."

I crossed the room and ran my fingers over my collection. The daggers and swords from so many travels with my father that I may never get to have again.

"Would it be okay if I went to get the notes? If Alizeh will take me I could be there before the guards and keep Dad company until they arrive."

"I think he'd like that." She slipped her hand onto my bicep and leaned her head of my shoulder. "He would be so proud of you right now. You will make a great king."

I dug an apple out of my bag and tossed it into the air. "Here you go, girl."

Alizeh clucked and snapped the apple in her beak.

I pulled out another. Her gigantic eyes widened even larger as she watched my every motion while I reared my arm back and launched it into the dusky sky. Another perfect catch.

I nuzzled in close to her wing as she pulled her head down and I pet her glossy feathers. “Thank you for your help, friend. I’ll never let anyone pin you down again.”

She rubbed her head against my shoulder. Maybe she understood. Maybe she didn’t. Either way, I owed her more than I ever thought I would. After Edwin had tied her down in the stables to keep my mother and me from escaping, I wouldn’t have blamed her for not coming back to the castle, but less than two minutes from when my lips emit a whistle and called her name, she arrived in the courtyard ready for the next adventure. A true friend.

Across the mountain, the temple roof glowed in the fading light as the sky burned brighter than it should for the approaching evening. I scanned the outside of the temple and my stomach hollowed. No one lounged in the peaceful garden. No one standing on the golden stairs. No life at all.

I’d expected it, but I’d still been hopeful. I tried not to go by Veda’s cottage. Even told myself about three hundred times that I wouldn’t and only stopped when I stood on her well-worn path with my hand knocking on her door.

No one answered.

It’s as if she’d disappeared along with her father. Maybe she was bouncing around oblivion bound by the fairy’s magic to be lost for the foreseeable future. I cringed and held my arm across my gut as the pain deepened, digging into my muscles and twisting my intestines. If she ever made it back, could she ever forgive me? Should she?

My father stirred in his cage. He clung to the bars and peered over at me and Alizeh, his furry paws hanging out into freedom while his animalistic eyes watched us move.

"Looks like someone else might need something to eat too." I pet her one last time and walked across the empty field toward the cage.

The makeshift canopy I'd created still held, although the wind had tried it's best to knock it down. A few slashes, claw-like marks, scarred some of the sheets, but at least he'd stopped and didn't rip it entirely. I flipped open the top of my bag. Berries, kiwi, and chopped up melon. Still warm slices of bread handmade just this morning. Wedges of gouda, havarti, and the sharpest cheddar from the market. And, just hidden under the rest of the bounty, the chunks of the richest chocolate I could find. My father's favorite weakness.

My father licked his lips with his wide pink tongue as I presented each of the snacks and slid them between the bars on the far side of the cage. He didn't rush at me or growl. This time he seemed calmer. Not quite human, but a lot less like an animal. If better conditions helped to keep him calmer, maybe there would be hope for him yet. Especially once we found a way to break the curse. And we would. I knew it. But how long that might take, I didn't dare think about that.

I held up the chocolate last and my father's stare locked on my arm.

"Mom told me not to bring it, but you know how bad I follow directions."

I slid it beside the assortment of cheese and backed away from the bars, then rested on the ground, my knees slightly bent. My father scrambled across the cage and scooped up a paw of raspberries and crammed them in his mouth. A few of the red gems fell to the side and rolled near his feet. He groaned as he chewed and swallowed, then moved on to the bread.

"Eat up, Dad. You need to keep your strength."

He stopped chewing and collapsed off his back haunches so he sat like me on the other side of the bars. He pushed one of the stray raspberries through the cage bars and nodded his head toward me.

"Thanks, but I'm okay." A familiar feeling prickled in the corners of my eyes and my throat started to ache. I coughed, but couldn't stop the flood overtaking me. I tilted my head back and closed my eyes. Drops of water dripped on my shoulders as a cool wetness fell on my cheeks. My hands twitched to wipe the tears away, but instead, I let them run. Let the horror and the heaviness of the past few weeks drain out and maybe even wash me clean.

"Everything is going to be okay now, Dad. Edwin is gone, the kingdom is saved, and we are going to find a way to break the curse so you can come home with us. Mom will make sure of it. She's so much more amazing than I ever thought. So strong. But she needs you to get better. She needs you to come back and be there for her. And you will, I know you will."

My voice started to crack as it fought against my gasping breaths. Each word a fight to force out.

"And I need you too. I should've been better. Paid attention. But I didn't. I know now that I can do this. I can be king, but it doesn't mean I don't want you there by my side as long as I can have you. Because I miss you. I want to be able to talk to you. To ask you questions. To tell you about the most amazing girl I met and how she broke my heart and ask you how I'm supposed to make it stop hurting if she doesn't come back to me. How I'm supposed to move forward in my life when I've made so many mistakes."

Dad crept over to the side of the cage and extended his paw out toward me.

"Thanks." I laughed through the sobs. I probably looked irrational to him. A crying, gasping mess. And I was. A mess. Or that's what it felt like.

I wiped my face with my sleeve and closed my eyes to let the warm breeze help dry my cheeks. I didn't know where that all came from, but it had been building up for a while. All the worry, all the pain, and all the fear slowly piled up inside me, but with the battle for the kingdom, I didn't have the time to tear it all back down. But now, with the threat of Edwin finally over it tumbled out uninhibited and unwanted. If this was victory, why did it feel so much like a loss?

Slow breaths. I inhaled deep and exhaled until my ribs collapsed against my lungs. Over and over until I started to feel some release.

A rustling noise poked at my ears. Scuffling sounds.

I snapped my eyes open. My father paced inside his cell. He pounded the bars at every turn and paced the other way, hitting the bars again. The clanging shook me out of my own head as my father reared his head back and roared at the sky.

"What's wrong, Dad?" I crawled across the ground nearer to the cage.

Squawk! Squawk!

A flurry of bronze feathers flapped on the far end of the yard. I peeled my stare away from my father. Alizeh tore at the ground with her talons, her head arched back as she let out pained cries. Tiny bits of fluff fell like snow around her, chunks of her feathers as she fussed and stomped about.

"Alizeh," I called, but she didn't look at me. "What's going on?"

The air thickened. Heavy and dense. Humidity mixed with gelatin. Almost tangible, weighing down on my skin like I could take a knife and cut out a slimy slice. The sun hid, leaving us in shadow as the temperature plummeted on the mountaintop.

To the east, the sky darkened. Thick gray clouds swirled in the distance until they converged into a stain of black on the horizon. Bolts of lightning shot through the center of the dark mass. Electricity sizzled in the air. Alive. Volatile.

I jumped to my feet and held my hand above my eyes as I stared into the anomaly. I'd seen storms before. Days of rain and thunder, and even hurricanes on the coast, but they didn't compare. This event, this thing, sprung from nowhere. No rain or sound followed. Just swirling nothingness and streaks of light. Could it be? Was this what Veda saw when she looked off her peak toward Urbis? Was this part of the darkness? The short hairs on my arm stood on end. How did the fairies expect me to fight a power that strong? I could never do something like that alone.

My father shimmied up the bars toward the top of the cage. He let out a deep guttural roar. Panicked. Maybe scared. Alizeh squawked louder, craning her head toward him then launching into the air and flying west, her majestic wings beating so fast they blurred.

"Wait," I yelled as I waved my arms in the air and ran after her.

Her bronze body shrunk until it reduced down to only a dot then disappeared.

I slapped my arms down to my sides. "Great. Now

how am I going to get home?"

A bright green flash illuminated the sky. I whirled around as the black clouds whipped faster in their circle. Around and around, drawing in all the light left. Faster, faster, then--poof! The entire concentration of clouds vanished in a blinding spark. It jolted through the atmosphere. I blasted backward, landing on my elbows in the dirt and smashing my head on the ground.

I held my forehead against the ache and looked up. The sun reappeared. The glorious spring day spread out above me as if it never left. Pain shot down my spine. I couldn't have imagined this, could I?

"Are you all right, Your Majesty?"

Two shadows loomed overhead as guards grabbed my arms and hoisted me to my feet. Dizziness rushed over me and I stumbled but the guards held me up until the feeling passed.

"Yes. Thank you. I think I'll be fine." I shirked out of their grip and shuffled forward.

"Are you sure, sir?"

I nodded and instantly regretted it. "Which one of you is in charge of this operation?"

One of the guards pointed to a decorated guard standing near my father's cage. He neared the bars as my father growled at him from captivity. The guard didn't flinch, taking the attack with stillness and unruffled nerves.

"I'd like to speak with him," I said.

The guards headed toward the cage and sent their superior to my side.

He rushed over and stood with a perfect shoulder-width stance and his hands clasped behind his back. "How can I be of assistance, my prince? We weren't expecting anyone to be waiting here for us. Has something happened at the castle?"

"No. As far as I know, the castle is fine. However, I wanted—"

I looked at the man standing before me. The short trimmed hair. The all-business expression. Ready to do my family's bidding without question. He'd likely been a pawn in Edwin's game and then passed back to me as if his life was merely a product to be bought or sold. And until now, I didn't even care. But maybe the end of Edwin's wave of terror could be the beginning of something better.

I extended my hand. "May I ask your name?"

His brow furrowed as if I'd presented the question in a foreign language. "My name, sir?"

"Yes, my family is asking you to protect my father and I realized I don't even know who you are. I'd like to change that."

I pushed my hand closer to him.

He looked at it strangely, then took it and shook firmly. "It's Merrick, sir. I've been a guard in your service for six years."

Six years and we'd only just met. Awful. "Well, Merrick, did you and your crew see anything unusual on your way up the mountain?"

He nodded. "A severe-looking storm was brewing in the east but it looks like it may have passed."

So I wasn't imagining it. Maybe it was only just a storm but the uneasy feeling that spread through my gut disagreed.

"And tell me, you hear things in the castle. In the city. Right?"

"What do you mean, sir?"

"Have you ever heard of anyone talking about something called 'the darkness'?" I leaned closer.

"Something evil perhaps?"

Merrick grimaced but remained steady on his feet. "No, sir. If there was something of concern I would report it to my captain. Is there any reason to believe that I've kept something from you?"

"No." I swiped my hand through the air and stepped back to give him more room to breathe. "I didn't expect that you would know, I guess I was just being hopeful. Thank you anyway."

I tapped him on the shoulder and walked toward the cage. Guards were already pulling out trunks of supplies and resting them around the outside of the cell as my father taunted them with his vicious paws. One guard shuddered and tripped over his own feet sending him flying to the ground.

I gave him my hand. "He's not dangerous if you treat him with respect. He's just scared, as I'm sure you would be if someone had you trapped like an animal. It's still your king in there, and I expect that he will be treated as such."

"Yes, sir," the guard replied as he clambered to his feet but chose to put distance between himself and the cage.

Merrick appeared at my side. "We will do our very best to make him comfortable, Your Majesty. The queen has been very particular in her directions and we will serve them to the letter."

"I appreciate that." I glanced up into the beautiful sunlit sky, still surprised at how quickly it had changed. "If I can get my friend to return I will get out of your way. Hopefully, the next time we see each other will be under better circumstances."

"Yes, sir." Merrick nodded as he assumed his militant stance again. "However, before you go, I haven't heard anything about a 'darkness' but there have been sightings of a few new faces hanging around in Mosa. Maybe they know of what you speak."

"Very well, Merrick. Thank you for that information."

I wandered near the edge of the peak and whistled for Alizeh. Her bronze body shone in the afternoon glow as she appeared over the clouds. A trustworthy companion.

But as I waited for her to land, my mind picked at Merrick's words. New faces in Mosa? With it nearly summer it could just be travelers passing through, nothing to be concerned about. But for some reason, the thought brewed a new storm, except this one raged in my head as lightning struck in my brain and warned me to proceed with caution.

15TH JUNE

I enveloped my fist in my right hand and pressed hard until my knuckles released with a crack that itched through my bones. I swapped hands and cracked again reveling in the relief that bordered on pain. Glancing at the door again, I paced the edge of the crimson and gold woven rug that lined the foyer stone floor. I shouldn't be nervous, but my feet refused to stay still while I waited.

"Are you expecting another invasion, my son?"

My mother descended the grand staircase and paused five or six steps from the floor. Her midnight-colored gown flowed around her as the silver filigree-stitched stars transformed a simple dress into the night sky.

"No, not today. Kalmin is coming over."

She laughed, the cheerful sound filling the foyer. “Well, that’s nothing to stress over. You boys have been friends for years, I’m sure whatever has transpired between you can be put in the past.”

“I hope so.” Except I wasn’t totally sure. Things had gone wrong for a lot longer than I initially thought. Not only did I need to make up for the things I knew I’d done, but there could also be a lot more I didn’t even know about yet. But it would be worth it. I knew it would. The time I’d spent lonely and isolated in the castle, I swore I’d never leave myself in that position again if I ever surfaced. It’s true, I could start over and look for new companions, but things with Kalmin seemed unfinished. Years of time and commitment to each other didn’t simply disappear overnight and salvaging that would be easier than losing him. Besides, I didn’t want anyone new in my life. I wanted him.

My feet twitched and I started my back and forth stroll again.

“I’m sure everything will be fine. Kalmin is a smart boy and he will make the right choice.”

“And what if the right choice is to stay far away from the poison of this family? A cursed king, an adopted prince with powers he doesn’t understand. It’s a lot for someone to have to absorb and still want to be around.”

My mother’s charming smile slid into a frown as she gripped the banister tighter, her knuckles growing whiter from the pressure. “Fallon Xavier Aldric, don’t ever let me hear words like that out of your mouth again. Our family has its problems but we love each other beyond all else. No matter what we go through, no matter what happens, we are still the same kind, generous, and loving people we always were. If your friend can’t see that then maybe you should start looking for someone smarter to spend your time with."

I inhaled, breathing in her words then letting them mingle and swim through my blood. How could she still hold so much faith after all she'd been through? But if she could do it, then surely so could I.

Just then the rumble of the entrance doors jerked me out of my own head. Daylight poured into the foyer outlining Kalmin as he stood on the threshold. He'd dressed up for the occasion. A long hunter green jacket hung to his knees with a collection of detailed silver buttons down the front. The crispest white dress shirt sat underneath, tight around his neck and looking horribly uncomfortable. But, his face appeared like stone, unreadable and difficult to break.

"You came," I said.

Neither one of us moved from our positions, either unsure or both of us feeling the need to stand their ground.

"Yeah, I did." The whisper of a smile slipped across his face. "Besides, when would I ever get an invitation to the castle presented by four fully armed guards? I figured I should probably make the trip."

"Well, I'm glad you came."

"Yes, it's a pleasure to have you in our home once again, Kalmin. I still need to find a way to repay you for providing me shelter through this whole ordeal." My mother's voice rang behind me, but I kept staring forward, still unable to move.

Kalmin took a step and bent down on his knee, his left arm sweeping across his chest. "My apologies, Your Majesty, I didn't notice you standing there. Forgive my rudeness."

"Oh hush, my boy. And stand up, you'll ruin your trousers. You are a friend to the crown and will be treated as such unless you give us reason otherwise."

"Thank you." He cast his stare to his shoes while he fingered his embroidered jacket cuff. "But, this time I intend to stay in the prince's favor as long as he'll have me."

A slight redness crested Kalmin's cheeks, likely the same shade growing on my own.

"I'd like that very much."

Kalmin took the last few steps into the castle. The guards quickly slammed the doors shut on his heels. Black dots speckled through my vision as the sun disappeared and stopped blaring into my eyes.

I swept my arm to the left and pivoted out of the way. "Should we head to the drawing room? I've already arranged for the kitchen to make your favorite apple tarts. You still like those, right?"

"Course. And if I remember correctly, the castle makes the best ones in the kingdom." He licked his lower lip and I chuckled.

"Still pliable with food and drink? I guess some things always remain the same."

He laughed and the sound destroyed the remaining tension in the room. "Why not? They are great things to surrender for."

My mother scurried down the rest of the staircase and whirled between us. "That's a nice idea, Fallon, but it's such a lovely day outside. Why don't I tell the kitchen to hold off on the pastries and you two head out for a while? Enjoy the beautiful weather and then come back here later. These cold stone walls will never beat a day in the sun."

Kalmin shrugged. "I heard they repaired the chess set in the square. That is if you don't mind losing in public?"

"I could be interested in a few games. But I doubt I'll be the one losing."

Kalmin smiled at the challenge and my shoulders relaxed, the tension of my rigid posture finally able to release.

My mother clapped her hands, a little too delighted about plans she had no part of. "Splendid. I'll tell the kitchen to expect you later."

She let out a tiny squeal, then disappeared across the foyer and down the hall.

"It sounds like she really wants to be rid of us," I said.

"It could be worse."

Yes, it definitely could be. Besides, a day out of the castle without some sort of nefarious mission would be a pleasant change of pace.

"Thank you for coming." I extended my hand and Kalmin shook it roughly.

"I missed you, Falls."

"I missed you too."

My mother was right, as always, it was a beautiful day to be outside. The sun shone its golden rays illuminating the city while a subtle breeze wafted through the streets to keep from being too warm and sweaty. It's as if she'd commanded this day to arrive and it did.

Reporters swarmed by the gate. Much less than over the recent weeks, but still fascinated to know about life behind the castle walls. Except, they'd never really have the full story. I paused and smiled allowing a few photos before ushering Kalmin over the bridge and into the city proper. Fighting the attention would only attract more and although I wished they'd all find something else to fuel their excitement, it was time I accepted it. I needed to stop hiding away from my obligations and show the people the true ruler I could be. That maybe I really did have potential.

The odd looks continued as we strolled the cobblestone streets, but I held my head high, smiling and nodding to anyone who cast a glance our way.

"So, you're really king, aren't you?" Kalmin asked as we slowed in front of the bakery, both of us inhaling the mouth-watering scent of fresh muffins floating out the open door.

"For now." I slowed down, letting myself revel in the lingering smell a bit longer. Banana, or maybe raspberry? "I'm still hopeful that they will find a cure for my father, but if the kingdom needs me, then I guess that's what I have to be."

Kalmin laughed and slapped me on the back. "Well son of a pixie, Falls. You might have finally grown up."

"Really? And where does that leave you?"

"Still trying—" His mischievous lips curled into a smile, but the joy in his eyes seemed stilted. "—but I'll get there."

He crossed his arms behind him and marched beside me, his posture straighter as if being around me suddenly required more pomp and circumstance. I cringed. If I wanted another advisor, I'd add another to the Council, but maybe things would take longer to repair between us than I thought.

"Hopefully, not *too* quickly. I'm going to need someone to keep all this importance from going to my head. Keep me fun and interesting so I don't bore all the patrons at the tavern." I nudged my shoulder into his.

He tripped sideways, almost falling into the street,

then regained his balance and nudged me back.

His jaw relaxed as he let out a bold, belly laugh. True emotion finally sparking in his expression. "Might be a big task, Your Majesty. You were never that fun or interesting to begin with."

"Then I guess I'll have to spend more time with you so you can show me how to be such a popular socialite. Dazzle the gentlemen, charm the ladies, and all that."

"I've been trying to show you for years, but you just never paid attention." He unhooked the top two buttons of his shirt and widened the area around his neck. His shoulders drooped and his steps started to regain the swagger I'd recognize anywhere. "However, what's this about charming the ladies? Don't you owe me a story about a girl?"

"Right." My brain drifted back to that night on the street. The panic in my veins. The hopelessness of the battle against Edwin. So much had changed in only a few days. Except, Veda still hadn't reappeared in Mosa, or at least not that I or any of the kingdom guards could find. Maybe she was lost in the fairy magic with her father, or in her typical style, she didn't want me to find her. "But, I don't think there is much story left to tell. I messed up pretty badly and I'm not sure if she'll be back."

"You were in love with her though, weren't you?"

I scoffed as I searched for anything more interesting to talk about. "Why would you say that?"

He skipped a few steps ahead and cut in front of my path, his arms crossed against his chest. "Because I've been around you my entire life. I've seen you with practically every girl in this city since your first kiss, and no one, not one of them made you look like I shoved a dagger in your side."

I cringed, the fictional blade plunging right in the fleshy spot Kalmin suggested. Maybe I did look a little upset? "Have you always been picturing stabbing me with a dagger?"

I pivoted to the left and tried to move around him, but Kalmin bobbed in front of me, refusing to let me pass without an answer. Like my own personal bridge troll.

"Enough, Falls. This girl. She's special, isn't she?"

"Is special? Was special? I'm not too clear on that right now." I gripped my forehead as sweat built along my hairline. The sun must have gotten hotter. "But I wish I would've gotten a chance to figure that out. Being with her brings me calm. Anchors me when I always feel like I'm floating. She's...I don't know...kind of like the best thing and the biggest disaster in my life so far. And I can't really get enough."

Kalmin chuckled and patted me on the shoulder. "Sounds pretty serious to me."

"But maybe just in my mind." I shrugged him off and continued down the street, following the web of cracks between the stones and letting the sun scald the exposed back of my neck. "Since when are you so interested in my love life?"

"Two reasons. One—" He held up his index finger. "—no matter what's happened I do want to see you happy. And two—" He held up a second finger, but looked away. "—all that stuff you said about your mystery girl. That's kind of how I feel when I'm around Sophia."

I halted and jerked my head up. Kalmin continued forward, leaving me behind before realizing I'd stopped, then turned around a wide-eyed look on his face.

"You and Sophia? When did that happen?"

Kalmin hung his head and gripped the back of his

neck. "It's still new. After you stopped coming around, things kind of took off. And I've actually been interested in her for a long time."

"Why didn't you just tell me?"

"I didn't want you to be mad. You're the prince. Any girl out there would line up to be with you. I don't have that kind of draw. And she was always hanging off your arm. How could I compete?"

I winced as I recalled how I'd treated Sophia and so many other girls in the kingdom. Like property. Playthings for my amusement. I'd have to add her to my list of apologies to the people I'd wronged, somewhere near the top.

I stepped forward, my shadow towering over him until he raised his head and dared to look at me, his eyes heavy.

"Don't ever hide something like that from me again. But does she truly make you happy?"

He nodded.

"Then she's lucky to have someone like you. As long as she doesn't mind me being around the two of you again?"

He glanced up cautiously. "Are you sure it's okay?"

"Of course, you deserve to be happy. Both of you. I wouldn't stand in the way of that, king or not."

He sighed as his body relaxed. The tension wound tight through his jaw and neck let go as we air rushed out at his mouth.

"Now are you ready for me to destroy you at chess?" I asked as I hurried down the street.

As I turned the corner at the bottom of the hill, Kalmin raced to catch up. We entered the square and a muffled din of voices flew at us. People were everywhere.

"What's this?" I asked as Kalmin appeared at my

side.

A large crowd had gathered staring up at a small stage constructed in the center of the square. On the stage, a mismatched group stood in crooked lines next to a rather overdressed man with a curled mustache who seemed to be running the show.

"Right. There's some writing contest awards happening here today. I read a sign about it somewhere but forgot."

The writing contest. Veda's writing contest? I sped forward to the back of the crowd and stood on my tiptoes trying to find her face up on the stage. A tuft of hair and flash of gray appeared behind a large muscular man in the front row. My pulse skipped in double time. Could it really be her?

"What's the big deal, Falls? Are you suddenly a huge literature fan now too?"

I glanced back at him and frowned. "No, the girl. Veda. She wanted to enter but I don't know if she submitted her entry in time."

"Well then, you'd better go find out." Kalmin laughed and slapped me across the back. "No wonder your mother suggested that I take you to play chess today."

"It wasn't your idea?"

He laughed harder. "No. She sent a message to me this morning saying you needed to get out of the castle and it would be a good suggestion. She is a dangerous woman, your mother."

"Of course, she is. She's the most powerful Aldric of all."

Kalmin nudged me with his elbow. "Stop thinking about your mom, Falls. Go get your girl."

A loud voice boomed from the stage. The stocky host stepped forward. "And now the prizes for best poem, long-form...”

He listed off the names as each contestant stepped forward to a rush of cheers and applause.

“Excuse me. Pardon me.” I weaved through the crowd, sidestepping my way between the bodies of the citizens as they grumbled at me.

Whispers erupted around me, my identity impossible to hide up close, but I didn’t care as I pushed my way through.

3rd place, Greta Halvorson. 2nd place...

The announcer’s voice grew louder as I approached. I twisted my head to try and find Veda among the contestants, but there were still too many in the way. A small opening appeared to the left and I lunged in that direction, my foot squishing something hard before hitting solid ground.

“Ouch,” someone groaned as I pulled my foot off theirs. A woman dressed in a white cloak cowered away from me.

“I’m so sorry, miss.” I winced. “I hope I didn’t hurt you.”

She looked back. Her ethereal blonde hair hung around her pained face as her ocean blue eyes glared up at me. I gasped. Golden rings circled in her stare. The same ones I saw in the mirror every morning. Like not one other person I’d ever met.

“Who are—”

The woman snapped her head away. “I have to go.”

“No. Wait.” I grabbed for her arm but the silkiness of her sleeve slipped through my fingers as she darted through the horde.

I started after her, jutting in and out between people, but her small frame fit easier than mine and gave her a generous head start.

And now the winners of our short fiction category. 3rd place, Oliver Hortensio.

Those golden eyes. Maybe that woman knew where I came from? She didn't look like anyone I'd ever seen in Aboria before. Too pale. Too spectral. But still impossibly beautiful. Did she have magical abilities like me?

2nd place, Stephano Cicero.

A space opened on the right. I pivoted and tried to jut ahead but the woman slid left and deeper into the crowd.

And 1st place with her heart-wrenching story of lost love "A Tale of True Beauty", Miss Veda Macario.

I stopped. The woman in white kept running. I glanced up at the stage as a familiar face stepped forward and the announcer lowered a large gold medallion over her head. The crowd around me cheered.

"Veda," I yelled as I waved my hands in the air.

I struck a burly gentleman beside me with my elbow. He frowned, then upon recognition stepped out of the way.

"Veda."

She placed her hand flat to shade her eyes and scanned the square. I jumped up, my arms flinging wild again. People backed away from me, gawking at my ridiculous display, but I didn't care. Nothing mattered.

"Veda."

Her head turned my direction and we locked eyes over the distance. Red flushed her cheeks and she stumbled back from the edge of the stage. She swung her head looking for an exit.

I rushed toward the side of the stage. "Excuse me. Pardon me. Sorry. Excuse me."

The crowd parted to let me through. I climbed the left stairs to the platform as she escaped toward the right.

"Veda, wait. Please stop."

Her hand hovered over the stair railing as she halted, and her head hung down. She gripped her hand into a fist and pumped it in the air before slowly turning on her heel. "Yes, Your Majesty."

The sarcastic tone of her words twisted the imaginary dagger in my side, sending a sharp pain through my spine. But I deserved it. I knew that. It still hurt, though.

I meandered through the other contestants and judges on the stage, each one of them frozen in place as if an evil witch had cast a sleeping spell over the kingdom. A similar hush fell over the rest of the crowd as they watched my careful steps that brought me closer to the one person I'd tried to forget and couldn't. She waited, her hands clenched in knuckle-white fists at her sides and a sad frown across her lips.

"What are you doing, Fallon?" she whispered as I neared.

My hands reached to hold her shoulders, to pull her close to me, but they resisted and dropped with a smack on my thighs.

"When you disappeared, I didn't know where you went. I looked everywhere. I even sent guards to find you, but you were gone. Where did you go? Why didn't you come back to me?"

A few murmurs started in the audience and Veda looked out over the captivated crowd, but for once whatever they thought didn't matter. Hate me if they wanted to. Throw more fruit. I wasn't leaving yet. Veda excelled at hiding and my heart couldn't take another vanishing act without hearing a reason this time.

"I don't know what happened. Everything went dark, then when I opened my eyes I'd somehow ended up lost and alone in the middle of the forest." She shuddered as the memory flickered through her eyes. "And you already know why I didn't come back."

"I don't though. Why do you think I pushed my way through the square screaming like a fool to catch up with you? I don't understand."

She lowered her voice and leaned closer. The sweetness of wildflowers clouded my head. An untamed jasmine flower.

"You're a prince. I'm just this—" She spread her quivering arms as her eyes welled. "I told you before, at the castle, guys like you don't end up with girls like me. We should just stop whatever this is now before either of us gets hurt. Before I get hurt."

"But..." I looked her over. Her quirky disheveled head to her sturdy, practical feet. If only she could see herself the way I saw her. How her beauty stole my breath every time we met. How it shone through her like a lighthouse calling me back to shore. Back to still waters. "Maybe you're right."

Her face melted as her body went limp. She pulled her hands into her sleeves and fought back her precarious tears. "See. Now can you just go."

"Except, I don't think that statement is true anymore. It used to be. I'll agree with you about that, but not now." I wrapped my fingers around her fist and teased it out into my palm. I covered it with my other hand and stepped closer holding it to my chest. Over my heart. "Guys like how I used to be don't belong with girls like you. That guy was weak, while you were strong. Where I was ignorant, you were wise. Where I was scared, you were steady. But being with you, and even being without you, over these past few weeks has changed me. It's made me question everything I am and everything I stand for. It's made me a better person, a bolder one. One who for the first time in his life knows what he wants and what he stands for. And that's all thanks to you. To the amazing person that you are. So, yes, guys like that jerk I was in tavern don't deserve good things in their lives, but now that I've been lucky enough to have it, I can't give it up. I just hope that you think the guy I am now is finally worthy of a girl like you."

Veda's hand trembled in mine. I bit down on the inside of my cheek. Had I made an idiot of myself? Maybe. But for her, I'd do it a thousand times to make her understand. To help her see how we fit even if it didn't seem like we did. I pulled her hand higher and pressed my lips against her soft skin. "And if you'd let me, I'd kiss you anytime, anywhere, no matter who was watching."

"This could be a huge mistake, Fallon," she said as her tears broke free and sailed down her cheeks.

"Or we could write the best love story anyone has ever read. If you'll let us try?"

"Don't make me regret this, my prince."

"I won't if you don't." I edged closer, our hands the only thing left between us. "Congratulations on your big win. I knew you could do it."

"Thanks." She picked up the medal and gleamed down at it with a satisfied smile. "I'm pretty excited about it."

I slid my hands around her waist as the heat of her body seeped through her clothes and alight my skin. I winked at her. "I think it might be my royal duty to kiss the winner."

She pushed up on her tiptoes and slipped her arms around my neck, locking her hands at the nape. "Only if you really want to."

"I really do."

My lips pressed against hers. Soft at first, waiting until she sparked alive under my kiss and pushed back with every ounce of fight I dreamed of tasting. The crowd roared. Whistles split through the air. We moved together, pushing and pulling, giving and taking, our lips telling stories our minds hadn't yet formed into words.

"Way to go, Falls," Kalmin hollered from somewhere behind us.

Veda giggled, the sweet vibration dancing across my mouth.

"Veda, meet my best friend Kalmin," I whispered.

"I can meet him later," she said as pulled away from my face, her hands still clutched tight around me. "I'll be around for a while."

I squeezed her tighter and looked out over the cheering crowd. My shoulders rolled back, my posture straighter as an overwhelming joy flowed through me. A lightness. It'd stopped the evil wizard, I'd won back the girl I loved, and I had a strong prosperous kingdom to rule. I'd gone through hell and come out the other side. I'd won.

Just then, a strange motion caught my attention in the far end of the square. The blonde woman with the blue and gold eyes stood near the alley watching us. I stared back. She pulled her cloak over her head then ran off, disappearing into the city.

16TH JUNE

"Stop it, Fallon. I can buy my own notebooks." Veda tried to reach around me but I puffed out my shoulders trying to take up as much space as possible while I tossed a stack of baht on the counter.

"I'm sure you can. But an award-winning writer like yourself should have the finest pages to write her dynamic ideas in."

She gave up and dropped her hands to her hips, maybe hoping that her glare would be sharper than her pointy elbows. "But do I really need twelve? I refuse to spend taxpayer money on frivolous things."

"Of course, you need them. One notebook for every month of the year."

The shopkeeper chuckled and counted the bills out on the countertop.

"Besides, I knew you'd never let 'frivolous' spending stand, so this isn't taxpayer money. It's hard-earned gambling money."

"Gambling? Really." Her lips curled up in a crooked line as she tried to fight the amusement breaking through her tough stance.

I shrugged. "High stakes chess game in the square. Kalmin and I beat a pair of travelers from up north. It's not my fault if they don't know their knight from their pawn."

She rolled her eyes. "You are ridiculous."

I grabbed the bag of notebooks from the shopkeeper and held them out for Veda.

"I know," I said with a flirty wink.

She shook her head then snatched the bag from my hand and headed back out into the street.

"Thank you, good sir." I tipped my hand at the shopkeeper and followed behind, the door slamming in front of me and nearly clipping my nose.

Outside the street bustled with people rushing left and right as they proceeded with their day. Ladies, gentlemen, even children tugging on their mother's hands filed in front of me, but no Veda. I shook my head and headed to my left.

"You really shouldn't do that." Veda leaped out from beside the shop.

I screamed.

She laughed and buckled over, her hands clenched across her stomach gasping for breath. "Serves you right for trying to spoil me."

My pounding heart slowed and I slipped an arm around her waist. "But what if I want to spoil you."

She flexed onto her toes and rubbed the tip of her nose against mine, then placed a quick kiss on my lips. I leaned in, trying to make the feeling last, but she wriggled out of my embrace.

"Thank you though. I do love the books." She held up the bag. "All of them."

"You know I would get you anything you wanted. You just have to ask."

"I know, but I don't expect you to buy me things. I don't need you to."

"And that's why I love to do it. Because it's not an expectation with you."

Veda grabbed my wrist and slid by my side underneath my arm. A slow, rolling fire built in my veins. Fire, but without the fury, I simply relished in the embers glowing between us.

"Now is there anything you expect of me, my prince?"

"No." I glanced down at her smile but it had faded. "Why do you ask? Has someone said something to you?"

"Not exactly, but it's still hard to see you in your world and know that I'm not one of those proper ladies that everyone would want you to be with. Maybe I should try a little harder if we are honestly going to make this work."

I gripped her shoulder and turned her to face me. "I don't want to hear you say that. If anyone is concerned with how you look or how you hold your tea, then they aren't listening to your words. You're smart and strong, and wearing a pretty dress isn't going to make you or your ideas more appealing."

She narrowed her stare. "You say that now."

"Yes, I do. And I don't want you making any changes unless you want to. If it's something you are interested in doing—not for me, but for yourself—I'll do whatever

I can to help. But don't think I care. Because I don't."

She sighed. "I'm not sure you're right, but I will think about it some more."

I placed my hand under her chin. "And then you'll talk to me and tell me what's going on before you do anything drastic. Okay?"

She nodded and pulled her head out of my hand then sidled back beside me as we strolled in silence through the city. The beautiful afternoon stretched out in front of us, all the plans and obligations I had back at the castle reeling over in my brain, but all I wanted was to stay here a little while longer and just be still.

But as we walked, a strange feeling crept up the back of my neck. Something heavy and foreboding. Like eyes staring through my skull. I glanced around. Just the regular citizens moving about their day. A few looked as they recognized me, but their quick peeks didn't feel the same. They didn't hold the same weight.

My stomach clenched and Veda twitched by my side. Could she feel it too or was it just my reaction making her uncomfortable? We turned the corner and a bright spark flashed ahead and to the left of us. I turned toward the disruption. The beautiful woman in the white cloak I'd seen at the writing contest stood in the opening to the alley, her sharp stare following our footsteps. The golden rings in her eyes glinted in the sun.

"Hey," I called. "You there."

The woman glanced back and forth, her eyes wide, then spun around and rushed back down the alley.

"Come on." I grabbed Veda's hand and ran across the street after the woman.

Dark shadows towered around us as we disappeared further into the center of the city. The pathways began to narrow, but the sound of the woman's feet pounding the ground ahead pushed me forward.

"Where are we going, Fallon?" Veda asked, her constant looking back starting to slow us down.

"Did you see the woman dressed in white standing by the alley? She has the same eyes as me. The same gold rings. I need to find her."

We twisted right, then left, then right again, the brick walls cold and ominous as we raced on. She'd been quick to escape me in the square, but now a second sighting and again she'd fled. Why was she running away from me? What did she know? We crested one final corner and I stopped quick nearly falling over my own feet. The walls stretched higher in every direction. A dead end. Nowhere else to go. But where was the woman in white? I rushed toward the wall in front of us and pushed my hands on the brick. It didn't move, no secret passageways here. I smashed my fist against the wall and a few specks of blood splashed across my knuckles as pain sparked up my arm. I hung my head.

"We must have taken a wrong turn. There's no way we'll catch up with her now." I rested my forehead against the brick, softer than my hand but enough to feel the sting through my skull. So close. But to what?

"Prince Fallon, we've been looking for you." A high-pitched saccharine voice rang off the brick walls.

I whirled around. The woman in white stood in front of the only exit, except this time she wasn't alone. Four other bodies appeared behind her from the shadows. Two men and two more women, nothing about them alike.

I jumped in front of Veda and gripped her hand. "What is going on here? The castle guards know to come looking if I don't check back in soon. Whatever you're planning, I suggest you don't."

"Then I guess we should make this quick, then shouldn't we?" The woman said as she stepped forward and let her companions pass to form a line in front of us. A solid wall we'd have to fight our way through if necessary.

I slid my switchblade from my pocket and flipped it open. The woman raised her hands. "We aren't looking for violence. We just want to talk to you. And since you've been chasing me for two days, I suspect you have your own questions to ask."

"Who are you?" I shifted Veda further back in the corner.

"I'm Eliana of The Vale. And these are my friends... my family?... We're not completely sure about all that yet. But we do know that shortly after we turned eighteen we each developed abilities that we can't explain. That we can't always control, does that sound familiar?"

I scanned the rest of their faces, each one nodding in agreement with Eliana. Was this some kind of trick? Only a few people knew about my powers and I trusted them, except for one who should be lost in another realm right now.

"What makes you think I'd have magical powers? That sounds preposterous."

Eliana shrugged and looked over at one of the other women. One who looked like she slayed dragons for entertainment. She gritted her teeth and shrugged back, but I cringed.

"Because we all know that you aren't the blood heir of the Aborian throne. You were left at the doorstep of the castle and the king and queen took you in. Or do you still think I'm lying?"

"Anyone could have told you that. It's a secret, but

not very well kept."

"All of us were adopted too. All of us left in different kingdoms eighteen years ago and all of us with strange powers. How many people do you know that have gold rings in their eyes? Until I met these guys I thought I was the only one too. So, Prince Fallon, stop fighting this and just tell us what magic you can do."

I surveyed them all through the darkness but even with the distance between us, gold flickered in each of their eyes. Could it really be true? I released Veda's hand and stepped forward. I closed my eyes as the tingle shot through my body. Long white-blond hair fell over my shoulders. My nose slimmed and turned slightly upwards. My hands shrunk as my fingers changed into daintier digits with longer feminine fingernails.

Eliana gasped. "It's as if I was looking in a mirror." She stepped forward, slow and measured as if approaching a wild bear. She ran her fingers through her hair on my head as her mouth fell open but silent. "It's incredible. Can you become anyone?"

I nodded. "Or at least I think I can."

One of the men crossed his arms, his own long locks falling into his eyes. Except where Eliana was light he emanated dark. "Not fair. How come he gets to shift into people? I only can shift to animals."

"We all have different powers, Castiel. And I'm sure your powers have their place."

"Can you all—what did he call it—shift?"

Eliana laughed, her voice light and airy like bells. "No. So far, just the two of you can change your appearance. The rest of us have other gifts. Deon can control plant life." The tall rugged guy in the corner raised his hand.

"Azia can control dragons. Blaise can manipulate water, and I can speak to animals. I'm not sure how everything ties together but that's what we're trying to figure out. To see if there are more in the world like us."

"Plus," the dragon tamer pushed her foot against the brick wall and stepped forward. "We're trying to figure out if these powers have anything to do with the strange happenings in our kingdoms."

"You mean the darkness?"I asked then glanced back at Veda. The uncomfortable look of shock still sat heavy on her face. As strange as this all sounded to me it must be a lot for her to take.

"I don't know what that is but if it's plaguing your borders then maybe," Azia said. "We're headed to Arcadia to look for any more missing pieces. Are you in?"

I grabbed the side of my face. Everything seemed to be coming at me so fast. I had a few days of downtime since the battle with Edwin and now this?

"I don't know if I can right now. My father has been cursed and turned into a beast. I need to find a cure and get the kingdom back in line before I could even consider leaving him."

Castiel sneered. "If whatever is affecting our worlds gets loose, you might not have a kingdom left to save."

Azia glared at Castiel and he looked away.

"Maybe defeating this thing, this darkness as you call it, will break the curse? If not, maybe we'll find someone with the power to fix him." Eliana extended her hand and flashed a tense smile. "We could really use you on the journey."

Veda clutched my arm, her cold fingers gripping tight into my skin. I looked back. Her face crinkled with worry, but she nodded her head toward Eliana. She'd been the one to tell me about the darkness in the first place. If anyone understood it would be her. She would sacrifice her happiness to do the right thing, but why did the right thing always need to be so hard?

So many reasons to refuse screamed in my head. I studied the band of unlikely heroes that circled around me. Could they really all be like me? Were we connected somehow? And the biggest question, what would I be giving up if I walked away?

"Curing my dad is the number one priority for me. If this mission goes awry, I'm out." I took Eliana's hand and shook it roughly.

Her eyes lit, bright blue and gold shining back at me. "You won't regret this."

I let go of Eliana's hand and pulled Veda closer to my side.

"I sure hope not."

~

"I don't think I've had a meal like that in, in well, ever." Deon rubbed his stomach as the entire crew wandered lazily into the grand foyer from the dining room.

Between the five strangers, they polished off platters of meats, cheeses, pies and anything else the kitchen could find to serve. I watched them all as we sat at the formal dining table, ensuring I ate my share before our journey, but still trying to piece together everything in my head. None of them looked much like me, except for the eyes. Those gold ringed eyes that I couldn't seem to forget. But, since I could make myself look like anyone I wanted to, maybe I didn't look like myself either? Maybe somewhere along the way, my undeveloped powers changed my face to blend in with the Aldric's, when I really looked more like Azia or Deon or even like Castiel. Every time I thought I figured something out two more questions popped up to replace it. A mythic hydra of mysteries.

"Yes, the kingdom of Alantis appreciates your uninhibited kindness, Queen Abigail." Blaise curtsied in front of my mother.

"No need for pleasantries, dear. You are most welcome here. And when you return, please remember to say hello to your parents for me."

Griswold appeared behind us with six matching shoulder bags. "The kitchen has also prepared some care packages to take with you on the journey. We wouldn't want the prince to go hungry, nor his companions."

Eliana took her bag and slid it over her shoulder. "Thank you. This will be extremely helpful. The long days are wearing on some of us a little more than others."

Griswold presented the bags to each of the travelers, but the stoic mask slid out of place when he reached me at the end of the line. "Be careful out there, Your Majesty."

"Oh, Griswold. I'll miss you too." I yanked him into a hug. His body tensed in my grip, but soon relaxed and for a moment I thought I felt him squeeze me back.

"Of course, my prince. The entire kingdom will be patiently awaiting your safe return."

I released him and he readjusted his jacket and cuffs, his eyes cast to the stone floor. He patted me on the shoulder without making eye contact then disappeared into the depths of the castle.

"My son, how will I ever spend the days without you?" Mom replaced Griswold in front of me, her gaze already watery.

"You can plan the days you'll spend with Dad when I return with a cure. Besides, you'll have Veda to keep you company and you can both sit and curse about me."

She slipped into my arms and I held tight, pulling her up so her feet left the floor. The smell of home flooded my senses and I fought to avoid joining her in tears not wanting to make a bad impression on the strangers that might or might not be my true family. We needed more than one meal before they would be let into my world. I already had enough love and people I cared about without them.

Mom nuzzled closer to my ear, a few drops of wetness falling on my neck and running under my shirt. "She's a good one, Fallon. I've never been so proud of you. Your strength, your integrity, and most of all your heart. Never lose your passion, my boy."

"I love you, Mom."

She squeezed harder. "I love you too. Now get going before I order the guards to lock you up and selfishly keep you here with me."

I let her go, my arms feeling painfully empty as she slipped away, then I swiped my arm over my eyes and blinked. Through the haze, the last of my potential regrets appeared. Veda's stood behind the crowd, her hands twisting together at her waist, a glum half-smile on her lips. We locked stares and she jerked her head toward the doors. I glanced at the others.

"Can I have a couple more minutes?" I asked as I took Veda's hand and headed for the outside.

Eliana nodded, but it didn't matter. No one was going to steal these last few minutes from me.

The guards opened the large castle doors and the golden sunlight streamed into the foyer. Another beautiful Aborian day and for the first time I actually wished for rain.

~

We strolled through the garden without a word, our hands clamped tight together and swinging between us as we walked. Doves sang us a soft mournful tune from their tree perches as the breeze rustled percussion through the leaves. The perfume of my mother's roses scented the winding path between the bushes and fountains. On another day, under other circumstances, this might have been perfection, but right then it felt like a funeral march.

"When all of this is over, I promise to take you anywhere you want to go. I'll show you the whole world and anything in it that your heart desires," I said finally piercing the quiet.

"You don't owe me anything. All I want when this is over is for you to return to me safely."

I stopped walking and used our joined hands to tug her closer to me. I placed my hand under her chin and propped her head up to meet my gaze. "Don't worry about that. I'll be home before you have time to miss me. And then we'll travel so much you'll beg to stay in for months after we return."

"I'd like that." She smiled but it looked hollow. No joy. No spark of happiness in her eyes.

"You are going to have the best time at the castle without me anyway. My mother is already looking forward to having another female around and I'm sure she will keep you busy. Make sure to get her to show you the library. You'll get lost in there for weeks."

Veda tugged her face away and wandered over to the rose bushes, then pushed her nose into the largest bloom to inhale the scent.

“If anything happens while I’m away. Something at the castle, or with my father, or if you ever just need me, send a note with Alizeh and I’ll come back immediately.”

She stood back and crossed her arms, still choosing not to look at me. “And if you ever decide that you just want to come home, then call Alizeh and she’ll bring you straight to me.”

“I will.”

I stood behind her and rubbed my hands along her shoulders the weight of leaving heavy on my back. If only this hadn’t happened so soon. We’d only just found each other again, but the pull of discovering where I came from had grown too strong already. I may never get a chance like that again. My destiny came looking and I couldn’t just let it go off to Arcadia without me. Plus, if I ever wanted the protection of the fairies, I needed to hold true to my promise about defeating the darkness. If I didn’t they might drop Edwin back into the grand foyer and sit around laughing in the rafters as he leveled the kingdom. I couldn’t risk that. Not for the citizens of Aboria. Not for my family. Not for Veda.

“Are you sure you’re okay with watching over my parents? I know it’s not the most exciting job but I need someone I can trust to tell me what’s happening and making sure that my father is cared for until I can bring back a cure.”

“Yes, of course. I’m happy to help try to clean up my father’s mess. It feels...I don’t know...cathartic somehow.”

“You and your father are different people. I don’t blame you for what happened.”

Her body stiffened in my hands. “I know, but I do.”

I turned her around gently, giving her the chance to resist, but she didn’t. I leaned down and brushed my lips against hers. She kissed me back, slow, pressing light like a whisper. I brushed her hair off her shoulder and slid my palm across her cheek, burying my fingertips in her locks, my other hand at the soft flesh of her neck. My head spun, drunk in the sweet taste of her and the delicious sensation of her skin against mine. I deepened the kiss. Stronger. Rougher. Wanting to brand myself with her lips so I'd never forget it.

She linked her fingers around my hands and yanked them away.

"Don't," she said breathlessly. "Don't kiss me like it's goodbye."

But maybe it was. She didn't know for sure and neither did I. I placed a soft kiss on her forehead and pulled her against me. Her arms wrapped around my waist and gripped tight enough to stop the breath in my lungs.

Eliana's melodic voice pierced the bubble around us. "Are you ready to go, Fallon? It's starting to get late and we'd like to make some ground before nightfall."

"Yeah. I'll be there in a minute," I said as my chin rested on Veda's head, the rumble of my words vibrating against her cheek.

Veda's arms slacked around my sides.

"Hey—" I bent my knees and rested my forehead against hers. "—make sure you fill those notebooks with as many stories as you can think of. When I get back, I'm going to want to read all your amazing work."

She nodded and peeled herself away. "Just make sure you hurry back so I don't run out of notebooks."

She took my hand and gave a sorrowful grin. We walked back toward the front of the castle, our steps slow and heavy. My five new travel companions stood at the ready.

“Time to go?” Eliana said.

I nodded and gave Veda a kiss on the cheek.

My mother hugged me tight, rubbing her hand along my back. “Find the cure, find your truth, then rush home. We’ll all miss you and be waiting.”

“I love you, Mom.”

Her eyes welled up and she wiped the tears away with her knuckle.

Now or never.

The five orphans paraded the cobblestone walk in front of me as the guards whisked open the gates. My heart skipped as we headed out and the iron gates creaked closed, the latch clanging in its place. The golden bridge to Mosa gleamed in the afternoon light. A road to a new beginning. A new adventure.

The shadow of the castle loomed behind us and cast disfigured shapes on the ground. I looked back—one last time—to the only home I’d ever known. I took a deep breath and closed my eyes, letting the image fade slow.

I’d promised I’d save the kingdom. Save my father. Save everyone.

It’s good to be king. Or at least that’s what they say. But was it, really?

DAUGHTER OF ALADDIN

GRAB THE NEXT BOXSET IN THE KINGDOM OF FAIRYTALES SERIES

Meet the Team

The Kingdom of Fairytales Series was a team effort. Below are the people that made it possible:

EQP Management: Rhi Parkes & J.A. Armitage

Our authors: J.A. Armitage, Audrey Rich, B. Kristin McMichael, Emma Savant, Jennifer Ellision, Scarlett Kol, Rose Castro, Margo Ryerkerk, Zara Quentin, Laura Greenwood and Anne Stryker.

Our Editor
Rose Lipscomb

Our Beta Team
Nadine Peterse-Vrijhof
Diane Major
Kalli Bunch
Stephanie Woodwood

Our Proof Reader
Tina Merritt

And to all the wonderful people who loved the world we created and reviewed our stories.
Thank you

READING ORDER

SEASON ONE
SLEEPING BEAUTY
Queen of Dragons
Heiress of Embers
Throne of Fury
Goddess of Flames

SEASON TWO
LITTLE MERMAID
Queen of Mermaids
Heiress of the Sea
Throne of Change
Goddess of Water

SEASON THREE
RED RIDING HOOD
King of Wolves
Heir of the Curse
Throne of Night
God of Shifters

SEASON FOUR
RAPUNZEL
King of Devotion
Heir of Thorns
Throne of Enchantment
God of Loyalty

SEASON FIVE
RUMPELSTILTSKIN
Queen of Unicorns
Heiress of Gold
Throne of Sacrifice
Goddess of Loss

SEASON SIX
BEAUTY AND THE BEAST
King of Beasts
Heir of Beauty
Throne of Betrayal
God of Illusion

SEASON SEVEN
ALADDIN
Queen of the Sun
Heiress of Shadows
Throne of the Phoenix
Goddess of Fire

SEASON EIGHT
CINDERELLA
Queen of Song
Heiress of Melody
Throne of Symphony
Goddess of Harmony

SEASON NINE
ALICE IN WONDERLAND
Queen of Clockwork
Heiress of Delusion
Throne of Cards
Goddess of Hearts

SEASON TEN
WIZARD OF OZ
King of Traitors
Heir of Fugitives
Throne of Emeralds
God of Storms

SEASON ELEVEN
SNOW WHITE
Queen of Reflections
Heiress of Mirrors
Throne of Wands
Goddess of Magic

SEASON TWELVE
PETER PAN
Queen of Skies
Heiress of Stars
Throne of Feathers
Goddess of Air

SEASON THIRTEEN
URBIS

Kingdom of Royalty
Kingdom of Power
Kingdom of Fairytales
Kingdom of Ever After

BOXSETS

AZIA
BLAISE
CASTIEL
DEON
ELIANA
FALLON
GAIA
HALIA
IVY
JAKON
KELIS
LYRIC
URBIS

www.ingramcontent.com/pod-product-compliance
Lightning Source LLC
Chambersburg PA
CBHW020244030826
48979CB00030B/2610/J

* 9 7 8 1 9 8 9 9 9 7 5 6 7 *